THE RED-KEGGERS

THE
RED-KEGGERS

By
EUGENE THWING

Illustrations by
W. HERBERT DUNTON

New York
THE BOOK-LOVER PRESS
1903

PREFACE

FOR the inception of this story of a Michigan farming and lumbering community, and for much of the material which has entered into its composition, the author is indebted to Mr. John W. Rhines. His long experience in that section of the country, his personal reminiscences, his acquaintance with men and women of the time, his graphic descriptions of places and incidents, and his constant and hearty co-operation during the progress of the work, have given the author substantial assistance, without which this task would hardly have been undertaken or completed. The author acknowledges also the courtesy of Mr. Edwin N. Burton in placing at his disposal the reminiscences of his brother, Mr. Frank S. Burton, from which such facts and incidents have been borrowed as have seemed needful for the purpose of this book.

LIST OF ILLUSTRATIONS

THE RED-KEGGERS

CHAPTER I

THE section officially known as Range 1, North, and Red-Keg, its focal point, were in the transition period between lumbering and farming. The combined cuttings of three contracting firms and several individual owners, amounting to some twenty million feet of sawlogs, had been sent down the river from Red-Keg and half a dozen other points extending ten miles along the bank. A hundred or more rivermen had gone down with the great drive to the booms at Saginaw, or farther on, and had made the river towns noisy with their customary revels. The camps in the woods had been dismantled, the swollen river had subsided, and comparative quiet now reigned in and around Red-Keg; but it was not the quiet of idleness. A different form of activity was gaining ascendency. Instead of the axe and the saw cutting their way through the forest, the plough was cutting its way through the fields. Instead of the crash of the noble pine, the growth of a century laid low in a moment, the tiny seed fell gently into the furrow. The spirit of destruction and death, which during the winter had stalked through the forest, now withdrew for a season, and the spirit of creation and life brooded over the fertile earth.

As the forest receded the farm took its place. Many

of the lumbermen of the winter became the farmers of the summer. Few of these men went down the river with the drive, and those who did go hastened back as soon as their work was done, leaving their companions, the roving lumber-jacks, to the drunken carouse which the holiday spirit, the sense of a year's work done, the relaxation from the intense strain of labor and danger, and the possession of a considerable "stake" seemed to make necessary, or at least inevitable. Nearly all of the farmers and other able-bodied men throughout the section made their winters profitable by working for one or another of the lumber contractors; or, owning timber land of their own, cut as much as they could with little outlay for additional help or equipment, travoyed their own saw-logs to the skidways, and later loaded them on sleighs and toted them to the banking-ground at the river to await the spring freshet. Thus there was for them no "off" season, no period for idleness, and no time in which those who cared for success could afford to waste strength and income in the prolonged debauch of the lumber-jacks. Yet the Red-Keg, the pioneer saloon from which the little town growing up around it involuntarily took its name, did a flourishing business from one year's end to the other. Its greatest revenue, of course, was in the winter and spring, when the lumber-jacks for miles around regarded the bright red keg fastened at the top of a pole in front of Pete's place as the beacon light which guided them to their ever-desired haven. "Pete's Place" was lettered on this red keg in scrawling characters quite in keeping with the sprawling characters so often found inside the saloon. Two hotels or boarding-houses, a general store, two company stores, and about fifty log- or board-houses, made up the rest of the village.

Five miles or more down the river was Midland City, the county seat. The state road ran north from Red-Keg some eight or nine miles, and then turned to the west for about the same distance, until it reached the village of Sixteen on the river about twelve miles above Red-Keg. The road and the river thus formed an irregular triangle. In the adjacent county, where the forest gave place, were numerous settlements and farms, locating themselves by the name of the village to which they chanced to be nearest.

District School No. 1, at Midland, was the rallying-place for the youth throughout the section who desired an education, or whose parents desired it for them, and the sturdy boys and girls thought nothing of walking five miles or more to and from school when the roads were good, or of riding the same distance in sleigh, buckboard, or even farm wagon, when snow or rain made walking out of the question. Although the railroad extended to Red-Keg, it was seldom used. Even some of the younger men employed in the lumber-camps, or on the farms, managed to get a few weeks of schooling during the fall and spring. For nearly a month after the wind-up of the logging season and the scattering of the gangs, the school at Midland continued its all-day sessions. Then, with its annual "exercises" and jollification, it closed for the summer, leaving the larger boys and girls free to help, according to their respective abilities, in the work of the farms.

Closing day at District School No. 1 was an event in which parents and friends as well as pupils took an active interest. From all parts of the section they drove in to enjoy the festivities. The forenoon was devoted to the regular routine work, the afternoon to speeches, recitations, and singing, the evening to games, spelling-bees, and dancing, usually lasting well on toward morning. This year Lettie Green, Norine Maloney, and Axcy Marthy were to "graduate," and the Red-Keggers were preparing to turn out in force to honor so important an occasion.

Two consecutive days of rare beauty marked the close of the cold rains and ushered in the season of the earth's awakening. With the warm south wind came the breath of flowers and songs of birds.

Strangely out of harmony with the joyousness around her, and in which she was expected to join, Lettie Green stood at her window with trouble in her eyes. A tear glistened a moment on her long lashes, and then slipped unheeded down her cheek.

A door behind her opened, and she turned quickly with a little cry of joy which as quickly died away. Then she flushed red at the thought that her aunt must have seen her disappointment and would know the reason for it.

"What on earth, Lettie! You've been crying; and to-day, of all things! What is the matter?"

"Oh, nothing, Aunt Lydia."

"No, of course not. Sam ought to have been here before now if he is going to take you to Midland. He went off hunting yesterday, and got too far, I suppose, but the other folks are sure to be along in a few minutes. You'll have to hurry and eat your dinner."

"He had no right to disappoint me the very first time," thought Lettie, as she followed her aunt downstairs.

The hasty meal was scarcely finished when Seward Rathaway drove up in his buckboard.

"Has Lettie gone?" he called.

"No, she's waiting for you," replied Lydia Green, appearing at the door.

"For me! Good!" exclaimed Seward, springing to the ground to assist Lettie into the seat. "Uncle Si and Mother Hawkins, Mr. and Mrs. Maloney, Norine, and Barney are close behind. We'll wait a minute and all go on together. Aren't you coming, Aunt Lydia?"

"Yes, I'll come down on the train with the Red-Keg folks. Sorry your mother isn't well enough to come. How is she this morning?"

"Pretty comfortable, thank you. To tell the truth, Lettie," he added in a low tone as he took his place beside her, "after the way you went driving with Sam last week, and the look on your face when you came back, I imagined there'd be little chance for me to enjoy such a pleasure as this again."

Lettie's face paled, and then flushed.

"Nonsense!" she replied.

When District School No. 1 was called to order for the forenoon session, the teacher noticed Jaky Strander, Rodney Bedell, Jim Gyde, and two or three of the other larger boys in their places, early, quiet, and serious,—all unusual symptoms with that particular coterie. A flash of expectancy which passed from one to another did not escape the schoolmaster, but he appeared to see nothing out of the ordinary.

Jaky, or "Babe," Strander, who had earned his nickname by his enormous proportions, and his weight of over two hundred pounds, was a clumsy round-faced fellow, always good-natured, always in mischief, the butt of practical jokers, and one of the chief of them himself. He was an expert log-roller, notwithstanding his weight, but very much less at ease within the narrow walls of the district school, and utterly unable to master the multiplication-table, although past twenty years of age. The difference between seven times eight and nine times six was an unfathomable mystery to him, but he could judge almost to a hair's breadth the probable movements of that most erratic of inanimate objects, the saw-log, whether in the water or on the skidway. Ashbel Fair, two years his junior, was his inseparable companion, a slender, bright-eyed boy, with light curls in a tangled mass over his head, witty, a favorite with the girls, punctilious in his attendance at school and his apparent obedience to rules, but ready to join in any lark, and always with the proverbial chip on his shoulder as a standing invitation to "scraps" for the slightest cause, or for no cause at all. He was never missing when a rollway was to be broken or a drive sent down the river, but he hurried back to school as soon as the excitement of the work was over, and he usually led his class in spite of time lost.

Jim Gyde, in other words "Shitepoke Jim," was twenty-two, and had been going to school since he was ten. Thoroughly careless and unruly, in the second reader and the primary arithmetic, he was still unable to write his name, and cared for none of these things. He stood six feet two in his stockings, had been the terror of all the teachers since he first came to school, and hesitated at nothing in the form of deviltry. He came or stayed away from school as he pleased, and even his father, who was school moderator, had no control over him. A typical woodsman and a champion "scrapper," he swung his long arms and bony fists with such effect that few cared to come within reach of them when they began to move. Only three persons had any power over him; they were Axcy Marthy, on whom he lavished his silent affection, Joseph Waters, the new schoolmaster, and Robert Allen, the backwoods parson.

Rodney Bedell and Bud Frazer were two lawless youths who sought to pattern themselves after Jim Gyde for bullying and after Ashbel Fair for mischief, following with alacrity either lead if it promised fun or fighting, terms which were almost synonymous with these young backwoodsmen.

Between fifty and sixty boys and girls from ten to twenty-two years of age were in their places waiting for the usual opening exercises. Something seemed to be in the air, and a furtive wink now and then from one or the other of the larger boys confirmed the suspicion which by some mysterious telepathic influence had communicated itself to most of the pupils. The schoolmaster showed no hurry to proceed with his reading of the Bible chapter. He first placed some of the lessons for the day on the blackboard behind the platform. Then he turned to the school and inquired:

"Jaky, how many are six times nine?"

Jaky was taken wholly unawares. He stammered, looked up at the ceiling, from one side to the other, rolled his eyes nervously, plunged his hands deeply into his pockets, and with a desperate effort blurted out:

"Fifty-six."

"How many of your lessons have you ready for to-day, Jaky?"

Again the unhappy youth squirmed under the searching eyes of the schoolmaster. The stillness was oppressive. Such a proceeding before the opening exercises and the reading of the roll was portentous of trouble.

"I've got my joggerfy and 'riffmetic all done," replied Jaky at last, with a vain effort to appear at ease.

"Very well, Jaky," said the teacher pleasantly, "come up to the platform. I will let you recite now, before you forget them."

Jaky hung his head, looked appealingly toward some of his chums, and, almost stumbling to the floor as he arose awkwardly from his seat, shuffled unwillingly toward the platform, his hands still up to his elbows in his capacious pockets. The others watched curiously every movement of schoolmaster and culprit.

"Step up here with me," said the teacher in a friendly voice, as Jaky hesitated at the edge of the platform.

Jaky did as he was bidden.

"Now turn your face to the school, so," taking the clumsy fellow by the shoulders and turning him around. At the same time he drew his own wooden chair from under his deal table and placed it directly behind Jaky: "Be seated, please," he continued.

Here Jaky mutinied.

"It's got pins in it!" he blurted, now almost beside himself with fear and embarrassment. Trembling from head to foot, he sidled away from the dangerous proximity of the chair, and in his excitement fell off the side of the platform and measured his length on the floor.

"Pins?" exclaimed the schoolmaster in mock surprise, as he took up the chair and examined it closely. "Why, sure enough! and very neatly and cleverly done, too," he added pleasantly.

"See here," he went on, exhibiting the chair to the school, "five gimlet holes bored through the seat in the form of a square, with one in the centre. These holes are nicely filled with wooden plugs, through the centre of which long, stout pins have been thrust, so that the points protrude nearly an inch upward from the seat of the chair. Isn't that a clever idea, boys and girls? Do you know that in an old city called Nuremberg, on the other side of the world, there is a pretty little contrivance called the Iron Maiden, which was constructed many years ago on a somewhat similar principle, only that it is much more elaborate, because the long iron pins were arranged to penetrate every part of the body from head to foot. Evidently a like genius invented this seat. It would be too bad to allow such a clever invention to go untried. Let us see, there are five of the pins. I will allow five of you to try the seat, one for each of the pins. Who shall they be?" and he glanced quizzically over the school, without resting his eyes on any one in particular.

Dead silence reigned. Even the innocent pupils were too much frightened to snicker, as they had been known to do when some unfortunate was caught in a scrape.

"Are there no volunteers?" asked the schoolmaster after a few moments. "In that case I shall have to issue invitations by name. Jim Gyde, Rodney Bedell, Bud Frazer, Ashbel Fair, and Jaky Strander, kindly step to the platform in the order I have called your names and sit down for a moment in this interesting chair."

Not one of the boys moved. Black looks and clenched fists, however, spoke eloquently of mutiny.

The schoolmaster gazed at his pupils a moment longer with his frank, courteous smile; then in an instant his face changed and became stern and set. His jaw squared and his eyes flashed. He stepped quietly to a small closet near his table, unlocked it, and took from it five new blue beeches and laid them in a row upon the table. When he spoke, his voice was very quiet and cold, but the ring in it was unmistakable.

" Jim Gyde, step forward, sir."

The young ruffian hung his head, spread his legs under the seat in front of him, and gripped his own seat, but otherwise made no sign or response. For about thirty seconds in the stillness of the schoolroom there was a contest of wills. Then Jim raised his head and met the steely gaze of the schoolmaster's eyes. Slowly he rose and stalked forward until he stood face to face with his master.

" You are to have your choice between sitting in that chair and a dose of the blue beech," said the schoolmaster, in the same quiet tone.

Another silence, while the bully measured his forces with those of the schoolmaster. Undoubtedly he had the brawn, and bone, and reach of arm, but there was something in the other which he lacked wholly. He could not understand it. He recognized it with anger and a touch of awe, and he yielded to it, as he had done before. He clenched his teeth.

" The beech," he muttered.

One of the five stout switches was made to do its work thoroughly and well, and was then thrown out of the window.

" Rodney Bedell," called the schoolmaster.

One by one the other four came forward and took their medicine, never dreaming of resistance after the toughest fighter in the school had been vanquished. All chose the beech, not because it would hurt less, but because they at least knew the taste of it, and moreover the other punishment would subject them to endless ridicule.

When the last of the five conspirators had resumed

"YOU ARE TO HAVE YOUR CHOICE BETWEEN SITTING IN THAT CHAIR
AND A DOSE OF THE BLUE BEECH."

his place, the schoolmaster rang his bell for order, called the roll, and then read the first fourteen verses of the twelfth chapter of Romans in a tone of voice very different from that which he had previously used. He remarked briefly on the value, the dignity even, of chastisement if administered and received in the right spirit. He spoke of the close relation between chastisement and love, and assured his pupils that he loved them, and did not wish to humiliate them or break their spirits, but that he wanted to lead them to respect themselves and turn their splendid energies into right directions. After reading the fourteenth verse he paused a moment, and looked kindly at the turbulent fellows before him.

"That is a hard precept to live by in this region, boys; but remember this: if a man respects himself men will soon learn to respect him, and nothing is a surer preservative of peace than mutual respect. Avoid quarrels if you can, but if one is forced upon you,—well, make it so hot for the other fellow that he will want to avoid them thereafter."

The lessons for the morning then proceeded without interruption, but the pupils recited mechanically and scarcely heard the questions and explanations of the schoolmaster. The one thing that occupied their minds was the startling event of the morning, and it was the one topic discussed when the school was dismissed an hour earlier than usual that the place might be prepared for the afternoon exercises.

"He knew all about it, and had everything fixed," exclaimed one and another. "How in thunder did he find out?"

CHAPTER II

"TIGHT fit, ain't it," remarked Hezekiah Bloag, as he edged his way to the front and squeezed into a narrow space on a bench beside Josiah Hawkins.

"Yes, there must be close to a hundred and fifty here, and it's only intended to seat eighty comfortably. We'll have more room to-night when the youngsters go home," replied Farmer Hawkins.

The little schoolroom platform was barely wide enough for six chairs in a row at the back. These were occupied by the School Board, consisting of Director, Moderator, and Clerk, the minister of the Midland church, Rev. Augustus Hayward, the itinerant preacher and missionary, Robert Allen, and Joseph Waters, the schoolmaster.

"This occasion marks an epoch in District School No. 1, and in the lives of these here young ladies who go out from its educatin' influence," said the Moderator in his opening speech; "but likewise it gives ye a chance to see the new schoolmaster, who, from all accounts, is as different from them who preceded him as the freshet that carried the drive down the Tittabawassee last month is from a spoonful of dishwater. Ye know my boy Jim ain't ezactly a baby. I don't fool much with him myself. Mr. Waters, here, larrupped him and four of his pals good and plenty this morning before the whole school, usin' up a blue beech on every mother's son of 'em; and all the time, they say, he was cool and quiet as though hearin' a class in spellin'. I wouldn't know where to pick out another man who could do the job. He's the kind of schoolmaster this district needs. More power to his arm, say I. We'll now hear the report of the Clerk for the past year."

One by one, the Moderator introduced the speakers of the afternoon. The Director, Ashbel Fair's father, spoke of the importance of a good school education in fitting young men and women for practical work even in the forest or on the farm. The city minister talked learnedly on no subject in particular until his hearers were glad to have him stop. The schoolmaster modestly begged to be excused from speaking.

"My boys and girls have already heard enough from me, and their parents and friends will be content if I stick to my work and let speech-making alone."

This, coming immediately after two long, prosy addresses, was greeted with hearty applause and some approving laughter.

Parson Allen could not escape so easily.

"Ye've been away all winter in the woods with the boys," said the Moderator. "If there's anything ye have to say to us people, now's your chance."

In a few simple words the stalwart backwoods parson spoke of some of the lessons taught in the wonderful school in which he and scores of rugged men had been pupils during the past winter.

"Our schoolmaster is stern and exacting, and our hours are longer than yours," he said. "We must keep at our lessons sometimes until after midnight, and start in again at three o'clock in the morning. It depends a good deal on the weather. But it's worth while, if the lessons are well learned. Most of the boys don't know that they are learning them, and I'm afraid they forget

them when school is out; but there's big hope for any
fellow when he gets his eyes open.

"In the first grade of our school out yonder in the
woods every chap learns four lessons in a wonderfully
short time. First comes patience. He needs it when
the roads are hard to make, when the snow comes too
soon and prevents the ground and the swamp from
freezing, when the horses break through the ice, when
a thaw stops the work before time, when the boss is
unreasonable,—at every point he must know his lesson
of patience by heart. Then there's endurance. When
a man must turn out of his bunk at two or three o'clock
on a frosty morning and fight against time in the teeth
of a biting wind or a driving snow for eighteen hours
or more at a stretch; when he must stand waist deep
in the water and floating ice of the river maybe half
the time from dawn to dark to gather and send forward
the stranded logs in the rear; when he must do the ordinary work of two or three men to win the battle with
time,—in all this he would fail if he had not learned
well his lesson of endurance. Persistence is another
of the lessons. Often the elements seem to mock the
mightiest efforts the men put forth. The labor of days
may be undone in a single night by a rain-storm or
a heavy snow. The same work must often be done
over and over again. Enough happens during a season's logging to discourage any but the most determined. Only by adding persistence to the other lessons
does the impossible become possible and a threatening failure is turned into success. Bravery also is
a lesson that is taught by every day's experience in
this great school of the lumbermen. I have seen, you
have all seen men go down under a mighty wall of logs
thirty or forty feet high to break a rollway or a jam,

when an instant's mischance might bury his mangled body under millions of feet of logs. Some of the bravest men in this region are right here in this room and belong also to this school, as well as to the larger one of the woods. Last month, in the jam below Red-Keg, when the tangle of logs resisted the efforts of the crews until they were almost driven to blow it to pieces with giant powder, who went down under the jagged mass and worked like demons until they tore out log after log and set the tangle free, barely escaping with their own lives? You know them. One was Jim Gyde. I thought he was here, but I don't see him. Another was Barney O'Boyle. There's Barney, now, and he needn't blush. Ashbel Fair and Jaky Strander were with them, and four braver boys I never saw. They have learned that lesson well. I hope they will all learn courage of another sort to add to their bravery.

"There is a higher grade in the school of the woods in which other lessons can be learned, and they are not so readily acquired. My friend Josiah Hawkins, whom I see yonder, has learned them well, and has long shown their effect in his beautiful life. One of these lessons is reverence. In the presence of the mighty forces of nature and the grandeur of the ancient forests, one is inspired with reverent awe for the great Maker and Ruler of all. Then the lesson of humility follows as one realizes the smallness and dependence of men. Lessons of self-sacrifice and brotherly kindness are learned by men who work together in common danger, exposure, and eager effort. There was not a man in any of the crews with which I worked who would hesitate an instant to leap to the assistance of a comrade in danger, though his own life might pay the forfeit.

"My one wish is that these lessons, learned unconsciously in the forest and on the river, may take possession of the boys and become the controlling impulses of their lives."

"Mr. Hawkins," called the Moderator, after Parson Allen sat down, "we would be glad to hear from you again. It's nearly five years since ye were Director of this school, and we've not seen much of ye in that time."

"Better let the young folks have a chance now. I guess there's been enough speech-making," replied Farmer Hawkins from his seat in the audience.

The Moderator accordingly announced that the program prepared by the school would be proceeded with at once, and he turned over the exercises to the schoolmaster. Axcy Marthy took her seat at the little melodion in the corner and in a moment the pupils and many of the visitors were singing lustily. Recitations, dialogues, and tableaux followed in rapid succession. A fat youngster in short "pants" and with a shrill, piping voice recited:

> "I wish I had a little wife,
>   A little stove and fire,
> I'd hug her like a lump of gold,
>   And let no one come nigh 'er."

A taller youth with aspirations to be a brave lumberjack made a bold attack upon "Spartacus." Little girls spoke dialogues. Lettie Green, after reciting with fine effect "The Baron's Last Banquet," received her school certificate tightly rolled and tied with a blue ribbon. Similar certificates were given to Norine Maloney and Axcy Marthy after their recitations. The latter brought down the house by an original sketch entitled "The Schoolmarm," in which she introduced

a clever caricature of the unfortunate dame whose brief
career at District School No. 1 had ended suddenly
during the last year, and whose unfinished term Joseph
Waters had just completed. The pleadings, the threats,
the tears, the nervousness, were reproduced true to life,
and the piece ended with the schoolmarm's absurd
attempt to drive her unruly brood out of the schoolhouse by flapping her apron at them with both hands,
stamping her feet, and crying "Shoo! shoo! go home!
shoo!"

As soon as dusk began to settle, nearly forty of the
younger children, most of whom lived in town, were
sent home, and a collation which had been prepared in
a neighboring house was brought in. All formality
and restraint disappeared, and the evening was given
over to fun and frolic. After the remains of the collation were cleared away, the chairs and benches were
arranged on opposite sides of the room and a spelling-
bee was organized, Axcy Marthy being named for leader
of one side and Lettie Green of the other. Each chose
her forces one by one alternately until the entire company of pupils, visitors, and school officials were ranged
on one side or the other, with the schoolmaster in
charge of "Sander's Speller." The battle raged for
over an hour, enlivened with frequent excited disputes
as to alleged partiality on the part of the teacher, or
bursts of laughter when the school officials or other
prominent personages were spelled down. Finally the
contest narrowed down to Lettie Green and the Midland minister on one side and Axcy Marthy and Ashbel Fair, who, with Jaky Strander, had returned in time
for the collation, on the other. The preacher was declared "out" for what he insisted was "only a slip of
the tongue," and Ashbel was so delighted that he failed

2

to watch his own defenses and went down at the very next word. Axcy and Lettie faced each other with flushed faces and shining eyes. They had proved their right to the leadership of their respective sides. It was now a duel to the finish, and more than ever demanded of the schoolmaster care in selecting the words, so that neither should gain an undue advantage. Several words had been spelled correctly by each of the girls when an interruption occurred. The door was thrust open and Sam Hawkins entered. He nodded to the few nearest him and made his way hurriedly to where Seward Rathaway was sitting. After a moment's whispering the two young men went out together. The disturbance was very slight, but it came at an unfortunate time for Lettie. At the next word she hesitated, stammered a little, and missed. Axcy spelled it correctly and was declared the winner. Both girls were extremely popular, so that congratulations were almost equally bestowed.

Livelier games were then called for: Blind Man's Buff; All Going 'Round the Levee; Button, Button; Strap; Lead; Whirl the Platter, and forfeit games of various kinds. Sam Hawkins and Seward Rathaway re-entered the schoolroom and were called to join in Blind Man's Buff, for which poor Jaky Strander had been compelled to play the blind man, his enormous size and awkward movements being counted upon to afford amusement and prolong the chase.

Sam excused himself and sought Lettie Green, whom he drew to one side.

"Awfully sorry I disappointed you, Lettie, don't you know. Got treed by a she-bear without my gun, and had to wait her highness's pleasure until this morning, when she went off to her young ones. Then I followed her into the swamp. Thought I might get you a nice skin; but the rascal gave me the slip."

"I did feel disappointed," replied Lettie, "especially—, but of course if you couldn't help it—; you'll stay now, and take me home to-night?"

"Really, Lettie, I'm awfully sorry, but Seward and I have got to go now; something important, don't you know." Then seeing Lettie's look of astonishment and reproach, and a suspicion of tears gathering, he added hurriedly, "Don't be foolish, Lettie, there's a good girl. . I'll make it all right," and he bent closer and whispered something in her ear.

The clouds partially disappeared from the girl's face, but she allowed Seward to get the benefit of an accusing flash from her eyes as he came toward her. He shifted uneasily, but said, with an effort to appear unembarrassed:

"You and Aunt Lydia can take the buckboard and drive back together with the folks. Sam and I have urgent business, and can't stay. Good night."

The two boys hurried off, attracting as little attention as possible to their departure. Lettie thought her evening was spoiled, but under the influence of the gaiety around her, her natural vivacity soon reasserted itself, and she joined in the games as though nothing had happened. The games of forfeit were most popular, and with Axcy Marthy, Ashbel Fair, and Barney O'Boyle as judges, the sentences imposed were sure to be ingenious and mirth-provoking. The dapper little minister of Midland was condemned to do a log-rolling act on an empty barrel provided for the purpose, and his carefully prepared gestures in the pulpit were never half so expressive as the impromptu ones with which he emphasized this performance; nor was his congregation ever so appreciative. With perfect good nature the precise little man made himself ridiculous and crowned his efforts with the expected downfall.

Big, jolly Pete Murray, who had the fastest horses in the district, and who drew the biggest load of logs ever brought into Red-Keg, was ordered by Ashbel Fair to thread a cambric needle in one minute, or kiss Axcy Marthy on the tip of her nose. Failing ignominiously in the first, he went at the second with a gusto, but made a slight mistake.

"Stop! that's my mouth!" screamed Axcy, laughing and blushing.

"Sure, right well I know it!" shouted the giant lumberman in glee. "An' it's a reward, not a forfeit, so it is."

"No fair! another forfeit! Make him pay another!" exclaimed the players from all parts of the room.

"Judge" Ashbel agreed, and demanded a story from the grinning Irishman.

"Good! a story! a story!" clamored the young people, who knew that Pete Murray was famous for his wonderful stories of the "ould sod," and that he always had a supply on tap.

Nothing loath, the jovial lumberman at once began a yarn that became taller and taller until it was drowned in the jeers and laughter of his hearers.

The next victim was "Babe" Strander, who was required to walk on a straight chalk line down the centre of the room, with a penalty of a pin-thrust from a pretty girl for every step which did not touch the line. Nearly every girl in the room had a jab at the poor fellow as the result of his promenade.

Ashbel Fair, falling, in his turn, under the condemnation of Judge Axcy Marthy, was ordered to preach

a five minutes' sermon to the Midland minister on the
sin of frivolity. Ashbel was disconcerted for a moment
only; then he showed that the mischievous girl had
not reckoned in vain on his wit and readiness for a lark.
He escorted the learned young domine with great dignity to a seat directly in front of the platform, mounted
to a place behind the teacher's table, and in solemn tones
delivered an impromptu discourse in which he imitated
the minister's own manner and gestures, and raked him
over the coals for imaginary offenses, until the audience
held their sides with laughter, and the poor minister
protested that it was he that was paying the forfeit, and
not Ashbel.

Hezekiah Bloag, one of the wealthiest men, and certainly the stingiest, in the section, being subject to a
forfeit, was called upon by the inexorable Axcy, the
only one who would have dared to do such a thing, to
make out a check on the bank of Midland for twenty-
five dollars for the widow of one of his men who was
killed in the rollway the month before. A cheer went
up as the forfeit was imposed; but Mr. Bloag refused
to be "bled" under such a pretence.

"For shame! Pay the forfeit! It's little enough
for ye to do," urged his neighbors and acquaintances,
vociferously.

Finally the stingy man went to the schoolmaster's
table and made out a check in due form for the twenty-
five dollars payable to the bereaved widow. A shout
of applause greeted the act, and Axcy Marthy was congratulated on scoring an unusual victory; but later,
when the check was presented at the bank, it was discovered that the old skinflint had written Bloog instead
of Bloag, and the check was not worth the paper it was
written on.

Barney O'Boyle had been enjoying hugely the forfeits imposed on the others, and was laughing boisterously, when suddenly his own name was called. He stopped short and stared at Axcy in bewilderment.

"Come, Barney, it's your turn."

"Faith, I'm a judge, ain't I?" asked Barney, hoping for immunity.

"Never mind, you've got to take your share. I'll act as judge," insisted Axcy, her eyes twinkling.

Accordingly the rollicking young Irishman, tall, lanky, and powerful, took his seat in front of the judge.

"What does a woman need most to keep house with?" asked Axcy.

"Pins," replied Barney with a grin. The rules required that the answer given to the first question should be repeated for every other question, and not another word should be spoken.

"What would you give the girl you love best for a wedding present?"

"Pins," said Barney, at the same time shaking his head vigorously to belie his word.

"What makes the best cushion for the teacher's chair?"

"Pins!" shouted Barney, and the roar of laughter that followed shook the house. Axcy cast a languishing glance at the schoolmaster and then, turning to Barney again, asked:

"What did the boys get who fixed the chair?"

"Pins!" and another roar broke loose.

"What would you do if you caught another fellow kissing the girl you love?"

"Smash his—! Begorry, I mean 'pins'; but he better not be tryin' it!"

"A forfeit! a forfeit!" came the cry in gleeful tones from all over the room.

Barney was covered with confusion. He had never declared his love to any girl, and his bashfulness made it seem impossible for him to do so, but the eyes of his friends were not blind. He feared now he had compromised himself.

"The sentence of the court is that you now sing a serenade to one Norine Maloney," declared Axcy maliciously.

Barney stared at his tormentor in despair, his face red as a beet.

"Sure, I can't do it. I'm no singer, an' I don't know no serrinades," he begged.

"Yes, you can, Barney. You are one of the best singers in the district, and the court will give you two minutes to think of a serenade. Surely you will not refuse to sing to such a nice young lady," replied Axcy, in her sweetest tones.

Barney glanced at where Norine sat blushing like a rose. He was seized with a fit of trembling, and looked around in vain for a way of escape. The clock ticked loudly on the wall. Barney scratched his head, and slowly a gleam of fun crept into his rough, honest face. The two minutes were scarcely up when he strode over to Norine, squared his shoulders, knelt on one knee, and began to chant in a solemn voice:

"Mid scenes of confusion and creature complaints,
How sweet to my soul is communion with saints."

An explosion of laughter and cheers put an end to the serenade, and it was conceded that Barney had turned the tables on his persecutors.

The games continued for some time longer, and then

the centre of the room was cleared, Jose, the champion fiddler of the backwoods, with two companions, struck up a lively tune, and in a jiffy the dance was in full swing.

Not until long after midnight did the jolly party break up. The new moon had set long ago, and only the light of the stars and the lanterns on carriages and wagons enabled the home-goers to find their way.

"Your room is all ready for you, Robert," said Mother Hawkins to the backwoods preacher. "You'll be with us soon?"

"To-morrow, perhaps, or Saturday," replied Allen.

Lettie whispered to her aunt, and the latter called Barney.

"I want to talk with Mrs. Maloney," she said. "You don't mind if Lettie and I ride in the family wagon? You and Norine can have the buckboard and return it to Seward to-morrow."

If Barney minded, he didn't say so, and Norine was not consulted, but she had reason to fear that her companion had lost his tongue on the long ride home. If she had known how much he longed to talk, she might have taken pity on him and helped him a little, but, instead, she repaid his taciturnity with a like silence, until he set her down at her gate. Then she said gently:

"Good-night, Barney."

"Good-night," he replied.

Joseph Waters, the schoolmaster, was boarding for a fortnight with Abe Davis, about a mile from the schoolhouse. The road zigzagged through a piece of swale. Houses were far apart, and on a dark night the road was uninviting. An old lumber shanty, about half-

"'MID SCENES OF CONFUSION AND CREATURE COMPLAINTS."

way to the right, was a favorite resort of the boys in
which to roast game or fish captured from woods or
river, tip the jug, sing songs, or smoke by the fireside.
The sturdy schoolmaster felt no fear in passing through
this lonely road on his way home, but his experiences
with the lawless members of his school had taught him
the wisdom of always being on his guard. He had told
no one how, going to the school very early on the
morning of closing day to make some preparations, he
had seen the five boys leaving the place, had quickly
discovered their trick, and made his plans for check-
mating them. He thought it better to keep them in
the dark. He was now debating with himself whether
he should accept the School Board's urgent invitation
to undertake another term. The work was hard and
the pay small, but something in his rugged nature
rebelled against the thought of retreat before those
young bullies.

"I had the upper hand to-day; but am I strong
enough to keep it?" he pondered. "There is something good and noble in their hearts, if it can only be
awakened to life. What grand men they will make if
they can be conquered without breaking their spirits.
Love is the only force that will do it."

A slight noise interrupted his thoughts. He was
just passing the shanty. Some one in a muffled tone
said:

"Sic 'im, Moscow; sic 'im!"

In an instant, from the deeper shadow of the shanty
a great body sprang out and rushed toward the schoolmaster. There was no time for thought. With a single leap the mighty brute cleared the ditch at the right
of the road and gathered himself for another spring,
his eyes gleaming through the darkness like coals of

fire. Joe Waters was an athlete and agile as an Indian. The instant the savage dog made his second spring the schoolmaster leaped to one side, and the brute, with wide-open jaws, passed him and was carried, with the impetus of his own bound, across the narrow roadway and into the ditch filled with water on the other side. His sudden fall and cold plunge surprised and dazed him for some seconds. Then, snarling and growling, he turned and laboriously climbed the slippery clay bank, panting with rage. Waters saw his opportunity, and planted a vigorous kick squarely under the jaws of the snarling beast. The dog slipped back, but did not lose his hold on the bank, and now, more infuriated than ever, pressed forward to what he knew was to be a battle to the death. The schoolmaster had whipped his revolver from his pocket, and waited only to get a sure aim. Almost before he knew it the brute was on him again. A second kick was not so fortunate. His other foot slipped in the mud, and before he could recover his balance the bloodthirsty beast had sprung for his throat. Unconsciously Waters had raised his left arm as a guard, and the iron jaws, instead of finding his throat, closed upon his wrist with a crunching that sent a wave of fire through his body. Then a flash burst from the revolver, the mass of dog-flesh quivered, the jaws loosened, and without even a groan the heavy body sank at the schoolmaster's feet, shot through the brain from ear to ear.

Waters struck a match and examined the dog closely. It was a Great Dane, notorious for its ferocity, and always kept chained at home by its owner, Jim Gyde.

"That settles it," muttered Waters grimly. "I shall stay."

CHAPTER III

Sam Hawkins never took kindly to work, study, or discipline. For years, as a boy, he had been hand-and-glove with the disturbing element in District School No. 1. When he was eighteen, his father, then a leading business man in Midland, and Moderator of the School Board, had sent him to college in an Eastern State, hoping that the training and discipline, the companionship of other young men, and the broader outlook on life and its possibilities there furnished might make a man of him. Sam, however, quickly formed a close friendship with two other wild, careless youths, Walter Hayward and Billy Axford, and developed still further the wrong side of his character. Seward Rathaway had persuaded his father to let him go with Sam to the same college, and the four chums, who soon became inseparable, styled themselves "The Invincibles." At the end of a four years' course, Seward, whose father had died the previous year, returned to Red-Keg, while Sam went with Walter Hayward to visit the latter's palatial home in New York. He returned in the fall, a vain, lazy youth, discontented with life as he found it in the backwoods, but without an aim or ambition to make a better way for himself.

Sam's father, finding that the strain of his business was undermining his health, and realizing, with pain at his heart, that his son could not step into his place, had sold out immediately after sending Sam to college and retired to a farm of two hundred and forty acres

about three miles north of Red-Keg, in connection with
which he owned also a quarter-section of fairly good
pine timber. This property offered Sam a good opportunity, but he scorned the work and refused to help on
the farm or in the woods. He quickly developed a
fondness for hunting, and spent most of his time in that
pursuit, as often as not being accompanied by Seward.
His good looks and a certain distinction of manner
made him for a time popular with the young people;
but his assumption of superiority, and his unconcealed
distaste for social intercourse with his neighbors, soon
isolated him from nearly all the better element.

"Can't bear the clumsy frolics of these country
gawks. They're an awful bore, don't you know," he
remarked to Seward, as they left the schoolhouse on
the evening of the closing festivities.

Upon Lettie Green, however, he conferred the honor
of an immediate regard, which for a time seemed genuine and deep, and the sprightly, ambitious girl repaid it
with a wealth of affection and an unswerving loyalty
for which many of the youths in the region had wooed
in vain. Her coquetry, hitherto her strong defense,
failed her when Sam Hawkins, fresh from the great
metropolis, laid claim to her heart. The innate selfish-
ness of the man showed itself on the occasion of the
school festivities, when he not only deprived Lettie of
his own promised escort, but dragged her cousin Seward away also to listen to his great scheme.

"I tell you I've made the greatest discovery of our
lives," he asserted again to Seward, as the two seated
themselves in the corner of a tavern well known to
Sam. "It will make our fortunes if we work it right,
don't you know. We must send for Walt and Billy at
once."

"For heaven's sake, quit beating about the bush, and let out your story," exclaimed Seward.

"You must swear not to reveal the secret to a soul. It would make it worthless to us if any one else should know of it."

"Oh, that's agreed, of course; go on with your tale."

"Good! My yarn to Lettie about being treed by a bear was partly true, don't you know; but I had my gun, and a shot only grazed the beast, and she slipped off into the swamp. I was bound to get her if possible, and followed the best way I could. There's a long ridge of rock running out into the swamp about six miles north of Red-Keg, and nearly three from the road. That's where I found myself after chasing the bear for half an hour or more. I came to a place where a point of flat rock dips down into a narrow lagoon. There I was stumped—couldn't go any farther, don't you know, and old bruin seemed to have given me the slip. Besides that, I was winded, and glad to sit down for a rest. It must have been a quarter of an hour later when out bobbed the old bear with two cubs on the opposite shore of the lagoon not more than fifty feet farther on. She saw me as soon as I did her and made a dive with the cubs into the water. Of course I let them have both barrels as quick as I could, but when the smoke cleared away not a sign of bear, dead or alive, was to be seen. It's hard to say whether I was more mad or puzzled, don't you know. They got away somewhere, that was sure, and the only direction seemed to be by water. I couldn't let them off so easy as that, even though it was getting late, so I crawled out on a log ten or fifteen feet into the lagoon till I could see that it bent around and widened out into what looked like navigable water. I got the log loose and managed to roll another one down beside it and fasten the two together with swamp grass and green branches. This made quite a respectable raft, and, with a long pole, I pushed out into the swamp. By Jove! I was on a regular canal. It twisted and turned to every point of the compass, and often I could hardly get my logs around the bends. Just as I was on the point of giving up and picking my way back, I heard falling water, and, around another turn——"

"Well, what in thunder are you stopping for?" exclaimed Seward, as Sam paused to make his announcement more impressive.

"An island!"

"Humph! Is that all?"

"All, man! A fairyland! A mystic isle, hidden from the world, with a big *cave*, a regular grotto, and a sweet spring of water! What more do you want? Isn't it just the place for the Invincibles, and our—our little—enterprise, don't you know?"

"That's so; it does sound interesting," admitted Seward.

"Interesting! We must send for Walt and Billy this very night," exclaimed Sam, in a tone which implied that he had given the matter all the consideration it needed.

"What! before I have even seen the place?" expostulated Seward.

"Not a day to lose," replied Sam. "That's why I bothered to come way down here to-night to see you. Had to spend last night in my new domain, don't you know; it got so late before I finished exploring it. Walt wrote in his last letter that he had about made up his mind to go travelling in Europe again with his folks the first of May, though he thinks it's an awful bore. He may be gone in a week. There's a train East from here to-night. I must get a letter off to Walt on that. You write to Billy, and both letters can go by to-night's train. Yours will be sent West from Saginaw and will get to Billy about the same time Walt gets his. We'll likely hear from them inside a fortnight."

Seward agreed, and the following letter was quickly prepared:

"RED-KEG, Thursday, April 22d, 1868.

"DEAR WALTER: I have made a grand discovery. I have unearthed a veritable Garden of Eden, and it is situated in the midst of this wicked portion of the earth. It is as secluded as though it were on the planet Mars. We intend to keep it so. Seward has written to Billy, and we both want you to come on here at your earliest convenience. Do you remember how we once longed for just such a secret place where we could carry on our 'experiments'? Well, we have at last found it, and it's just an ideal spot. Come prepared for roughing it for the summer. Hastily but sincerely yours,

"SAM."

A copy was written for Billy Axford and both were taken to the agent at the railroad station, who agreed to see that they were despatched on the night train.

"I suppose we may as well go back now," suggested Seward.

"Oh, you don't care for those kindergarten games," replied Sam. "Besides, the less questioning we have to submit to the better for us, don't you know. They don't expect us again to-night."

"Well, where shall we go? I don't propose to walk home seven miles this time of night. There is no train till morning."

"Bedell will lend us his buckboard and we can both go to your house, get some sleep, and start early for our new possessions," said Sam.

Accordingly they hunted up Rodney Bedell's house. He was out, explained his mother, but of course he would be pleased to let Sam and Seward take the buckboard; no, she didn't know where Rodney was; she supposed he was at the school dance.

Before the sun was up, the two young men were on their way to the great swamp. Seward's excitement rose as his chum dilated on the beauties, the mystery, and the possibilities of the hidden island. As to its inaccessibility, he had ample evidence before reaching the end of the trip. The swamp covered hundreds of acres in the heart of the forest, and was impassable on foot. A man cared little for life who would attempt to cross it. Sink-holes were numerous, and the surface of the ground was covered with fallen timber criss-crossed and piled up until it presented an impenetrable barrier to progress. Even in the severest winter weather the sink-holes were seldom frozen hard enough to bear the weight of a man. The place had attractions for neither farmer nor hunter, lumberman nor trapper. A few tamarack-trees remained standing here and there, dead, with their bare limbs spreading spectre-like over the uninviting scene of desolation. This swamp was apparently as impenetrable and as safe from encroachment as the famous "valley of death" of Southern Arizona. At a certain place a ridge of sand and rock, as Sam had said, ran out from the forest far into the swamp, forming a narrow cape. At the end it tapered gradually down to a low point of flat rock which dipped into one of the countless lagoons of clear deep water. There was no beach or muddy bank, and nothing to distinguish the pool of water, as seen from the rock, from any of the numberless sink-holes of the region.

Sam had provided himself with rope, hammer, nails, and axe. Reaching the rocky point, they proceeded to reconstruct their raft with three logs, well fastened together, and each man cut a stout pole. As they pushed off, it seemed to Seward that they would surely run plump into the tall, rank grass at what appeared to be the other end of the lagoon; but in an instant he saw an opening to the left into a second lagoon, which also seemingly ended abruptly. This opened in like manner into a third, and so on.

"Talk about exploring!" exclaimed Seward, as they worked their long raft with difficulty around the short bends in the channel; "no one would imagine there was anything but swamp here, surely."

"That's the beauty of it," replied Sam; "and we can close the opening from the first lagoon with an artificial hedge of swamp grass rigged up to look like the real thing from a little distance. Then we might be in the heart of Africa so far as any attempts to find us are concerned."

"We'll need an Indian canoe and paddles," said Seward, after the end of the raft had become entangled two or three times in the grass at the sides of the canal. "That is the only proper way to navigate these waters."

"Yes, we shall want at least two of them when Walt and Billy come," assented Sam. "There! Don't you hear the waterfall?"

Seward listened a moment, and then exclaimed:

"Right you are! I suppose we ought to shout 'Land! land!' only it seems to be water."

"You'll see the land quick enough," laughed Sam.

3

Another turn, two or three hard pushes with the poles, and the two explorers, huddling together as far as possible at the rear of their raft to tip the forward end up, drove the three logs upon a shelving rock similar to the one from which they had embarked, but presenting to the water a concave edge like a horse-shoe, and thus forming an excellent boat-landing.

"Splendid!" shouted Seward, as he sprang ashore. "You failed to do it justice, my boy; it's a paradise!"

The beautiful island on which they landed presented a striking contrast to the surrounding dreary desolation. It was perhaps ten acres in area, and was nicely timbered, free from underbrush, and provided by nature with a copious spring gushing out of a ledge of rocks. This spring was clear and limpid as crystal, cold, and refreshing, and never-failing. It was the source of a deep, quiet stream that cut its way through the bog with apparently no fall or current. From the island it circled around to the north a short distance, and then branched, one fork continuing in a northerly direction, the other southward to the rock from whence the young men had come. There was no apparent outlet in either direction. The north branch led up to the extreme southern end of the burnt hills, and ended abruptly at the foot of a gigantic willow-tree. Both branches were equally hidden in the tall grass of the swamp, and both gave access to the island from points several miles apart.

"Come up and see our grotto," called Sam, leading the way directly over the centre of the island, which was its highest point, and from which they could see the swamp in all directions. In the distance the forest and the hills were visible, but this particular bit of land was not high enough to be distinguishable from the swamp or the forest. Near the northern end of the island was the cave, running into the ledge of rocks from which the waterfall issued on the south. It was a really wonderful cavern, large and roomy, with an opening high enough to enter while standing erect, and broadening within to a diameter of nearly twenty feet and a height of twelve to fifteen. Two or three other smaller chambers connected with the first, and from the farthest a small opening let them out again to the surface of the island. A circulation of air thus kept the interior dry and habitable.

"With a little digging and clearing and fixing up, we can make those caves as snug and cozy as a castle," declared Sam.

"It can't be beat, that's a fact; but it will take money to fit the place up. How are we going to get it?" asked Seward.

"Leave that to Walt and Billy. That's what they are good for," replied Sam with a laugh. Then, as though announcing his guiding principle, he added: "What's the use of sweating when you can let somebody else do it for you?"

They were strolling through a clump of pine-trees on their way to the farthest end of the island, when Seward suddenly exclaimed in an excited whisper:

"Look, Sam! Get your gun ready; you're a better shot than I am. There!"

Turning in the direction indicated, Sam observed a large wildcat creeping toward them. As he raised his rifle, the beast turned to retreat. A bullet stopped him, and he rolled over with scarcely a struggle.

"We're not the first inhabitants, at any rate," remarked Sam. "I'm glad that chap didn't find me last night. We must thrash the island thoroughly before

establishing an abode here.   And now to business.
You remember old Pomp and his wife?"

"Who took care of the Invincibles' house at college?
Yes."

"When the boys come we'll send for that old couple,
and Pomp can help us prepare our 'experiments.' You
remember he said he was an old hand at the business
before we picked him up.   The woman can cook and
keep the place in order.   Pete will be glad to assist at
the business end.   Meanwhile, we can improve the ac-
commodations of the castle."

The forenoon quickly passed in thus exploring and
planning, and, after eating a luncheon hastily put together in the morning, the two conspirators returned
to their raft and pushed off into the lagoon.

"We must drive in to Midland this afternoon with
Rodney's buckboard," said Sam.   "You can take yours,
too, and we can return together."

Half-way to Seward's house, they were overtaken on
the road by Ros Whitmore, who pulled up his horse
and greeted them cordially.

"We missed ye last night," he exclaimed, "and you
missed a mighty good time.   What took ye off so sudden?"   He looked reprovingly at Seward.

"Something else on hand," replied Sam, shortly.

"We were called off on urgent business that came up
unexpectedly.   I was sorry to miss the fun; but business before pleasure, you know," explained Seward, in
a more conciliatory tone.

Ros Whitmore was everywhere popular.   He made
friends by showing himself friendly.   Though devoted
to his own large family, and working hard to keep those
of his fourteen children who were dependent upon him
supplied with the necessaries of life, he yet found time

and occasion to exert himself for others. He had already done Seward more than one good turn, and the young man did not wish to offend him.

"Now look here," went on Ros, with animation, "it's just sheer luck that I met ye. I can't get everywhere, and there's heaps o' ground to cover. You two can help a sight—Hold up, Jenny, we'll be goin' soon.

"Ye see, it's this way," with a turn of the line around his hand to restrain his impatient horse; "Parson Allen has been workin' all winter out among us boys and the shantymen in the woods, and never got a cent. Why, bless your heart," as he saw a look of surprise on Seward's face, "he could have earned his stake with the best of 'em, ef he'd been a mind to, but that dear saint wouldn't let his name go on no time book, 'cause he said he wanted to be free to go and come from one camp to another as he felt called to; and he worked with the men just to git the chance to be with 'em close, on their own ground, and talk to 'em, and let 'em see he loved 'em, and didn't set himself up above 'em, and to show 'em a man could work hard in the woods night and day 'thout swearin' and drinkin' and fightin'. Lord! he wouldn't take no pay, though he done as much real work as any, and done it clean as a whistle, too. That kind of pay warn't what he was after. He figured that ef he took pay the boys would jest think he was there for what he could earn, and wouldn't pay no great 'tention to him. Anyhow, that's the way your father thinks he figured it," glancing at Sam.

"What has all this got to do with us?" asked Sam, impatiently.

"The pint is jest this. As I said, the Elder ain't got a cent to show for his winter's work. Maybe you two don't know that he's been doin' that same thing every winter goin' on six, seven years in this region, and he don't get no regular pay for preachin' and ministerin' from Red-Keg to Sixteen, and all the settlements hereabouts the year 'round."

"How in the world does he live?" asked Seward.

"Jest as it comes to him. He says all is the Lord's, and he is the Lord's, and the Lord will provide ef he sticks to the Lord's business; and to tell the truth, I ain't never seen him goin' hungry or naked, and wouldn't allow it ef I did, neither would any one else as I know of."

"Very good; glad to know the good man is so well off," said Sam sarcastically, as Ros paused an instant. "Just now, we've got business in town, and must leave a discussion of the Parson's self-sacrificing labors and his providential rewards till a more leisure hour, don't you know."

"Hold on, don't get uneasy," went on Ros, good-naturedly, "I'm comin' 'round to the text in my usial backhanded fashion. The fact is, us boys, meanin' me, and Pete Murray, and Bob Landseer, and Tom Moore, and Barney O'Boyle, and John Maloney, and some others, have talked it over with Farmer Hawkins, and decided to give the Elder a darnation party."

Seward laughed. "A donation party, you mean," he said.

"Course I do. It ain't no swearin' matter. I want you to help."

"Excuse me; that's a line of work I'm not acquainted with," sneered Sam. The mention of Barney O'Boyle's name as one of the movers in the affair had especially riled him. He had taken an immediate dislike to the outspoken, independent young Irishman, whom he had found occupying, as he thought, a too important place in his father's household.

"Is there *any* line of work—?" began Ros Whitmore. Then he laughed. "It's nothin' but to let folks know," he said. "Bein' so scattered, it takes everybody to spread the news. To-day's Friday. The Elder is comin' up to the Hawkins place to-morrow to stay two, three weeks. May hold prayer-meetin' in the ell on Sunday. We lay out to have the darn—donation party Tuesday afternoon. We want every man we can git aholt of in time to come, and especially the women, and every mother's son and daughter must bring some donation, don't matter what, 'slong as it has *value*. So long, boys, glad I met ye," and Ros gave Jenny the rein and was soon out of sight.

"Well, I'm not!" ejaculated Sam, replying to Ros's last remark. "It's a pretty state of affairs to have the house turned into a parsonage and filled with psalmsingers, and a hired laborer strutting about the parlor as master of ceremonies. You won't get me into such a mix-up." He waited a moment. Then he laughed grimly and added: "Our castle on Mystic Isle will be likely to find me a more constant visitor than I thought, don't you know."

CHAPTER IV

"THAT dear woman certainly does have her share of trials, Robert. Little Ben is wasted to a shadow with the rickets; Ray broke his wrist falling over the stone wall; Tilly can't seem to get rid of that cough; Bess got the end of a needle in her thumb; Tom lost his shoes in the creek and was nearly drowned fishing for them. I don't remember the rest, but it seems to me that all of them are doing something to add to the general worry. Yet Jule hasn't a word of complaint, and by the way she sings about the house you'd suppose there wasn't a cloud in the sky."

Mother Hawkins finished laying away her wraps, and sat down in the calico-covered rocking-chair with a sigh of relief.

"You have been out to The Corners?" asked Allen.

"Yes, there were so many things the dear lambs needed, and so few hands to do them, now that Jenny and Lucy are out at service."

"You are always ministering, Susan. It's the 'inasmuch' way," said Allen, smiling.

"Oh, it's little enough I can do, and I guess it don't count much, except as a means of grace to my own heart," replied Mother Hawkins. "Now with you it's different; you have come to be a real necessity, and the people are at last beginning to realize it."

"Every man is necessary to God's plan in some way, Susan; but no man can claim any credit for doing what has been put upon him to do. I need to do the work for my own sake, just as you have said yourself. 'For though I preach the gospel, I have nothing to glory of, for necessity is laid upon me; yea, woe is me if I preach not the gospel.' Paul must have remembered his great sin, and felt a deeper sense of need when he wrote that. And I can say with David, '*My* sin is ever before me.'"

"But remember, Robert, *He* cast it all behind his back long ago," said Susan, gently.

"Yes, and He has given peace in place of bitterness; but He gave also work as a necessary condition to peace."

Mother Hawkins was silent.

Presently the minister said, in a low voice that choked as he spoke:

"I cannot forget Ruth, Susan."

Mother Hawkins made no reply, but soon a tear, followed quickly by another, rolled down her cheeks into her lap.

"Come, Mother, let's get dinner out of the way early," said Farmer Hawkins, bustling in. "I'll talk with Robert a while." Then he added in a whisper as his wife came toward him: "They'll be here along about three o'clock. I just saw Tom Moore. He says there'll be a crowd."

"You mustn't go out this afternoon, Robert," he said, after Mother Hawkins had left the room. "Some of the neighbors were talking about dropping in for a friendly call. They haven't had much time to visit with you since last fall, and we ought not to let the neighborly spirit die out."

"Little fear of that, I judge, while there is such hospitality to be found as this home always affords," replied the minister.

"I've just got that acre and a quarter lot cleared of stumps," continued Farmer Hawkins, ignoring the bit of flattery. "I paid Ros Whitmore a hundred dollars to do the job, but although he managed it well, so far as I could see, I'm afraid he lost money on it. I've given him another lot at the same price with not more than half the number of stumps, so I guess he can average up all right."

"Stump-pulling is the worst feature of farming in this region, truly," said the minister.

"Yes, and you can't dodge it any more than you can dodge the stumps themselves when you try to plough a field which has not been cleared. If they would only decay in a few years, one might wait, but they all have to be grubbed and pulled, one by one. It adds quite an item to the cost of land."

"But not when you get the original yield of timber," said Allen. "Your neighbor Maloney gets enough from his logs on one acre to pay for pulling stumps from several others, with some to spare."

"To be sure, and I'm glad for John. If any man deserves to succeed, he does. His eight years' struggle with the wilderness is only just beginning to yield him a little comfort. Barring his clump of good pine, his choice of land was not fortunate. Too much sand in some places, too much clay in others. He might have had this quarter as well as not, before I took it into my head to come out here."

"Does Maloney ever hear from his folks?" asked the minister.

"Only now and then from his brother Orrin. John is too proud to make advances, or to accept favors from those who cast him off because he married the girl he loved. He cherishes no resentment, I believe, but he is bent on making his own way."

"His brother Orrin was always his friend, was he not?"

"Yes, but not openly. He is still in partnership with his old father in Belfast, and while the latter lives, Orrin wishes to keep peace with him."

"John made a pretty fair haul of logs this spring. Why don't you cut some of yours, or sell the stumpage?" suggested the minister, who saw with a lumberman's practical eye the values in Farmer Hawkins's outlying quarter-section of pine.

"I suppose it will have to come to that soon," replied Josiah, "although my quarter is hardly first-class lumber pine. I have thought of organizing a camp of my own down there, taking out a shingle-mill, and cutting the logs into shingles on the spot. There will be quite a yield, I know. Perhaps I may do it next winter."

"You can have your pick of the boys, that's certain," said Allen, approvingly.

"The truth is," went on Josiah, "I have never yet been able to cut trees without a pang. I love them—all of them—and some of them in particular. You see those noble oaks, and that big beech yonder, and those maple-trees?" he said, rising and leading the minister out upon the veranda. "Did I never tell you what a struggle I had with my men, when clearing the farm, to make them leave those beautiful trees untouched? All over the place I tried to preserve for shade and ornament certain trees on which I had fixed my affections; but the boys would persist in consigning my leafy pets to the axe or the flames. The workmen meant well, no doubt, but indifference, thoughtlessness, and habit led them to sacrifice my idols in spite of repeated warnings. I never could impress upon them the value, still less the beauty, of a good green tree in the right place. One of the strongest reasons I had for buying this particular section, aside from John's earnest wish that I should be his neighbor—a feeling, by the way, which I shared—was the fact that it contained such a variety of trees, many of them growing free in clearings, as if they had stepped out from the crowded forest to stretch their splendid limbs and plume their gorgeous foliage in the broad light of day. It was October, just after Sam went to college, when I took my first trip through this section. Those very trees over yonder were in a blaze of glory. I loved them at first sight. There were hundreds more like them scattered over the farm that was to be. I succeeded in saving less than half of my chosen friends; but they have been a comfort to me these five years. The first year, when my head was still weary from too close attention to business, those dear trees whispered peace and rest to me. I have never been reconciled to the warfare against the trees that has gone on around me all this time."

"Yet in this way is our frontier pushed forward, our great industries developed, our lands cleared for cultivation, and countless thousands given employment," urged the minister.

"True; I know it. The spirit of business seems to prevent the growth of sentiment. The forest must be overcome, must die under the bite of the axe and the gnawing of the saw. It is everywhere a death struggle with the issue never in doubt, and the slaughter becomes more wholesale each year. Yet I know of some men who, like myself, destroy trees while they

love them. They spare when it is not necessary to
kill. They plant other trees. Their orchards early
cover the ground laid bare, and their homes are surrounded by trees for shade and beauty. I wish there
were more such farmers in this region. Yet I shall
cut my pine in due time."

Robert Allen did not challenge further discussion,
and they returned to the house. After a few moments
he asked, reminded by Farmer Hawkins's casual mention of his son:

"Where is Sam, now? I have seen him only once
or twice since he returned from college. I should like
to know him better."

A weary look came over the father's face. He did
not reply at once, but his friend and minister read the
testimony of a heart's sorrow in lines which he had not
observed before.

"I wish you might," said Josiah presently. "He
needs some stronger influence than mine to come into
his life. His college experience did not have the effect
I hoped for."

The minister waited in silence for him to continue.

" 'A foolish son is a grief to his father and bitterness to her who bare him,' " muttered Farmer Hawkins,
more to himself than to Allen, and he did not observe
the strong emotion which overspread the minister's
face.

"There was another such boy once," the latter whispered.

After a moment Josiah Hawkins raised his head and
looked into his friend's face with a sudden intensity of
appeal.

"Robert," he said, "do you suppose if you were to
make a special case—if you would take it as a particu-

lar burden on your heart—the Lord might let you be
the means——"

"Josiah," interrupted the minister, "I was once hungry and you gave me meat, naked and you clothed me.
More than that, I was fallen and you lifted me up, an
outcast, and you took me in. Do you think there could
be any joy so great for me as to be the means in God's
hands for returning to you in like kind the bread you
cast upon the waters so long ago?"

"God help you, Robert!" breathed Josiah Hawkins,
grasping the backwoods minister by both hands.

But Sam was sowing the wind and was destined to reap
the whirlwind before he listened to the still small voice.

Dinner was eaten in unusual quietness. Sam came
in after the meal began, replied shortly to remarks addressed directly to him, and went out before the others
finished. Barney, the life and sparkle of every family
or social gathering, had not yet returned from his
errands with Tom Moore, the big lumberman and village constable, Barney's particular friend.

"Have you any new books since last year, Josiah?"
asked the minister, as they arose from the table.

"A few choice ones," leading the way into the sitting-room and unlocking the large glass doors of the
bookcase. "These friends are the rivals of my trees;
but often I can enjoy communion with them both at
the same time. For example, I never enjoy the companionship of this author," caressing a volume of
Thoreau, "so well as when close to the trees that he
loved as I do."

"I'll spend an hour or so with these friends of yours,
while you are making ready to receive our other friends,
your neighbors" said Robert Allen, all unconscious of
the purpose of the gathering that afternoon.

"Parson, ahoy!"

The stentorian voice of Barney O'Boyle broke in upon the quietness of the minister's reading and caused him to shut his book in a hurry. Going out to the veranda, he found five or six buckboards, farm wagons, and ox-teams drawn up in the road before the house, and filled with a shouting, laughing crowd. There were John and Mary Maloney, and their daughter Norine; big Pete Murray and his wife Kate, with two buxom girls, Katie and Sally; Bob Landseer, with Hetty his wife—"humly as a hedgehog, but ther ain't a bigger heart from Maine to Californy," Bob was wont to say affectionately. In front of all were Tom Moore and Barney O'Boyle, like great rollicking brothers.

"Bein' as we're the committee, we laid out to git here early," explained Tom; "and how be ye, Elder? Jumpin' kangaroo! yer right there," he exclaimed, releasing his own great paw from the parson's iron grasp.

"Committee?" queried Allen, puzzled. "I'll call Mr. Hawkins."

"Lave Uncle Si wherever he is," said Barney. "These folks are after comin' to see yourself; an' there'll be more of them before there's less. Sure, it's your turn, intirely, to-day. Out with ye, ladies an' gintlemen, an' pay your respicts to the best friend ye have in the county."

Down came the mothers and daughters from their seats, laden with bundles of all sizes and shapes, and all began to talk at once.

"We made this at the quiltin' bee last winter, and it has nigh twelve hundred pieces in it, and soft wool linin'," said Hetty Landseer, giving the minister a huge parcel from which at the same time she deftly stripped the covering. A gorgeous quilt of many colors was revealed.

"I never had sech good luck dryin' apples," broke in Kate Murray, putting down by the parson a big calico bag crammed full of the dried fruit. "Them's from the South orchard, and I find them the best flavor," she explained.

"Pumpkins," said Sally briefly, as she and Katie, who had lugged a heavy basket between them from the wagon, set their load down in front of the bewildered minister.

"Dried, of course," added Katie, "but prime for pies and sech."

"Here's six pairs of woollen socks and some warm mits for driving, that mamma and I made off and on through the winter. I guess they'll fit you all right," said Norine Maloney, putting the parcel in the minister's hands.

"When you women stop to catch your breath a minute, we'll speak *our* little piece," called out Bob Landseer. "They's a load o' spalts out here for ye, parson."

"An' stave-bolts," cried Pete Murray.

"An' heading-bolts." added Tom Moore.

"Sure, this ain't much account; put it in your pocket an' say no more about it," said Barney, handing the parson a folded paper.

"You might let this go with it," said John Maloney, thrusting another slip into the preacher's hands.

Robert looked vaguely at the papers and saw that they were due-bills on the general store in Red-Keg. All this time he had been standing in one place fairly overcome with astonishment and emotion. The rapid fire of gifts and talk had left him no chance to ask questions or speak his thanks.

" Well, Robert, what's the matter? You look mixed,"
exclaimed Farmer Hawkins, coming from the doorway,
where, with Mother Hawkins, he had been watching
the scene.

" And no wonder," said Allen, regaining his voice.
" What is all this about, and why are these things
here? "

" You've been giving to us freely the best you have
for years. Now your friends want to give you something," answered Hawkins.

" Here's Jake Vogel an' Grat!" cried Barney. " You
ain't seen Grat since last year, Parson. He's lavin'
his dad behind for a tall bye. He's for the woods next
fall, so he says."

Lettie Green with her Aunt Lydia, and Dan Underhill, Arch Fellows, Joe Reon, and Ned Blakely, with
their wives, drove up. New arrivals began coming in
a steady stream, each with a donation of some kind.
Money was very scarce Trading was done with due-
bills and orders—often called " white horses "—or with
supplies, or any articles of market value. Therefore
the great store of mink, coon, bear, wolf, wildcat, otter,
beaver skins, dried apples, dried sweet corn, dried
pumpkins, spalts, stave-bolts, heading-bolts, snow-shoes,
woollen socks and mitts, blankets, fishing-tackle, school,
drain, township, and state orders, pension vouchers,
due-bills for shoes, groceries, and dry-goods, hand-made
quilts, pots of preserves, etc., with which the minister
found himself surrounded, all represented so much cash
value, and could be sold or traded off to suit his own
needs.

" A Donnybrook Fair, so it is!" cried Pete Murray,
delightedly, as he examined the wonderful display of
gifts.

4

"But where's Ros Whitmore?" asked Farmer Hawkins suddenly.

"Drove to Midland this mornin'," answered Bob Landseer, "to make a little trade an' bring back two storekeepers to bid against this Red-Keg scalper for the Elder's extry stock," and he gave Jake Vogel, the genial storekeeper of Red-Keg, who had brought as generous a donation as any one, a resounding whack across his shoulder.

"Good fer Ros," laughed Vogel. "But I reckon them Midland fellers won't get much, 'less it's suthin' I don't want. The on'y man I'd be afraid 'ould bid too high is old Bloag. He ain't comin', I hope?" and Vogel put on a look of great alarm.

"Did ye ever hear tell how he found only twenty-three eggs one mornin' in the nests, an' driv' to the store with the old hen in a box an' kep' her there to make up the two dozen? An' begorry, she did it," said Pete Murray, as soon as he could be heard amid the laughter that followed Vogel's question.

"Thet ain't so bad as the time he took the schoolmaster hum from church an' kep' him talkin' in the settin'-room all afternoon 'thout a bite to eat, while one after 'nother o' the fam'ly, includin' the old deacon himself, sneaked out o' the room to git their dinner," related Bob Landseer.

"To hear him prayin' in meetin', 'O Lord, Thou knowest we are as prone to wander an' go astray as the sparks are to fly upward,' ye'd think the old skinflint hed a realizin' sense of his wickedness; but I hev my doubts on thet pint," said Dan Underhill.

"Sure, he preys durin' the week as hard as he prays on Sunday, but it ain't the same kind," remarked Pete Murray.

"WHAT IS ALL THIS ABOUT, AND WHY ARE THESE THINGS HERE?"

"Here comes Ros up the road, now," said Farmer Hawkins, "and there are three men with him."

"An' one o' them is the new schoolmaster!" shouted Barney. "It's a fine boy he is."

The coming of the schoolmaster was greeted by all with pleasure. He had shown good mettle, and his neighbors were anxious to know him better.

"Sorry Jule couldn't come," said Ros. "She's tied up with a sick baby; but she would have it I must take that shoat of ourn to town an' git the most I could for it. We thought ye could take care of this bit of paper better than to have the pesky young critter runnin' 'round."

As he handed the due-bill to the embarrassed minister, Mother Hawkins whispered to Josiah: "There's real sacrifice. I know they were laying store on that shoat." She thought a moment, then she added anxiously: "Are you sure Ros will come out well with that new lot of ours, Josiah?"

He smiled and whispered: "He'll clear fifty dollars easily."

The conversation went on merrily in parlor, on veranda, and on the greensward in front of the house. The minister went from group to group with words of thanks and friendly inquiry. Among the sturdy farmers and lumbermen, he presented no mean figure. Somewhat under the average height, his shoulders were broad and square, his head erect, and his eyes clear and keen but full of a deep tenderness and sympathy that went straight to the heart. Long ago he had been through college, but none of his backwoods flock knew of it, and few knew or remembered what he had been before he came among them uninvited, unassuming, simple, direct, and loving in his practical ministry, without salary or home that he could call his own. At rare intervals they had seen the flash of a fire within, which let them know that he could make the wildest of them tremble if he chose; and his self-repression placed no discount on his influence with men unaccustomed to control themselves.

At an early hour Mother Hawkins announced that she had brewed a cup of tea, and led the way into the big ell of the house where prayer-meetings and sometimes preaching services were held when the minister was there, and above which Robert Allen had his own rooms. Two long, broad tables were spread with pies, cakes, baked beans, and other light refreshments. The tea was brought in by a bevy of girls who volunteered for the task, and the assembled Red-Keggers prepared to demonstrate that their appetites were ready on the instant at the call of duty.

Just then several new arrivals made their appearance. Seward Rathaway and Sam Hawkins came in, Sam taking a seat at once near Lettie Green, and Seward entering into conversation with the nearest group in such a matter-of-fact manner that their entrance was scarcely noted. The couple who followed them created a sensation.

"Axcy Marthy! Good for you! How are you? Set right down an' have some tea," greeted her from a dozen or more of her friends. Her companion was welcomed with brief nods and a few exclamations of "How d'y, Jim!" but the looks of astonishment and the whispers that ran around the tables spoke more eloquently. Axcy was fully conscious of the sensation she had made, and she enjoyed it. More than that, she was a little proud of the power she had over the lawless young giant whom so many others feared.

"How ever did you get *him* here?" whispered Lettie Green as soon as she could get near enough to Axcy.

"Told him if he wouldn't take me I'd ask Ashbel Fair," replied the roguish girl, with a chuckle. "I guess he didn't imagine Mr. Waters would be here, though," she added, with just a shade of apprehension, as she glanced from the schoolmaster to the corner where her escort had seated himself and was glaring from one to another with a hunted look in his eyes.

The schoolmaster had spoken to him with a friendly "How are you, Jim?" but he had pretended not to hear or to see him, and passed to the opposite end of the room.

Mother Hawkins bustled in with a tray of teacups.

"I am going to wait on you people who came so far myself," she said, going straight to Jim Gyde first. "I made this myself. You never tasted my tea before; won't you have some?" and she thrust the cup into Jim's unwilling hand. "Axcy, this is for you. Now I guess you all are served. No, you haven't any, Mr. Waters. Do try a cup."

As the schoolmaster turned in his seat to take the teacup, Mother Hawkins noticed for the first time his bandaged wrist.

"Sprain?" she asked. "I have some splendid liniment if you would care to try it."

"No, it is not a sprain," answered Waters, looking directly at Mother Hawkins, but in a tone much louder than was necessary to reach her ears. "I got a rather bad bruise the other night, but it will be all right in time."

"Well, don't catch cold in it. Fortunate it's the left one, isn't it? Another cup of tea, Mr. Landseer?

Why, certainly!" and the good, motherly woman hurried away to the kitchen.

Presently Mr. Waters rose, and, passing from one to another of his acquaintances with a word or a nod, gradually made his way, without attracting attention, to the corner where Jim Gyde sat, as nearly alone as he had been able to contrive.

"Glad to see you here, Jim," he said. "We are all glad of a chance to show our good will to Mr. Allen."

Jim Gyde did not speak, but his eyes shifted here and there as if looking for an avenue of escape.

Waters looked quickly around to make sure that no one was listening. Then he said in a low tone:

"Sorry I had to kill Moscow the other night. There was no choice; if I hadn't, he would have killed me."

"Good riddance!" muttered Jim under his breath. The schoolmaster's ears were sharp.

"Perhaps," he said quietly, with intentional misinterpretation. "He was a dangerous brute to be at large."

The young man glared, but made no reply.

"Jim," said Waters, after a moment's silence, "men often do not know their own possibilities. A lot of good raw material goes to waste because a good many men do not discover the gold in themselves, and even imagine it does not exist. Now, I am going to tell you, as a friend should, that I believe you have a rich vein of gold in your make-up. If you will set about to discover it, you may make yourself rich, and others, too."

Jim Gyde stared at the schoolmaster in sullen astonishment, wondering vaguely if he had gone mad from the bite of the dog.

"I don't know what ye mean," he said at last.

"Think it over. It will come to you. If not, let me

know, and I will explain. But Jim, I expect one day to see you a leader of the men in these parts—a leader in nobility of character, as you now are a leader in physical daring and bravery. The pure gold is in you; I am sure of it. And remember, Jim, I am your friend, and shall be glad to give you a brother's help whenever you will accept it. Here's my hand on it."

But Jim Gyde was too bewildered to respond, either by hand or by tongue, and with a commonplace remark, in a louder tone, calculated to put the young man more at his ease, Waters left him to himself.

A group of young people had inveigled Pete Murray into telling stories. Suddenly a burst of laughter testified to one of his hits.

"Oh, we can't hear," called Axcy at the opposite end of the table. "Please speak louder, Mr. Murray."

"Sure, with pleasure. What was it ye missed?"

"Silly! How can I tell, when I didn't hear it?"

"Well, can ye tell this: What is it that falls without breakin' an' breaks without fallin'?"

"Ain't you the tease, Pete Murray! You know I can't guess conundrums," laughed Axcy.

"Give it up?"

"Yes, without trying."

"Sure, night falls without breakin', an' day breaks without fallin'. Thought everybody knew that," said Pete Murray, mockingly.

A sudden stillness spread over the room, as the merrymakers became aware of angry voices near the door.

"Certainly, I'll repeat it, if you didn't understand. I object to being dictated to in my own house by an ignorant hired laborer. If that isn't plain enough, I might add that your vulgar efforts to pose as one of the family don't go down with me. I'll thank you to go back to the cow-yard where you belong, and stay there."

Barney O'Boyle stood erect, and stared at Sam Hawkins as though still failing to grasp the meaning of his insulting words.

"You're after losin' your wits, man, I'm thinkin'," he said slowly.

"I'm in more danger of losing my birthright, if your little scheme works," snarled Sam.

"What do ye mane?" demanded Barney, pale and quivering.

"Mean? Why, I've come to the conclusion that you are trying to wheedle my father into leaving you his property, and that's why——"

Barney sprang at him in a whirlwind of rage.

"Ye lie, ye whelp! an' I'll soon——"

"Barney, lad, sit down here; I want to talk with you."

A grip like steel drew him away from Sam, and, turning, he found himself looking into the deep, quiet eyes of the minister. Under that steady gaze, the fire in his heart died slowly away, and without a word he sank into the seat beside Robert Allen.

Farmer Hawkins led his son into another room.

"Sam," he said, and his voice trembled, "such conduct disgraces you, and it shames your father and mother before their guests." The bitterness which he strove to repress began to sound in his tone, and he stopped abruptly.

"Why do you persist in making an enemy of Barney, when he would gladly be your friend?" he continued, presently. "He has never harmed you, and I am sure he never will if he can help it."

"I can't bear the lout," growled Sam.

"He hasn't had your education, Sam; but that is not his fault. He has as true a heart as ever beat, and there is not a man or woman who knows him who is not proud to have his friendship."

"He puts on altogether too much importance for a hired man to suit me. Why can't he stay where he belongs, and not interfere with his betters?" said Sam crossly.

"His betters?" asked Farmer Hawkins. "Who are they? So far as I am concerned, and I think I speak for my neighbors in there as well, Barney is our social equal. He came here as the friend and companion of John Maloney years ago, and he consented to help me with the farm only because Maloney urged him to do so out of friendship to me. He might now be in business for himself if he wished. Some day he will, doubtless, and then I shall lose him."

"Not till he gets all he can out of you, I'll bet," sneered Sam.

"That is nonsense. Barney has given more than he has received. I am surprised you should allow yourself such silly suspicions," said his father, with another involuntary touch of irritation.

Sam walked to the window, thrust his hands into his pockets, and scowled out at the setting sun.

"It was stupid, I suppose, to make such a scene in there before everybody," he said after a while.

"You are not going to leave them to think so ill of you?" asked his father.

Another pause followed, while Sam watched the changing colors in the sky with unseeing eyes. Then, with a muttered imprecation, he turned and went to the door of the room where the friends and neighbors of his father and the minister were gathered, and looking about until his eyes rested upon Barney, he said:

"Barney O'Boyle, I take back the stupid things I said a while ago. It was vulgar to make a scene here, don't you know. But more than that I'll not say."

He walked away without waiting for a reply, but the dark look had not left his face.

Not until the auction sale was fairly under way did the assembled Red-Keggers regain their jovial spirit. The bidding was lively, Tom Moore, as auctioneer, spurring all hands on to do their best. The three store-keepers were required to pay in cash for all they bought. Some of the articles even brought fancy prices, the purchasers having a mind to boast of owning something that had "belonged to Parson Allen." Counting the due-bills, orders, etc., a total of over seven hundred dollars was realized. Some things selected by the pastor for his own use were not sold. Among these articles were a rifle and an outfit of fishing-tackle, things which the busy and serious-minded minister had never heretofore found time to use.

CHAPTER V.

LETTIE GREEN walked up the road from her home in company with Sam, early the following morning. A red spot glowed on each cheek, and a frightened, appealing look was in her eyes.

"What shall I do, Sam?" she moaned. "I never thought you could be so cruel; oh, what shall I do?"

"Now, please, Lettie, don't be so upset over a thing of no importance at all. It will be all right one of these days. I only meant it in fun."

"Oh, Sam! how can you say that?"

"But it's so. I tell you, you are making it altogether too serious. It will be for a short time at most, don't you know. Can't you take my word for it that I will make it all right as soon as I can possibly see my way clear?"

"I don't know, Sam; I'm afraid. You have been so different the last few days."

"Nonsense, Lettie; you only imagine it. Several things have happened lately to bother me, don't you know, and some matters of business. I really couldn't help it last Thursday, as I told you. I was disappointed, as well as you."

"But you acted so strangely yesterday."

"Oh, I say, can't you forget that, Lettie? Barney riled me beyond endurance with his airs and his impudence in telling me what to do and what not to do. Besides, I apologized. What more could you want?"

"I didn't mean that, Sam.   I meant that you acted as if—as if you——"

"As if what?"

"As if you didn't—care for me."

"Now that's simply your imagination again, Lettie. Of course I care for you.   I'll show you, when I can get money enough of my own to live decently.   Why, I didn't want to come in at all yesterday, in spite of Seward's insisting; but I knew you would be there."

"Couldn't you live well enough with your father and help make the farm pay, Sam?"

"Surely, Lettie, you don't want to live on a farm in the backwoods all your life, do you?   The city is ever so much better for a girl of your beauty and intelligence."

"I don't know, Sam.   I think I would be contented here—with you."

"Well, I'm sure I wouldn't.   I should want my wife to move in better circles than among these ignorant country louts.   Just wait a while, and when my plans succeed you shall have a taste of real life in the city— perhaps New York.   Think of it!   Apartments in a fine house, a servant to do the work, stylish clothes, the theatres, balls, society—why, it's the only way to live.   That's the kind of life I was cut out for, and you were, too, don't you know; and that's the life we shall have some day, Lettie."

The girl's face cleared and her eyes sparkled as Sam drew the glowing picture.   As he finished she said, doubtfully:

"Are you sure, Sam?"

"Of course I am sure.   Now I have an appointment with Seward and must hurry on.   Remember, and be patient."

"I'll try," said Lettie; but Sam never noticed, as she turned to retrace her steps, that the sparkle had gone from her eyes and left the wistful expression and a half-suppressed fear in its place.

"Thank goodness that's over with!" muttered Sam, with a breath of relief.

His appointment with Seward had been offered on the spur of the moment to cut short an embarrassing conversation; but he stopped at Seward's house on the way home, as a matter of habit, only to find that he had gone to the village. But Sam was not sorry, in the circumstances, to miss spending the afternoon with Lettie's cousin. He preferred the comfortable feeling of self-congratulation with which he regarded his interview with Lettie rather than the shame of which he was even now dimly conscious, and which Seward's company might tend to keep alive. Left to himself and the free exercise of his own sophistry, which lulled his conscience without really deceiving him, his complaisance and consequent good nature increased, and when, after dinner, Robert Allen, taking advantage of his approachable mood, asked him to try his new rifle, and then challenged him to a day's hunting bout in the woods, Sam agreed almost before he knew what he was doing. Second thought made him regret his promise, and he tried to postpone the trip indefinitely on the ground of a previous engagement with Seward. The minister would not listen to it, and offered to call on Seward at once and get his consent to the alteration of his plans. Then he began to discuss the trip and the subject of hunting with such a lively interest and evident appreciation that Sam found it impossible not to warm up to him. He was surprised at the hearty, jovial, unassuming manner, the easy carriage, and the enthusiasm which animated the man whom he had regarded as wholly given up to serious things, and an enemy of all sport and all sportsmen. He felt himself yielding to the genial influence, and actually started out in the morning with more real pleasure than he had believed could be possible.

The section of woods agreed upon was along the Sturgeon Creek, to the eastward of the Hawkins farm. Sam had no mind to take the minister anywhere in the vicinity of Mystic Isle, which lay in the heart of the forest and swamp to the northwest. He was less familiar with the Sturgeon district, but preferred a tramp through this comparatively unknown region to the embarrassment which an effort to avoid the neighborhood of his hidden island might involve.

Just before sunrise they were on the road. The clear, fragrant air and the rosy glow in the east promised a beautiful day, the last of April. The roads, still soft from the spring rains, were dry enough for comfortable walking, even if the heavy boots of the men had not made them indifferent to such conditions as mud and water.

"We'll keep up the road half a mile or so and then turn to the right into the woods till we pass through our section of pine and the huckleberry swamp beyond," said Sam. "There we'll take a short cut to the Sturgeon by the new trail blazed last winter. We can save at least three miles to the bend of the river, and perhaps stir up something on the way."

"Isn't that near where Rousheau lives?" asked Allen.

"Who?" queried Sam.

"Jacques Rousheau, an old lumberman; must be a French-Canadian," replied Allen.

"Oh, I guess you mean Old Leatherback. Yes, he

lives in the bend almost surrounded by the river. I don't know as I ever heard his name; never cared enough to ask. He's nothing but a rough, ignorant lout, such as one sees so many of out here, don't you know."

The infelicity of this remark to the minister struck Sam as soon as he had uttered it, and he looked around quickly to see if Allen resented it; but nothing of the kind was apparent in his face. On the contrary, his reply seemed to indicate that he heartily agreed with the sentiment.

"They are rather deficient in culture," he said, "and they have never had the advantage of much book-learning. What they do know has come to them in other ways, more direct perhaps. But did you ever notice, Sam, that these people, even the most ignorant of them, really have a great respect and admiration for book knowledge, and are quick to recognize the superior position it gives those who have it?"

"Can't say that I ever did," replied Sam. "In fact, it always struck me just the other way, don't you know."

"Well, it's true, and the curious thing about it is that the ones who sometimes appear the most indifferent, or who actually scoff at knowledge acquired in schools and colleges, are often the very ones who have the most real regard for it. Their scorn is a mask to hide their own sense of lack. Deep down in their hearts they feel it and wish they had had more 'school-in' in their younger days. I've heard more than one of them say as much."

"I don't see what good it would do them if they had it," argued Sam; "they couldn't use it cutting logs and digging fields."

"Oh, yes they could," protested Allen. "Even a lumberman or a farmer is worth more if he can add the knowledge acquired from books to that acquired from his own experience. He can always fill a better position, and his influence is greater if he has the sense and ambition to make use of the knowledge he has acquired."

Sam wondered if the last remark was aimed at him. He had the uncomfortable feeling of being hit, and cast about for a different topic of conversation, but Allen showed no desire to relinquish the subject.

"Not only that," he continued, "but these people are always willing to follow such a man if they can respect his manliness as well as his education. There's a man down near Midland who has more money than any three of his neighbors put together, but you would never know it by his appearance or behavior. He never seems to spend any of his money if he can help it, either for his own good or any one else's. Those who don't know him would imagine him to be as poor as Job's turkey."

"I suppose you mean old Bloag. He's a fool,— stingy as he is rich," said Sam, not understanding at once the turn in Allen's remarks, but glad to have them directed at any one except himself.

"Just so," went on the minister; "it's natural to feel that way about any man who has something valuable but refuses to use it for himself or others. It doesn't make much difference whether that something is money or a college education."

"Here's where we strike into the woods," exclaimed Sam, hastily turning to the right from the road at a point where an old and partly overgrown lumber path pierced the forest. The rising sun was beginning to send horizontal rays across the tops of the trees, but

barely enough light filtered through to the path to enable the two men to pick their way. For some time
they went on in silence, too much occupied in following
the path to give attention to conversation. Sam welcomed the interruption. Until he could get the minister's mind filled with the sport on which they were
bent, he preferred to hear from him as little as possible. His own ideas did not come very freely, and it
seemed that the more he tried to think of something
to say which would not suggest any moral application,
the more difficult it became to speak at all. Yet he
was by no means sure that the minister had intended
anything personal. Probably he was too ready to put
on a coat which seemed just about his size. After a
while he remarked:

"This isn't much of a thoroughfare, but it's better
than we'll get in the new trail over by the Sturgeon."

"Oh, this is not so bad," replied Allen. "I suppose
there will be no path at all through the Sturgeon
woods."

"Not where we go—only a blazed trail; but we'll
have more light then."

"This path leads through your father's pine, I believe
you said," remarked Allen.

"Yes, we shall come to it in about half an hour, and
beyond that is the huckleberry swamp."

"Your father said the other day that he might cut
his pine next fall for shingles. What a splendid chance
that will give you to learn the lumber business and get
acquainted with the men."

"Humph! that would be delightful, no doubt, but I
haven't any special hankering to be a lumber-jack myself or to mix in with them, either, so the splendid
chance hardly appeals to me, don't you know."

Sam had allowed more of a sneer to creep into his voice than he realized, but the minister took no notice of it and continued in the same hearty manner:

"You see, it will be your father's camp, and doubtless you can have more or less charge of it if you like. That will put you at once in a position of authority, and may be a stepping-stone to something bigger later on if you make the most of it."

"The chances are he'll make that—that Irishman boss," said Sam, bitterly.

"Probably he will—if you refuse to take it," answered Allen, quietly; "but if I know Farmer Hawkins, he would much rather see his own son lay claim to the position; and believe me, Barney wouldn't for an instant dispute your right."

Sam made no reply. He was compelled to admit to himself the truth of what the minister had said, but the admission brought him no satisfaction, and the impulse to act on the suggestion that he should claim his rightful share in his father's enterprise, though it did come to him for a moment, was quickly subdued by other thoughts. He gave his attention to the woods about him. The light was increasing steadily, and it was possible, soon, to see everything in detail within the comparatively narrow limits of vision. The larger pine-trees in this section had been cut some years before, and in their place had grown up among the smaller pines a forest of hemlock, poplar, birch, and balsam, and a tangle of brush and vines.

Denizens of the forest were astir in great numbers. The cheerful notes of robin, thrush, catbird, and chickadee, and the coarser tones of bluejay and crow blended in a woodland chorus which struck a responsive chord in Allen's breast. Familiar as he was with these voices of the wildwood, his sympathetic nature was always attuned to them and ready to thrill with the rhythm of their song. To the birds, to the squirrels in the beech-trees, to the timid jack-rabbits who scurried away in the underbrush at the approach of the two men, to the gentle doe, who, sniffing them from afar, vanished almost before she was seen, Allen felt his heart cry out: "Be not afraid! I am your friend, though you see me armed with the weapon of an enemy. It is not you that I hunt."

Sam heeded neither the songs nor the singers. The question suggested to him by the sight of every living thing was whether or not it was available as game. Birds, squirrels, rabbits, doe were not regarded as game, so he ignored them. He kept in the lead when he could to avoid unpleasant conversation. As the forenoon wore on very little was said by either except the commonplace remarks provoked by immediate circumstances. Just after passing through the great huckleberry swamp and striking into the new trail through the Sturgeon forest, the minister thought he saw a bear. A movement among the branches of a tall young pine caught his eye, and looking sharply he saw a dark figure through the thick foliage.

"There he is, Sam; look!" he exclaimed in a loud whisper, pointing upward.

"What? Where?" asked Sam.

"A bear! Don't you see him, there, on that branch?"

Both men stared into the tree, but could not at first make out clearly the figure which undoubtedly was crouching on one of the smaller branches. Suddenly a change of position disturbed the foliage and revealed the quarry.

"A porcupine!" exclaimed Sam in disgust.

"Sure enough," replied Allen; "not much of a find, after all."

"No, but we may as well bring him down. The pesky things are no good, and they ruin every dog that tackles them. You take a shot at him, parson."

"All right," agreed Allen, and taking deliberate aim at the porcupine, he fired. As he lowered his rifle he looked to see the animal fall from his lofty perch. On the contrary, however, he humped up his spines for an instant and then settled back with a firmer hold on the limb.

"Better try it again," said Sam with a smile. "He doesn't seem to mind the noise."

"Well, I'll try to give him something more than noise this time," replied the parson, laughing good-naturedly at Sam's sarcasm.

With a still more careful aim Allen fired his other barrel; but the porcupine paid no more attention to it than he did to the breeze which gently swayed the tops of the trees.

"Guess I'll have to let you have him," said Allen, taking a seat on the trunk of a fallen tree and proceeding to reload his rifle. "I used to be a pretty good shot," he added, "but for the last twenty years I haven't practised much."

"Yes, it's a peculiar mark, and wants an experienced marksman, don't you know. I'll settle him," said Sam, as he sighted his Enfield.

Once, twice, three times he blazed away, but the porcupine sat unmoved upon his pine bough, from which he had gnawed a long strip of the tender sweet bark, a favorite repast with this animal. To the rain of shot he seemed utterly indifferent.

"That plagued beast must be bewitched—or else I am," cried Sam, giving way to his vexation. "I'll bring him down if it takes all day."

Again he aimed with unusual care and pulled the trigger, but with no better result.

"Let us give up the porcupine and go on in search of better game," suggested Allen. "This chap is invulnerable, apparently, and he isn't worth so much powder and shot."

"I'll be hanged if I go till that porcupine comes down," replied Sam, his face red with mortification that he should make such a poor showing at his first trial before the minister.

Three times more he banged away in vain. The animal once or twice bristled up and then seemed to cling tighter than ever to the slender limb which bent beneath his weight. The minister at last, seeing the useless rage into which Sam was working himself, interfered and asked for another trial, promising to bring the victim down with two shots. Sam stepped aside with a poor grace.

"I'll bet you fifty—" he began, and then, remembering who his companion was, he stopped.

"I don't bet; but I'll show you a trick that I've seen worked before on these fellows."

Up came the parson's rifle to his shoulder, where it rested firm as on a rock.

"You'll never hit him, aiming that way. He's more to your right," Sam was remarking, when both barrels of Allen's rifle spoke in quick succession. At the same instant there was a crack, and down came the porcupine, bringing his branch with him.

"'When the bough breaks the cradle will fall;
And down will come baby, cradle and all,'"

sang the minister, as he stood his rifle against a tree and began looking for a club. His bullets had so severed the limb that it would hold no longer.

Sam forgot his vexation in his frank admiration for the parson's marksmanship, and he manfully congratulated him on his skill.

"You could have done it just as well, my boy, if you had thought of it," said Allen. "But I think I've been told that the spines or quills of the porcupine form an armor that sheds bullets as easily as a duck's back does raindrops. Very likely you hit the rascal with every shot."

"That's so, perhaps I did. I'd rather believe in the armor than think I missed so many shots," replied Sam, completely won by the minister's ready tact and generous praise. As they pushed on through the woods, he found himself on a more friendly and intimate footing with the parson, and he listened with surprise to Allen's stories of adventures, his descriptions of places and things, and his many scraps of useful information, drawn from his long experience and close observation in the forests, on the streams, and with the pioneers of the section.

At noon they sat on the banks of the Sturgeon to rest and eat their luncheon. No big game had been found. Both hunters were tired with their long forenoon tramp in and out of the woods, through the swamps of black ash and huckleberries, and along the shores of the river; but patience is one of the first requirements in the outfit of the hunter. They were not discouraged. Something worth while would turn up during the afternoon,—or they would turn it up.

For an hour or two after finishing their lunch they explored a thick jungle of tanglewood skirting one of the numerous lagoons near the Sturgeon. Here they confidently expected to find a quarry, and here, indeed, they discovered unmistakable signs of bear. Following the tracks they came to the edge of the swale and waited quietly for some minutes with eyes and ears alert for the slightest movement. Presently Sam pointed excitedly to a spot about forty yards distant where the tall grass was being disturbed by some unseen cause. Neither man spoke, but eyes and gestures were eloquent, as without a sound they prepared for whatever might come. It was impossible to tell whether the supposed bear was alone or not, whether a coward or a fighter. If a coward, he might slip away before they could get a shot at him. A fight would be preferable to a flight any day.

A moment later the hunted animal sniffed the enemy. Raising himself upon a fallen log he peered above the swamp grass, espied the hunters, and with a grunt of disapproval dropped down and disappeared before either of the two sportsmen could aim a gun or pull a trigger.

"Well! That bear is taking no chances," exclaimed Allen, as for an instant they watched the rapid retreat of bruin and noted the direction by the waving grass.

"Come on, we mustn't let him escape!" cried Sam. "He's the biggest one I've seen yet. There's no use trying to follow him direct. He's making across the swale and isn't likely to stop until he gets to the other side, anyhow. Our game is to catch him in the huckleberry marsh beyond. We'll have to head him off. You go to the north and I'll go to the south, and we'll meet on the other side of the swale. If you run across him, take him just behind the shoulder or in the snout, don't you know, and he's yours."

Sam rattled off his instructions in breathless haste and hurried off.

"Right you are, my boy!" called the parson after him, as he himself turned in the opposite direction.

The circuitous trip through the tanglewood was not so easily or speedily accomplished as the comparatively short distance would indicate at a glance. Fully half an hour passed before Allen found himself in the big huckleberry marsh where the going was not so difficult. The ground was covered with gray moss and occasional rocks, and the high-growing huckleberry, or blueberry, bushes were scattered over many acres in thick clumps, higher often than a man's head.

Allen looked in vain for any sign of Sam or the bear. It was impossible to see more than a few yards in any direction, and he proceeded cautiously toward the point where Sam should have entered the marsh. He hesitated to call out, fearing to warn the bear of his proximity. Presently a movement among the bushes about twenty feet directly ahead of him attracted his attention, and he stood still to listen.

"There is his lordship, now," he mused. "If he will only show himself, or grunt out a statement of his exact position, I will present him to Sam as a trophy of our first hunting trip."

With his gun at his shoulder he waited, but the bear did not appear. Instead, he heard a low but distinct noise like a string of metallic beads rubbed together.

"A rattler! Mr. Bear has stirred up a nasty customer; but he saved me from running against it, so he has my gratitude."

Allen began to make a detour as noiselessly as possible, to get within sight of the bear which he supposed was on the farther side of a large bush. He had gone about half the short distance when the same low, threatening sound reached his ears again. It sent a disagreeable chill over his body. Twice before in his life he had come in contact with the deadly massasauga, or swamp rattlesnake, and he knew enough of its fearful power and venom to dread it most heartily. He hesitated whether to go on or to hasten away from the spot; but in a moment, reflecting that the snake would hardly leave its present position while in a fighting mood until it had sprung upon the enemy which had disturbed it, he pushed on more quickly in his circuit to the farther side of the bush. A few steps brought him in full view of a sight as startling as it was unexpected. Coiled in the midst of a thick clump of bushes, which had been rudely pressed apart, was the massasauga. His ugly, bulldog-shaped head was thrust up about a foot from the centre of the coil, and was moving back and forth with a dizzy sideways motion. His wide mouth was stretched open, and the long, forked tongue flickered to and fro, as though with an eager relish for its victim. Just behind the head, but protruding only about half as high from the centre of the coil was the horny tail with its string of rattles. No bear was in sight, but standing directly in front of the deadly snake, and scarcely arm's length away from it, was Sam Hawkins. He seemed rooted to the spot and powerless to move. Surprise, terror, repugnance, and a strange look of fascination struggled together in his face. His hands were raised as if to ward off a blow, but he made no effort to escape or to defend himself. Meanwhile the rattlesnake showed every sign of intense rage. His head swelled, and then flattened and darted hither and thither, the beady eyes gleaming wickedly. His tail buzzed round and round, giving forth at intervals the sharp metallic rattle which is always recognized as the warning before an attack. Those who have heard the sound say it can never be forgotten.

The minister took in the scene in an instant. Sam was in deadly peril. It was universally believed that the massasauga gave three warning rattles before striking. Allen had heard two, but he could not be sure whether he had heard the first. There was not a second to lose. Instinctively he clubbed his rifle, and, springing forward, dealt a crushing blow at the rattle-snake. The butt of his rifle struck a hidden rock and broke into splinters, and the barrel flew out of his hand. The rattlesnake was only stunned for a moment, and almost before Allen could recover from the shock of his own blow, the snake began to show fight. With-out a thought of risk, quick as a flash, Allen jumped at him and planted his left foot about eight or ten inches below the ugly head. The rattlesnake squirmed and twisted in the soft ground in frantic efforts to escape. Then he struck his fangs against the minister's tough horsehide boots, which fortunately were proof against his attacks. A cold sweat broke out on Allen's body as he realized his position. To hold the writhing snake seemed impossible. To allow him to escape was almost certain death, so loath is the massasauga to abandon a foe until he has bitten him to his heart's content. The barrel of his rifle lay just out of reach. Sam stood near by in a daze, and seemingly unable to help himself or the minister. Allen paid no more attention to him than if he were not there. His whole thought was bent upon getting his rifle barrel without releasing the snake. Glancing quickly around, the branches of the huckleberry bush brushed his face. Eagerly he grasped a long slender branch and broke it off. Making a loop he reached it out toward his rifle barrel and just succeeded in hooking the branch over the end and slipping it along to the middle. A quick jerk, and the steel weapon was in his hands. In a moment he had beaten the life out of his venomous foe. The rattlesnake was about an inch and a half in thickness and about four feet long, sinewy and strong. He had eleven rattles and a button, showing him to be thirteen years old. Allen had fought him in silence, and when he saw the dreaded reptile lying at last dead and mangled at his feet, he turned away and sat down wearily upon the rock which had wrecked his new rifle. Even his strong frame could not withstand, for the moment, the feeling of weakness and reaction which followed a battle with the deadliest inhabitant of that wilderness.

Sam came to himself with a gasp and a deep sigh. He sprang to the minister and grasped him by the shoulder.

"You saved my life! You saved my life!" he exclaimed, nervously. "Did he bite you? Are you hurt? I couldn't have moved to save my soul, though I knew he was going to strike. I never met one of those devils before, and I hope to God I never shall again. I've heard they can hold a man in a spell so that he can't move hand or foot. I never believed it; now I know it's true. I felt it the minute I saw him, and I knew what he was, though I never saw one before. You saved my life, Mr. Allen; and you risked your own to do it."

Sam was more overcome by the incident than the minister, and spoke quickly and excitedly, without a trace of his usual affectation. As the minister listened, he recovered his own calm self-possession and hastened to divert the young man's mind from the horror of his recent plight. Picking up the splintered butt of his rifle he looked at it with a rueful smile and held it out to Sam.

"Guess I'll have to give up hunting," he said with a laugh; "I don't seem to know how to handle a gun after all. This pretty new toy had a short career."

"But a glorious one, by Jove!" broke in Sam. "It came to its end in saving my worthless life, and I'll make it good just as soon as I can."

"Thank God!" exclaimed Allen.

"Why, of course; why shouldn't I?" asked Sam, surprised at the minister's fervency.

"There is no reason why you shouldn't, and every reason in the world why you should. I earnestly hope you will do it."

"I'll borrow the money to-morrow, and get you one just like it if Jake has another in his store. If not, I'll go to Midland," said Sam, slightly nettled that the minister should press the matter so hard.

"I wasn't referring to the rifle, Sam. I don't care for another one," replied the minister, quietly.

"No? What then?" asked Sam, more than ever puzzled.

"I'm glad to have disposed of my rifle in the way I did, Sam. Perhaps it can be counted as a part of the investment," replied Allen, enigmatically.

"What investment? What do you mean?" persisted Sam.

Allen glanced at the sun, and then looked at his watch.

"It's growing late," he said. "If we want to get home by dark we must go on at once. Come, we've had hunting enough for one day; let's have a nice friendly chat on the way home."

He linked his arm affectionately through Sam's, as they turned toward the western forest, and for some moments the two walked on in silence, having found the corduroy road which ran through the swamp.

"That trifle of killing the snake, even if I was fortunate enough to save you from being bitten, doesn't measure how much I think of you, Sam," said Allen, presently. "I wish I could do more than that. I know you don't like to have me preach to you; but we're here all alone together with no inquisitive ears to hear what passes in confidence, and there are some things I want to say, just as an elder brother who loves you and longs to do something for you. Won't you let me, Sam?"

The moment which the young man had dreaded since the trip was first planned had arrived. He was painfully ill at ease; yet the feeling of resentment which he had expected, and which, indeed, he had depended upon to inspire a suitable retort to any such advances, was strangely lacking. A sense of his own unworthiness crept into his heart and made any resentment hard to rouse. With the self-abasement came a feeling of the minister's strength and manliness, and his unassuming goodness. Even some slight thrill from his great, loving, eager heart seemed to find a sensitive chord in Sam's breast, and as he thought of the unhesitating bravery with which the minister had risked his life for him just now, all his opposition melted away, and he stammered, with a choke in his throat:

"Why—why—of course, you can say what you like —I mean—it's very kind of you to take so much interest in me. I don't know why you should."

"I do take an interest in you, Sam,—more than you

can think; because I care for you,—and for another reason, that you may know some day."

He drew Sam's arm tighter in his own, and continued in a tone of friendly intimacy, softened by the deep earnestness and solicitude which he could not repress.

"I spoke of the broken rifle as a part or the investment. It could be only a very small part, of course. Did you ever think of the $1,200 spent for your four years' college course as an investment?"

"No—I never thought of it just that way," admitted Sam.

"But it was, nevertheless. The business man invests his money in his store, the speculator invests in a gold mine, the trustee invests in government bonds. They all expect to get the money back for themselves, or some one else, with interest; and they always do, if —if what, Sam?"

"Why—if the security was good, I suppose," said Sam, flushing uncomfortably.

"Exactly; if the security was good. A father invests $1,200 in his boy to give him a college course. More than that, he invests untold prayers, and self-denial, and tears, and heart-yearnings that cannot be uttered. Will the investment pay? Was the security good? Or was it—was it—like the shares in a gold mine which I bought one time, many years ago, in the hope of getting rich without working? The certificates were elegantly printed and emblazoned with big gold seals, but—they weren't worth a cent. The security was worthless."

The minister was silent for several moments, and Sam did not venture any reply. The picture startled him. He seemed to see himself in a mirror, but looking as he had never looked before. He caught his breath, and asked himself again and again, "Am I worthless? Am I really worthless?" It was a relief to hear the minister's voice again; but the words startled him afresh. They answered his latest thoughts. Had he spoken them aloud?

"Sam, no *man* is worthless. That's the grandeur of being a man. There's something in man that's wonderful and mysterious. It is awful, when you come to think of it; yet it is splendid and inspiring. A man may not realize that it is there. It may never work its wonders through him, because he smothers it; but it is there, always there, through boyhood, through young manhood, through old age. It is ready and waiting, waiting, waiting to thrill him through and through and make him perform mighty deeds and stand as a king in the earth. That wonderful thing is in *you* this very moment, Sam!"

The minister's earnest words had come with more and more intensity of feeling as he went from sentence to sentence, and the last one was spoken almost in a whisper, as he clutched Sam's arm in an eager grasp. The young man was trembling with a fear that he could not understand. He felt the mystery and the throb of earnestness in the minister's strange words, but he could not guess their meaning. At last, unable to endure the silence, he asked, hesitatingly:

"What is it?"

"The breath of God," said Allen.

Sam shivered. After a moment's pause the minister quoted in a low tone, but with thrilling emphasis:

"'And the Lord God formed man of the dust of the ground, and *breathed into his nostrils* the breath of life; and man became *a living soul*.' A living soul, Sam,— living by the breath of God in your nostrils. Isn't it a wonderful thought—awful, but glorious? And why did God breathe His own breath into man? He had a purpose. Listen: 'And God said, Let us make man in our image, after our likeness; and let them *have dominion* over all the earth . . . and *subdue it.*' You see, God never intended man to grovel, or be content with little things or a narrow life. He set him on his feet and told him to be a king. And so he can be; and so *you* can be, Sam."

"How?" asked Sam, as the minister seemed to be waiting for him to speak.

"First of all, and most important of all, by making war upon your worst enemy and conquering him, by crushing out his opposing forces and weaknesses, by re-creating in him a new being, by giving his good qualities a chance to grow, by ruling over him wisely, firmly, unyieldingly. When you have done that you will be a king, ready for wider conquests."

"My worst enemy——?"

"Yourself! You must either conquer or surrender. One means kingship; the other is slavery. Why, Sam, man!" cried the minister, stopping suddenly in the road and facing the young man, his eyes blazing with enthusiasm, "you are not cut out for a slave. You have it in you to rule. Be what you have it in you to be. Grapple with yourself and win. It will give you a confidence in your own power, and an outlook into the future that will surprise you. These backwoods are just the place for a rough-and-tumble fight to the finish with the worst enemy, and probably the only enemy, you have. You think there is nothing here for a college man to do and be proud of? Don't be fooled; that's one of the lies your enemy tells you. Through his eyes, the opportunities here don't look attractive.

Get away from *him*, and you won't be so anxious to get away from *here*. Then you can dominate circumstances, and not let them dominate you. The world owes you a living, but it won't pay the debt of its own accord. You've got to get out and collect it. And let me tell you, if you are not spry, that debtor will palm off on you a poorer living than belongs to you. It depends on you to collect the full amount."

The two men were approaching the forest, and as the open road grew shorter the minister's enthusiasm increased, and he spoke rapidly, realizing that conversation would not be so easy after entering the narrow, irregular path through the woods.

"Look here, Sam," he continued, "any man can walk on a smooth road. It takes more grit and determination to push on over a tangle of logs and brushwood. Just so, it will show the man in you if you make an honorable place for yourself right here among these backwoodsmen. They will see it quickly enough, too. Who knows but they may want to send you to represent them in the outside world some day? The only safe rule here, or anywhere, is not to be satisfied with anything short of the best you can do, and the most honorable position you can occupy. That's the way men move on. Hold your head high among these rough, true-hearted men, Sam—not to look down on them, but to compel them to look up to you. I'm so anxious for you, my boy. It almost seems as if the investment had been my own. I want you to be such a man in your most secret life that when you look at yourself in the glass you can say, 'Sam Hawkins, I'm proud to know you.' Then you can depend upon it that others also will be proud to know you. Dear me, here we are at the woods again. I've preached quite a bit for a hunter; but Sam, my boy, think of what I have said, and whenever you remember it, remember that I said it because I love you. I hope you will come to me for help whenever you need it."

Sam muttered an almost inaudible "thank you" and went on in silence. Allen made no further trespass on his thoughts, hoping and praying that something of his hurried talk would find lodgement; and, indeed, Sam was more impressed than he had ever been. A struggle was already begun which made him glow with hope and purpose, or tremble as he felt the strong hold of his evil life upon him. Could he break away from it and be a man such as the minister had pictured? Why not? It would be hard work; but the minister had seemed so sure, and he must know something about men. It would be a relief to get rid of the heavy feeling of discontent which came, no doubt, from doing what other people condemned, and avoiding what they regarded as duty. Probably they were right. In fact, of course they were. He was no fool. It was all well enough to pretend to his folks, and to Seward, and the rest, that he had a perfect right to do as he was doing; but in his heart of hearts, where no one but himself could see, he knew that it was all a lie. "Where no one but himself could see?" Another shiver ran over him as he repeated the words and realized their awful error. Surely, it would be worth any amount of struggle to set himself right in the eyes of the *two* who could read his heart. How fine it would be to feel that he was really master, that he could fill a high place, that he could compel others to look up to him—even these ignorant louts, as he had called them. Were they not better than he, after all? The young man's heart was sadly torn with the contending thoughts and questionings which had taken possession during the past hour. He was almost persuaded. Perhaps he would talk with the minister to-morrow of his own accord.

The homeward trip was accomplished without adventure or further conversation. As they approached the house, Sam saw Seward coming toward him and waving a paper in his hand. After a hurried greeting to the minister, Seward dragged his friend out of hearing and exclaimed excitedly:

"They're coming, Sam, both of them! Here are the letters."

"Who?" asked Sam in bewilderment.

"Walt and Billy!"

That night Sam could not sleep. The conflict raged fiercely. A new element had been introduced by the two letters, which, although expected, had come at such a critical moment. He would like to take up the new life which the minister had made so attractive, but he was already committed to the three "Invincibles" and their scheme for Mystic Isle. It was too late to back out. This was the end of all his feeble bouts with his evil genius, and at last he accepted it as the inevitable. But what about the minister? He was more than ever afraid of him now. And he had saved his life! More than that, he had twice told Sam that he loved him; and Sam believed it. What should he do? He could think of nothing but the coward's refuge. He must keep out of his sight, or at least avoid being alone with him for a single instant. Yet he wished—but no, it was too late—too late.

CHAPTER VI

ALL that summer Sam kept his resolve not to see
the minister. During Allen's absence from the farm
when visiting and preaching at other villages and settlements throughout the section, Sam came home as
usual; but when the minister returned from his trips
and made his home with Farmer Hawkins, Sam remained away on one pretext or another, spending his
time in the forest, on his "Mystic Isle," or with Walt
and Billy at the home of Seward Rathaway. The four
"Invincibles" were together most of the time, "camp-
ing, fishing, shooting," as they claimed when questioned
concerning their occupation, but always "too busy"
when called upon to take part in any of the affairs
which interested their neighbors.

Toward Lettie Green, Sam's attitude was one of
friendliness, patronizing tolerance, or impatience. It
varied as her behavior to him varied. He desired quiet
complaisance on her part with the existing state of
affairs. Some demonstration of affection he permitted,
as his due. Too much irritated him, and anything like
reproaches or pleadings angered him. By degrees the
proud but infatuated girl, stung by his indifference,
suppressed her own feelings, and cast about for some
means to occupy her mind and give her a stronger sense
of independence.

There had long been need for a school in Red-Keg
for the smaller children who were unable to make the
long trip to Midland. More than once Lettie had

heard the subject mentioned, always coupled with the regret that no one with the necessary courage and qualifications could be found to attempt the uninviting task. The conviction grew upon her through those summer weeks that this was her opportunity. Her father, Andrew Green, was at home so little that she hardly thought of consulting him. Boss for a firm of lumbermen, he was engaged in the forest some ten miles up the river during the winter, and in the spring he went to Saginaw on business and remained away a large part of the summer. He never found time to be on intimate terms with his daughter. Her aunt would hardly prove sympathetic, Lettie feared. She sought the advice of Mother Hawkins.

"My dear child," said she, "you could not find a nobler work—if you think it would not be too much for you. The dear lambs are growing up like so many young pine-trees—tall, and straight, and strong—and with just as little brains. Only I'm afraid you will not find them quite so steady."

"They're more like wildcats, I guess," said Lettie.

"Yes, they will need taming before they can be taught anything; but—if you are not afraid, dear—we will stand by you."

Lettie's next visit was to her friend Norine Maloney, to whom she confided her plan. There she found sympathy and admiration for her pluck.

"But, oh, Lettie, do you think you can stand it? It wouldn't be so bad if you were only going to have the little girls, but there'll be a crowd of boys, and some of them are dreadful," said Norine doubtfully, as the probabilities of the case began to dawn upon her.

"I know, Norine; I've thought it all over; it will be

hard; but I must do something. Working around at home doesn't take up my mind enough."

Norine noticed a plaintive tone that was new in her friend's voice and wondered at it, but she only said, encouragingly:

"If anybody can do it, you can, Lettie. Have you told any one else?"

"Only you and Mother Hawkins; but I want you to come with me to see Mr. Waters. He'll know just what I ought to do."

And so one bright morning the two girls drove down the river road to the home of the Midland schoolmaster. About half-way between Red-Keg and Midland was the farm of Hal Marthy, and Norine suggested that they turn in for a few minutes to pass the time of day with their friend Axcy. As they approached the house Lettie exclaimed:

"Why, there's Mr. Waters now, and talking to Axcy!"

She pointed to where the two stood, near the gate, engaged so earnestly in conversation that they did not observe the newcomers until the buckboard came to a stop near them.

"My, how you startled me!" cried Axcy, flushing a little at sight of her friends. "What brings you down here?"

"We were on our way to see Mr. Waters, and we just stopped in to see you first. Now we find you both at once," replied Lettie. "And it seems you have the first claim to him this morning," she added, a little maliciously.

"Mr. Waters came to see me on business, but it can wait just as well as not," said Axcy, fully recovered from her momentary embarrassment.

"Business?" said Lettie, with just a perceptible lifting of her eyebrows. "Oh, well, that's what we came for, too; but don't let us interrupt. Rock can rest in the shade a while, and I'm going to get a drink. Come on, Norine," and the two girls, springing lightly to the ground, started toward the well.

"Let me help you," said the schoolmaster, hastening after them and grasping the windlass.

"Why not tell Axcy, too?" whispered Norine. "It can't hurt; she's a dear."

"I don't know," replied Lettie, doubtfully; then, holding the brimming dipper poised in her hand she said, looking first at Axcy and then at the schoolmaster:

"Mr. Waters, I want to start a school at Red-Keg for the small children, and I came to talk with you about it."

"How funny!" cried Axcy, looking at Mr. Waters knowingly.

"Why is it funny?" asked Lettie, piqued that a matter so serious to her should be regarded as a joke.

"Only as a coincidence," said the schoolmaster; then, glancing at Axcy and receiving a nod of permission, he continued:

"Just now I was asking Axcy to help me in teaching the younger children in my school so that I may have more time for the older scholars, and she was on the point of consenting—I hope—when you drove up."

"But I didn't consent," said Axcy laughing, "and I won't consent, unless Mr. Waters promises to help you all you want him to," she added, putting her arm affectionately around Lettie.

"Agreed!" exclaimed Mr. Waters, delightedly. "Why, District School No. 1 is getting to be a full-fledged normal school. Two-thirds of its graduates become teachers in their first year. Tell me what you want me to do, and I shall be very glad to help you, Miss Lettie."

Lettie explained that she hoped he would speak to the members of the School Board and find out whether or not her school would have to come under their jurisdiction, and if so, what arrangements could be made for a schoolroom, her salary, and other preliminary matters. If the district School Board had no control, some arrangements would have to be made with the people of Red-Keg themselves.

Mr. Waters agreed to make all the necessary inquiries, and encouraged Lettie to go ahead and interest the parents in her undertaking. He promised to help in every way possible.

"I wonder what Jim Gyde will say to Axcy helping Mr. Waters in the District School. He's awfully jealous," observed Norine, as the two girls drove homeward.

"Do you think Mr. Waters is—do you think he might—care for her?" asked Lettie.

"I don't know, you can't tell. He's big, and strong, and handsome, and—a gentleman," answered Norine, absently. Both girls seemed to be thinking of something else more than the subject of their conversation.

As the weeks passed and everything contributed to the advancement of Lettie's enterprise, her own courage waned. The more certain of accomplishment her purpose appeared, and the more hearty the approval and co-operation of her friends and the people at large, the more doubtful she became of her ability to grapple with the task. It grew more forbidding as it came nearer, and she began to look for obstacles, which, however, did not turn up. So many children were promised as candidates that she was compelled to rule out strictly all who were able to go to the Midland school. It was only an experiment, she said, and she could not undertake too much at first.

With many misgivings, therefore, she set out for the village one morning in September. A vacant log-house, formerly belonging to a well-to-do lumber contractor, had been cleaned and fitted up for the school. It stood scarcely a mile from her house. Many of her friends had offered to accompany her and help her during the first day, but she feared such a reenforcement would be regarded by her pupils as an evidence of her own timidity or lack of sufficiency, and so she declared her purpose of starting alone.

A boisterous crowd of girls and boys, some with their parents, was awaiting her at the schoolhouse, and set up a clamor of welcome. Her heart sank at sight of them, but with a bright smile and a cheery "good morning, children," she pushed her way past them into the schoolroom, took off her hat, and without waiting to consider the novelty of the situation, rang the bell on her table to call the children together. About forty boys and girls, ranging from six to fifteen years of age, crowded around her. They were a noisy, dirty, un-tamed, untaught herd. Some had shoes and hats, most had neither. Less than a third of them were dressed with any regard to appearances; but Lettie thought nothing of this. She was looking at the bigger boys and girls, and wondering if she had not made it clear that they were not to be admitted.

"This school will be for the younger children only, at least this year," she announced. "All boys and girls who are over twelve will have to leave the room."

Disappointment showed itself on several faces, and a chorus of protests came from the older children; but Lettie was determined.

"I cannot go on until you do as I ask you to. You ought to go to Midland to school. I did when no bigger than you. Perhaps next year—but, no, I can't make any promises. You must go out now, that's certain."

Grumblingly, about ten of the larger children shuffled out. They were not so anxious to attend school as they were to gratify their curiosity as to the new school-teacher.

"Now I will take your names for the school roll. First——"

"Mine first!"

"No, mine!"

"Git back! I goes down first."

"I'm bigger'n you!"

The pushing and pulling and shouting threatened to result in a fight immediately. One little girl began to cry because a rough boy had stepped on her toes.

Lettie rang the bell desperately, and exclaimed in a voice which she tried to make stern and commanding:

"Boys, be quiet at once. I shall begin the roll with the littlest girl, and end with the biggest boy. Now Betty, dear, I guess you are the littlest, so here it is—Betty Underhill—first on the list. Now, Julia Fellows, Dotty Johnson, Mamie Murray, Lu Blakely," and so on.

"Matt Reon," she said suddenly, looking suspiciously at the tall boy who had first insisted on having his name head the roll, "you are fourteen if you're a day. Why did you stay when the others went out?"

"I dunno, Miss; me mother said, bein' they was a

school here, I had ter come. I ain't fourteen 's I knows of."

"Very well, I will put your name down for the present, but you must behave, or I can't let you stay."

"Yes'm."

The Whitmore household was represented by Ray, Tilly, Hank, Tom, Carrie, and Ros, Jr. Jake Vogel sent John, Ida, and Tene. From Red-Keg homes came also Andrew and Arch Barrow; Alice, Bessie, and Pete Doane; Ike, Mary, Christy, and Viola Bowe, and others.

"Teacher!"

The grimy hand of little nine-year-old Dotty Johnson appeared above her frowzy head.

"What is it, Dotty?" asked Lettie pleasantly.

"My maw says as how you must give me four lessons a day."

"We'll see," said Lettie, continuing with her roll of pupils.

The ignorance of some, the precocity of others, and the general lack of home discipline and restraint made Lettie's task a hard one.

Matt Reon was the proud owner of a cent and kept flipping it in the air to arouse the envy of the less fortunate boys.

"Put that in your pocket, Matt," commanded Lettie.

"Yes'm," said Matt, giving the cent a final flip for luck; but the luck was against him, and the cent fell to the floor. Instantly the other boys scrambled for it, pulling, pushing, and hitting. The teacher's voice was drowned in the frightful din. As a last resort, she rang her bell sharply. There was a momentary lull in the noise, and Matt succeeded in snatching his cent from the smaller boy who had found it.

"Boys, take your seats this minute! Matt Reon,

put that cent here on my table until after school. Such behavior is disgraceful. I won't allow it!" exclaimed Lettie, almost distracted. When at last she was ready for her first class, the sun had almost reached its meridian. She took from the drawer of her table a carefully prepared order of exercises, looked it over a moment, and then glanced at the little clock on her desk. "It's nearly noon, now," she said, "so I will excuse the younger children from their lessons while I try the older ones in spelling, and find out what classes to make. Tom, you may go over and sit with your sister Tilly and take care of her. Ike, you are too big a boy to be bothering Kitty White like that. Come up and sit on this seat near my desk."

About half of the pupils were selected for the spelling class and arranged around the wall.

"John Vogel, you take the head of the class; Hank Whitmore next; then Kitty White," and so on until the class was complete."

"Teacher!" bawled Dotty Johnson again in defiant tones, raising her hand as high as she could reach and snapping her fingers impatiently.

"Well, Dotty?"

"Ben't I goin' ter git a lesson? My maw——"

"Keep quiet, Dotty, till I get through with this class. Now, John, you may spell 'bear.'"

"B-a-i-r, bair," said John.

"Next, Hank, you spell 'bear.'"

"Don't know how," frankly admitted Hank.

"Well, Kitty, you may try."

"What kind of bear?" asked Kitty timidly.

"Bear, an animal."

"Oh, teacher, I know now!" exclaimed John, a gleam of intelligence in his eyes.

"All right, John, you may have another try," said Lettie.

"B—a——"

"Teacher! My maw says—" again broke in the obstreperous Dotty.

"Dotty, if you say another word before this class is through, I shall have to punish you. Now, John, try again."

"B-a-r-r."

"Teacher!" both of Dotty's hands were up now, and her voice indicated outright rebellion. "My maw says——"

Lettie, her patience sorely tried, started toward the frowzy little recalcitrant. Before she could reach her, however, the midget was dodging around the back of the room. Back and forth she darted, with Lettie after her, until, reaching the door, she ran out, her hair streaming in the wind and her chubby feet making tracks for home. The whole school was in an uproar, and most of the pupils rushed out to see the fun.

"Run, Dotty, the teacher's after ye!" yelled a mischievous imp.

"Come back an' sass her some more," called another. "She dassn't hurt ye!"

Nothing more could be done that forenoon. Lettie was tired and unstrung, and made no attempt to follow the little vixen farther. She sat down at her desk and gave way to tears, as the only thing left to do.

"Teacher, I'm so sorrow."

Demure little Tilly Whitmore, the only one who had not left the room in the stampede, put her hand caressingly on her teacher's arm.

"Don't try, teacher," she said with a sob in her own

voice. Then, impulsively she threw her arms tightly around the discouraged teacher and sought to comfort her.

"Dear little Tilly! If they were all as kind as you are I would have no trouble;" and holding the sweet little sympathizer closely to her, she kissed her tenderly, while the tears flowed unrestrained.

By the time the noon hour had passed Lettie felt her courage returning, and as the children came tumbling in from their romp in response to her bell, she nerved herself for the afternoon's work. The primer class was called to the recitation seats, and the smiling little faces helped her. She began to feel something of her opportunity for moulding these young lives. In recognition of the compact of sympathy formed during the noon recess, little Tilly Whitmore was placed at the head of the class, and she held her green-covered primer proudly as she spelled out the lesson and exhibited her knowledge of the alphabet and the words taught her by her mother at home.

"T-h-e, the, c-a-t, cat, the cat, i-s, is, the cat is, o-n, on, the cat is on, t-h-e, the, the cat is on the, m-a-t, mat, the cat is on the mat."

She looked up, expecting a word of approval.

"Say that agin, an' I'll punch yer head!" shouted Arch Barrow.

Tilly looked frightened; but the threat was not aimed at her, for Arch followed it up quickly with a blow at his seat companion, without waiting for him to "say it agin." A rough-and-tumble fight began at once, and again the school was in an uproar.

Lettie realized that she must show more strength and authority than she had done in the morning, or she would quickly lose control of her school. She caught her breath with a little gasp, and without a word stepped forward and seized each belligerent by the ear and dragged both boys toward her desk. Ignoring their howls and protests of "I won't do it no more, teacher," she stood the offenders with their faces to the wall. After an hour of such durance they very meekly begged to be forgiven, and returned to their seats.

The primer class had finished, and the first-reader class was in a line before Lettie, when the door opened, and in walked Dotty Johnson, as defiant as in the early morning. She went coolly up to the teacher and handed her a dirty, crumpled note, meanwhile keeping an eye on the door.

"Mis greane i want to tel yu thet mi darter Dotty must hev fore lesuns eech da an yu atend to it an not driv her hoam eny moar onles yu want to git liked i wunt taik nun ov yer impertens nether bewair. Mrs. jhonson."

Lettie took the note without a word, her face showing at first a pink flush. As she read, a paleness and rigidity took its place, and when she looked up, the pupils saw an expression of austerity and determination that surprised and quieted them.

"Dotty," she said, "do you wish to belong to this school?"

"My maw says—" began Dotty retreating.

"I don't care what your ma says. I want to know if you are coming to this school, and intend to obey your teacher?"

"My maw——"

Lettie was too quick for the little rebel this time, and caught her in both arms. The child screamed, and kicked, and attempted to bite, but her teacher held her fast until she became quiet; then without a word she drew her slowly up to the desk. As she did this the door was pushed ajar, and the ugly, mannish features of Dotty's mother appeared. There was a threatening scowl there. Evidently she had come with Dotty to see that she did not receive the promised punishment. Lettie, fortunately, did not see the scowling face, but she still held the note in her hand. There was no disorder in the school now. All were quiet and expectant. Dotty was hanging her head. Her lips pouted, but she looked somewhat subdued and frightened. Lettie looked at her silently for a moment. When she spoke, her voice was very gentle.

"Dotty, don't you want to be a nice little girl, so people will love you, so I can love you, too, and so you can be a help to me?"

Without waiting for a reply, she twined her arms around the child and kissed her forehead. This was too much, and the little girl began to cry hysterically. A look of astonishment spread over the ugly face at the door. In another moment, like a frightened deer, the woman was running away from the presence of the girl who, as she afterward declared, must be a saint.

Firmness and gentleness had won the day, and Lettie had established herself in the hearts of her pupils and gained their respect, the first requisite to cheerful obedience. The rest of the session passed busily and pleasantly. Just as school was dismissed, Ros Whitmore drove up in his farm wagon to fetch his little flock. After a few hearty words of congratulation and compliment on the completion of her first day as the prettiest schoolmarm in the county, he smilingly handed her a note which Mrs. Johnson had just given him and begged him to deliver. It was profuse in apologies.

Lettie read it with flushed face and tear-dimmed eyes. Dotty and Tilly, her little tormentor and her little comforter, each received a good-night kiss. Folding the two notes together she tucked them safely into her reticule as tokens of her first school trial and triumph, and hastened away to find Norine.

7

CHAPTER VII.

As soon as it became known that Farmer Hawkins intended to get together a crew of his own to cut the pine on his quarter-section, so many of his friends volunteered to join him that he determined to engage no strangers at all, but to organize the camp with his neighbors and acquaintances only. He resolved, in his own mind, also, that the winter's work should not be all drudgery, but should be made pleasant by good-fellowship and occasional social relaxation, and by as much physical comfort as was compatible with the proper conduct of a lumber camp.

The quarter-section of pine lay to the westward of the farm, between it and Sturgeon Creek, to which stream the logs, if intended for the booms, would have to be hauled and then sent down to the Tittabawassee. Farmer Hawkins, however, had decided to cut the logs into shingles on the spot and, after their weight had been reduced by drying, haul them direct to the railway at Red-Keg. Accordingly he rented a portable shingle mill at Saginaw, brought it up the river in sections, and erected it in the midst of his timber. Near the mill he built a large "shanty" for the crew. It consisted of two separate buildings standing some fifteen feet apart. For the walls, instead of logs, he used pine-boards set on end. The roofs were of shingles. The space between the buildings was roofed over, but left open at the ends. One building was to be used for the camp kitchen, and contained, besides the cooking-range, shelves, and supplies, two large board-tables, with benches, at which the meals would be served. The other building was the men's camp, with a double tier of bunks on each side, and in front of them a long bench, called the "deacon seat." In the centre was a round stove for heating. A short distance from the shanty were the stables and shop built of logs with board roofs.

"Sure, the byes will be snug and asy here. It's a sight better nor Green an' Binker's camp on the Big Salt last winter," said Barney approvingly, as he inspected the completed quarters.

While Farmer Hawkins was nominally boss, he had placed upon Barney the actual duties of foreman, recognizing his more intimate knowledge of the work and his fitness for aggressive leadership of the men in the ways to which they were accustomed.

A fine, jovial crew of about twenty men was gathered, including several like Ros Whitmore, Pete Murray, and Bob Landseer, who had farms or timber of their own, and who postponed their operations for the season in order to join the Hawkins camp. At Pete Murray's suggestion, Jim Gyde, Ashbel Fair, and "Babe" Strander had been asked to join, because of their strength and skill in handling the logs, and their natural enthusiasm for the work of the lumber woods. Jim Gyde, however, for some unexplained reason, seemed reluctant to accept. Rodney Bedell and Bud Frazer came because the others did. Lon Hawley, an expert shingle-sawyer, whom Barney had met in one of the mills at which he himself had worked in previous winters, was brought from Saginaw, a fact which showed that Barney was free from jealousy and rather liked good wholesome rivalry that made the blood tingle. Moreover, he knew his own powers, and did not fear that he would be bested by any shingle-sawyer in the country. Young Grat Vogel, keen for his first winter in the woods as a real lumber-jack, was engaged by Farmer Hawkins for his father's sake, and for his own. Joe Reon, Ned Blakely, Dan Underhill, and Arch Fellows were there. "Old Leatherback," a veteran swamper, had begged for a job, and had brought his friend "Red" Lampheer, an uncouth shantyman, from the Sandytown settlement. The reputation of the last two was not very savory, but with the "wild" element so distinctly in the minority, no trouble was feared. As a matter of course, Barney had persuaded his friend, big Tom Moore, to come with him. No company would be complete in Barney's opinion without Tom. Sam Hawkins and Seward Rathaway had been asked to form part of the crew, but Sam vetoed the proposition, saying that he did not know the trade of the lumber-jack and had no desire to learn. Speaking for Seward, he declared that together they had other plans for the winter. Walt and Billy had returned to their homes, it is true, late in the fall, promising to come again in the spring and stay through the following winter "for the hunting," but Sam and Seward still claimed to have interests which demanded their attention, though what these interests were no one seemed to know.

The crew took possession of the camp in September and began at once making small roads leading away in every direction through the timber, but all focussing at the mill. Through these roads the logs would be hauled, or travoyed, to the long skidways at the side of the mill where was located the drag-saw. From these skidways, instead of being loaded upon heavy sleighs, as would be the case if the logs were to be hauled to

the river, they were rolled upon the "carriage" which
ran under the drag-saw. Here they were cut into
proper shingle length of sixteen or eighteen inches.
These short sections of logs were called bolts.

The first fall of snow in November found the roads
finished, the ground frozen hard, and Hawkins's camp
ready for an aggressive attack upon the forest.

"Be up wid ye, byes! She's here!" cried Barney,
as he burst into the men's camp at four o'clock one
morning and stamped the snow from his legs. "Now,
be the powers o' smoke, we'll be makin' her hum!"

In an instant the camp was alive with noise and action. Voiceful yawns, grunts, snarls at the cold, crisp
oaths, the kicking on of frozen boots, the swashing of
water, the slamming to and fro of the door, and then
the welcome call from the kitchen, "Brekfus ready!"

Pell-mell for the other part of the shanty rushed the
crew, stumbling through a huge drift of snow which
lay between.

"Gee! she's snowin' yet, fit ter bury the lot of us!"
grumbled Babe Strander, wallowing up to his hips in
the fluffy mass.

"Colder 'n seventeen devils!" exclaimed Grat Vogel,
as the sharp wind howled through the clearing, driving
a cloud of fine white flakes within.

"Yer right there, bub," observed Ros Whitmore
with a laugh. "Devils is usially hot, 'cordin' ter my
knowledge."

Into the cook's den they tumbled, chaffing, scolding,
laughing. The two long clothless tables were fairly
splendid in the light of the lamps, with rows of bright
new tin plates, each guarded on the right flank by a
deep basin, or dipper, filled with a steaming fluid that
appeared as if it might have been dipped from the

Black Sea.   Piles of bread, white and brown; pyramids
of potatoes, "biled with their clothes on," and sending
up their quota of fragrant steam; great yellow hunks
of butter; fried pork, swimming in its own fat; black
molasses; various table utensils of the strictly useful
rather than ornamental class, and last but not least, at
each end, beans in the original packages, that is to say,
in the kettles in which they were baked.

"Pitch in, boys!" cried Reon, the cook.   "They's
chuck a plenty for all, sech as 'tis, an' it's good 'nuf fer
anybody whut they is of it."

With this statement all hands agreed, and "fell to"
with the beautiful and primitive simplicity and eagerness which mark the banqueting of half-famished
wolves.   No grace was said.   The minister was not
there.   These men had their share of his ministrations
during the summer.   He felt called to other camps
where, as at no other time, he would have opportunity
to get hold of the roving lumber-jacks.   Once or twice
during the winter he would visit Hawkins's camp out
of regard to his friends there employed.   Even Farmer
Hawkins could not get down from the farm every day.
Breakfast thus proceeded without any polite ceremony.
It does not take a very long time for twenty stalwart
and hearty men to consume a handsome quantity of
"chuck."   Meal-time never fails of a welcome.   Farmer
Hawkins had provided a liberal supply of good things,
and his neighbors and helpers always did it ample justice.

"What say, Barney?" asked Ros.   "Is this here
goin' ter keep up all day?"

"It's meself would like to know," replied Barney.
"Be the way she's comin' now, we'll be nadin' the
plough, if it lasts the day out."

"It's a roughish storm to work in; but we've all seen wus, an' likely to again afore we git this here pine all cut into shingles," remarked Bob Landseer.

"Please pass them beans, an' never mind the storm; I guess we uns isn't sugar nor salt," called Ned Blakely from the middle of the table.

"More wash, cookee," demanded Underhill, passing his basin to the cook's assistant for another filling of hot black tea.

"Ain't yer hash-traps full yet?" exclaimed Reon the cook, after he and his assistant, the cookee, had been flying about like veritable "devil's darning-needles" for what seemed to him as long a time as ought to suffice to satisfy the most voracious appetites.

Heedless of the cook's impatience, the scene of gormandizing went on until the inner man cried "hold! enough!" Then the teamsters, the choppers, the sawyers, the swampers, and the loaders, arming themselves with their appropriate implements,—chains, axes, peavies, cant-hooks, etc.,—pushed boldly out into the whirling, driving storm, all bustling and hastening, as was their wont, to see who should accomplish the greatest amount of work for the day. There were three teams of horses, and a separate crew for each, each with its complement of men for the various kinds of work. The mill would not start up until the skidways were filled, so the entire force of men was first set to work felling the trees, cutting them into lengths, and hauling the logs to the skidways. Thus they began in earnest to devour Farmer Hawkins's pine forest.

Another week passed, and the mill was going in full blast. The weather was clear and cold. A steady stream of logs to the skidways kept the mill supplied. Barney had transferred to Tom Moore his duties as foreman, in order that he might devote his time to his specialty as shingle-sawyer. He and Lon Hawley worked side by side, and kept their saws hot, with a good-natured, though none the less keen, rivalry for the lead in numbers of shingles completed in a day. First one and then the other would show a winning score, but the margin was slight. The rivalry became contagious, and the men of the outside crews soon caught it and dropped in between trips to learn how the race stood. Partisanship developed. Each man had his backers, though, of course, Barney, who was well known and immensely popular, received by far the most general support. The Midland contingent, for once, was divided, Ashbel Fair and "Babe" Strander rooting for Barney, while Rodney Bedell and Bud Frazer declared for Lon. Jim Gyde was watchful but silent and non-committal. Ned Blakely and Arch Fellows favored the lean, long-limbed Yankee. Most of the others, with the possible exception of Old Leatherback and Red Lampheer, who appeared to take no interest in the matter, stuck by the no less lanky and agile Irishman. Curiously enough, neither of the real contestants seemed to care whether his superiority was believed in by the crew at large or not. Their whole attention was bent upon their work and the effort of each to demonstrate to the other his own unbeatable speed.

Finally the interest became so acute that some one suggested a match to settle the question of superiority definitely. The idea found immediate favor. The day before Thanksgiving was selected, and an extra holiday for all hands except those necessary to run the mill was declared. The mill was cleared of all rubbish. The skidways were filled with the best logs obtainable.

The tramway was examined and put in good running order. The fireman had placed ready to his hand an extra supply of well-dried spalts and edgings to keep a full head of steam all day. His machinery was all clean, oiled, and inspected; the belts made taut; the drag-saw and shingle-saws newly filed and "gummed," that is, the spaces between the teeth made deeper, to allow free play for the sawdust.

News of the match spread throughout the surrounding country, and visitors from other camps and mills secured leave of absence, that they might witness the contest between two of the fastest sawyers in the whole region. Even the women, taking advantage of a clear crisp day, came out to the mill and brought extra supplies of good things for the boys to eat. Sam Hawkins and Seward Rathaway yielded also to the general excitement, and found their way to the seat of battle. A certain hope, strong in Sam's breast, led him, more than anything else, to see the match.

The evolution of a pine shingle is a simple and rapid process, fraught with dangers to fingers and hands in proportion to the speed attempted. The rough pine-log passes under the drag-saw, is cut into shingle-lengths, or bolts. A bolt is seized the instant it drops from the saw by an axman, who sets it on end and with a few quick strokes of his axe deftly removes the adhering bark and "sap," that outer portion of the wood through which the sap or pitch of the tree runs, and which is worthless for lumber or shingles of the better grades. He then splits the bolt into halves or quarters according to the diameter of the log, often leaving small bolts whole, and tosses the clean shingle bolts to the sawyers, by whom they are placed upright in the sawing machine. There they are held in place by spiked rollers above and below, are rapidly slipped back and forth with an alternating slant to right and left, and thus are sliced into rough shingles, thick at one end and thin at the other, with jagged edges, corresponding with the split sides of the bolt. As these shingles fall from the saw, they are picked up by the man who runs the "edger," a large revolving disc with keen, chisel-like knives, like those of a plane, radiating from the centre on its inner surface. The shingles are slid along a table into a slot where the edges press against the revolving disc and the knives remove with lightning rapidity all rough or uneven edges. The shingles are then tossed to another man, the "packer," who places them into the packing-machine, where they are made up into bunches ready to be stored away in the drying-house. By this last process the weight of a bundle of shingles is reduced nearly one-half.

The most expert edgers and packers had been secured to assist at the match, for the double purpose of taking care of the shingles promptly, as they fell from the two saws, and to insure against accidents which often resulted from an effort to speed when the skill was not equal to the test.

The sound of the whistle had scarcely died away at six o'clock on the morning of the day of the match, when the wheels in the mill began to move; the first log, specially selected with a view to making good bolts for the start, was rolled upon the carriage, and before the drag-saw had fairly gained its momentum, was in place for the first cut. The log was made fast; the saw descended, and, with a shout, the first bolt was rolled to the axman.

"That's a darlin'!" exclaimed Tom Moore, the master of the axe, as he clipped off the sap, cleft the bolt into even quarters, and let them fall all together at the hands of the rival sawyers.

Barney and Lon each grabbed a section at the same instant, and in the wink of an eye the sharp "ping" of the saws was heard as they bit into the live wood. The tone deepened into a hum, then ended with a "zipp" as the first two shingles dropped off. Instantly the same note was repeated—over and over again, with hardly long enough intervals to mark them as separate sounds. In a steady stream the shingles fell upon the edger's scaffold.

Chip, chuck, chur-r-r-r, went the edger, as, with a flip and a flop, first one edge of the shingle and then the other was pushed against the sharp chisel-bits.

"Who won first blood?" yelled Jaky Strander, meaning the first shingle to the edgers.

"Both kem together; no advantage," announced Ros Whitmore, who watched at that point.

Sawdust and edgings began to fly at a lively rate. Full steam was up at last, and the match was on in earnest.

According to the rules adopted, only number one shingles, without "shake" or sap, were to count in the score, the narrowest shingle of this class being six inches in width. This required good judgment in getting the bolts to the saw, a bolt under one management often producing several more shingles of the first class than it would yield if first set to the saw some other way.

Few visitors had arrived so early in the morning, but Farmer Hawkins had made it a point to come for the very beginning of the match. The other men of the crew who were not needed for the actual mill-work found places of vantage and spurred the two sawyers on with encouraging shouts and scraps of advice, or engaged in speculations as to the outcome.

Both men seemed to be putting in their best work, yet as the morning advanced Lon Hawley was seen to be forging steadily ahead. His lightning-like movements, his flashing eye, and his strict attention to business resulted in a gain that grew alarming to Barney's friends, as Ros Whitmore marked the tally from time to time on a large board. Barney appeared to pay no attention to the score, but chaffed good-naturedly now and then with his partisans.

"Tech her up, Barney; yer runnin' a bit slack, ain't ye?" urged Tom Moore, after an hour or so waiting to see whether Barney would try to cut down his rival's lead.

"Sure, it's asy I am in mind an' body," said Barney. "Ye'll have no nade to worry before the day is inded."

But Tom continued to worry. He could not bear to see his friend dropping behind.

"Keep it up; you're a winner, Lon!" cried Rodney Bedell, who with Sam Hawkins and Seward Rathaway stood near the Yankee's machine. Sam made no effort to conceal his pleasure, but said nothing.

The stack of bundles was growing to considerable proportions, and orders were given to take them at once to the drying-house and thus make more room for visitors who were constantly arriving. Lon was working at top speed, excited by his own lead and determined to maintain it. The edgers and packers were compelled to strain every nerve to handle the flood of shingles.

"Bedad! but they're the fast sawyers," exclaimed Pete Murray to a newcomer.

"One of them is," sneered Sam, indicating which one by a jerk of his thumb.

A gleam crept into the eyes of Barney O'Boyle, but he gave no other sign that he had overheard the remark.

"Come, Barney, quit playin' with 'im, an' pull out; show yer friends what ye can do." Bob Landseer's voice betrayed real concern.

Barney allowed his eyes to rest quizzically on his friend's face for the briefest fraction of a second, then he went on with his work, cool and collected as before.

"Time enough, Bob," he said.

Dinner hour approached. The relative positions of the contestants remained the same. The whistle blew, and the saws stopped. Ros Whitmore announced that Lon Hawley was a whole bundle, a quarter thousand shingles, in the lead. Barney's smile vanished. The lead was larger than he thought. At that moment, glancing about the crowd of spectators, he saw Norine Maloney standing near the door. She smiled, but looked disappointed. Barney's eyes glistened, his jaws set firmly, and with erect figure and elastic step he walked out of the mill toward the shanty.

"What's ailin' ye, me boy?" asked Pete Murray, as he and Tom Moore hastened after Barney. "Sure, there's no sawyer in the State would be runnin' away from ye with a bundle o' shingles before dinner if ye were feelin' loike yersilf."

The smile came back to Barney's face.

"Would ye mind puttin' your hand there a bit; an' there?"

Tom felt of his friend's forehead and wrists, and exclaimed:

"Cool es a cowcumber, an' not a drop of sweat!"

"See any shakin'?" asked Barney again, as he stretched out his arm and held it rigid.

"Nary a shake," said Tom.

"Now ye might go look at Lon; an' don't be after worryin' yourselves grayheaded fer what ain't loikly to happen."

"Two extra tables were spread for dinner in the men's camp, to accommodate the crowd of visitors. Excitement over the match ran high, but did not dull the appetites. Barney's friends were puzzled at his poor showing, and could only hope that he had greater things in reserve. Farmer Hawkins, when appealed to, declared Barney would come out all right, he felt sure. On the other hand, the partisans of Lon were jubilant, confident, and boastful. Lon himself was in high feather and declared he would certainly gain another bundle during the afternoon. He admitted that he had "put in his best licks" from the start, and was glad of a resting spell; but he explained that everything depended upon gaining a commanding lead early in the game. "It sorter puts the other feller under a handicap, an' takes the nerve out'n him," he said.

Jaky Strander had something on his mind, and it made him fidget until he got it off.

"Guess I'll bet five on Lon ter win this 'ere match," he said, taking care that Barney should not hear him.

"Thought ye were for Barney," said Tom Moore, in surprise.

"Yes, thet's right; my feelin's is with the under dog, but my money's on the top one. Any feller want it?"

No one seemed in a hurry to cover the bet, and "Babe" laughed jeeringly.

"Lon's got ye all scared; looks like a sure thing.

Gee! ef Barney ain't got a backer, guess I'll hev ter bet th' other way."

"Give Ros yer money, ef yer so anxious ter lose it; here's five ter cover it," said Tom; and each man wrote on a bit of paper his I. O. U., and deposited it with Ros Whitmore.

Sam had been watching the transaction with flushed cheeks. It was exactly what he wanted to do himself, but he had hesitated to take the initiative. Now, however, waiting only until his father was away at the other part of the shanty in his capacity as host, he pulled out two ten-dollar greenbacks, and exclaimed loudly:

"Here's twenty, spot cash, on Lon,—that is, if any of you is foolish enough to bet against a sure winner." The last words were spoken with an unmistakable sneer.

Astonishment showed itself on all faces. Barney heard, but quickly turned away. Norine also heard and gave a little sniff of indignation.

"How'd he come by twenty dollars—greenbacks, too?" whispered Bob Landseer to Dan Underhill, who sat near him.

"Not by workin', I'll venture. Mought o' borried it from them city chaps who spent the summer here," speculated Dan.

Pete Murray spoke up promptly:

"Is it twenty dollars an' no more ye want?" he asked.

"Why, I thought twenty was about right, don't you know," replied Sam, a little flustered.

"Ye'll not be after makin' it forty, maybe?" persisted Murray.

"Well, no; to tell the truth, twenty is about my limit just now," said Sam, still more nervous because of the other's calm assurance.

"Right ye are. Jes' pass up the green ter Ros fer

safe houldin'.   Here's what'll kape it from bein' lonesome."

The wagers added fuel to the excitement, and all
were eager for the struggle to be resumed.   Before the
noon hour was over the mill was crowded, and those
who could not get in waited around the door until some
of the spectators should come out and give them a turn.
Lon stood at his machine with a smile of confidence,
and acknowledged the congratulations and admonitions
of his party while waiting for the whistle to blow.
Barney pushed through the crowd at the last moment
and paid no attention to the great cheer of welcome
and encouragement that greeted him.   He reached his
place just as the whistle blew.

The machines had been set in motion a few moments
before the blowing of the whistle, so that no time need
be lost.   Both men began at once rushing the bolts
through.   Tom Moore wielded his axe with fury and
precision to keep a pile of bolts ready.   The drag-sawyer
called for an additional helper.   The watchers looked
eagerly to note the first sign of any change in the score.

"Barney's gainin'!" yelled Grat Vogel, of a sudden,
trying to jump into the air.

"Shet up! He ain't; Lon's got him beat," said Ned
Blakely, crowding in front of the boy.

But Barney was gaining, and the first bulletin exhibited by Ros Whitmore showed that the margin between
the contestants had narrowed considerably.   With coolness and good judgment he picked up the bolts invari-
ably with the best side ready, and before they were
fixed on the rollers the carriage was in motion.   Every
bolt was made to yield its utmost of No. 1 shingles.
His speed seemed to increase steadily as the hours
passed.

A shudder went over the spectators as the murderous teeth of the whirring saw caught his smock and ripped the sleeve. Barney did not even withdraw his hand, but went on with his work as if nothing had happened.

Near him Lon was working like a madman. The same driving speed of the morning was maintained. He fairly hurled the bolts through his machine. Barney's coolness worked on him like a constant irritant. He saw his margin of lead slipping from him, and was determined to keep it. His power was being exerted to the extreme limit, but the strain of the long forenoon was beginning to tell. He began to show nervousness, and to cut too many narrow shingles.

The weather grew colder as the afternoon waned. Steam was harder to make, and the fireman called for assistance. The crowd of onlookers shifted uneasily, unwilling to lose sight of the exciting match, yet unable to endure quietly the piercing cold. The shingle-mill afforded no more shelter than a thin roof, and a single thickness of boards stood on end for walls. Yet in spite of the snapping frost, the workers now all perspired as freely as in July; and the men spectators, first in one position and then in another, stuck doggedly to the mill, or made brief visits to the cook's den or the men's camp to get thawed out. The women made their headquarters in the cook's shanty, and received news at intervals, or ran over to the mill for a brief sight of the contest.

As the last hour drew near, the cold was almost forgotten in the tingle of excitement. The fire under the boiler cracked and roared under forced draught. As the steam came up, part of it would blow off.

"Jump onter thet 'ere safety-valve, and hold her

down!" yelled Lon, as he heard the escaping steam.
"We want every bit o' power in the boiler." Without
looking to see whether his demand was complied with
he bent still more furiously to his work.

"Babe" Strander quickly planted his great bulk
astride the offending valve. Higher and higher rose
the steam. Faster and faster dropped the shingles on
the edgers' scaffold. The machinery was rushing at a
terrific rate.

"Look out! She'll bust!" cried Ros; but nobody
"looked out."

Just then a bulletin went up.

"Tied, by thunder!" yelled Ashbel Fair.

The shout from the crowd drowned the noise of the
machines for an instant. Lon swore a fierce oath, and
with fire in his eye grabbed a bolt.

Barney gave no heed to the cheers. He was looking
anxiously at his machine. It seemed to be losing
speed. Soon the saw stopped altogether. The arbor
had become choked with gum, ice, and sawdust. Only
an instant was needed to discover the mischief, and
only a few moments to clean away the dirt; but these
few moments were precious, as the other saw was
whirring spitefully on, and Lon was regaining the lead.
With the stoppage of Barney's saw, the belt had been
thrown and had to be replaced. Fully ten minutes
were lost.

Barney's blood was up at last, and he let out the last
wrap, as he faced the task of regaining in an hour's
time the loss of ten minutes, besides the necessary
margin for winning. He had saved his strength during
the early hours, and had gauged that of his opponent,
but had not looked for so severe a finish. A stoppage
of Lon's saw with the accumulation of the day's gum

and dirt put them on even terms again. Then the race waxed hotter.

"Cut yer gov'ner belt!" shouted Fellows to the engineer. The latter, without a moment's hesitation, whipped out a big knife, and with one slash severed the belt. The loosely built mill seemed like to fall to pieces over their heads.

"I can't stand this much longer," wailed "Babe," from his hot seat on the safety valve, his face red as a boiled lobster.

"Cawn't ye?" cried Lon. "Move one pound off'n thet valve, an' I'll make jelly of ye!"

Round and round flew the shafting. Again Barney, who had forced himself into the lead, was put out of it by an exasperating delay. A squeak, another, another; then a smell of burning oil and sawdust gave notice that a hot journal must be attended to.

"For the love of hiven! grab some snow, quick!" called Barney, and a dozen hands obeyed.

The cooling was the matter of a moment; but the oil-cup had to be cleaned and refilled with oil, before the machine was again in commission. Lon was a score of shingles ahead.

"Half an hour more!" cried Ros.

"Hit 'er up, Barney!"

"Keep yer nose in front, Lon!"

"You kin ketch 'im yet, Barney!'

"Yer a winner, Lon!"

"Five on Barney!"

"Five here, on the winner!"

Everybody was shouting, and nobody paid attention to any one else. The two men were straining every nerve. The machinery, with no governors to check it, was racing madly. Still the fireman piled dry spalts and edgings into the furnace. "Babe" Strander squirmed in agony, but clung to the safety valve.

"Five minutes to six!" said Ros, consulting the engineer's clock.

The bedlam of voices suddenly ceased. All were too excited to talk. A new log rolled upon the carriage. The bolts fell one by one. Tom Moore caught the first, denuded it, and laid it in quarters just in time for the sawyer.

"Yer journal's hot, Lon!" exclaimed Blakely, but Lon paid no heed, as he reached for one of the new quarters.

"Don't ye see 'er burnin'?" insisted Ned.

"Let 'er burn and be——"

"Ping! r-r-r-r-r-zip!"

Not Lon's, but Barney's saw gave forth the startling sound. A villanous pine knot lurked in his bolt, and every tooth of his saw succumbed in the contact.

A groan of dismay; a half-suppressed shout of exultation; then a flash, and a wail like a demon spirit. Lon's saw turned a cherry red, and clogged itself in the "shaky" ice- and gum-filled bolt he had just picked up. Both saws were out of the race and the shrieking of the six o'clock whistle drowned all other sounds.

"Lon wins!"

"How so? Barney's ahead."

"No, Lon."

"What say, Ros?"

"Wall, Barney he's a full dozen shingles to the good. I reckon he must be the winner," declared Ros.

Then, in the midst of the shouting and cheers, Barney grasped Lon by the hand and threw his left arm around his antagonist's shoulders in a brotherly embrace.

"Bedad, yer the foinest sawyer I've set me two eyes on; an' ye gave me such a rub, I thought I was licked. It's proud I am of ye."

The hearty sincerity in Barney's tone went far to take the sting out of the defeat, and Lon roused himself to take his beating manfully.

"Guess I'll hev ter own up ter being licked fair an' square by a better man," he said, returning Barney's grasp.

Sam Hawkins was trying to sneak off unobserved to hide his chagrin and disappointment; but Pete Murray and Ros Whitmore stopped him. "Here's yer twenty, Sam. Pete, here, says he has no thought o' keepin' it," and he thrust the two bills into Sam's hand.

"Not keep it! Why—he won it—didn't he?" exclaimed Sam, in surprise.

"Sure, I'll not be takin' money I've not earned, from the son of me friend Hawkins," said Murray. Then he added, "I made quick to take yer bet to kape it from fallin' into the hands of some one who might not fale the same way."

Sam sheepishly pocketed the money and hurried away. Tom Moore was not so soft-hearted and felt no hesitation in taking "Babe's" money.

"'Tain't safe to bank too heavy on the top dog early in the game," he remarked. "The under dog is sometimes playin' possum."

A glance from two bright eyes was Barney's reward, —the only reward worth counting.

CHAPTER VIII

SATURDAY night, after Thanksgiving, Jim Gyde turned his team of horses over to the stableman with a muttered exclamation which the other did not understand, and marched off at once to the men's shanty. Without a word to the half-dozen men who were there before him, he sat down on the deacon seat in front of his bunk, and, resting his head on one hand and his elbow on his knee, proceeded to wrestle with the problem which had been bothering him for several weeks. During the past three days it had reached an acute stage, and he felt that the time had come for a fight to the finish. The supper call from the cook's shanty sounded, and the other men scrambled off. Jim sat still on the deacon seat, and only a slight scowl gave token that he heard the call usually welcomed so eagerly. Presently he stretched out his legs, and forming a bootjack with the toe of one foot and the rim of the stove he drew off his heavy boots and placed them before the fire to dry while he held out his stockinged feet to the red glow of the stove for the same purpose. A pungent odor of steaming leather and wool quickly asserted itself in the close atmosphere of the shanty. Jim's movements had been almost automatic and unconscious. He was still absorbed in the struggle which raged within. Rodney Bedell and Bud Frazer came in from supper and stared at him in surprise.

"What's up, Jim? You look like a funeral. Ain't you goin' to grub?" asked Rodney.

Jim started and shook himself together.

"I'll go when I like," he replied shortly; but at that moment his face lost all the perplexity which had furrowed it with wrinkles, and a look of determination and purpose transfigured it. He pulled on his boots and went at once to supper. Then, gathering together the few personal belongings which he had at the camp, he quietly slipped away, taking care that no one should be aware of his going. An hour or so later he presented himself at the Hawkins Farm and asked Josiah Hawkins for his "time," meaning his pay for the time he had worked and his release from further duty. Persistent questioning failed to get from him any reason for his sudden desertion. He had no grievance, he said; nothing had gone wrong; he felt fit as ever, and liked the work, but he wanted to quit. With a kind word of regret, and a cordial invitation to come to the Christmas jollification which had been promised for the members of the Hawkins camp, the farmer paid Jim and let him go. Barney O'Boyle, when appealed to, could not explain Jim's action. Even Ashbel Fair and the other boys from Midland had not been taken into his confidence.

"Now that I think of it, he's been actin' kinder queer-like the last month," said Barney; "kapin' to himself sorter quiet an' peaceable. Sure, he's after givin' Red Lampheer the cowld shoulder entirely. Him an' Red were the divil's own twins for trouble up the river last year. It's my opinion there's somethin' on his mind."

Farmer Hawkins laughed and said: "I should hardly regard that as a bad sign. A little thinking will do him good. If you hear from him, let me know."

Meanwhile, Jim Gyde had gone from the farm directly

to Red-Keg. The night was cold and clear, and he walked rapidly along the snowy road, reaching the village about nine o'clock. Almost unconsciously he turned in the direction of Pete's saloon and "hotel," the Red-Keg, from the window of which a cheerful light seemed to invite him to enter. He stepped upon the low platform which served as a piazza, and raised his hand to push open the door. Then he hesitated, and let his hand fall slowly to his side.

"'Tain't 'xactly the place to begin," he muttered, and stole softly away.

A little farther up the street was Jake Vogel's store with his house adjoining. Both were in darkness, but Jim, after a moment's deliberation, pounded on the door of the house with his fist. Presently a voice within demanded to know who was there, and then the door was opened and Jake Vogel appeared holding a smoking kerosene hand-lamp above his head.

"Great beanstalks, Jim! What brings ye to the Kag this time o' night, an' what kin I do for ye?"

"Nothin', 'cept give me a place to sleep till mornin'," replied Jim.

"Ye kin hev Grat's bed ef it's long enough," said Jake, as he shut the door; "but I thought ye was workin' in Hawkins's camp out by the Sturgeon way."

"I've quit," said Jim, so shortly that Jake was constrained to keep his curiosity to himself, and he showed the young man to a small room on the next floor, remarking:

"This here's Grat's room; don't know what shape it's in; guess ye'll hev to make out by yerself; the old lady's in bed."

"I'm much obliged, an' I don't need no waitin' on,"

said Jim. "I might o' gone to Pete's, or to Ferd's, yonder, but—but——"

"Never mind," interrupted Vogel, "ye're welcome here; make yerself ter hum." With this, Jake retired, taking his lamp with him.

Early on the following morning, after a quick but substantial breakfast, Jim started off again along the river road to Midland. Later in the forenoon numerous conveyances would pass along that road with Red-Keggers on the way to the Rev. Augustus Hayward's church. It was just as well to be early and avoid meeting acquaintances who might ask embarrassing questions.

The intense cold of the past three or four days was moderating, and already the snow was beginning to soften in the morning sun. A thin sheet of ice had formed over the Tittabawassee since the last snow fell, but it was likely to break up with one warm day. The naked trees between the road and the river afforded free glimpses of the frozen stream, glistening like silver in sharp contrast to the bronze-like boles. On the other side of the road the forest was broken at intervals by the clearings of lumbermen or farmers, and in most of these clearings the houses of those who had thus slain their thousands in their battle with the forest stood a short distance back from the road. Overhead, the road was arched, for most of the distance, with great branches, which in summer shut out the heat of the sun and in winter mitigated the fury of the storm. A beautiful road it was for those who had eyes to see.

Jim Gyde cared for none of these things; he did not know of their existence. The road was a way from Red-Keg to Midland, that was all—or, not quite all. His stride grew slower as he approached a clearing about a mile from Midland.   Just within sight of a neat farmhouse he stopped and gazed eagerly at veranda, windows, doors, grounds.   Nothing seemed to reward his search, for the longing look did not leave his eyes. He started to enter the gate, hesitated, and then hastened on his way, with a spring in his step and the light of a strong purpose kindling anew in his face.

"Not now; not yet," he muttered, and then, with a grim smile, "thet 'gold' first, for her, an'—him."

Jim's father was surprised when his son stalked into the house on Sunday morning.   He had regarded him as fixed for the winter at the Hawkins camp.   Failing to get any explanation, however, for his sudden throwing up of a good job, he satisfied himself by administering a tongue-lashing, which was received in silence, and then left his son to his own devices.   The injunction, "Father, provoke not your children to wrath," was not a part of old man Bill Gyde's rule of conduct. He would have been surprised if any one had told him that his "line upon line, and precept upon precept," and his adherence to the command, "Thou shalt beat him with the rod and shalt deliver his soul from hell," had wholly failed in Jim's case because the necessary admixture of love had been lacking.   Jim, in his younger days, had hated his father.   Now, when he himself was larger and stronger and able to resist the long-accustomed switch, his hate had changed to contempt.   The tongue-lashing had lost much of its sting, and reminded him, more than anything else, of the rapid and futile stabs of a venomous snake held prisoner under the sole of a thick horsehide boot.   Therefore he ignored his father's reproof and kept his own counsel during the remainder of the day.

Monday morning dawned amid a whirl of snow.   The

wind blew a gale from the northeast. It had grown colder again over night. Joseph Waters rubbed the sleep from his eyes at daybreak and cast troubled glances out of the window as he dressed.

"Bad day; not many out; I must get around early and warm up," he soliloquized, as he noted how the mercury had sunk nearer to the bulb in the thermometer nailed to the frame outside his window. A few minutes later he repeated the same observation to Dame Bedell, who stood over a crackling hard-wood fire in the kitchen preparing breakfast. In his "boarding 'round" itinerary, the teacher of District School No. 1 had, the week before, taken up his brief abode with the parents of one of his pupils, Rodney Bedell.

"You're 'bout right, teacher," responded Dame Bedell briskly, as she thrust a fresh stick into the stove and jammed it down into place with the poker. "I'll hev your breakfast ready in a jiffy, an' ye can git off as soon's ye like."

The school was but a short distance from the house, and as soon as Waters arrived, he set about building a fire in the long box-stove with its antique drum on top. Pine chips, and dry spalts, and heavy sticks of beech and maple, full cordwood length, were soon blazing and snapping. The fire roared through the long stovepipe, the sides of the old stove became cherry-red, and the drum threw out a cheerful warmth which soon reached the remote corners of the room.

Waters looked for a slim attendance at this first session of school after the Thanksgiving holidays. The storm would keep many of the little ones away who loved to come, and some of the older children who were glad of any excuse to be absent. His assistant, Axcy Marthy, would come in spite of the storm; he felt sure of it. She had almost never missed a session as pupil, and now, as assistant teacher, regularly appointed at a salary by the School Board, she was, if possible, still more faithful. The little ones worshipped her, and considered it the direst misfortune if kept at home. Her winning smile and merry laugh, and her natural roguishness and love of fun made her the comrade of them all; while the forceful dignity with which she controlled them when she wished commanded their respect and obedience. To Mr. Waters she had grown indispensable. The work of the school proceeded better, the deportment had improved, and he found himself taking real enjoyment in the performance of his arduous task. He sometimes questioned with himself what had wrought the change in behavior among many of the formerly unruly boys. Was it his own firmness, or the presence in the room of Axcy Marthy as assistant teacher? And what had wrought the change in his own attitude to the school? Last year he had entered the room in the morning with a sense of taking up a burden or beginning a struggle. In the evening he departed with a feeling of relief. He had even debated seriously whether to accept a reappointment. This year he experienced unmistakable pleasure as he began his day, and curiously failed to welcome its ending. Perhaps he was not fully conscious of this reversal of feeling. Perhaps he did not realize this Monday morning, as he wound the school clock and set it by his watch, that his only thought with regard to the half-hour remaining before school time was one of impatience for it to be gone.

One by one the pupils struggled in from the storm, shutting the door with difficulty against the wind and the whirl of flakes. They shook the snow from coats and wraps, stamped their feet, and gathered around the big stove in the centre of the room. Cheeks were aglow and spirits rollicksome after the battle with the elements. Some of the smallest children, living near at hand, had been brought, bundled up, by their fathers or big brothers. At nine o'clock between thirty and forty pupils were present, but Axcy Marthy had not come. Just as the teacher reached for the bell-rope, one of Axcy's anxious pupils, who was posted at the window and peering through the flying snow, called gleefully:

"Here she comes—I guess! Way down the road. The wind is mos' blowin' her to pieces."

Instantly a dozen more children were wiping the steam from the windows on that side of the room and straining to catch a glimpse of their "own teacher," who had fought her way through the storm for more than a mile, and now seemed exhausted and almost helpless in the wind and drifting snow.

Waters glanced through the window and then sprang for his overcoat and cap to go to the girl's assistance. As he stepped out into the road he saw a tall man hurrying toward Axcy with the evident purpose of rendering aid. A moment more, and Waters saw to his surprise that the man was Jim Gyde, who, as he had thought, was ten miles away at Hawkins's shingle-mill. He watched the two until satisfied that no further help was needed, and then re-entered the schoolroom to await their arrival.

"Well! Thought I'd never get here! What a storm!" exclaimed Axcy, as she burst in, panting and laughing.

Jim shut the door and stood by it, looking sheepish and uncomfortable, his frame towering above all the other pupils and even the schoolmaster himself, who extended his hand cordially.

"Glad to see you, Jim. What brings you down here so far from the camp?" he asked.

"Why—I—ain't it school time? I b'long here, don't I?" replied Jim, fidgeting awkwardly.

"Certainly! Glad to have you. Pretty rough outside, isn't it?" said Waters, still puzzled, but quick to see that the young lumberman did not want to be questioned. Probably this was simply another of his many whims, which had so long kept him from making progress in anything that required persistent application.

School was quickly in session, and Jim glared at the lesson that had been given him to study as though he would devour it, book and all. Now and then he dug his fingers into his hair and scowled at the page in a sort of suppressed fury. Real study was so unusual with him that it almost baffled his most determined efforts to keep his mind on the lesson, and he was angry at his own seeming inability to conquer what the smaller pupils found so easy. A feeling of shame grew strong in him as he began to realize his own ignorance, but he only went at his task with more fierce determination, which made the sweat stand out on his forehead. Waters noticed with interest and curiosity the evident struggle in which the young man was engaged. He had never seen him tackle his lessons in such a manner before. Something was behind it, and it must be something out of the ordinary. He would watch and wait.

At noontime the storm had abated somewhat. Most of the children had brought their lunch and gathered in groups to eat it; but Jim plunged out into the drifts as soon as the bell rang for noon recess. He had recited once during the forenoon, and had surprised himself no less than the schoolmaster and the other pupils by spelling several words correctly. He had a vague dread that compliments and questions might be waiting him, so he fled precipitately the moment the bell rang. Waters noticed this also with a smile.

Just as the school was reconvened, not a moment sooner, Jim returned and took his seat, and the painful struggle of the forenoon was renewed. After another creditable recitation Waters covered him with confusion by commending him before the school. Moreover, he determined to speak personally to him after school and encourage him to go on with his good work; but the young man disappeared the instant school was dismissed.

Several days passed in this way, and the schoolmaster watched with growing interest and wonder the dogged persistence with which Jim stuck to the work. His progress was marvellous, for him. Waters had tried every day to find an opportunity to talk with him alone, but the young man avoided everybody. Twice as Waters left the schoolhouse in the evening he caught a glimpse of Jim, apparently hanging around and waiting for him, but as soon as he approached, Jim went away.

"The boy has something on his mind and he wants to tell me, but can't screw up his courage. I'll have to help him," concluded Waters, after the second experience of this kind.

The next day was Friday, the last school day of the week. Before dismissing the school, Waters announced the names of six pupils who were requested to remain for a few minutes. Jim Gyde was among them, much to his surprise. After the others had gone, the schoolmaster began to dismiss the six, one at a time, with a

word or two concerning their studies, until only Jim
was left.

"I want to speak to you, Jim; and I think you want
to speak to me; but you've kept away from me so persistently that I had to resort to this little ruse to get
hold of you." Waters laughed as he made this frank
confession, and took a seat near Jim.

"Now tell me all about it," he continued. "What's
got into you? You're a new man. Why, do you
know, Jim, you have really accomplished more in this
one week than you ever did before in a year. It has
been hard work, I know. I admire your pluck. At
this rate you'll do wonders by spring. What does it
all mean?"

Pleasure, surprise, and chagrin betrayed themselves
in the rugged face of the young lumberman. The
schoolmaster's hearty praise pleased him, but he had
flattered himself that Waters understood exactly the
reason for his changed conduct.

"You don't mean to say—that is, you haven't forgot,
have ye, what you said at the parson's party?" said
Jim, hesitatingly.

"No, Jim, I haven't, surely; and you haven't forgotten it? You said then that you didn't understand me,
but you have never asked me to explain. Did you
figure it out for yourself?" asked Waters.

"You said as how I had gold in me an' didn't know
it, or some such talk as that. I didn't know what you
meant then, an' I ain't jes clear now, but I couldn't git
it out o' mind ever sence. I kinder figgered you was
usin' fancy talk, like the parson does in preachin', an'
meant that I didn't amount to much, but could if I laid
out to do my best."

Jim was painfully embarrassed at having to explain

himself to the schoolmaster, but now the ice was broken he was resolved to make his intentions perfectly plain. Waters could scarcely refrain from a smile at the reference to his style of language, but he replied seriously and kindly:

"You came pretty near to it, Jim; I did mean that you could amount to something if you would rouse and use the good qualities that are in you but that had been neglected. A manly character—bravery, honesty, kindness, worthy ambition and the pluck and ability to achieve it—this is the gold in a man. When he finds it and uses it, he makes himself rich, and his friends, too. I'm glad you've struck the vein."

"I ain't so clear on that," said Jim, "but if it's so, as you say, an' I can git ahead, an' make up for lost time, an' be good fer suthin, I want to. I don't know much —not as much as the other fellers—an' I thought maybe I oughter come back to school this winter 'stead of cuttin' logs."

"Yes, there are some things a man must get before he says good-by to school-books, if he wants to take any kind of place among his fellows. We'll crowd a lot of good, practical, every-day learning into the remainder of this school season, and you will be surprised at the results in the spring. I shall be only too glad to help you all I can."

Waters spoke heartily and rose as he concluded, to indicate that their understanding was complete, and the purpose of the conversation achieved. Nothing more remained but to go home. But Jim kept his seat, and cleared his throat in the manner which always intimates that there is something more to say.

"That ain't quite all, Mr. Waters," he said, with some hesitation. "You told me that time you was my

9

friend, an' would always be willin' to give me a brother's help if I'd take it—didn't you?" The question was added with a sudden tone of anxiety lest he had presumed too far.

"That's right, Jim. I meant it, and I'll stick to it. Nothing will give me more pleasure than to help you on in the way you have chosen. Do not hesitate to call on me for anything you need that is within my power to grant."

The young man seemed to be laboring under a suppressed excitement, which made it difficult for him to speak. The schoolmaster's hearty and unqualified promise of help stirred him strangely.

"I have no right to ask it; I know I ain't," he said, hoarsely. "I ain't forgot how I set the dog on ye, an' how ye never told on me, an' even offered to be my friend. It was a dirty trick. I hated you that day fer thrashin' me; I hated you worse fer killin' Moscow, an' I hated you again fer forgivin' me an' makin' me ashamed o' myself. Then, 'long in the summer, I didn't hate you, an' felt more ashamed; an' I thought about all you said, an' made my mind up to try an' make up for it, an' show you,—an'—another reason. I meant ter come ter school at the start, but the boys got me out ter the mill before I knew it. Then I thought I'd wait till spring, but the more I thought, the more I couldn't wait, so I quit an' come here. Now I'm havin' the cheek ter ask favors of the man I tried ter git done up."

"Never mind the dog, Jim," said Waters. "I don't regret the episode at all. I believe it was the means of bringing us together. We'll be all the better friends because of that little affair and this frank talk. If there is any other favor you want to ask, don't hesitate. If I can, I will grant it gladly."

"There is!" exclaimed Jim. "I don't know why I come to you for it, 'cept that you're the only man who could do it, an' you are goin' to help me be somebody, an'—an'—you're a square man."

Jim paused a moment, at a loss how to proceed. Waters said nothing, but waited.

"I said I wanted to try what ye told me, an' show you they was somethin' decent in me," continued Jim, after a moment. "It was no more'n fair to you, after the way you'd treated me; but there's somebody else I want to show, too—somebody I want to make myself fit for. I ain't good enough now, I know, but you said I could be, an' you promised to help. If you'll do that, maybe in a year or so I'll be fit to go to her and tell her, an' ask her ter have me. Mr. Waters, you've been talkin' about the good in me—the gold, ye called it—an' about ambition, an' all that. Let me jes say this—there's nothin' in God's world will bring 'em out like the love in me for that girl, an' the hope of makin' her my wife. If they's any gold, it's for her, an' if—if ye could, sometime, speak a good word for me to Axcy, it would be the biggest favor ye ever did, an' more'n I deserve."

Would it not, indeed! Jim had been so absorbed in his appeal that he did not observe the pallor which spread over Joseph Waters's face as he listened, nor the look of horror and anguish which distended his eyes, as the full significance of Jim's request struck him with cruel force. A complete realization of his own feeling for Axcy seemed to come simultaneously with his comprehension of Jim's desire, and he cringed as from a blow. It was impossible to answer Jim's request at once, and he rose hastily and walked toward the door to conceal his emotion. His limbs seemed weak and trembling and threatened to give way under him. Only an instant passed, though it was like an hour to him, when he heard Jim's voice again, away off in the distance, it seemed.

"What's wrong? Don't go yet, till you've answered me," he was saying. "You offered me your hand, that time, and a brother's help, an' I was too much of a fool to take it. Would you mind—shakin' hands now, ter show you meant it, an' that they ain't no hard feelin's? I'm only takin' you at your word, ain't I?"

With a supreme effort, Waters controlled himself and turned to Jim, who had risen from his seat. He extended his hand, and the young man grasped it eagerly.

"Jim," said Waters, his voice husky and uncertain, "you can make a worthy man of yourself if you stick to your resolve. The help I have pledged you, I shall give, you may be sure. The matter of your—love for —a noble girl is between you and her alone; but do not doubt that I shall speak well of you whenever you deserve it. Good-night."

Jim strode away satisfied. Waters remained for a few moments to lock up, scarcely conscious of what he did; then he walked slowly away toward his home. The suddenness with which the double revelation had come to him unnerved him and made it impossible to think clearly. He knew that he had come to a crisis in his life. He felt as if an abyss of darkness and death had on the instant opened in front of him and behind him, where just before all had been bright and promising. Now a step in either direction meant disaster and heartbreak. He entered the Bedell home and sat down to supper because it was there awaiting him. After sitting awhile without eating, he excused himself to the good dame who kept house alone while her husband and son were away to the lumber-camps, and went to his room. There, alone, in the cold and the darkness, he tried to find the bearings and steer the course of his storm-tossed soul. The case seemed hopeless. Over and over again he repeated, "I love her—I need her; he loves her—he needs her. I am pledged to lift him up, to help him gain the prize of manliness. Must I sacrifice myself—and her—to do it?"

Joseph Waters was a true man. He was sturdy, stubborn, and conscientious. When once he had decided that a certain course was the right one, he would not hesitate to follow it, no matter what the cost; but while he was true to others and to his sense of right, he was true also to himself. To be guilty of an injustice to himself was a sin only a degree less than injustice to another. He believed it to be his duty to gain every good thing, every advantage, every joy for himself which could be gained without depriving another of his due. The problem which now confronted him was unparalleled in its complexity and its promise of pain for himself and others, however it might be solved. The more he wrestled with it, the more hopeless it looked. To conquer the unruly spirit and arouse the dormant ambition of Jim Gyde was an undertaking which he had specially chosen and made one of the most earnest purposes in his work at District School No. 1. He had chosen it partly because of a genuine interest in and wish to benefit the young man, and partly because of the very difficulty of the task itself. It was his nature to try things that others regarded as impossible, to do things that others would not do. Moreover, he regarded the training of the minds of his pupils in school studies as only a part of his work with them. He had the missionary spirit combined with that of the pedagogue. From the very first, he had recognized that the Midland school, with its element of half-grown and fully-grown young backwoodsmen, lawless and uncouth, was the field of labor which needed him. When he was tempted to leave it, his stubborn nature seized upon the incident of the dog and threw it into the balancing scales. They tipped at once to the side of staying, and Jim Gyde became his special aim. Strangely enough, God seemed to have given him, in his very first conversation with the fellow, a word which had struck home. He had pledged himself to stick by Jim and help him in his struggle for a new life, and the young man had accepted his pledge and held him to it. Ambition and purpose had sprung into fierce life and seemed to be sweeping the lad on with resistless impulse. All he asked was the co-operation of the man who had promised to be his brother. That was all, indeed! To Joseph Waters it was *all*. What fearful sacrifice had Jim unknowingly demanded? He had innocently and trustingly confided to his new-found brother that the one thing he cared for, the one thing he needed, was the love and companionship of Axcy Marthy. He had known it in his heart before, but now his roused ambition and aspiration to be a worthy man among men seized upon his great love as the reason for all ambition, the incentive and support of all worthy effort. Without it that ambition and purpose would die as suddenly as they had burst into life, so Waters feared; yet how could it be possible for Jim to possess the priceless thing so much desired? Another desired it with equal ardor. To another it was the thing needed, the pearl of great price for which all else must be sacrificed, and that other was Jim's teacher, and friend, and brother, who had promised to help him to gain the prize of manly effort. Now, should he rob him of the prize which he had declared was the object of this effort; or should he allow himself, in the fulfilment of his pledge, to be robbed of that which had been slowly tightening its hold upon his heart, through months, though he knew it not, but which now, when demanded by another, suddenly revealed itself as the greatest thing in the world for him?

How was she affected? Surely her welfare and happiness must, after all, be the deciding factor. Was he not better fitted to provide both? With his education and refinement, and his work, would he not be a more suitable and congenial companion for a high-minded girl like Axcy Marthy? Would it be right to her to relinquish her to an ignorant, uncouth lumberman, however good his purpose might be? "God, I thank Thee that I am not as other men are . . . or even as this publican." The involuntary thought of this ancient boast smote him like a whip. Had he not assured Jim that the discovery and development of the good in him would make him rich, and others, too —that he expected to see him, one day, a leader of the men in these parts—a leader in nobility of character, as in bravery and enterprise? What better should a woman want in the man of her choice? Her choice! Waters shivered in the cold of his room as his thoughts suddenly turned in a new channel! Was Jim the man of her choice? He remembered now the occasions when he had seen them together, not many, but full of meaning, as they stood out before his mind. There was the donation party to Robert Allen. What could have brought Jim to such a place, and so soon after the commission of his abortive crime against his schoolmaster, except the fact that Axcy wanted to go with him? And the other morning in the snow-storm, had they not both looked conscious and embarrassed as they came into the school together? Every word and look which Axcy had bestowed upon the young man assumed an exaggerated significance in Waters's mind, as he tried to guess at her feelings toward Jim and himself. The result of this analysis was not conclusive. He felt confident of his own ability to win Axcy if he tried, and he felt painfully aware of the probability that, if he held aloof, Jim Gyde, after coming into his new estate of manhood, might in his own simple, direct, and passionate manner lay successful siege to her heart. Thus he came back to the starting-point. The problem still remained to be solved by the ruin of his hopes or Jim's. Either thought was intolerable. Had he been given such strong and unexpected influence in the young man's life only to deal him a cruel blow that might crush him lower than he had been before, and make all future effort in his behalf worse than useless? A bitter feeling of resentment surged up within him, and for a moment he regretted that he had succeeded in winning Jim's confidence. If it had not been so, he would now be free of all obligation and free to compete with the young lumberman for the love of Axcy Marthy. Such feelings, however, were too foreign to Waters to flourish long. He crushed the thought back angrily. Faithlessness to Jim would be faithlessness to himself. The entrance he had gained to Jim's heart had been granted him in answer to special prayer. Should he reproach God for giving him what he had earnestly asked for? Whether faithfulness to Jim included the giving up of his own heart's desire, the blasting of his own life forever, was another question. He sought in vain for the answer.

The night grew colder, and Waters at last became conscious of the cold. He undressed and went to bed with an agonized, wordless prayer for help.

CHAPTER IX

THE night passed; the morning came, and found Joseph Waters still in the throes of his heart struggle. The help he had cried out for in the darkness had not come, and the light which greeted his eyes did not penetrate his soul. He seemed farther than ever from a solution of the bitter problem. His own insufficiency to cope with the question, which he felt must be answered without delay, angered him, while his failure to receive an answer to his oft-repeated appeals to a higher Power surprised and troubled him still more. His head ached; his mind was confused with the conflicting thoughts, yet he could not dismiss the subject for a moment. He knew there would be no peace for him until some decision was reached, and not even then unless it was a decision which would satisfy his sense of right. If it were only a matter which he could talk over with some one; but who was there with whom such a personal and sacred matter could be discussed? Suddenly he thought of Robert Allen. He knew him only slightly, but he had been deeply impressed with his quiet strength, his deep sympathy, and quick insight. If any man could help him, he was the man. Fearing to hesitate, when perhaps the thought of Allen had been sent to him in answer to his prayer for help, he yielded to the impulse, and after a hasty breakfast, started off with Rodney's horse and cutter to find the backwoods minister.

Parson Allen was not an easy man to locate during

the winter, as he was in the habit of visiting several lumber-camps, for a week or two at a time. Waters had no idea where he was at present, but he believed Farmer Hawkins could tell him, and thither he went without delay. The eight-mile drive was accomplished in little over an hour, and Farmer Hawkins and his wife were surprised to receive so early a call from such an unaccustomed visitor.

"Joseph Waters! Well, this *is* a treat!" exclaimed Josiah, coming out of the barn just as the schoolmaster drove into the yard. "To what good fortune—?" then, seeing the other's gloomy face, which still bore traces of his sleepless night and mental struggle, he said, anxiously, "No trouble, I hope?"

"Oh, I just took a notion to look up Mr. Allen and have a little talk," replied Waters, non-committally. "I thought it might save time to find out from you where he is."

"You never thought straighter to the mark in your life," said Farmer Hawkins, heartily. "Robert is due to spend Sunday here and hold a meeting for the boys down at the shingle-mill. He is up at old Bloag's camp on the Tobacco, now, and may get down here before dinner, or maybe not till afternoon. You come right in and stay to dinner. I'll tend to the horse."

Mother Hawkins bustled in from the kitchen, wiping her hands on her apron, as the two men entered the house.

"Here, Mother, you know Mr. Waters, the schoolmaster at Midland. He was up here to Robert's donation last spring. Seems as if he might have found the place again before now, though he did have to go down to Saginaw for the summer. Anyhow, here he is, and he's going to stay to dinner, and wants to see Robert more than he does us. You give him a talking to while I put up his horse."

"How he does run on!" laughed Mother Hawkins, as her husband, after his jovial introduction of the schoolmaster, left the room.

"Come right into the sitting-room and I'll light the fire," she continued. "It's all made and ready, but Josiah don't get much time to sit down till after dinner, and I'm in the kitchen all morning. You'll find some books here you may like to look at. Wish you could get to see us oftener."

"You're very kind; I'd like to; perhaps I will of a Saturday now and then,' replied Waters, his heart soothed by the hearty hospitality of these people, and especially by the motherliness in the good woman's tone and manner.

"Do!" she exclaimed, "and I'll have some of the girls here to dinner if you like. You don't see much of your old pupils now, do you? You know Lettie's doing wonders with those children of hers. They fairly idolize her. Poor little Tilly Whitmore is almost heart-broken because she can't go to school, even in the sleigh, these stormy days, on account of her cough, and Lettie, tired as she is after school, goes clear out to The Corners almost every other day to visit the little mite. She says she owes all of her success to that child's sweet sympathy and comforting on the first day when everything was going wrong."

"I've heard great accounts of Lettie's school several times this fall. She's a plucky girl," said Waters, forcing himself to take an interest in other matters than the one which absorbed him.

"Indeed, she is," assented Mother Hawkins. "She has her school crowded in the worst weather, and I don't know what she will do when spring comes. You wouldn't believe the number of children there are around Red-Keg. Guess we'll have to build a school-house soon."

"Yes, you need one, and so do we at Midland," replied Waters.

"Guess you'll get it before we do. I hear you have Axcy helping you. She's another smart girl, and lively —my! I wonder she can keep serious long enough to teach lessons all day. Really now, Mr. Waters, isn't she more of a distraction than a help? She's so pretty——"

"Axcy is a perfect success as a teacher, and a great help," interrupted Waters, hastily. "How is Norine? I haven't seen her since last spring."

"The dear girl is at home, helping her mother, though she runs over to see me almost every day when it doesn't storm." A sudden wistful tenderness crept into Mother Hawkins's voice as she spoke of the girl who had been as a daughter to her ever since she had come to the farm. The poor sorrowing mother, failing of the love which her own boy seemed unable to feel, and yearning for that giving and receiving of affection so necessary to every mother's heart, had lavished her love upon the child of her neighbor and friend Mrs. Maloney, and found joy and comfort in the warm, un-restrained affection which Norine gave her in return. Mrs. Maloney, sure of her own first place in her daugh-ter's heart, never felt the slightest twinge of jealousy, but declared that it would be impossible for her Norine to be loved too much. If God saw fit to give her daughter two mothers, she would say, and a heart big enough to love them both, sure, it was a matter to be thankful for, like all the other blessings.

"She is a very clever girl, too," went on the school-master. "She is more quiet than some, but very faithful and sweet-spirited. You must find the Maloneys delightful neighbors in every way."

"Why, they are our most intimate friends," exclaimed Mother Hawkins. "We have known them ever since they came from Ireland with Barney. That little girl, —she was but a child then—how she has grown! You may wonder at me, Mr. Waters, when I tell you that I couldn't love an own daughter better than I do her. Sometimes, when I look into her soft brown eyes, with their tender, caressing look, and kiss her rosy cheeks, plump and fresh as a ripe cherry, I feel as if she really does belong to me after all, and that somehow God made a mistake in giving her to another mother. Then I pray Him to forgive me for such a wicked thought, and thank Him that he has filled her brimming full of love and lets me have a share of it."

"I imagine Barney would like a share of it, too, wouldn't he?" remarked Waters, with a faint smile.

"To be sure he would, and he has it, if he only had the gumption to see it, the big goose!" laughed Mother Hawkins. "He worships the ground she steps on, but he mustn't know how she feels toward him until he sees for himself, or screws up the courage to ask her; so don't you tell him what I said. Barney is a good boy," she added, with a sigh. If only she could say the same of Sam.

Farmer Hawkins, after unharnessing the schoolmaster's horse and putting him snugly into a warm stall, had finished the necessary morning chores, brushed up, and now returned to the minister's guest, who, for a while, would be his. Mother Hawkins started up as she saw her husband at the door.

"Lands! here I am with my sleeves up and my hands rolled in my apron, gossiping away like a quilting-bee, and my work all standing around the kitchen. You come right in, Pa, and sit down with Mr. Waters till dinner-time," and with a smile and flurry of gingham apron the good woman disappeared through the door which led to her domestic laboratory.

"So this is your day off, is it, Mr. Waters," said Farmer Hawkins, as he adjusted the drafts of the stove and sat down opposite the schoolmaster. "I'm taking a holiday myself to-day on account of Robert's coming. Ought to be down to the mill, you know; but, really, I'm not needed much, Barney looks after everything so well. He knows the business better than I do, but I play boss some days."

Hawkins stretched out his legs to the fire and settled more comfortably in his chair, with a genial smile at his guest. The thought of Barney always gave him a contented feeling, when it was not coupled with a thought of his own wayward son. Waters assented politely, but ventured no remark, and the farmer presently exclaimed, as a new idea came to him:

"By the way, have you seen anything of Jim Gyde lately? He quit work about a week ago, without giving us any reason. Barney said something seemed to be troubling him."

"He came back to school last Monday," replied Waters.

"Well, well! that is surprising," said Hawkins, with a laugh. "He is hardly the man I should expect to throw up a good job to tackle school-books. I'm afraid he's too restless to stick to anything long, and yet it's too bad to see such good raw material going to waste."

"He means business this time, apparently," replied

Waters. "He has been digging along furiously, and, as I told him yesterday, has done more this week than he ever did before in a year."

"You don't tell me!" cried Farmer Hawkins in genuine surprise. "Something must have moved him mightily. Barney evidently was right when he said Jim had something on his mind. How do you account for it, Mr. Waters?"

"He has suddenly discovered the hidden man in him —his plus identity, you might say—which, moved by new purposes, and armed with pluck and potency of will, starts out to subdue difficulties, and create a place for itself. Who shall attempt to explain it? God uses the chance word, sometimes, to startle such a slumbering giant into life."

"Just so," said Hawkins, with a sigh; "the chance word; while the fervent, agonizing prayers of father and mother sometimes go on for many years unanswered. Why is it? Why is it?"

The question was not addressed to Mr. Waters. It was murmured in a low, musing tone, as an oft-repeated soliloquy which the anxious father had found very bitter to the taste, and which sorely tried his sturdy faith in the availing power of prayer. For some time neither man spoke. Waters took up a book and tried to read, but his mind would not admit other subjects than the one which had brought him in search of Parson Allen. The delay in seeing him, and the conversation with Farmer Hawkins and his wife had made him begin to question the wisdom of confiding his difficulty with even such a man as Allen. Could any man, whoever he might be, dictate acceptably the course he should pursue in so personal an affair of the heart and the conscience? Did not his very manliness and self-respect demand that he should fight his fight out alone? If the issue should be against him, no one else would share the responsibility. What man living was there who could enter into his inmost soul and understand his feelings and his motives well enough to help him to the right decision? During the long forenoon, he debated this new phase of the question. Farmer Hawkins and Mother Hawkins came and went, and endeavored to entertain him, but he could not rouse himself long from his abstraction to display genuine interest in their kindly attentions. Finally Mother Hawkins, with her woman's intuition, took her husband aside and said:

"Better let him alone, Josiah. He came to see Robert, and there's something on his mind that he can't get rid of till then. Just let him be."

Allen came soon after noon, and dinner, which had been delayed somewhat in hope of his arrival, was speedily announced. Waters had concluded to keep his own counsel and work out his own salvation as best he might. He responded, therefore, to the minister's friendly greeting without restraint, and joined with the others more freely in the chat of the dinner-table. After the meal was finished, Farmer Hawkins remembered an errand to John Maloney's which required immediate attention. His good wife retired to help her woman in the kitchen, leaving the minister and the schoolmaster to enjoy each other's company alone.

"You've only been in this part of the country a year or less, haven't you, Mr. Waters?" asked the minister. "Did you ever see a logging-camp in full swing? If not, you must come up to Mr. Hawkins's place sometime and watch the men. It's an inspiration. They work as if their lives depended upon getting the great-

est possible number of logs to the mill before sundown. They are a stalwart, happy, true-hearted set
of men."

"I should enjoy seeing the camp, immensely," said
Waters, "but I am usually busy at the same time
your loggers are, and it has never occurred to me to
run away from my work to inspect theirs."

"What's the matter with taking a jaunt up to the
camp now?" exclaimed Allen, with animation. "You
have the afternoon, and so have I. Hawkins has deserted us, and the boys will be glad to see us both. I
expect to preach up there to-morrow. Let's go and
look over the ground now."

The minister's enthusiastic suggestion met a ready
approval. Having abandoned his original purpose,
Waters was at a loss to account for his unexpected
visit, and was glad to occupy the afternoon with some
definite enterprise. Accordingly, making their excuses
to Mother Hawkins, and promising to return for supper or stay to eat the meal in the cook's den at camp,
as inclination prompted, the two men departed on foot
through the snow for the shingle-mill in the woods.
Although fully aware of the fact that Waters had
driven eight miles from Midland in the early morning,
especially to find him, and recognizing the probability
that this unusual performance betokened some particular errand, Allen betrayed no curiosity, but left the
schoolmaster free to choose his own time and manner
for introducing the topic of his concern. He did not
dream that that topic was the very one Waters had resolved not to introduce.

"The crew at Mr. Hawkins's camp is made up almost
wholly of his friends and neighbors, I understand," said
the schoolmaster. "It must be very pleasant for all

hands, if too much sociability does not interfere with the work."

"On the contrary, it spurs them to greater endeavor," replied Allen. "Every one of them would give his right hand for Uncle Si, as they call him. He has endeared himself in unnumbered ways to them all. Then there's Barney. He stirs them up like a streak of lightning. He loves Uncle Si as a father."

"It's a wonder Mr. Hawkins's own son doesn't take a hand in the work," said Waters. "One would think he would welcome such an opportunity, on his own father's property, to get a practical training. They say he doesn't care much for work of any kind."

The minister's face clouded.

"It is a wonder," he admitted, gravely. "If ever a boy preferred husks to the meat of his father's table, Sam is such a boy. I had earnest hopes for him at one time last spring, but the coming of two careless fellows with whom he had been intimate in college, destroyed, at least for the time, the impulse in the right direction which seemed to have sprung into life."

"It seems to me I've heard about those boys," replied Waters. "Seward Rathaway is with them, too, isn't he? They call themselves 'The Invincibles,' I believe."

"Yes, though what they are invincible in I can not guess, unless it be in their determination to shun all honest work. They were inseparable all summer and fall, and stayed away most of the time in the woods. Some say they were not as idle as they appeared. As nearly as I could find out, they have fitted up an old hunting-lodge and intend to hunt and trap on a large scale next year. Well, I suppose that is better than doing nothing. The most discouraging feature is the intimacy they seem to have formed with the Red-Keg saloon-keeper, Pete."

"Is there no way of breaking up this little clique of so-called 'Invincibles,' if it stands in the way of interesting Sam in something better?" asked Waters, somewhat vaguely. He felt hardly equal to wrestling with another problem just now, but he recognized the great interest Allen took in Sam's welfare. "Seward is a very clever chap, also," he continued, "and he would soon settle into something worth while if wrong influences could be withdrawn."

"I believe so, with all my heart," agreed Allen; "but I have sought in vain thus far for some means to counteract the wrong influences. It is hard to say what should be done."

"These two boys—what are their names—come from some distant States, do they not?" asked Waters. "Could you not write, or Mr. Hawkins, to their parents and kindly advise them to keep the boys at home?"

"Perhaps," said the minister, doubtfully. "It might not accomplish the desired end, however, and if it came to the ears of the boys themselves, might do more harm than good. A way, the right way, will be provided, if God wills, sooner or later. It is a comfort to know that we do not need to solve all the perplexities of life, even the ones that concern us most closely, but that they can be safely left to a higher power to solve for us—yes, and the right answer reached, where we too often would reach the wrong one. There is One who knows the end from the beginning, and He can take our snarled affairs and make them straight. You know the saying that 'man's extremity is God's opportunity.' After doing our best we can remember that

'it is good that a man should both hope and quietly
wait for the salvation of the Lord.'"

Waters listened to the minister with a strange thrill.
Surely here was the answer he had been groping for
during the past twenty-four unhappy hours. How
simple and inevitable it all seemed. There could be
no other answer. Without a doubt he had been sent
to Robert Allen to receive it. What mattered that he
had not told him of his trouble? Allen had been giv-
en his message to deliver. Must he not deliver it just
the same, even if the one for whom it was intended kept
silent? Waters turned to the minister with shining
eyes.

"You are right—God bless you," was all he said, but
peace had entered his soul.

The trip to camp was an enjoyable event. Barney
and the other men welcomed them hilariously. They
stayed to "grub" in the cook's den, and shared the
"wash" and the "chuck" with the lumbermen on
equal terms. Waters inspected the shanties, the mill,
the stables, the tools, the newly cut logs, the roads
through the snow—everything connected with the
work of logging and shingle-cutting—with all the enthusiastic interest of one who has never seen these
things before. Allen noted his companion's changed
demeanor and shrewdly guessed that his errand had
been achieved in some mysterious manner. Late that
evening they returned to the farm and meekly bore the
mock reproof of Farmer Hawkins for running away
from him when he had taken a holiday especially to
entertain his guest. To make up for it he insisted that
Waters should stay over night and hear Allen preach
to the men in the forenoon. He could drive home at
his leisure after dinner. The schoolmaster consented,

although he thought to himself that nothing the minister could say on the morrow would help him more than the brief message he had delivered, all unknowingly, to him that day. His course was clear now. He would not attempt to decide between his duty to Jim and his duty to himself. He would certainly perform to the full his duty to Jim, as he saw it, but that duty did not include any unnecessary or conspicuous self-effacement. On the other hand, he would take no advantage himself that would imperil any happiness that might be rightly Jim's. Axcy should be free to choose between them, uninfluenced for or against, so far as he was concerned, and let Providence decide the issue. In no other way could Waters feel conscience-free.

Through the months that followed, he had many anxious days and nights, but on the whole he adhered faithfully to his resolve. Jim made rapid progress in his studies, and in the general development of a manlier character. He paid no aggressive suit to Axcy. He was biding his time, unaware that anything in her or another was working against him. Whether or not the quick-witted girl divined anything of the situation with regard to her two silent rivals, she maintained an undisturbed balance, and bestowed her gracious favor impartially upon both. Without apparent planning she managed to go to social gatherings, such as the Christmas-tree party at the Hawkins farm, the quilting-bees, the husking parties, the dances, etc., in company with Lettie Green or Norine Maloney, and her friends never guessed that two of the best-known men of the region would have given all they had to assert the right to be her escort for all time.

CHAPTER X

"HELLO, there, Sam! I've been hunting for you,"
cried Seward Rathaway, as he spied Sam Hawkins
coming out of Jake Vogel's store and Post-Office one
morning, late in November, of the following year.

Sam started, and thrust a letter hastily into his
pocket.

"I'm not so hard to find as to need much hunting,
am I?" he said, crossly.

"Well, now, you needn't get mad," replied Seward.
"I have important news, and we must get together at
once and decide what to do. Uncle Sam has taken it
into his head to send a little bevy of sleuths on a trip
through this neighborhood to try to locate a certain
'Mystic Brand' whose fame seems to have spread beyond our humble domain. I just got the tip from Pete.
He thinks there are three of them in all. One chap
—sort of an early bird trying to catch the worm—is
here now, down at Pete's."

Sam paled for an instant as he heard Seward's statement; then, with an air of bravado, he exclaimed, with
a short laugh:

"So! on to us, are they? Well, we're ready for
them, aren't we? Where are Walt and Billy?"

"They're out at Mystic Isle. We better go out and
talk it over. Don't let that chap in Pete's see us,
though he's more than likely asleep by now, after his
nice little tramp last night."

"What tramp? What do you know about him, anyhow?" asked Sam, impatiently.

"Oh, he walked down from Beaverton, a little matter of thirty miles or so," laughed Seward. "Pete told me the whole story. It's a good one, but rather long. Wait till the other boys can hear. I don't want to tell it twice."

About noon Sam and Seward arrived, tired and hungry, at their secret resort on Mystic Isle. During the two seasons that Walter Hayward and Billy Axford had been with them, the large caves on the island had been comfortably fitted up for living purposes, and other improvements had been made, Walt and Billy supplying the needed cash. The old blind negro and his wife, who served them at college, had been installed as caretakers and cook, and were faithfully devoted to the interests and comfort of their young masters. The whole establishment was sufficiently novel and in contrast to the ordinary affairs and environments of the Red-Keg section to please even Sam's contemptuous fancy. Walt and Billy were eating a substantial dinner prepared by old Sue, when Sam and Seward broke in upon them. After acquainting the former with the facts, the two late-comers joined in the repast. The story as told by Seward was in substance about as follows:

Jack Mann had been repeatedly to the North Shore for consignments of the "Mystic Brand." He did not know nor care who placed it there nor whence it came. All he knew was that through the agency of Pete someone paid him well to take loads of corn to a certain out-of-the-way spot, leave them there, proceed to another cache near by, pick up the supply of "Mystic Brand," carry it further up, and transfer it to whomsoever might be waiting with the proper countersign. Pete had given him to understand that the continuance of this job, and the certainty of pay, depended upon keeping a close mouth. He drew his own conclusions and kept mum; but the ease of his work and the immunity enjoyed thus far had made him a little careless. Yesterday he had taken a supply of the goods as far as Beaverton, and was transferring it to a tote-team in charge of a French-Canadian whom he had met before on similar occasions, when he was approached by an affable fellow who took him into the tavern and plied him with drink. As usual, Jack became loquacious, and it was not long before his newly made friend had secured admissions enough to hang him, if hanging were the penalty for moonshining. Pete happened to be up there, and he spotted the fellow at once, so while the sleuth was filling Jack up, Pete went out and started the tote-team off in a hurry. By the time Vidocq got through with Jack, there was only the confession of a drunken man left, and the real evidence was well on its way toward the throats of a thirsty lot of French-Canadians at Camp Number Ten, away up on the Salt. The fellow looked chagrined when he discovered that he had been tricked, but he did not dare to make any protest. There stood Pete, with the "city" constable by his side, each smoking villanous pipes, and discussing the prospects for a good cutting of logs for the winter.

"Excuse me," said the sleuth, "but did you see which way that tote-team went that was out here just now?"

"The one with the grey and the black hitched to 'er?" asked Pete, innocently.

"Yes, that's the one. Which way did it go?"

"Went over toward Sixteen, didn't it, Mack?" Pete replied, turning to his friend the constable.

"Yas," drawled Mack. "The feller's nigh over to the Ox Bow by this time. He's a mighty fast traveller that. What did ye want of 'im? Goin' along deown his way? Ef ye want ter ketch 'im it's time ye were hurryin' up," and so saying Mack turned to Pete again, and the two went on talking just as though nothing had happened.

"Pardon me again, but can I get a teamster to drive me over to the Ox Bow, so as to catch that man before he gets any farther?" said the stranger, again addressing the constable.

"Ye mout and ye mout not," said Mack, drily. "Leastwise not onless ye tell me what ye want to ketcn thet feller for. Ef ye want 'im to take ye on a ride up to the head of the jam er thereabouts, you'll find 'im a mighty accomerdatin' feller. But ef ye're after 'im fer any—any—purpose other'n peaceful ones ye mout as well tackle a catamount, and a hungry one at that, as to tackle Pierre Badeau; eh, old boy?" turning to Pete.

"Betcher life," said Pete, giving a vigorous puff at his pipe.

"But, say, my friend," continued Mack, "ef ye need any assistance I'm the constable hereabouts, an' mout be of sarvice to ye."

They palavered for some time in this manner, and finally the stranger said he thought, as it was getting late, he would stay at the tavern all night, and he went inside again, expecting to find Jack dead drunk, lying on the bench where he had left him. He was dumfounded to find that his supposed prisoner had flown even as had the teamster. He was nonplussed, but dared not make his identity known as yet. He had intended merely to shadow Jack, and at the right time catch him when he could scoop in the gang and claim the reward of a thousand dollars offered for the arrest and conviction of the offenders. Except for the watchfulness of Pete and some of Jack's chums, who spirited him away, suspecting that a trap was being set for him by the oily stranger, his plan might have succeeded. As it was, he could hardly conceal his surprise and chagrin.

Suspicion having been directed to him, some of the fellows loitering around the bar got their heads together and held a conversation in low tones for a few moments, after which one of their number, Jim Lampheer, or "Red," rawboned and lank, stepped out from among the group, and, approaching the stranger rather unceremoniously, remarked:

"Ye seem to be a stranger 'round these parts. Mout I ask yer business?"

"That's a great deal like impertinence, isn't it?" observed the detective.

"Impertence or no impertence, we want ter know yer business, an' we're goin' ter know it, too. P'r'aps yer mout fust tell us jes' why ye got thet feller drunk in yere a little while ago?" and Red Lampheer came up closer. Looking down in contempt upon the now frightened minion of the law he continued in tones that left but one interpretation:

"We know who ye are. Ye're one o' them sneakin', meddlesome tenderfeet as comes up yere 'bout once a winter spyin' inter other folk's business. We're goin' ter give ye jest ten minutes ter git outen this camp, an' ef we ever see ye agin in these parts we'll run ye through a rollway. D'ye understand?"

"But, my friend, I am a stranger here, and there's no stage running out of here for several days——"

"Walkin's good enough fer the likes o' you, eh,

pards?" and a loud roar of approval emphasized the necessity for prompt action.

"Five minutes," roared Red, and the detective set about preparing for his hasty departure. When the time had elapsed, the unwelcome visitor was counting curves on the Tittabawassee pike down toward Red-Keg, where he arrived the next morning after having walked the entire thirty miles during the night.

Pete followed on horseback about a mile behind the fellow until he reached the Salt Licks trail, and then he deviated off on that and arrived at the Keg ahead of the chap. Seward was at the tavern when Pete arrived, and was at once made acquainted with the circumstances. Then Pete shaved up, changed his clothes, and went to bed for a little sleep. When he thought it was time for the fellow to arrive he took a chair with Seward out on the veranda and waited. He knew if the stranger came to Red-Keg, his was the only place at which he could put up, as the lumbermen's boarding-houses were full, so he and Walt waited with easy assurance. They were soon rewarded by seeing the man coming down the road. He was tired and muddy; but as he approached, his countenance lighted up, and, reaching out his hand to Pete, said, very cordially, but with surprise in his voice:

"How in the world did you get here? You surely never passed me on the road, for I walked like one possessed. How did you get here ahead of me?"

"Guess ye must be mistaken, pard," replied Pete, as he took the man's outstretched hand. "I've never seen ye afore; but I don't mind shakin' the hand of a stranger. Come in an' have a nip; ye look tired. My friend, Mr. Rathaway," turning to Seward. "Come in, gentlemen, and let's have suthin'," and Pete led the way into the saloon.

"Surely I saw you, or your ghost, or your double, up the road," remarked the stranger, wiping his mouth.

"Where wus ye?" queried Pete.

"At Beaverton, thirty miles up the road."

"Ha, ha, ha! Ye're not the fust one to be fooled thet way. Ye see, we're brothers—twins—an' our mother couldn't tell us apart. Well, thet's another on me," whereupon Pete took down his best bottle for the stranger.

"Ye don't mean to say ye've hoofed it down frum Beaverton in the night, do ye?" went on Pete, taking an apparent interest in the fellow.

"That's what I did," he replied.

"What d'ye do thet fer?" persisted Pete.

"Well, you see I came across there from Sixteen by way of a friendly tote-team. I'm simply travelling through this pine wilderness with a view to hunting up some possible paying properties to buy, and also to have a little outing. I didn't seem to make a very good impression up there, and so——"

"I see, I see," broke in Pete, with another of his guffaws, "an' ye were invited to leave! Ye're not the fust one treated thet way up to Beaverton. They're kind o' exclusive like, an' don't take kindly to strangers. But ye'll find it different here 't the Kag. We're all cosmopolitern like, an' here's one o' the jolliest fellers you'll ever meet. Shake again with Mr. Rathaway. Ef ye stay long hereabouts, he an' his pals 'll show ye 'round in style, eh, Seward?"

Seward was quick to take advantage of the opening so cleverly provided by Pete, and replied, heartily:

"Certainly, I shall be glad to show this gentleman

around if he is looking for a good time. We have a
nice stretch of hunting woods, and if you are anything
of a huntsman we will give you lots of fun."

The stranger declared he would be delighted—that
he would probably remain in the neighborhood several
weeks, and that he considered himself fortunate indeed
to have fallen into such agreeable company.

"But for the present moment," he exclaimed, "I am
most interested in the wants of the inner man, and I
must ask if I can get something to eat. I am about
famished."

"Certainly," said Pete, "breakfast is still on; come
into the dinin' room an' fill up. In the mean time ef
ye'll give me yer name. We don't keep no register.
I jest keep the names in my head."

"My name is Barker—James Barker, from New
York."

"Long ways frum hum, eh?"

"Yes, rather far. This is my first visit to the lum-
berwoods," he volunteered, following Pete into the
tavern.

Seward waited around until Barker came out from
breakfast and then told him he would see him the next
afternoon and introduce him to his friends. Then as
soon as the man retired to his room to rest after his
fatiguing tramp, Seward hastened to acquaint the other
boys with the situation.

"Well, we're up against it," said Sam, after Seward
had told his story. "Now the question is, how shall
we throw the chumps off the scent?"

"We must get out to the old lumber-shanty over
on the Salt, and have that for headquarters while
this gentleman is around," said Seward. "We will
fit it up as a hunting-lodge the same as we did last

year, and when we are out on a tramp we'll take him there."

It was agreed that Seward and Walt should go to the Keg on the following day for the purpose of entertaining the visitor. Sam and Billy were to repair to the lumber-shanty and prepare it for habitation. Seward and Walt were to come out that way in a day or two and bring Mr. Barker, who was to be tendered the freedom of the place. Accordingly. about noon the next day, Seward and Walt started on their return trip to the Keg, reaching there by three o'clock. Barker was sitting on the veranda in front of Pete's place, talking with the proprietor. As the boys came up, he arose to meet them, and Seward introduced Walt.

"Sorry I couldn't find Sam Hawkins and Billy Axford," he explained, "but I learned this morning that they had gone off on a hunt and might not be back for two or three days. They are nice fellows, just the kind to go out running deer with. Sam is a little inclined to be egotistical, but we all have our failings. You will like him when you know him. We four were chums at college, and we have formed an alliance since we graduated that has afforded us much pleasure, and as you are out here for pleasure we may as well help to make your stay as pleasant as possible."

"That is very kind of you, I am sure," replied Barker. "I shall be delighted to meet your friend. What kind of game do you find in this region?"

"Nearly everything from squirrel to bear, and from jack-rabbit to deer. There are plenty of raccoons, wolves, wildcats, wolverines, and porcupines in the woods, as well as beaver and otter. If you care to go out with us we can be sure of good sport, and very likely may run across Sam and Billy at our hunting-lodge up on the Big Salt."

Barker expressed his readiness to join them at the earliest possible opportunity, and it was agreed that they should start for the hunting ground on the following day.

Before evening a heavy rain set in, and for a time threatened to cause a postponement of the trip. The Invincibles welcomed the downpour because it would obliterate all tracks leading in an inconvenient direction. Toward morning, however, the rain ceased, and the air became cold and crisp. Seward and Walt sought Pete's place early in the forenoon, where Barker joined them in a few minutes, announcing himself as ready for anything.

"Ye oughter hev different togs than them," ejaculated Pete, as he eyed the amateur Nimrod with looks of disapproval.

"These are all I have. I couldn't take my baggage across to Beaverton from Sixteen, and so it is there yet. I have ordered it sent here, however, for I think I shall be pretty well contented in this hospitable hamlet for a few weeks."

"Them store clothes o' yourn wouldn't last till ye got out to Sturgeon slough, even goin' by the State road, say nothin' o' goin' through the timber, as ye orter," again insisted Pete.

"Pete is right, Mr. Barker. You'd better try to get a suit more like ours," added Seward. "Perhaps Pete has something he could lend you for the present."

"Yas, I can let him have the rig as belonged to thet feller as was all chawed up in the rollway last year. He was about your size, an' I 'low, you won't mind usin' 'em, will ye? He had all his duds at my place, an' no one hes ever claimed 'em, so you mout as well put 'em on, eh?"

Barker consented, and in a short time reappeared with more suitable hunting apparel, whereupon the trio immediately set out for the woods. They followed along the bank of the Tittabawassee for several miles, ate their lunch about noon, and then struck into the woods to the northward in the direction of the lodge provided for the occasion. Through brambles, briers, fallen logs, swamps, and upturned roots, the party wended its way for four or five hours, until from sheer exhaustion Barker dropped upon a log and declared that he must rest.

"You mustn't give out yet," said Seward. "We have still three miles to go before we reach the lodge. There you can have a good night's rest. So keep up courage."

"I suppose I must. Don't you get tired, or lose your way?"

"Oh, no. When we first came we did, sometimes; but now you can neither lose nor tire us. If we should leave you here you would never get out in the world. Can you tell in which direction you are now going?"

"Not for the life of me. As nearly as I can guess, we have been proceeding southward, have we not?"

"Just the opposite," said Seward. "See the moss growing upon the bark of these black-ash trees? Do you notice that it extends only about half-way around the trunk?"

"Yes."

"Well, there you have the woodsman's compass. The side showing the moss is to the north."

"Well, I declare, I never knew that before. It is

wonderful how nature provides even a compass for the use of man in the wilderness," exclaimed Barker.

It was getting so close to sundown now that the boys urged their guest to another effort, and off they started toward the camp. These three toilsome miles nearly finished the tenderfoot, who had not yet recovered from the effects of his thirty-mile tramp from Beaverton; but the boys, while pretending to sympathize with his evident suffering, were inwardly chuckling at the ruse they were playing, and the fun they were having at his expense. At length, as they arrived at the clearing, in the centre of which stood the lodge, the poor fellow gave a cry of satisfaction, remarking that if it had been an Indian camp, or a bear's den, he would have welcomed it, for he was ready to drop from exhaustion.

Sam and Billy were waiting for them, and Barker was introduced with due ceremony, after which he begged to be allowed to rest, and was at once put to bed in a "bunk" on the wall. Daylight came, eight, nine, ten o'clock, and still he slumbered. The boys had been up since sunrise skirmishing for breakfast. When Barker finally began to bestir himself, he found that he was lame in every joint. His feet were swollen, and he felt generally the worse for wear, he said, but was greatly interested in his surroundings. The interior of the old log shack had been fitted up gorgeously with skins of all kinds. The logs had been well "chinked" and filled with moss. Deer antlers were numerous, and several bear heads scowled down from the walls.

Barker's nostrils caught the smell of a savory steak being broiled in the old fireplace at the far end of the shanty, and this served to recall his slumbering appetite. He was the guest of a lot of jolly boys, and he was as much interested in Sam and Billy as he had been in Seward and Walt. He partook ravenously of the steak and called for a second portion, which he devoured with undiminished relish. When informed that it had been taken from the choice quarter of a bear he was somewhat incredulous. To prove their assertion they took him outside the cabin and there exhibited the carcass of bruin, who had been sacrificed the day before. Barker agreed that the steak was most delicate, and expressed his willingness to be fed upon it indefinitely.

"How long have you been in this paradise of Nimrods?" he asked, after he had taken a mental picture of all the surroundings.

"Oh, we have occupied this place as a rendezvous for the past two years, ever since Walt and Billy joined us," replied Sam, "and we find it a jolly place to stop, when out hunting. We are all by ourselves and monarch of all we survey, don't you know."

"But how am I to get out of here?"

"The same way you came in."

"Is there no nearer way?"

"Not so direct; but there is a logging road which runs out to the Big Salt from here, and by walking about twice as far you could reach Red-Keg by way of the Sturgeon road. But it is a stupid way—no game, and nothing but sand and mud to walk through—much worse even than climbing over logs. You will soon get accustomed to roughing it, and you won't mind such a little tramp as you took yesterday. We must take another little jaunt this afternoon in order to limber up your stiff joints, or you are liable to get foundered, like an old horse."

"But I want to return to Red-Keg yet to-night. I am expecting a couple of friends up to-morrow, and I must meet them. So if you will start me on my way, I think I will reach there all right by way of the logging road."

"We will at least see you safely to the Sturgeon road, and if we start in time we may meet the stage which makes the weekly trip to Sixteen and return. It is due at Red-Keg to-night at seven."

"All right, boys, I will attempt it, though I am almost as sore as though one of your rollways had run over me. I am very grateful for your kindness; but as my friends are coming I will not attempt to impose them upon your hospitality."

"You are welcome to our cabin. The latch-string is always out, and whether we are here or not, just come at any time and bring your friends and make yourselves at home," said Seward, warmly.

Later in the day the whole party started through the woods to the road where Barker hoped to meet the stage. Their arrival was well timed, for they soon heard the rumble of the old stage-coach coming toward them at a rapid rate. The jehu was a Frenchman noted for his intrepidity and his ability to swear. He was urging on his horses, as the sky was again overcast, and already a fleecy snow had begun to fall which portended a blizzard before many hours.

Just as the clumsy vehicle was rounding a curve a short distance above, where the five men stood, Mr. Barker stepped hastily out into the road, and called to the driver to stop.

The hunter's garb is fantastic, something like that worn by Daniel Boone in his day, and in the gloaming it looks much like that worn by the Indians. With an oath that rent the stillness of the air, the driver of the stage brought his horses back on their haunches, throwing the half-dozen occupants together in a heap inside. In an instant a carbine was levelled full at Barker's head, and the Frenchman ordered " Hands up!"

At this critical juncture the Invincibles gave their old college yell, adapted by them for use in this wilderness, and instantly the carbine was lowered; but those inside of the stage were frightened nearly out of their senses. Order was quickly restored when it became known that a hold-up was not intended, but that simply a new passenger was about to join them.

"Well, I'll be blowed! Where in the world did you come from, Barker?" spoke somebody from the interior of the stage.

"Same to you; I certainly never expected to see you here," answered Barker. "Come out and meet my friends. What! Dabney here, too? Well, well!" he continued, taking the hands of his friends and shaking them at the same time.

"I was just on my way to Red-Keg, where I expected to meet you to-morrow, supposing you would come up on the railroad," he continued. "Why did you come across this forsaken way?"

"Oh, we just learned you had roughed it over and we thought we would do the same. So we followed your trail. You didn't leave a very savory reputation at Beaverton, and we came near being lynched when we reached there. We were——"

"Sh! not so loud. Be careful. We are pleasure-seekers, and land hunters," interrupted Barker in a low voice, but not so low as to escape the quick ear of Seward. Then in a louder tone: "Yes, they certainly lack hospitality to strangers out there. I was unceremoniously ordered to depart, because they did not know my pedigree, and I walked all the thirty miles to Red-Keg in the night."

After introductions and a short parley it was decided that Barker and his friends should leave the stage and all go out to the cabin together. So dismissing the stage driver, the Invincibles and guests set out into the woods, while the jehu shouted to his steeds, and was soon lost to sight in the fast-falling snow and approaching darkness.

As the boys had feared, the quiet was of short duration, for before the party reached the cabin, the wind had risen, and they were in the midst of a whirling blizzard, which threatened to freeze or bury them before their retreat could be reached. The lodge was a welcome refuge to the four boys as well as to the fatigued and nearly frozen sleuths. The latter still believed that their mission was unsuspected by the Invincibles, and the boys were careful not to dispel this delusion. The Invincibles had this advantage—they were on their guard and sure of their enemy, while the detectives were hunting in the dark, hoping to land big game. There was only one secret-service man in the trio, Mr. Lawrence; the other two were amateurs looking for fame—and shekels.

"Whew! what a terrible night," said Mr. Lawrence, as they opened the door, and a gust of wind carried a cloud of snow in with them.

"Mighty comfortable place, this, for such a night," remarked Barker, remembering his snug bunk and sound sleep of the previous night.

The logs which had been left in the fireplace still glowed, giving a cheery aspect to the place, and when a few pine-knots had been fished from the "loft," there

was enough light and warmth to fill the place from end
to end.

After a hearty repast they sat around the fire to
spend a cosy evening.

"Don't know that this weather is at all suggestive
of mosquitoes, but, as I came through some of these
swamps, it occurred to me that in the summer you
must have a vast number of those pesky fellows to
contend with," remarked Lawrence, half interroga-
tively.

The Invincibles looked around at each other, and
then Seward, seeing no one else ready to respond, remarked nonchalantly:

"Oh, yes; but we don't mind them now. After a
year or two one learns how to avoid them. When I
first came out here, though, I was reduced twenty
pounds in two weeks from loss of blood. The critters
would bore through my buckskin shirt, my boots—in
fact there was no getting away from them. They
would follow me all day, and the same hungry crowd
would be after me at night. They——"

"Indeed!" broke in the three strangers in con-
cert.

"True as gospel," asserted Billy. "I have seen
them so thick on Seward's back that when I struck
them the blood trickled down and spattered into my
face!"

"Oh, yes, I know that mosquitoes, even though
they're not aristocrats, and have no pedigrees, are often
full of good blood," assented Lawrence.

"Don't you know, my dear friends," interrupted
Sam, seriously, "that some varieties of these insects
grow to a prodigious size up in some part of the State
among the swamps and rivers? Why, I've heard from

good authorities that the biggest ones are used by the raftsmen bringing up the 'rear' for snubbing-posts. They make them put their bills into the ground—. What in the deuce are you laughing at?" he exclaimed, glancing with an injured air at the three strangers.

"What Sam was saying may seem slightly exaggerated, but it is not overdrawn," interrupted Seward. "You know truth is stranger than fiction. These beasts are always the most obstreperous about rafting time. Only last year a rafting party of five men with two yoke of heavy oxen went up here to the Ox Bow, and began work. By noon of the first day the oxen were reduced to skeletons, although their drivers fought the pests all the time. The men had their peavies along. Don't know what a peavy is? Well, it is a strong pole about eight feet in length turned round, bulging below the centre, and smaller at each end. In the lower end is driven a strong sharpened spike about six inches in length and nearly an inch square, and to hold this securely and strengthen the handle, several bands of iron are driven on, the last and smallest one acting as a ferrule."

The seriousness of Seward during this description riveted the attention of the hearers, who listened with respectful silence.

"Each workman finds one of these peavies a necessity, and always carries one when at work, either on the drive, rollway, or rear. Well, on this occasion, when the noon hour came, the raftsmen had arrived at an old shanty something like this, into which they went to prepare their noonday meal, leaving their peavies and oxen outside. You may not believe me, but just one hour later, when the men went out, neither oxen nor peavies were anywhere to be found!"

"What had become of them?" timidly inquired Barker.

"Well, they had disappeared as though by magic; but a careful search disclosed some heaps of fresh bones lying near by. A great humming noise was heard, a cloud obscured the sun, and looking up, the men saw that the cloud was formed of mosquitoes, and the larger ones, which were the queens, were perched upon the tall pines picking their teeth with the peavies," and the speaker ducked just in time to save his head from contact with the snowball which Lawrence had all the time been rolling out of the drift of snow, let in when they arrived at the shack.

The wind shrieked, the logs in the fireplace crackled and spluttered, the pine-knots glowed fitfully, and all tongues were silent for the space of three minutes and seventeen seconds by the watch.

CHAPTER XI

THE next morning found the skies again clear and the air keen and bracing. Everywhere, without, the earth was buried under a billowy and rippled sea of dazzling white, against which the dark boles and branches of the trees stood in naked contrast after their battle with the wind.

"Just the day to run down deer," declared Seward, as they sat at breakfast. "I move we all go out on a hunt. Our larder needs replenishing. No game, no dinner."

Dabney agreed without hesitation, but Barker rubbed his limbs reminiscently, and remarked that he was willing to defer another day's hunting until some later date. Seward turned to Lawrence, who had remained silent, and said:

"You will join us, of course, Mr. Lawrence? We are sure to stir up some big game to-day, and will show you what real sport in these woods is like."

Lawrence chewed his steak meditatively for a moment, and then replied, slowly:

"Thank you; to tell the truth, however, I am not much of a sportsman,—though I have hunted, on occasions. Perhaps if I tell you a little experience on my last deer-stalking expedition, you will understand my weakness. It was up a little farther north than this. I was on a trip with a party of enthusiastic huntsmen at their urgent invitation, although I made no pretense of being able to shoot anything. They had a fine outfit, including a pack of hounds. We chose a promising section of country along a beautiful stream, and I was assigned to a ' runway ' upon the heavily timbered flats of the west side. There I sat, pursuant to careful instructions, very quietly for a period as long, perhaps, as fifteen or twenty minutes, my piece cocked, my eyes open, awaiting almost breathlessly the advent of game. It didn't come, and the pastime grew monotonous to me. I arose and looked about to see whether I might, perhaps, catch a glimpse of dog, hunter, or deer. I saw nothing. Then I listened for the baying of the hounds; but not a bay could I hear. I leaned my rifle against a thorn-bush which grew near the bank of the stream, and began to divert myself by picking up pebbles from the beach and making them 'skip' across the rippled water. Tiring of this amusement after a while, I strolled carelessly down the beach, picking up small pebbles, when of a sudden I became conscious of a slight but peculiar sound in the woods just over the bank, which at this point was a little higher than my head. I crawled cautiously up the turfy terrace, mounted the huge trunk of a prostrate, wind-thrown elm, and peered into the dense covert of the forest. Very soon I discovered what had caused the sound, and it was with difficulty that I repressed an exclamation of delight. Right across a little bayou in front of me and distant not more than thirty yards, daintily cropping the herbage that grew on a verdant knoll, was a fine yearling doe. The exquisitely beautiful creature had not observed me, and for several minutes I sat motionless enjoying the picture. How graceful those limbs! That slender, willowy neck! How large and lustrous those glorious eyes!

"Why didn't I shoot? Shoot her! Why, by all the

vandals and bloodthirsty savages of the forest! Shoot that delicate, fairy-like thing! Not if I had a whole arsenal at my command!"

Seward and Walt shifted uneasily, Billy coughed slightly, and Sam smiled sarcastically and opened his mouth to make some comment, but Lawrence continued:

"I assure you I had no more thought of attempting to kill that beautiful, harmless animal than I had of killing myself. I was merely sitting there ('like a bump on a log,' as my discoverer afterward more forcibly than poetically put it), mute with delight and admiration, when a crackling in the brush to the right sent my timid beauty flying deep into the forest, and brought me to my wits and to my feet.

"'Was that a deer?' demanded the harsh voice of one of the hunters who had come out with me.

"'Ye-es,' I stammered.

"'Why didn't you shoot?' He asked this question with rather more than impatience in his tone.

"'Why—why,' I answered, in confusion, 'I didn't have my gun here.'

"'Where is it?' he demanded, in disgust.

"The truth is that I had forgotten all about the gun, and it was still standing leaning against the thorn-bush some twenty perches up the stream. And, will you believe it? that man was actually angry with me. He abused me ferociously—and he had always been one of my very best friends, too.

"'You'll never make a hunter!' was the emphatic declaration with which he concluded his tirade. That was an unkind cut. A hunter! Hadn't I found? and, as it transpired, wasn't I the only one of the entire crew who did find a deer that day? And therefore I still insist that I was not only a hunter, but a remarkably successful one. As to being a *butcher*, that was quite another matter. I've always had a lingering suspicion since then that in the ordinary acceptance of the terms 'hunter' and 'sportsman' they are necessarily synonymous with 'butcher.' Of course I don't mean any aspersions on you, my good friends; but you can see that I would make rather unprofitable company for you on the proposed deer-running trip to-day."

Sam laughed. "It is fortunate we are not all so tender-hearted," he said. "I know some hungry men who would have no dinner to-day. Besides, how about the ravages of wolves and other troublesome beasts?"

"Oh, don't understand me as being opposed to the shooting of dangerous animals who are the natural enemies of man, or those which are necessary for food. I can hunt without mercy—on suitable occasions," said Lawrence, smiling. Then he added, quickly, "I have known of many instances, however, where men have slaughtered hundreds of helpless doves, simply to display their marksmanship, or have shot down beautiful song-birds for no better purpose than to give some vain woman the pleasure of wearing the murdered little beauties on her hat."

"You are right there!" exclaimed Seward. "There is too much of that kind of sport. We do not indulge in it."

By the time breakfast was over, it was agreed that Dabney should exchange clothes with Barker and join the Invincibles in their hunt, while the other two visitors remained at the lodge. The hunters set off in two divisions, Seward with Dabney in one direction, Walt, Billy, and Sam in another.

"Let us round up at the western edge of the swamp.

I saw a new runway down there the other day, that looked promising," called out Seward, as the friends separated, Seward and Dabney taking the shortest cut.

In the course of an hour Seward declared that they were in the vicinity of game. They had struck the deer trail, or runway, which deer and other animals followed to find water, making a well-beaten path. The hunter waits near this path, and if he escapes the keen scent of the game, he will be sure, soon or late, to see one or more of the timid animals go by. As the two men stood for a moment, considering whether to remain there or go farther toward the swamp, they heard behind them the patter of hoofs, and the terrified snort of a deer in distress. They jumped to one side just in time to avoid being run down by a big buck, who rushed past with a murderous catamount firmly fixed upon his shoulders. With each bound of the deer the claws and teeth sank deeper into the quivering flesh.

Seward raised his rifle and fired two shots in rapid succession at the cat; but still the buck kept up the terrific pace.

"Come!" shouted Seward, and the chase was on. Neither paused for breath. The deer would keep to the runway until it fell exhausted, and if the pursuers could maintain a reasonable speed, they might overtake the fleeing buck before the cat had made an end of him. Snow-covered brambles caught their clothes, hidden logs their feet. Down they went, time and time again; but nothing daunted, they raced on. Dabney kept close with his companion, and in the excitement did not feel the pain of bruises or the lacerations from the cruel briers. Almost before either man was aware of it, they had reached the margin of the swamp. Here a terrific fight was going on. The stag had run under the limb of a tree which had dislodged the wildcat. Quicker than a flash the deer had turned on his foe, and with lowered head was striving to disable him. Both were too much occupied to notice the approach of the hunters, and the battle was a royal one. The cat, hungry already with a taste of blood, was making fierce efforts to again mount the back of the buck, who, though weak from the loss of blood, led in the fray, his eyes gleaming wickedly. The cat parried in vain for an opening; the deer was ever on the alert. Now on the aggressive, now on the defensive, the combatants rushed around and around in a little open space on the margin of the swamp. It was soon evident that the deer could not hold out much longer, as he began to stagger, and the fire was leaving his eyes.

Up to this time the hunters could only gaze in awed silence and admiration at the prowess of the timid and gentle deer, fighting so gallantly with his terrible antagonist. But now Seward, reloading his rifle, raised it to his shoulder, took deliberate aim, and pulled the trigger. As the report rang out, the catamount gave a shriek of pain and anger, and turning upon his new foes, only a few feet away, the enraged beast made a furious spring at Seward. The latter had anticipated the move, and instantly, while the cat was still in air, not six feet from the muzzle of his gun, the other barrel barked, Seward sprang to one side, and the monster dropped like lead at the very feet of the two hunters, shot through the heart.

The deer, at this unexpected dénouement, turned and made a dash for the swamp, hotly pursued by Dabney. The buck proceeded but a little way before his feet became imbedded in the quagmire, and Dabney, nothing daunted at the fight the fellow had put up against the cat, rushed impetuously after him. The deer remained quiet till Dabney came within a few feet of him and had drawn his hunting-knife to despatch him. But the inexperienced hunter had reckoned without his host. With a last desperate effort the monarch of the forest, driven to the last ditch, freed himself and made a rush at his new foe. Dabney, now realizing his peril, sought to retreat, but his own feet were entangled in the swamp, and he could not escape. In an instant he was battling for his life with a deer brought to bay. Hoofs and horns were used with powerful effect, and by the time Seward's attention was called to the new arena of battle, Dabney was almost past help. Picking up the latter's rifle, which had been dropped in his haste to get at the deer, Seward took aim at the beast's head, and none too soon the bullet went crashing into the stag's brain. This was an enemy against which the gallant buck could not contend. The fire of battle died out of his eyes. His noble form quivered, and he fell crashing to the ground, where he lay, motionless forever.

Seward turned his attention to Dabney, and found him covered with blood, his face badly cut, his clothes torn, and his body so deeply imbedded in the mire that he could not draw him out. To add to the situation the poor fellow had fainted.

Reaching for his revolver, Seward fired five shots in the air. Almost instantly an answer came, not far away, and soon the other hunters came in sight. Having heard the first firing, they were hastening to the scene of the scrimmage.

After considerable effort, Dabney was extricated from his muddy bed, and soon regained consciousness. No bones were broken, but he was plentifully supplied with cuts, bruises, and rents in his clothing, made by the stag's sharp hoofs.

Turning their attention to the cat, they found him to be one of the largest of his species, four feet long and armed with magnificent teeth and claws. A few strokes of the knife, and the pelt was off. Sam, Billy, and Walt then went after the deer, and having quartered him, started for the lodge, each, except Dabney, who was scarcely able to walk alone, carrying a portion of the quarry.

Lawrence and Barker stood watching the departing Nimrods till they had disappeared into the woods. Lawrence, ever on the alert, observed the flutter of something falling to the ground as Sam drew a handkerchief from his pocket. As soon as the party was out of sight, and Barker had re-entered the cabin, he went to the spot and picked up a letter.

"All is fair in love and war," he soliloquized. "In my business, one must not stop to consider the niceties too closely. It is necessary at times to do things that are distasteful, like reading another man's private correspondence, for example. These boys are certainly hail-fellows-well-met, generous to a fault, and perhaps as straight as they seem to be. I hope so; but there are several things I must find out before I give them a 'clean bill.' Hallo! this letter is not addressed to Hawkins. I will look at it, and put it back where I found it, if it contains nothing of importance. Barker need not know anything about it."

Thrusting the letter into his pocket he returned to the shack. Barker was sprawled out among the furs, half asleep.

"Come, old man, we have work to do. There's no

12

time to sleep while we have this place to ourselves. Let's nose around a bit and see if we can find any clews. If these young fellows are not the ones we are after, we shall have to start on another tack inside of a week."

"All right, John; only for heaven's sake don't talk so infernally loud," grumbled Barker in an undertone. "Some of these skins may hide a pair of ears that we haven't counted on."

Lawrence laughed, and then remarked good-naturedly: "You are right. It is well to be discreet as a matter of self-discipline, although I have no doubt that we rule this roost alone just now. However, we will quickly find out if there are any secrets here. I confess, it begins to look as if we are barking up the wrong tree, notwithstanding the tip we received."

With a show of admiration and curious interest they set about a careful examination of the place, and were not long in satisfying themselves that there was nothing "queer" about the house or premises, for not the smallest nook or cranny was left unexplored.

"Well, what do you think about it?" asked Lawrence when their work was completed.

"No sign of anything wrong here, that's sure; and the boys seem all right. We are not apt to find much moonshine here," replied Barker. So saying he stretched himself out again in the bunk from which his partner had roused him to make the search.

Lawrence strolled out of the cabin, saying he would like to have one more look around before the hunters returned. As soon as he was alone he inspected the letter which Sam had dropped. It had been posted about a month before at Belfast, Ireland, and was addressed to Barney O'Boyle. The envelope had been torn open at the end. As Lawrence read it, a look of astonishment and perplexity spread over his face, and his lips puckered into a long, low whistle.

"Oh, ho! There's a colored gentleman in this wood-pile somewhere. Either Sam Hawkins is personating the said Barney O'Boyle, or he is appropriating his mail. There's a girl in it, too, with a pretty name—Norine. This is interesting enough to investigate a little on my own hook. Meanwhile I shall hold fast to this little missive. Mr. Samuel Hawkins will pass several uncomfortable moments when he misses it, and will finally conclude that he lost it somewhere in the swamp. It's just as well that he hasn't seen *me* yet, but only my sandy-haired friend Lawrence. I may want to meet the gentleman again before long."

The detective carefully adjusted the yellow mustache which had adorned his face since his departure from Sixteen the day before. Re-entering the lodge, he roused Barker to tell him that he had decided to push on to Red-Keg at once, leaving his two allies to conclude their investigation of the Invincibles at their leisure.

"I am expecting certain important papers to reach me at Red-Keg, and they may even recall me from this section," he explained, "but if I do not return, or you do not see me at the village, I will leave word for you there. Convey my regrets to our kind hosts, and tell them I hope to see them again some day," and after getting Barker to tell him all he knew as to the best way out of the forest, he was off.

When the five hunters returned, they found Barker still lying at his ease in the bunk. He was alarmed when he saw Dabney, but catching sight of the ugly head of the catamount still attached to the skin, he felt that his friend's appearance was amply accounted for.

When told that it was the deer instead of the cat that had created the havoc, he was astonished beyond measure.

"I thought the cat had been trying to make a meal of you," he exclaimed.

"Where's Lawrence?" asked Dabney, looking around.

"Oh, he is no kind of sport at all. About an hour ago he started off for Red-Keg, leaving nothing but regrets. Said he expected to hear from his house, but I have an opinion that there is a girl in it, so I let him go without much protest."

The next few days were uneventful. Lawrence had not returned, and it was supposed that he had been recalled as he had anticipated.

Before the week was over, Dabney and Barker were convinced that they must look elsewhere for "moonshine" and rewards. They parted from their jovial hosts with genuine regret, declaring that the few days spent in their company had been a delightful event in their lives. The Invincibles accompanied them to Red-Keg, where Barker found a note from Lawrence which read as follows:

"Nothing can be accomplished by remaining here now. I am going further up into the woods, where I hope to be more successful. Will see you later."

That was all.

The same evening the train took away two detectives, completely outwitted, not knowing what move to make next, but bound for Saginaw, from which place they would plan a new start. They scarcely concealed their discomfiture, and the Invincibles were jubilant accordingly.

CHAPTER XII

"THANK goodness, we have gotten rid of that gang of spies. I was afraid they would give us more trouble than they did, don't you know," exclaimed Sam, as the four Invincibles met again in their snug quarters on Mystic Isle, the day following the departure of Dabney and Barker from Red-Keg.

"That's a fact, they were easy," replied Seward. "They have gone off, I'll venture to say, prepared to give us the best of reputations 'to whom it may concern.'"

"Don't be too sure," broke in Walt. "They were almost too easy to suit me. It may be a bluff. I hope we have seen the last of them, but it will do no harm to be on the lookout, and go slow with the Mystic Brand for a while."

"It's all very well to talk about going slow," remarked Billy, "but we need the money. We have been doing nothing for the past week, and we can't afford to remain idle. Since the old man reduced my allowance, this is my principal source of income. I don't look for any further interference from the reward hunters, and I vote to go ahead."

"Well, boys, you have all had your say; now listen to me. I have something else in mind that is more important to me, don't you know, than all the moonshine that we can turn out in a year. I can't tell you all the details just now, but I may want your help before long. Are you with me?" queried Sam, earnestly.

"Well, you say it's more important to *you*. Where do we come in? We've always stuck together and I guess we will now, if there's anything in it for all," said Billy.

"That's the idea," agreed Walt; "mutual interest, you know."

"Oh, it's not likely I'll forget those who stand by me, even if it is a personal matter," replied Sam. "Besides, it needn't interfere with our business here. I merely want to be sure of your help if I should need it."

"What's your game, then?" asked Seward.

"I can't give you all the particulars now," answered Sam, "but to begin with, I may as well say that I have set my heart on winning that little beauty, Norine Maloney, for my wife."

"What are you talking about! She and Barney O'Boyle have been in love with each other for years. You haven't a ghost of a show there," exclaimed Seward, in astonishment.

"Now look here, my boy, don't you get a headache on my account," replied Sam, somewhat nettled. "You ought to know that I am not in the habit of going into a thing without considering it beforehand, and what I undertake I generally put through, don't you know. As you say, Norine and Barney have been fooling around together for a long time—too long—nothing has come of it. That big calf of an Irishman don't know enough to come to an understanding with the girl, and she is more than likely to get tired of waiting for such a dullard and be only too glad to take a gentleman who has gumption enough to ask her, and I flatter myself that she could do worse than to accept the emperor of this fair island."

"How about my cousin?" inquired Seward, with

rising anger. "She has shown a decided preference for you herself for the past year or two, and it was understood some time ago that there was an understanding between you. The rest of us boys think you are very lucky in having such a pretty girl at your beck and call. Surely you do not mean to give her the cold shoulder?"

"Nonsense!" exclaimed Sam, uneasily. "Lettie's a nice girl, but she hasn't any claim on me. I may have paid her some attentions, but I don't see how that prevents me from choosing another girl for my wife if I like. You are not likely to object very much. I know you would be only too glad to get Lettie yourself. Just now she seems to be completely taken up with that school and pack of ragamuffins of hers. I have more than one reason for preferring Norine, and my mind is made up to have her."

"If she will have you. I suppose that side of the question is worth considering," said Seward, flushing with annoyance. "It is the general impression that the young lady considers your room slightly more desirable than your company."

"I don't care *that* for the 'general impression,'" cried Sam, snapping his fingers. "Do you suppose I am going to allow that lanky Irish farmer, or a girl's silly whim, or a 'general impression' to stand in my way? However, it may require a little manœuvring. I have a plan by which Lettie can help me. If that fails, I may call upon my friends, the Invincibles."

"What deviltry are you up to, I should like to know?" broke in Walt. "I don't see what the Invincibles have got to do with your love affairs, anyway."

"Explain yourself a little more fully, Sam," said Seward, quietly.

"What's the use, if you're all against me?" snapped Sam. "We may as well dissolve partnership right now, if it has come to that."

"Not at all," said Seward, still controlling himself; "we haven't declared against you; we merely want to hear your plan. We can't go into a thing of this kind blind. What is it you propose to do and what do you want us to do?"

Sam hesitated a moment and glanced doubtfully at one after another of his three companions. He distrusted them; yet he feared to admit his distrust by refusing to confide in them. Presently he said:

"I may not have to ask anything of you, after all. I have an idea I can work things around my own way by the use of a little diplomacy. I know Norine doesn't care for me—that is, at present—but perhaps I can make her. It is devilish unpleasant to think that stupid Irishman can always stand in my way. He must be made to give her up, or she to give him up—I don't care which. Lettie can help me, if, as you say, she is at my beck and call, and is willing to sacrifice her own feelings a little for my wishes. She can make herself fascinating enough if she likes, and is something of a coquette—if she hasn't forgotten it. Why shouldn't she try her wiles on Barney for a change. Of course I'll have to put her up to it somehow. If that pans out, and he should appear to neglect Norine, my chances with the latter will increase, though, of course, I don't want Lettie to suspect that part of it. Then, if all goes well, I won't have to bother you fellows at all; but I am determined to put the thing through in any event, and I want to feel that, if need be, I shall have you to fall back on. Let's settle it now; can I count on you or not?"

"Villain!" muttered Walt under his breath; but Sam's eyes were on Seward, and he did not notice the expression of disgust on Walt's face.

"Well, I've got this to say, so far as I'm concerned," said Seward, harshly; "in the first place I don't believe you can carry that very pretty scheme through. It's not a small matter to trifle with the affections of one girl, to say nothing of two. Lettie will hardly consent to be your tool in any such business—not if I know her. You may get her to do a good deal if you lie cleverly enough, and I do not question your ability in that direction; but for all she is so devoted to you, she is a proud little woman and will not stand to be humiliated or insulted. In the second place, my advice to you is to make the most of the business we are in as long as you can. It is what we came together for, and is the only thing that will keep us together here. I imagine Walt and Billy will not care to stay out in this neck o' the woods just to help you in your love affairs and dirty private schemes. In the third place, I consider your proposed treatment of my cousin Lettie, to say nothing of Norine and Barney, as scoundrelly and cowardly in the extreme, and I'll be shot before I'll have anything to do with it."

Sam sprang to his feet, his face purple with rage and his fists clenched. The other boys also sprang up hastily, and for a moment a fight seemed imminent; but Sam counted the forces against him and decided that as they might be three to one, it would be better to avoid a personal encounter.

"Hang it all, Seward!" he snarled, "what do you mean by such insolence? I won't take it from you nor anyone else. It's come to a pretty pass when you can preach to me about what I ought and ought not to do. I wouldn't have said a word about my plans, only I thought we were sworn friends, ready to help each other in everything, and lo and behold, you flunk and play the baby act at the very first——"

"Hold on, Sam," interrupted Walt. "There's no baby act about it. I agree with Seward in every word he said. This isn't a matter the Invincibles want to be mixed up in. We may be criminals in Uncle Sam's eye, because we don't share our profits with him, but there are two ways of looking at that. This job of yours is very different, and I confess the thought of it turns my stomach, although I'm not especially interested in either of the young ladies. If you want to hold the corporation together, I advise you to see when you're outvoted and let personal interests go when they interfere with those of the concern."

Sam scowled and kicked viciously the head of a wildcat which glared at him from among the skins on the floor of the cave. He was rapidly turning the subject over in his mind, and in a few moments replied sulkily:

"Oh, very well; if you're all so hot over it, we'll call it off and say no more about it, though I don't see why you should be so squeamish all of a sudden. I suppose we'll have to stick to business this winter, spies or no spies, and get in some money. If you only knew it, I have had a better eye to business than you gave me credit——"

Sam stopped suddenly. He had put his hand into his inside pocket while speaking, then into his other pockets in rapid succession.

"What is the matter?" exclaimed Billy. "You are as white as a sheet, Sam. I declare you are really trembling."

"I—oh, nothing. That is—I think I have lost something. Excuse me, I will look around my bunk," and Sam, greatly agitated, hurried off to another of the group of caves which formed their remarkable establishment.

"There's a nigger in the wood-pile somewhere," said Walt. "Sam has not unbosomed himself as fully as he might. I only hope he won't get us entangled in more than our contract calls for."

Billy Axford had taken very little part in the heated discussion aroused by Sam's astonishing proposal.

Later in the day, however, he found opportunity to speak to Sam alone, and recurred to the subject confidentially.

"I didn't see that anything could be gained by causing a split," he said, "so I kept quiet; but if there's any money to be made in working the scheme you have in mind, just count on me for any help you may want. The gov'nor don't like my staying out here instead of sitting at a desk in his office, and when he wrote reducing my allowance for this year, he intimated in no gentle terms that if I stay out here after this winter there'll be no allowance at all, so it's make or break with me—or else go home like the prodigal son."

Sam seized his friend's hand enthusiastically. Here was unexpected help.

"Thanks, old fellow!" he exclaimed. "It'll be 'make' this time. If we put this thing through, I'll line your pockets well, and we needn't let the others in at all. If it comes to a pinch they will have to stand for their share whether they like it or not."

As the winter wore on, the Invincibles applied themselves to their business with more industry than ever.

Their "hunting and trapping" trips were more frequent and protracted, and to keep up appearances they
began to despoil their lodge in the woods and even
their island caves of some of the accumulated pelts in
order to make a display of bringing them to market.

In all of this activity Sam bore his share with less
and less regularity. Night and day he puzzled his
brain for some means to cause an estrangement between Barney and Norine. He went out of his way to
make himself agreeable to the unsuspecting girl, and
showed her parents more courtesy and attention than
he had ever done before. He took especial care that
Barney should not notice his behavior for fear it might
spur him on to declare himself. Moreover, Sam renewed his attentions to Lettie, who, in spite of her
school work, had been unable to overcome her infatua-
tion, as some of her friends regarded it, for Farmer
Hawkins's son. She was overjoyed at what she
thought was his reawakened love, little dreaming that
he merely-sought to assert his influence over her sufficiently to bend her to his wishes. Whenever he could
contrive it on one pretext or another, he brought Lettie
and Barney together and made sure that Norine should
hear an exaggerated version of the meeting. He hardly
dared to ask Lettie outright to attempt anything like a
wilful flirtation with the young Irishman, preferring to
accomplish his purpose, if possible, without revealing
his hand. He found his task harder than he had anticipated, though Barney's natural gallantry and his frank
friendliness toward Lettie, as Norine's friend, helped
the plot not a little. After Barney had been trapped
several times into taking Lettie to her home from the
Hawkins farm in the evening, and once from her
school, Sam had the satisfaction of seeing unmistakable

signs of trouble and resentment in Norine's manner
when told of the affairs. Without apparently intend-
ing to do so, Sam succeeded in conveying to her mind
the interpretation suited to his purpose. In the absence of an understanding between Barney and Norine,
neither felt like calling for or giving an explanation,
but Norine did not come so frequently to see Mother
Hawkins, and the dear, loving heart began to wonder
and grow sad. Her health had been failing for some
time, and she needed more than ever the sustaining
power of filial love.

Spring was approaching, and Sam grew impatient.
Norine's doubt concerning Barney did not seem to pro-
duce any kindlier feeling toward Sam. She began to
connect all her trouble with him, and, without understanding the reason for it, to fear him and shun him.
He determined on a bold stroke. The last dance of
the season would be held at Sixteen, Saturday, May
6th. If he could arrange it so that Lettie should go
with Barney, or, at the least, so that Norine should believe they were going together, he might take advantage of her pique and take her to the dance himself
and settle things that night. Lettie would have to help
him whether she liked it or not, and the sooner it was
understood the better.

After considerable thought he contrived what seemed
to him a plausible argument intended to convince Lettie
of the necessity of her going to the dance with Barney;
but when he explained it to her she refused indignantly
and then burst into tears. She pleaded that Barney
cared nothing for her; that he was devoted to Norine,
and would wish to take her; that Norine was her
best friend and she could not think of offending her;
that what Sam proposed would be dishonorable, and,

moreover, might subject her to suspicion and humiliation.

Sam broke in upon her protestations and insisted that Norine and Barney were out; that Barney would be only too glad to take her, and Norine wouldn't care; that he was giving up his own hoped-for pleasure in taking her, because special reasons of great importance to him required that she should go with Barney. She should know all in good time. If she cared anything about pleasing him, she would yield her preferences, this once, as he had, and make sure of doing as he requested. It might take a little time to arrange, but she could do it if she was a mind to use her cleverness a little to accomplish the desired result. After the thing was over, he would reward her in a way she would like best.

With sophistry and flattery and promises he so confused the poor girl that before she realized what she had done she agreed to attempt the task from which her soul revolted. Her mission was foredoomed to failure, and she knew it, yet she persisted hopelessly. As the time for the dance drew near, she contrived to speak of it often, and let fall numerous remarks to the effect that Norine was planning to go with Sam Hawkins. One day, after calling attention to the fact that Sam's arrangement to take Norine left herself and Barney without companions, she asked him if he would not like to take her, and finding that he did not respond with alacrity, she begged him to let her go with him to show the others that they were not limited to one companion.

Barney was puzzled and embarrassed. He admired Lettie for her beauty and vivacity, and for her devoted work among the children of her school, but he was unwilling for more reasons than one to accede to the proposition she had made. At last he told her bluntly but kindly that he was very much flattered by her willingness to go to the dance with him, but that if he could not take the girl of his choice, whom he had been expecting to take, he would go alone.

Poor defeated Lettie could only implore him not to tell any one that she had been so unmaidenly as to ask him to take her, and then hasten away to drown her humiliation in tears in the privacy of her room.

The meeting with Sam the following afternoon on her way home from her school was a bitter experience for the proud girl. When she told him of her defeat and added that Barney would surely ask Norine to go with him when he discovered the truth of the matter, Sam flew into a rage, and made the girl who had humiliated herself in the effort to serve him, the victim of his wrath. The interview was brief and bitter.

Lettie stood still for some minutes after Sam had gone, her breath coming in short sobs, and her cheeks alternately paling and flushing. A struggle was going on in her heart between the love which dwelt there supreme, and a stranger which came to wrest it from its throne. The sun was sinking toward the western forest. The unhappy girl looked down the road in the direction Sam had taken, and then, turning, fled to her room and gave way to passionate tears.

Sam was boiling with wrath, as he strode along the road to the village. He saw his cherished schemes threatened with defeat. Nothing but desperate measures could win for him now. He inferred from what Lettie had told him that Norine still thought Barney was planning to take her rival to the dance. If anything was to be done it must be done quickly. He would make a last attempt with the girl himself, before she had a chance to come to an understanding with her Irish lover. As he neared Red-Keg he saw Norine coming up the road alone. Now or never, he thought.

CHAPTER XIII

"Let up, you Irish devil! Let up, I say! Do you want to murder me?"

"Begorra, no! Murderin' is not in my line, me boy. I've given ye less than ye desarve, but if ye're sorry for what ye done, git up and apologize to the lady like a man."

"I'll see you in —— first!" snarled Sam, springing to his feet and whipping out a revolver. Before he could pull the trigger, however, the brawny fist of Barney O'Boyle flashed out and sent him measuring his length again in the mud of the road.

"So that's it, is it, me foine college-brid gintleman? Faith, ye're whipped an' don't know it. We must lave no grounds for unsartinty this time," and heedless of Sam's howls and curses Barney rolled him over on his face in the mud, and seizing a stout switch from the roadside began to apply it vigorously to the back and legs of the prostrate man.

"Oh, Barney, please let Mr. Hawkins go now. I think he is sorry, and surely you have punished him enough."

"Well, well, Miss Norine, if you intersade for the man as has insulted and threatened ye, I reckon I'll have to let him go, but first we must put that shooter where it can't go off."

As he stooped to secure the revolver which lay on the ground near Sam, the latter suddenly drew up his feet and aimed a vicious kick at Barney's face, only missing it by a hand's breadth as Barney dodged to one side.

"Ha, ha! but that was meant well, if it did miss. If it's kickin' ye would try, ye'd better practise up a bit. Ye might employ Pete's old mule for a teacher while he's not workin'," and Barney laughed mockingly as he still held Sam down in the mud, while he picked up the revolver and threw it over the fringe of bushes into the river about fifty feet from the road.

"I promised Norine to let ye go, but, begorra, yer face is so dirty with the mud, and yer blood is so hot with wicked feelin's that I'm a mind to give ye a dip in the Tittabawassee to clane the one an' cool the other."

Lifting Sam Hawkins to his feet, with a quick motion Barney caught both of his arms, pinned them behind his back, and rushed him through the bushes down to the river's edge. Then kicking his feet from under him by a skilful twist, he rolled the thoroughly beaten man into the cold water.

"Now, me boy, I'm through with ye. Swim around a bit an' cool off, or go home an' hang yerself up to dry. I'll lave the decision to yerself, while I see Miss Norine home," and Barney rejoined the frightened girl in the road.

"I'm not through with you, Barney O'Boyle!" shouted Sam, as he crawled out of the water. "By the eternal, you shall suffer for this!" and instead of turning in the direction of his home, Sam started off at a rapid pace for Red-Keg.

"Come, Norine, it's time for the likes of you to be home. There's a good two miles yet to walk an' yer mother will worry her dear heart out of her mouth if ye're not home before dark."

"Oh, Barney, I'm so afraid Sam will seek revenge

"SWIM AROUND A BIT AN' COOL OFF, OR GO HOME AN' HANG
YERSELF UP TO DRY."

on you for this afternoon. He is not one to forget such a beating as you gave him!"

"An' the longer he remembers it, the better for him an' for you. He'll not be so likely to annoy you with his attintions. As for meself, I'm thinkin' I'll be a match for him if he wants to try another bout."

"It is not that, that I am afraid of, Barney. You are more than a match for him in a fair fight; but he may resort to underhanded means to be revenged. Sam would not stop at anything, however dishonorable, I am afraid, to gain his purpose."

"There, now, Norine, don't you be after troublin' yer pretty head. Barney O'Boyle will carcumvent the rascal if he tries any dirty tricks. By the way, Norine, I have a bit of news for ye that's been spilin' for the tellin', an' I might as well——"

Barney stopped suddenly, looked up and down the road, cleared his throat, took off his hat, brushed his hair up from his forehead with one hand, put on his hat again, glanced sideways at Norine, and then walked on in silence.

Meanwhile Norine looked at him with her bright eyes wide open in expectancy which soon changed to surprise at Barney's silence.

"News, Barney? For me? Well, why don't you tell it to me? I'm waiting."

"Well, you see, Norine, I—that is—don't you see, I —faith, Norine, I'll tell ye this avenin' after supper."

"Now, Barney! Why can't you tell me at once? I shall die of curiosity if you don't," and Norine lifted her rosy face beseechingly to that of the stalwart young farmer by her side, and pulled on his sleeve with a teasing and at the same time caressing touch that made the young man's blood tingle.

"Sure, Norine, who could resist ye? Will ye be so smilin', I'm wonderin', after ye hear the news? It's just this. I—was thinkin'—I mean, I thought, maybe —Howly Saints! what was that?" Barney jumped suddenly, as a dismal "Hoo—Hoo—! Hoo—Hoo!" sounded from the woods that lined one side of the road.

"Pshaw, Barney! that was only an owl."

"So it was, the varmint! I must be narvous. By the way, Norine, are ye goin' to the dance at Sixteen to-morrow three weeks?"

"I don't know yet. Why?"

"Well, I heerd ye were goin' with Sam. I'm thinkin' ye'll not do that same after what happened this afternoon?"

Barney looked quizzically at his pretty companion, and a grin struggled with the anxious look in his honest eyes.

"Who in the world said I was going with Sam, I should like to know? Me go to the dance with Sam Hawkins? Well, I guess not, indeed!" and Norine gave her shoulders a little shrug of disgust, and then broke into a merry laugh.

"Surely, you didn't believe a word of that, Barney? I have detested that man for some time, and after to-day I fear him. It is too bad, but I'm afraid he is breaking his dear father's and mother's hearts. But who told you I was going with Sam, Barney?"

"Lettie said as how you were goin' with him, least-wise, that he wanted ye to, an' she thought ye would."

"Lettie is mistaken. Perhaps Sam told her a false-hood. She likes him so well herself that she imagines every one else does, and she can't understand why I do not. I have never told her my reasons, because it would only hurt her, and she is a dear good girl. She is blind to Sam's faults, and cares more for him than he deserves; but she is a charming companion, and I suppose you will have a nice time with her at the dance, won't you?"

There was a slight quaver in Norine's voice, although she strove to conceal it.

"Ye'r jokin', Norine! I never went to a dance with Lettie in me life, an' I'm not likely to. She's a swate girl an' all that, but if I can't take the one of me choice, faith, I'll take no one," and the decision manifest in Barney's voice left no uncertainty as to his intentions.

"Whom are you going to take, then?" asked Norine, her words exhibiting a great deal more curiosity than she really felt. She did not look at Barney as she waited for the answer.

"Sure, it'll be no one unless it's yerself," replied Barney; then he added, "I'll borrow Rock and the buckboard, an' the trip will be nice an' asy. I'm thinkin' there'll be a full moon, an' barrin' rain, the road will be middlin' dacint. It's the last dance for the sasen, an' we don't want to miss it. Ye'll go, Norine?"

"Yes, since you are not going to take Lettie, I will go with you, and be pleased; but is that the news that you were going to tell me, Barney?"

"Well, not exactly; that is—why, here we are at your gate, Norine, darlint, an' it's supper-time. The news can wait until——"

"No it can't, Barney. It may be something I would like to tell the folks. Why not let me have it now?"

"Faith, Norine, it consarns only yerself—an' me. It's just this, darlint, I love ye, an' I want ye for me own little wife. Norine, tell me—why, what on airth are ye laughin' at?"

"Why, Barney! that's not news. I've known that

for ever so long," and Norine tried to hide the blushes that swept over her pretty face by laughing merrily.

"Ye don't say! Who tould ye?" exclaimed Barney, hardly knowing whether to be pleased or provoked.

"Why, you have told me yourself hundreds of times, in every tone of your voice and every glance of your eyes. You told me again this afternoon when you defended me so bravely against Sam Hawkins—yet—I—am—glad to hear you tell it to me now, Barney," and Norine looked up frankly into the blushing face of the manly swain, who had been taken so much by surprise by her unexpected reception of his avowal.

"God bless you, Norine, darlint! I thought it would be news to ye. But maybe you have—ahem—have ye any—any—news for me, swateheart?" Norine dropped her eyes from his face. Her head drooped lower and lower, and the rich blood came and went in her sweet face and neck. She stood silently twisting her bonnet strings for what seemed to Barney a long time. At last, his boldness returning as hers seemed to be waning, he reached out one big brawny hand and took possession of one of her little ones. Still the silence continued. He gathered in the other little hand; then he drew her nearer, and a strong arm stole around her shoulder.

"Look up, little swateheart, an' tell me the news, the blessed news,—if ye have any for me."

A sly glance, another blush, and then the answer came, in a voice so low that Barney had to bend his head closer to hers to hear.

"It—wouldn't be much more like news than yours was, because—because I've loved you almost as long as you have loved me."

The sweet confession ended in almost a whisper.

Barney's face was very close to her as he listened. Just the least upward turn of the rosy face below his— was it an invitation, or only a permission? He never stopped to consider, but took quickly what the gods put within the reach of his lips. Then, with a sudden movement, and a whispered "Come after supper," Norine had freed herself and was flying away to the house, leaving Barney standing in the road trembling with his happiness.

CHAPTER XIV

THERE are some fires which water will not quench. The blaze in Sam's breast had grown into a conflagration as he crawled out of the Tittabawassee and continued his interrupted way to Red-Keg.

"I'll be even with that —— Irishman, and pay the score with interest," he snarled between his teeth. "And that hussy who flies to his arms for protection —I'll bring her off her high and lofty perch before she's many days older. They shall both rue this day's work. What would the boys say if they were to catch me in this fix? Just wait a bit; my time'll come soon."

Blinded by his rage, and wholly occupied with his ugly thoughts, he hurried along the road, utterly oblivious to everything else, until suddenly glancing up he found himself almost face to face with Robert Allen, who was walking rapidly toward him. Without stopping for a moment to think what he should do; without responding in any way to the minister's hearty greeting and anxious inquiry, Sam turned and dashed into the woods at the side of the road and ran and scrambled through the trees and underbrush as if in mortal fear for his life. For several minutes he kept up his wild flight regardless of direction, until at last, becoming aware that he was not pursued, he sank trembling upon a bank of moss, his heart thumping in his breast painfully. The minister! Of all men the one he wanted least to see. And why? Why had he instinctively fled from the man who was probably the best friend he had in the world? Like a flash he recalled the minister's words and looks a year and a half ago, when he had talked to him after saving his life. He had told Sam that he loved him. What other man, even his father, had ever told him that? Yet Sam dreaded the very sight of him. Yes, as he sat there trembling in the gloom of the forest, he almost felt that he hated him. Why had he come along just in time to see him in such a predicament? Why did his tender and entreating words persist in plaguing Sam? He ground his teeth in wrath, and choked back fiercely the still small voice that had suddenly made itself heard for a moment in his inmost heart. He deliberately turned his mind again to Barney and fanned his vengeful rage into a blaze again.

With some difficulty he found his way back to the road and turned again toward Red-Keg, keeping a sharp lookout against further undesirable meetings. When he reached the village, shortly before dark, he hastened at once to Pete's and put on a dry suit of clothes, borrowed from the saloon-keeper, while his own were dried before the fire. While waiting about the place, and repeating to first one and then another curious questioner a lying account of Barney's attack upon him, he caught sight of Jim Gyde coming out of Jake Vogel's store. At first he paid no attention to him, but a moment later an idea took possession of him, and he went to meet the tall young lumberman.

Sam's contempt for and indifference to the people among whom he lived had caused him to remain ignorant of many things concerning them which were matters of common knowledge throughout the region, and this ignorance now led him into a humiliating blunder. He remembered Jim Gyde as one of the most reckless and lawless of the boys in the Midland school when he himself had attended there. He had heard once or twice since then of Jim's scrapes, and he had been told of the terrible thrashing the fellow had received the day Lettie and the other girls graduated. Whenever Sam had seen him, he had been vaguely impressed with his size, his strength, and his generally forbidding appearance. He assumed that he was the same kind of a man now, and just as ready for mischief. Perhaps he would be just the one to enlist in Sam's plan of revenge. The fact that Jim might be one of Barney's friends never occurred to him. He accosted the young man, much to the latter's surprise, and with a jocose reminder of old school-days, which Jim received in silence, he asked him to walk down toward the river a little way, as he had something particular to tell him. As Jim wonderingly complied, Sam told his version of the trouble with Barney, and asked Jim to help him "get square with the Mick." Jim listened with a curious expression in his face, which the gathering darkness hid from his companion.

"An' what can I do?" he asked. "Have you anythin' in mind?"

"Well, not exactly, don't you know," replied Sam. "I thought you'd be a match for him in anything, almost. But say, they're going to break the rollway soon, ain't they? You'll both be there, I suppose. Why not dump him in, or something?"

Jim grunted nervously, and if Sam had been watching him closely he might have noticed a peculiar twitching of the long fingers which were suddenly drawn from his capacious pockets.

"Do you happen to know, Mr.—Sam Hawkins, that to 'dump him in, or somethin', while the logs are rollin' would mean that he'd git chawed up an' spread along from here to Midland 'most as sure as we're standin' here? Is that your lay?—or do you jes' want to thump him an' call it square?" Jim leaned forward and peered into Sam's face as he spoke.

"Oh, of course I didn't mean to ask you to kill him outright," said Sam, rather taken back. "I thought a good ducking and scare would serve him right for what he did to me. If he got any more than that it would be his own lookout. He pretends to be so smart on the river."

"You sneakin', lyin' coward!" cried Jim, giving way, at last, to his wrath; "you know right well what happens nine times out of ten to any man who gits off his feet in the rollway. You've picked up the wrong man this time to do your dirty work. Hold on there!" he exclaimed, grabbing Sam by the shoulder, as the latter was turning hastily away. "I ain't through yet. You've picked up the wrong man, as I was sayin', an' you might have knowed it if you hadn't been too stuck on yourself an' too busy doin' nothin' to notice anybody else. I see I'll have to tell you that I ain't the Jim Gyde you used to know. More'n a year back I turned over a new leaf an' started in to be somebody an' behave like a man, an' it strikes me you better do the same thing. I'm ashamed to talk to a man who's been to college an' had the chances you've had, an' tell him what he ought to do; but if you don't look sharp, Mr.—Sam Hawkins, you'll git left back in the ruck, an' rough chaps like me, who mean business, will git ahead of you."

He loosened his grip on Sam's coat; but as the latter wrenched himself away, he sprang quickly forward and seized him again.

"I forgot to tell you another thing," he said. "Bar-

ney an' me are special friends. We've worked side by
side in rollways before, an' likely will in this one. I'll
keep my eyes peeled." With this parting shot, he let
the discomfited and angry plotter go.

Sam was fairly choking with shame and rage and
unable to make any retort to the tongue-lashing he had
received from one whom he had considered so greatly
his inferior. The thought of a lecture from the minister was bad enough, but that this coarse, ignorant
logger should presume to preach to him was intolerable. Moreover, the truth in what he had said
stung Sam to the core. He hastened back to Pete's
and began to drink recklessly. As the fumes mounted
to his head he talked more and more loudly, heedless
of who might hear him. A stranger, clad in a loose
flannel shirt, and trousers tucked into high boots, sat
near the door. A short thick overcoat, a stout stick,
and a small bundle lay on the floor by his side. He
listened for a while to Sam's angry tirade against Barney, and presently, strolling up to the bar where Sam
stood, he said, confidentially:

"Look here, partner; I used to know a young fellow
of that name some years ago. Wonder if it could be
the same. He played me a dirty trick, and I've been
biding my time ever since to get even."

Sam glared at the man for a moment, and then asked
rudely:

"How should I know?"

"It ought to be easy enough to tell if it's the same
one," replied the stranger. "The chap I knew, con-
found him, came from Ireland about eight or nine years
ago with a family by the name of Maloney. I met him
in New York soon after he landed, but he went West,
and I lost track of him."

"He's the man all right," growled Sam, eyeing the stranger with new interest. "He's here, just out of the village, and I'd like to break his neck."

"Just what I've said myself many a time. Have one on me," rejoined the stranger, calling Pete, who placed a fresh bottle before them.

"What did he ever do to you?" asked Sam, as he accepted the glass the stranger had filled for him, but did not notice that he had forgotten to fill one for himself.

"Oh, he—that is I—why I did him a kindness in New York, and he repaid it with—the meanest trick I ever had played on me. I don't like to talk about it," he added, to explain his hesitation, "but if I could only get hold of him again, I'd—come sit down over in the corner, my friend, where we can talk without being heard, and we'll let our genial host here keep us supplied with refreshments as we want them."

Sam yielded, glad to find any one with a grievance against Barney who would listen sympathetically to his story of wrongs—and, perhaps to his plans for revenge. His rage at Barney and at Jim Gyde, and the conflicting emotions aroused by the sight of the minister, had caused him to lose his self-control, and he drank more freely than was his custom, growing more and more confidential with his new friend at the same time. An hour or so passed, and the stranger rose with a yawn.

"Guess our young friend ain't used to much indulgence," he remarked to Pete, with a laugh. "He seems to be getting sleepy. Better let him bunk here if you've got any room."

"That's all right; I'll 'tend to him," replied Pete. "He kin hev the room he an' his pals hev used before. He'll be all right in the mornin'."

When morning came, however, Sam was far from all right. His head ached, and he felt ugly clear through. An important meeting of the Invincibles had been appointed for that morning at their regular rendezvous. He was in no mind to go, but he feared what the other boys might do in his absence, so he braced up as best he could and started for the island. The Invincibles were not in the most friendly state of mind when the time for the meeting came and Sam had not arrived. They waited impatiently until dinner-time. After dinner their displeasure began to find vent in remarks that testified to Sam's waning prestige as leader. Yet they had no choice for the present but to stick together. Shortly after dinner Sam's call was heard at the south landing, and old blind Pomp, who had replaced his sight with some other mysterious and almost equally serviceable sense, hastened off in the boat to bring his young master to the island. In a few minutes Sam entered the cave and threw himself down upon a seat without a word of greeting, but looking tired and ugly.

"What's up, old man? You look as if you had been trying to act as peacemaker between two gangs of rivermen. Nothing wrong, I hope?" inquired Seward as cordially as possible.

"Everything's wrong, wrong as hell," growled Sam; but except for a fictitious account of his fight with Barney, the boys failed to get anything from him in explanation of his present mood or his intentions for the future. The meeting was called to discuss plans for getting more corn to the North Shore without arousing suspicion, and increasing the output of "Mystic Brand" to meet the large demands from the numerous logging-camps where the men had finished their spring cleaning up and were indulging in their usual spree before resorting to the rollway. After the Invincibles had finished their deliberations, Sam, with a cautious sign to Bill to join him in a few minutes without letting the others know it, strolled off toward the other end of the island. There the two young men remained in earnest conversation for some time, after which they separated and returned to the cave from different directions. Already the Invincibles were "a house divided against itself."

Lettie Green left her room Saturday morning under the spur of a new resolution. There was something she must know at once. The burden on her heart was too heavy to carry alone. She sought out Norine, that she might ask her the strange question which she believed could only be answered one way, yet which she dreaded might bring another answer. Norine was shocked at her friend's haggard face and swollen eyes, and with a quick rush of sympathy she put her arms around her and led her into the fields, where they could be alone.

"Tell me all about it, dear," she said, soothingly.

"Norine," exclaimed Lettie, hysterically, "tell me truly, do you love him? Do you care the least bit for him? I don't believe it, but I must hear the truth from your own lips," and she looked beseechingly into the astonished eyes of her friend, and found that she was blushing furiously.

"Why, Lettie, dear, how you surprised me. Whom do you mean?"

Lettie's face grew suddenly red, and her eyes dropped before Norine's astonished gaze, as she said in a low tone:

" Sam."

"Sam Hawkins! How can you—" began Norine, with flashing eyes and a voice full of scorn; then as she saw her friend's look of pain and anxiety, she continued more softly, "No, Lettie, I certainly do not love Sam in the very least. I fear him. You do not know. Why do you ask, dear?"

A look of relief struggled with the pain in the unhappy girl's face as she replied: "I know you love Barney, and God bless your love. He is worthy of it. If only Sam—. Oh, Norine, you do not know what torture it is to love and remain unloved—to love and to know the one you love is unworthy—to love and be spurned, and still to love—to feel your love turn to hate, and then feel the hate melt away in the love that will not quench—to dishonor yourself for the sake of that love, and know that you have gained nothing by it after all. God help me—I could not keep it to myself any longer."

Norine made no reply, but simply drew the heartbroken girl closely in her arms and shed tears of sympathy which were more eloquent than words.

CHAPTER XV

THE early morning sun was shining through the tree-tops; the moist fragrance of spring filled the air, and forest birds were singing a welcome to sun and flowers. There was something singing in Barney's heart, too, as he strode along through the woods on the way to Red-Keg. The song in his heart found expression in the rhythm of his buoyant steps and the cheery whistle that came from his lips. He had won his dear love. What mattered all else in the world? His little rub with Sam the previous afternoon was hardly worth a thought, certainly not a regret. He had borne his own indignities a long time patiently, for Uncle Si's sake, and he was rather glad of an excuse to settle with Sam on some one else's behalf. Besides, had it not supplied just the spur his courage had needed to make the long-deferred avowal to Norine? Now his heart was as light as a bird, and he wondered why he had waited so long. To commemorate the happy occasion he was on the way to Red-Keg to look for a present for his "swateheart."

Barney's progress toward the village and his blithesome whistle were suddenly interrupted by a rough challenge: "Hold on, there, Barney O'Boyle! Not so fast ef ye please."

A tall, heavy-set man sprang into the road from behind a large tree and barred the way. He was clad in similar fashion to Barney, in rough flannel shirt and long-legged cow-hide boots, and he carried a stout stick.

Barney gazed at him a minute in astonishment, and then broke into a hearty laugh.

"What on airth do ye mane, Tom Moore, by skarin' the life out o' me like that? Was ye waitin' for me?"

"Thet's jes what I was, Barney. I arrest ye, in the name o' the law," and big Tom Moore stepped nearer and placed his hand on the other's shoulder.

Barney did not move a muscle, but stared into Tom's face for several seconds before answering. He could not imagine the cause of this strange act. He and Tom Moore, the village constable, were bosom friends, and he suspected a joke, but Tom Moore was not given to playing practical jokes on his friends, so Barney looked at him earnestly to make sure whether he was in earnest. A tell-tale twinkle stole into the stern eyes and quickly disappeared, but Barney saw it.

"An' what might ye be arrestin' me for, yer honor?" he asked, banteringly.

"Fer fellernously assaultin' an' attemptin' to murder one Sam Hawkins—to say nothin' o' givin' him a bath in the Tittabawassee agin his will, an' with his cloze on."

As Tom Moore finished stating his charge, his face relaxed, a grin spread over it, and in a minute both he and Barney were laughing aloud together.

"I couldn't keep it up, Barney," said Tom at last, in quite a different tone from that which he had lately assumed. "Folks that ain't got a guilty conscience don't skair wuth a cent; an' when ye saw through the joke so easy, I had to give in. Sam made complaint agin ye last night for tryin' to murder him, an' wanted me to put ye in jail, but I laughed at him an' told him I'd hear your story fust. Are ye goin' to the Keg? Ef so, I'll walk along with ye."

"It's little story ye'll nade, I'm thinkin', Tom. Ye know Sam Hawkins, an' ye know me, an' to come to the pint, ye must have seen how Sam has been pesterin' Miss Norine with his attintions. She's towld him repatedly that she can dispinse with his company an' not pine for the lack of it, but the rapscallion refuses to take the hint, an' buzzes round her like a pesky horse-fly. The more she won't, bedad, the more he will, an' yisterday he had the impidence, consarn 'im, to waylay her on the road and threaten her, sayin' he'd have her whether she liked it or not. The brave little girl scorned him, an' the varmint was makin' a grab for her, when I made me ontray like a play-actin' hero. About that same minit Sam Hawkins got taken weak in the knees, or somewhere, kinder suddint like, an' lay down in the mud. Somethin' must have made the gintleman narvous, for in two more minits he was foolin' with his pistol, an' I thought it me duty to relave him of it for fear he might think it wasn't loaded, an' hit somebody. There bein' nothin' better for him to do just then he lay down in the road agin! Faith, it was a shame to lave him go home all over mud, so what did I do, in the kindness of me heart, but try to clane the mud off with a stick, which same bein' not quite satisfactory, I helped it out with the water of the Tittabawassee. The last I seen of him he was bathin' there quite paceable."

"Ye done right, Barney, so far as I can see," declared the constable, heartily, "but I'm afraid ye'll hear from Sam in a way ye least expect. He's one to nuss a grudge till doomsday, an' he's sworn to git even with ye."

"Begorra, let him try it on—when he fales the nade of another bath," laughed Barney.

"It's not fightin' he'll try next time. Ye may rest sure of that, Barney, an' ye'd best look out for his tricks. He'll be up to some devilment, I'm afraid. He wuz mad clean through las' night, an' made no bones o' sayin' he hoped ye'd git kilt in the rollway nex' week."

"In which same I'll decline the honor of obligin' him. Ye better tell him to be keerful himself. I've noticed that them as wish others harm are ginerally the fust to git hurted."

"Thet's so, Barney, but he won't git hurt in the rollway, fer the very good reason that he won't be there; it's too much like work for him an' his pals. The chances are they'll be off somewhere in the woods doin' the devil knows what."

"It's true, ye are, Tom; the b'y's not much good at all. His college larnin's made him lazy, but he kapes the devil busy findin' mischief fer his idle hands to do. His good owld mother an' father are breakin' their hearts for him, though he ain't wuth it."

"I seen Sam talkin' to a strange chap at Pete's las' night," resumed Tom, "an' I didn't like the looks o' the feller. He's never been roun' these parts before, an' he came from nowhere. Fust anybody knowed he was sittin' round in Pete's jes' as cool an' comftable 's if he'd lived here all his life. When he heard Sam lambastin' ye, he kinder jined in sympethetic like, an' then he an' Sam sat down in a corner together an' was talkin' kinder low an' quiet fer 'bout an hour. I kep' my eye on 'em, though o' course I couldn't go near enough to hear anythin'. The chap didn't leave until Sam had drunk hisself pretty near under the table, an' Pete had ter drag him up-stairs an' put 'im to bed."

The two friends had now arrived at the village of

Red-Keg, and Barney was on the point of excusing
himself to Tom in order that he might perform the
errand on which he had come to the village, when Tom
suddenly nudged him and remarked:

"See that dark-lookin' feller with the black whiskers,
talkin' to Pete? Thet's the chap Sam was chinnin'
with las' night. Let's see what he has to say."

"Mornin', Tom; mornin', Barney," called out Pete
as he saw the newcomers approaching. "Let me in-
terjuce this here gentleman, Mr. Jim Lane, who came
to this metropulus to start a store. I've been tellin'
him 'tain't no use. One store an' one gin-mill is 'bout
all we need here jes now, an' sence he's seed the place,
he's come 'roun' to my way o' thinkin'; thet so, stranger?" concluded Pete, turning to the man he had just
introduced.

"It looks that way, indeed," assented Mr. Lane.
"I was led to suppose your town was larger. I think
I shall have to look elsewhere; but I am glad to meet
you, gentlemen. What names, did you say?"

"This here's Tom Moore, constable, an' t'other is
Barney O'Boyle, thet lives with Farmer Hawkins, three
miles up the road. Guess I forgot ter give ye their
hull names before," apologized Pete.

Lane extended his hand, and the others took it somewhat grudgingly. Barney noticed that the stranger
eyed him more than once with peculiar interest.

"I am told that you expect to break the big rollway
in a few days. Is it much of a sight?" asked Lane.

"Bet yer life!" exclaimed Pete. "Biggest rollway
ever piled here or anywhere on airth. Ef ye ain't never
seen one, ye'll think it's a sight. They's nigh on seven
million feet o' logs down there now, an' some loads
ain't in yet. Besides that, they's other rollways along

up the river for fifteen or twenty miles waitin' for the
freshet."

"That being the case, I think I'll stop and see the
job done, provided it will be soon. I can't wait more
than three or four days."

"They calc'late ter do it Monday, the 17th, or Tuesday at the latest, an' to-day's Saturday, so ye'll not
have long ter wait. Ef ye're a mind ter, we'll go down
t' the river an' see it now."

Barney and Tom Moore consented to join them,
though ordinarily they had very little use for Pete's
company, and all four were soon at the place where the
great rollway was being filled in. The stranger exhibited the liveliest interest at once as he saw the immense
pile of logs which reached from the high bank of the
river on one side, more than half-way to booms which
marked the edge of the mud flats on the opposite side,
and extended for a distance of over half a mile up the
river, and which was being heaped up by means of
skids until the top was twenty or thirty feet above the
higher bank and fully sixty feet above the water.

"Surely all those logs didn't come from hereabout!"
he exclaimed. "And how in the world can their owners tell them apart and separate them after the rollway
is broken?"

"Them logs hev been comin' here all winter from all
pints o' the compass," began Pete, with great relish.
He was never so happy as when imparting information
—or gossip—to an interested listener. "Some fellers,
small lumbermen, settlers, an' the like, bring mebbe
one small load a day with the on'y ox-team they got.
Then agin they'll be the big operator thet sen's in a
dozen ox-loads, or mebbe a hull train-load from up the
line. Big an' little, all goes in together to make the

pile ye see. Every log is scaled an' branded on the end before it goes in, an' every man kin tell his own logs, when it comes ter siftin' 'em out at the booms down the river."

"How do they start that great pile of logs moving? It looks to me as if nothing short of an earthquake would do it."

"Wal, ye see, looks is deceivin'. What with the river bein' swollen at this time o' year, an' nateral tendency o' logs to roll, like as not one man kin do the trick."

"One man! Surely you are joking," exclaimed Lane.

"Fact, my friend; but it's mighty resky. Thet pile o' logs hes ter be started from the bottom, an' it ain't no job for any man thet's skeery. Es I say, one man *might* do the trick alone ef he got holt o' the right log at the bottom, but more'n likely they'll be a dozen or twenty at p'ints along the river, an' maybe they'll break the rollway in two or three sections. Anyhow, ye'll see 'em go down there at the fut o' the pile o' logs, squint along close ter the water, till they git their eyes on the log thet looks ter be the lock fer the hull combination; then with peavies or cant-hooks they'll yank the log out, an' the chances are thet before ye kin say 'Jack Robinson' more'n once, down comes a few thousand logs, rollin', crashin', splashin', an mebby the hull rollway is on the move."

"Wonderful!" exclaimed Lane; "but what on earth becomes of the man who loosened the first log? I should think he would be crushed to death in an instant."

"Oh, he's used to it, an'——"

"What! used to being crushed to death?"

"Course not! used to breakin' rollways, an' he kin most gener'ly look out fer hisself. Some o' the fellers roun' here have broke so many thet they think no more of it than eatin' their breakfas'. Barney, here, is a cool han' at the job, an' like's not will be in this one—eh, Barney?" and Pete turned a questioning eye on the young Irishman.

"I'm thinkin' they'll want all the help they kin get, an' ye'll be likely to see me there—if me huntin' ingagements will allow," assented Barney, grinning suggestively.

Lane's interest seemed to increase, and he turned to Barney as though on the point of speaking to him, but instead he said to Pete:

"Do you mean to tell me that men can go down into the river under that mountain of logs towering sixty feet above them, loosen a key log here and there, which lets the whole mighty mass down like an avalanche, and yet escape with their lives?"

"Yep; thet's right. I've seen Barney, here, an' many another like him, go down under the front of a rollway, pick out a suspicious log at the bottom, flop his cant-hook 'round it, an' give it a yank as unconcerned like as a dentist turn-keyin' an obstrep'rous tooth. With a crash an' a roar down comes the logs, an' fust thing ye know, there is Barney hoppin' an' trippin' on the rollin' logs, like the bareback rider in the circus, till, when they hev stopped movin', he's standin' on the logs at the top o' the heap, smilin' an' wavin' his han's an' makin' his bow to the cheerin' public on the bank!"

"That is certainly a marvellous feat!" declared Lane; "but are there not accidents often?"

"Sometimes, but not so often as a stranger might

think. Las' spring, Moses Hawley was tryin' to break the rollway. He got holt o' the right log, sure 'nuf, but there ain't been nothin' seen o' him sence. Mebbe ye'll see his widder—thunder! there she is now; see her walkin' along the river-bank up yonder es though she war lookin' fer somethin'? Poor critter, she's a little gone in the head, an' she comes here every day, rain or shine, lookin' fer Mose. Yer can't make her b'lieve she won't find him some day."

"Let us hope she will," said Lane, quietly. Pete laughed at what he thought was intended as a joke, but Barney glanced at the stranger with a quick thrill of surprise.

"Is there no other way to break the rollway? Couldn't they fasten a rope to the key log and pull it out?" asked Lane.

"Nope. Rope's been tried, but it gets tangled with the logs an' makes a jam. Onct I saw a yoke o' oxen thet was haulin' on a rope get pulled in an' rolled into jelly afore any one could cut the rope. The man-way's the surest an' best."

"Why can't they——"

"Hey, there, Pete! The boys is breakin' loose up in the Kag. Better come up before they's any broken heads an' glass," and Bob Simons, the saloon roustabout, after coming near enough to yell out this bit of information to the proprietor of the Red Keg, turned back to the scene of the scrimmage, Pete following in a hurry.

"What's the trouble?" asked Lane, addressing Barney.

"Faith, it's nothin' but two river teams been fillin' up, an' gettin' frisky. They're after finishin' their work up the line, an' have a day off till the rollway is broken. Them teams are jealous, an' it's likely they been disputin' which could do the biggest stunts. Once they git at it, begorra, they're wuss than Kilkenny cats, an' won't let up till every mother's son o' thim is laid up for repairs. Pete's gone up to protict his property."

"Why don't you go up there, Mr. Moore, and put a stop to the row? Some one may be killed. Aren't you constable?" inquired Lane, evidently surprised at the apparent indifference of the village officer.

"Ye don't understand the situation, my friend," replied Tom Moore; "but ye're right in sayin' some one might be killed ef I mixed in. Those fellers dɵn't allow no interference in their little fun. The feller thet tries to play peacemaker must make his will fust. I'd as soon try to arrest a pack o' wolves as them rivermen when they're drunk an' ugly. They's only one man in creation 't I know of thet kin go up against that crowd an' not git hurt; an' he ain't here."

"Who is he? He must be a wonder, if they're as bad as you say."

"Parson Allen; he *is* a wonder," replied Tom. "He knows every mother's son of 'em, an' kin handle 'em like babies, drunk or sober; but they ain't nobody else kin go near 'em, an' he may be ten miles or more from here."

"But suppose they should kill some one?" persisted Lane.

"Wal, 'twouldn't be much loss, ef 'twas one o' themselves, an' they don't bother the citizens o' the place, ef the citizens don't interfere with them. The two teams fight it out between themselves, an' when one side licks, thet settles it, an' the victors stan' treat."

"Pete's turnin' the varmints out into the street,"

remarked Barney, pointing in the direction of the saloon.

As he spoke, the sound of shouts and curses was heard, and with a rush and a tumble the drunken, fighting crowd shot out of Pete's place into the street just ahead of the trio. Toques, smocks, boot-packs, heads, heels, and fists were mixed in savage *mêlée*. A heavy bottle was raised high in air and brought down with murderous force upon the head of a drunken brute. He went down like a polled ox. A rough boot-heel, reinforced with nails and calks, was planted ruthlessly in his face. The fight was more than usually fierce, and the opposing gangs seemed to be evenly matched.

"That is downright brutish," exclaimed Lane, turning away in disgust.

"Yep, it is unpleasant, but ye can't do nothin' to stop it, away out here in the lumber region," said Tom, glancing at the stranger in some surprise that a man of his appearance should be disturbed by a rivermen's fight. "One hundred or so able-bodied citizens would git the wust of it ef they interfered with them fighters, so we let 'em have it out in their own way. It's only when they git drunk thet they fight!"

"Look at that, Tom, look!" exclaimed Barney, suddenly. "Parson Allen's at them!"

As he spoke, a violent eruption seemed to be taking place in the dense crowd of struggling rivermen, and as the writhing mass split open in the middle, the sturdy figure of the backwoods minister emerged, dragging two of the combatants by the collar. Placing them beyond reach of each other, and speaking a few quick, low words that seemed to galvanize them to the spot, he sprang back into the *mêlée*. With astonishing strength and disregard of the flying fists, bottles, and stones, he grabbed two more of the brawlers and yanked them away from the mob. He spoke to no one at first except the men whom he had captured, and his words to them could not be heard above the shouts and curses of the fighters. Twice again he repeated his surprising assault upon the mob. Then, as the men began to realize who it was that was interfering in their row at the risk of his own life, a remarkable change took place. Some of the rivermen slunk away shamefacedly. Others seized those of their own party and compelled them to stop fighting. As the noise grew less, the minister was heard talking pleasantly, calling them "my boys," and telling them they must stop such "rough play" and save their prowess to wrestle with the logs on Monday. The fight was over, and the bruised and disabled were helped away almost before the three men who had been watching from a distance could realize what had happened.

"Wonderful!" exclaimed Jim Lane, at last.

"Yes," remarked Tom Moore; "thet's the man I jes' told ye about—the only man in the State of Michigan, or anywhere else for thet matter, who could a'done what ye seen jes' now."

CHAPTER XVI

JIM GYDE felt that he was indeed a new man. His statement to Sam had been no idle boast. He was not the Jim Gyde of a few years ago. All who knew him had seen the change, and now he realized it himself. A winter and spring of hard study, a summer of farming rendered more than usually strenuous by the effort to gain as much time as possible for work at his books, and then a full season of logging in Pete Murray's camp, had wrought wonders for the young man. His development surprised even the optimistic schoolmaster, who, having settled the question with his conscience, bent all his energies to the task of helping Jim to make up for some of his wasted time. Robert Allen, during his visits to Pete Murray's camp, noticed the transformation that was taking place in the young man and became greatly interested in him. An intimacy sprang up between them which gave the minister opportunity to arouse Jim's concern for the welfare of his soul as well as of his mind and body. His whole outlook on life was changed and broadened. In the steadfast, unflinching working out of his own salvation he tasted happiness for the first time in his life. He was worth something after all. He would count as a man among the best men of the woods. He would keep on as he had begun and be ready to step up to something higher whenever the chance presented itself. For the present season his work was almost finished. After the rollway had been broken and the

drive sent down the river, he would be free to go where
he pleased. And where would he please to go? Jim's
blood tingled as he thought of the one who was the inspiration and support of all his earnest efforts. The
schoolmaster? Ah, no! His word had roused him;
his faithful, patient help had led him on and encouraged
him; without him — but, there, why not admit truthfully that another face was before his eyes, another
voice in his ears, another purpose spurred him on.
The schoolmaster, bless him, was simply the way by
which Jim might reach that which he greatly coveted.
He had shown now what he could do. His performance thus far was eloquent of future possibilities.
Was it not time to claim his reward? Jim could admit
of no negative answer. His mind had been made up
for weeks that as soon as this season's work was done
and he had drawn his "stake," he would ask Axcy
Marthy to be his wife.

Pete Murray's logs were all in. He was always the
first to break camp. His example was an inspiration
to his men, and the enormous loads which came to the
rollway from his camp were the pride of his men and
the admiration of all others. Jim Gyde had just come
down from camp on Friday when he met Sam Hawkins.
He was staying with Jake Vogel while waiting for the
breaking of the rollway. Saturday and Sunday were
off days with nothing to do. Jim found almost before
the sun cleared the tops of the trees that this period of
waiting and suspense was going to be unendurable.
While actively engaged in the strenuous work of the
logging-camp he could possess his soul in patience, but
now there was nothing to distract his thoughts from
the one who had so long monopolized them. Why
should he wait, after all? Was not to-day, his day of

leisure, as good a time as any to lay claim to his great happiness? A peculiar weakness stole over him as he thought the momentous hour had come. The very act of deciding to do what most of all he desired to do, aroused, suddenly, a spirit of temporizing and procrastination which he resented even while he cherished it. Nevertheless, while the contest of his emotions and inclinations raged within him, he proceeded to make himself as presentable as possible, yielding to the dictates of some inner arbiter who advised him to take a walk down the river road toward Midland. It would do no harm, anyway, to walk past her house. If he should be so happy as to see her he would be well repaid. He need not say anything unless he wanted to.

As he approached Hal Marthy's farm, he caught sight of a tall, graceful figure which came down the driveway from the house and started up the road ahead of him in the direction of Midland. His pulses leaped into tumultuous action as he recognized Axcy. She was hurrying, and the fact roused him like a challenge. He could not let her escape. His long, rapid strides brought him up with her in a few moments. She greeted him with unfeigned cordiality and pleasure.

"Why, Jim! You *are* a stranger. I haven't seen you for more than six months. Are you back for good?"

"Murray broke camp yesterday, an' I came down to the Keg to wait till it's time to break the rollway. It's a big one. They count on doin' the job Monday," answered Jim, relieved, in spite of himself, that it was possible to talk at once on commonplace topics.

"I'm coming up to see it," declared Axcy, with enthusiasm. "I never do get tired of seeing that great pile of logs go rolling and tumbling down into the river, and you poor men scrambling out of the way. It's awfully dangerous—but it's exciting. Are you going to be down underneath again?"

"I s'pose so," said Jim. "They'll be a dozen or more of us down there. Say, Axcy, do you know how much I'll git for this season's work?"

"No—let me see—oh, maybe a hundred dollars," replied Axcy with some hesitation, not knowing whether Jim's industry at school had extended to his camp life. In other seasons he had earned scarcely half a full season's pay, because of his irregularity.

"Over two hundred dollars!" he announced proudly. "They's only two men in the camp thet'll draw more'n that."

"My! that's splendid," exclaimed Axcy. "You must have worked hard."

"I did," he admitted. "I'm always goin' to work hard after this. Some day I'll be a rich man."

The sturdy confidence in his tone did not wholly conceal a slight questioning, almost pleading, note which sounded strangely in Axcy's ears. She glanced quickly at him, but glanced still more quickly away when she found his eyes fixed on her face.

"That will be fine, won't it?" she replied, with an effort to appear unconcerned.

The breeze played with a stray lock of hair, blowing it now and then across her cheek. Jim watched it, fascinated, silent, greedy. Suddenly the fire in his heart flared up.

"Axcy," he said, hoarsely, "I love you!"

The girl started and caught her breath. "Oh! Jim, how you frightened me! If you do that again, I shan't let you walk with me," she exclaimed, with an uneasy laugh.

Jim ignored her interruption, and continued with a half-suppressed fierceness of desire:

"I love you! I want you. I want you for my wife!"

"Jim! Jim! Please don't," cried Axcy, facing him, genuinely frightened this time, and quick distress and pity gleaming in her eyes.

"Don't?" repeated Jim. "Does that mean you won't have me? Quick! Tell me, does it mean that?"

Axcy looked away and toyed nervously with a fold of her dress. It was hard to reply to such a big, passionate questioner, when the answer could only give him pain. But Jim would not wait.

"Answer me, for God's sake, Axcy! Don't you see I'm waitin'? Will you have me?"

"Jim! I can't, I can't!" moaned Axcy, cowering from him as if she feared a blow, and little realizing that with her simple words, "I can't," she was delivering a blow more cruel than any the young giant before her could give with all the strength of his brawny arm. Jim quivered and paled for an instant, but a dull red flush quickly flooded his face as he took up her words again.

"'Can't!' An' why not? Ain't I good enough? Haven't I stuck to schoolin', an' learned to read, an' write, an' figger? Haven't I give up drinkin', an' deviltry, an' fightin', 'cept when I can't help it? Haven't I been tryin' for more'n a year to be a clean man, an' worth somethin'? Why? All 'cause I wanted you, an' wanted to make myself good enough for you—though partly, I'll allow, 'twas to please Schoolmaster Waters. If I ain't good enough yet, I'll keep on, if you'll——"

15

"Don't Jim! It isn't that. You are good enough, but—I—I——"

She could not go on, neither could she conceal the blush that had colored her cheeks when Jim mentioned the schoolmaster's name. The young man had noticed it, but did not at once connect it with its cause. His whole attention, for the moment, was on the question and her reply. Now he stood regarding her in perplexity and bitter disappointment.

"Then why can't you, if it isn't that? Do you understand? I love you. I must have you. I've been lookin' forrard, an' plannin', eager, but keepin' quiet, an' eatin' my heart out, too long to take any such answer as that. Why can't you? You don't mean it, Axcy; you're teasin' me."

"No, Jim, I wouldn't do that," said Axcy, gently, recovering her self-control. "I like you, Jim. You've made me respect you, too, this last year. We've been good friends. Can't we keep on being friends?"

"I want love! I want a wife!" cried Jim, passionately. "Do you s'pose I could ever look at you or talk to you without thinkin' of that? Why can't you give me what I want?"

"Because, Jim—because—it isn't mine to give," said Axcy in a very low tone, while Jim bent toward her in his eagerness. As the meaning of her words forced itself into his brain, he straightened up with a gasp.

"Oh—h!" he said, and the word was a groan. For a moment he stood looking at the girl he had hoped to make his partner and his inspiration in the struggle for a better, broader, nobler life upon which he had entered. The mainspring of his ambition and purpose seemed broken in him. A heaviness settled upon him, and the light of day grew dim. Then his square jaws closed tighter, and without a word he turned on his heel and strode away. He chose no direction. He knew not where to go—only to be alone, where none could see his hurt. Pity he dreaded. Even sympathy he shunned. No one should know, because no one could help him. No one? A thought came unbidden of one who understood him, and who might know just how to deal with this trouble. Perhaps if he went to the schoolmaster—another thought flashed upon his mind and drove all else away. He stopped suddenly. The next instant he was hastening back to the girl who had sunk down on the bank by the roadside, and, with her face in the hollow of her arm, was finding a woman's relief from the strain and pain of the episode just passed. Jim stood before her.

"Axcy, look up!" he said, harshly.

She lifted two startled, tear-dimmed eyes and looked at the young man.

"Tell me, Axcy, is it him—the schoolmaster?" he panted.

The tell-tale blush was hidden quickly as the girl's face went down again into the hollow of her arm. She said not a word, but a movement of her head gave an affirmative reply only too plainly understood by the unhappy man.

"Him!" he whispered through clenched jaws, as he turned away again from the sobbing girl. "Him! who pretended to be my best friend! Him! who's been tellin' me how much there was for me in life if I'd make myself worthy of it. And now he's robbed me of the *only* thing I want—oh—curse him!" A fierce oath burst from his lips, and he brought his great clenched fist to his shoulder and thrust it down again in impotent rage. So this was his reward for all his hard work; this was the "brother's help" which had been given him. He would not have dreamed that Waters could be so false. All these months, while he had worked and studied to make himself worthy of the girl of his choice, the schoolmaster had been making love to her behind his back, thought Jim, even after he had told him of his own great love.

"What a fool I was!" he muttered, as he pushed on blindly along the road. "Why didn't I see it? Why did I wait so long?"

He remembered the events of that last winter in school as if it had been yesterday. The reason for the schoolmaster's strange behavior when Jim first told him of his hope with regard to Axcy was plain now. Why hadn't he suspected it then? He tried to think of any other significant words or acts, but could recall nothing else that might have roused his suspicion. That was the worst of it. He took it for granted that Waters, put on his guard from the very beginning, had governed himself accordingly and had taken unfair advantage of his absence. It seemed like tearing out his very heart-strings to believe the man guilty of such baseness; yet Axcy had confessed the truth. Jim had lost his love and his friend at the same moment. What was there left for him now? He tumbled on in the direction of Midland, though he was unconscious of time or place. The sound of hurried steps behind him suddenly brought him to a halt, and Axcy stood again before him, breathless, panting, her bonnet off, and her hair flying loose about her flushed face.

"Oh, Jim—!" she cried brokenly, "Jim, please— *please* don't tell him!"

The young man gazed at her dumfounded.

"What—who?" he asked, at length.

"You know; what I told you. Oh, why did I say it? You forced me to. Please—promise me, Jim, that you won't tell him."

"I don't understand," stammered Jim. "Do you mean that I ain't to tell the schoolmaster thet you— you—love him, an' so can't hev me? Is thet what you mean?"

Axcy nodded her head and tried to hide her face from Jim's searching gaze.

"Why! don't he know it already?" exclaimed the unhappy fellow.

"I never told him—nor anybody, before," murmured the girl.

"Didn't he never ask you?" demanded Jim, almost fiercely.

Axcy shook her head.

"An' didn't he never tell you he loved you?" cried Jim, still more imperatively.

Another shake of the beautiful bowed head, and then the poor girl began to sob hysterically.

"He hasn't yet," she faltered, "but—oh, please, Jim, don't ask me any more, and please don't tell him."

For a moment Jim made no reply. He was weighing the new admissions and readjusting his verdict on the schoolmaster's conduct.

"I'll not tell him," he said, at length. "He'll find out soon enough for himself if he don't know already, but," he went on passionately, "he can't care for you as much as I do, Axcy. It seems like I couldn't live without you, now, after lovin' you, an' waitin' for you so long. You say he never asked you—never spoke to you? What right has he, then, to keep you away from me? Don't you think you could care for me if you tried—a little? I'll wait as long as you say. Won't you try, Axcy?—I love you so!"

He waited, but no reply came from the sobbing girl whose face was persistently turned from him. He took a step nearer and laid his hand on her arm.

"Axcy!"

There was a world of longing and entreaty in his voice as he spoke her name. Her sobbing became audible. She was so sorry for Jim, but she wished he wouldn't torture himself and her any longer. His cause was hopeless.

"I can't," she said again. She felt his hand drop from her arm, and heard his footsteps growing fainter and fainter. When she looked up again she was alone in the road half a mile from her home.

CHAPTER XVII

THE sun had not begun to redden the east when Barney was up and busy with his Monday morning chores. Farmer Hawkins expected nothing of him this morning, but Barney was unwilling to leave any of his ordinary tasks to Uncle Si, so he clipped an hour from his usual sleeping time, and by sunrise was ready to start for the river where the great rollway was to be broken up and its contents started down the swollen current.

As he left the house, he met Norine Maloney running up the road.

"Good mornin', an' what brings ye here, like a lark, with the sunrise, darlint?" exclaimed Barney, as he opened wide his brawny arms, caught the breathless girl, and administered a hearty salutation. She squirmed out of her prison, shook the tumbled hair back from her blushing face, and cried:

"Oh, Barney!"

"I am that same," replied the young farmer.

"Barney, *please* don't go down under the rollway this morning. I was afraid I should not catch you before you went, so I ran all the way here." Norine stopped short for want of breath.

"Not help break the rollway, is it, darlint? An' why shouldn't I do it? They'll be nadin' all the men they kin git fer the job, an' I promised to help. I'm jes' goin' down now, Norine. What did ye want me to do?"

"Oh, Barney, I had such a horrid dream last night. I saw you down in the river, and the logs had just started to roll. You looked so happy and seemed to be looking up at me. All of a sudden somebody gave you a push, and you fell into the water, and the logs came rolling down, down, down on you by the hundreds and thousands! I screamed and tried to look away, but I couldn't. I had to keep looking, and the logs kept rolling, and rolling, as though they would never stop. If I shut my eyes I can see them now. Really, Barney, you mustn't go down. I can't let you."

"Faith, darlint, 'twas only a drame, an' drames go by opposites, ye know. I must help, 'cause I promised to, an' I couldn't be backin' out now. Ye wouldn't have me tell any o' the b'ys thet it war on account of a drame?"

"But I am sure something will happen, Barney. I have a presentiment. Can't you stay away—for my sake?"

Barney was sorely puzzled, and he stood still in the road and scratched his head several minutes before answering. At length he looked around and exclaimed with a kind of desperation:

"Where's thet varmint Sam Hawkins an' his three good-fer-nothin' chums? Bring 'em on, the hull four of 'em, an' let me lick 'em all togither fer insultin' Miss Norine Maloney. Let me *do* somethin'—anythin' fer this little swateheart! Begorra, what wouldn't I do fer ye, darlint; but ye see the difficulty is, ye want me to do *nothin'*. Not bein' used to thet kind o' work, I don't know how to do it. Sure, Norine, ye wouldn't hev me begin sarvin' ye by shirkin', an' loafin', an' breakin' me word? I tell ye what, darlint; come to the river with me an' kape yer swate eyes on me while

I'm at work, an' ye'll be my protictin' angel, so ye will."

Without waiting for any reply to his harangue, or for any further protest, Barney took Norine by the hand, and together they hastened on toward Red-Keg and the rollway.

Many were there before them, and others came later. Some were there to work and risk their lives. Others came only to look on, and cheer if need be. Pete's tavern was deserted, even by the roughest of the river element, for this was an occasion when cool heads and steady nerves were all-important.

The rollway had reached enormous proportions. The contour of the river at this point was particularly favorable for constructing and handling a large rollway, and for this reason had been chosen by the railroad company and other large operators, who brought their logs here from distant points, as the nearest available outlet to the Eastern markets. Many small operators had banked their logs at other points farther up the river to save the time and labor of toting them to Red-Keg. Here, however, where the main rollway was always constructed, the Tittabawassee formed a crescent about half a mile long, the village lying within the crescent. The shore on this side was high and precipitous. On the opposite side, away from the village, the land was so low that in the spring the river overflowed the bank and covered a wide strip of mud flats. Piles were driven along this shore and immense boom logs fastened to them with chains to define the channel of the river and keep the logs from floating over upon the flats. About half a mile below Red-Keg the lowlands came to an end, and the river, with a sharp bend away from the crescent, flowed between high banks on either side. At this point the drivers had work to keep the logs from jamming. It was the only really difficult place on the river, and the watchfulness and agility of the rivermen could be counted on to prevent trouble even at this point in all ordinary conditions. To lessen the probability of choking this bend with too great a rush of logs at one time, the expedient had recently been adopted of breaking the rollway in two or three sections, beginning at the lower end, the contour of the bank rendering this feasible.

The great rollway now reached from end to end of the crescent, and extended half-way across the river to the opposite booms. The top was sixty feet above the swollen stream. It had been building all through the winter, and layers of snow and ice deposited by the season's storms helped to cement the massive logs together. Along the base, the turbulent water, augmented by heavy rains and melting snow, swept on with growing force, whirling against the edge of the rollway, and gurgling and hissing through the crevices with an impatient, taunting call to the sleeping giant to awake and join in a wild revel.

Pete Murray, Andrew Green, John Maloney, and the others who were responsible for the affair had chosen the time for breaking the rollway with that unerring precision which comes only from long experience and constant alertness. The freshet was approaching its height. In three more days the waters would begin to subside; but then the great drive of logs would be well on its way to the booms at Saginaw and below.

Crowds from the surrounding district and from Midland filled Red-Keg. Even Joseph Waters, whose school was represented in the force of workers by more than a few sturdy fellows, gave the remainder of his pupils a holiday, that he, and some of them, might see the rollway broken. Robert Allen, the minister, who, although a skilled logger, made no claim to proficiency as a riverman, joined Waters as a spectator.

Gossip was rife concerning the plight of old Hezekiah Bloag, whose logs were in a fair way to be stranded up on the Tobacco River, above the village of Sixteen. He had always been noted for his close-fisted habits and his meanness to the men in his camp. Only the worst class of loggers would work for him. This season he had exceeded the limits of their endurance, and his entire camp had mutinied and refused to complete the work until he paid them a certain amount. He stood out obstinately against their demands, while the men employed their idleness by drinking and fighting. When Bloag saw the freshet coming and tried to compromise with his men, preparatory to eventually yielding, they were too drunk and ugly to listen to him, and thus the matter stood when the time came to break the rollway. Very little of Bloag's cutting had come to hand, and very little sympathy was expressed by his neighbors, nearly all of whom had suffered at one time or another from the old man's meanness.

As one result of Bloag's hang-up, "Red" Lampheer, his foreman this year, was absent from the breaking of the rollway. His dare-devil recklessness usually made him a conspicuous figure on the river. With such men as Barney O'Boyle, Jim Gyde, "Babe" Strander, Ashbel Fair, Tom Moore, Ned Blakely, and scores of others, ready to the call, however, the daring but quarrelsome Lampheer and his gang were not sorely missed.

Andrew Green and Pete Murray rounded up the men and, dividing them into the various gangs, despatched them to their places. A dozen expert rollway breakers were assigned to the lower section of the huge rollway which was to be released first. Barney gave Norine's hand an encouraging squeeze, and, grasping his peavy, mounted the towering pile of logs with the others of the gang. Jim Gyde was close to him. Quickly they disappeared over the brink of the rollway and began the perilous descent to the water's edge. The assembled crowd could only hold its breath and watch for the outcome.

Barney went over near the middle of the section, the most forbidding and dangerous point of all. As his hat disappeared from sight, a little woman pressed her way through the crowd, and, standing as near to the edge as was safe, fixed her eyes anxiously on the spot where her lover was last seen.

Minutes seemed like hours. The spectators were growing nervous. The suspense to Norine was almost unbearable. She clasped her hands tightly and breathed a prayer. Then she waited as patiently as she could. Her eyes never wandered for an instant from the spot where Barney had disappeared. She seemed to see again the frightful dream, and the logs rolling down, down, down, upon the man she loved. None of the spectators could see the workmen, and this made the strain of suspense more intense.

Soon a shout was heard from below, and the watchers knew that the crisis was at hand. As some huge monster, disturbed in sleep, stirs, yawns, and then is still again, a rumbling was heard through the great pile, low and ominous. The mass of logs began to move, slowly and with lazy deliberation apparently, and then it stopped. The right log or logs had not been released. There was another wait. Suddenly the great mass moved again. This time there was no uncertainty, no hesitation. Thousands of the foremost logs went tumbling and rolling down, a mighty, rushing avalanche, into the swollen river. The rollway was broken.

All eyes were strained to catch sight of the men who were risking their lives in the raging current below, seemingly at the mercy of the wild deluge they had let loose. As the logs went tumbling down, and the huge pile began to melt away into the rushing stream, the men were seen to rise and leap with marvellous agility and rapidity from log to log until they reached the top. A shout of triumph rang from the throats of the assembled throng on the shore, because of the success and bravery of these men; but Norine shivered, and sought out Axcy and Lettie, that their companionship might take her mind away from her troublesome dream. When she looked again down into the river, she saw Barney hard at work with his peavy urging on the rolling logs into the foaming current. Near him, engaged in the same work, was Jim Gyde.

It was now time for the "drivers" to take their places. These men mount the logs as they are floating down the stream and keep them moving. Experts are needed for this work, also, and it is only a shade less dangerous than breaking the rollway. With high boots, having calks in the soles to prevent slipping, and with peavy in hand, these men skip from log to log, and wherever a tendency to "jam" is observed they seek out the offending log, straighten it around, and soon the mass is again moving. Drivers are stationed, also, at points along the river, wherever the formation of the banks makes jamming liable, and there they watch the passing stream of logs like hawks, ready to dart out and pounce upon any one which threatens trouble.

The first break loosened and sent down into the stream many thousands of logs and kept a full force of drivers busy.   There were, however, two more sections of the rollway with nearly twice as many more logs to be released and cared for.   The greatest disadvantage of breaking the rollway in sections was that a larger number of men were required.

"Now's the time we could be usin' old Bloag's gang," remarked Pete Murray to Lettie's father, as he began assigning the remaining men to their places and realized that the supply would be hardly sufficient.

"Call for more volunteers.   There must be some men able to lend a hand in this crowd," said Green.

A dozen additional men were quickly hunted out. Among them, Jim Lane offered himself.   Neither Green nor Murray had ever seen him before, and they hesitated.

"Are ye shantyman, or riverman, or what?" asked Murray.   "Ever break a rollway before?"

"No—not exactly," admitted Lane; "but I'm willing to begin.   Always have to begin sometime, you know. I'm something of an acrobat, and I've ridden floating logs before.   Guess I can help juggle these without breaking my neck."

"Wall, ye've got nerve, an' mebbe ye can.   Here's a peavy; git out there where ye see them two, yonder," pointing to where Barney and Jim Gyde were at work; "but, begorra, yer blood is on yer own head ef ye git kilt."

Lane hastened out upon the logs with an alacrity which surprised those who thought he was going to almost certain death, and more than one protest was heard among the onlookers; but Murray shook his head and grinned. "Take a fool fer luck," he said; "guess he'll pull through."

"His boots ain't calked!" exclaimed one man. "He can't stand on them logs. Call him back an' make him fix his boots, anyhow;" but it was too late, for Lane was already out of hearing.

Barney and Jim Gyde greeted the newcomer with some surprise and suspicion. Barney remembered what Tom Moore had told him of the stranger's conversation with Sam Hawkins, and of Sam's expressed hope that Barney would be killed in the rollway. If this was a plot he would take care not to be caught napping, and he felt conscious that among the moving logs on the river the advantage was his; therefore when the stranger asked him what he could do to help, Barney replied, shortly:

"Faith, if ye'll moind yerself, an' kape right-side-up, I'll wrastle the logs."

Lane said nothing, but watched the young Irishman closely, and when the opportunity came, assisted with a skill and display of muscle which commanded Barney's admiration.

"Ye're right handy fer a beginner," he remarked, finally; "but moind ye kape back by the boom logs when we let this next rollway down."

It required but a few minutes to start the pile of logs moving a second time. As before, they moved almost imperceptibly at first, but soon it seemed as if every log were a living thing, or that some great up-heaval was taking place and toying with the heap as a child would play with a handful of jackstraws.

It was time for the men to appear at the top, and all but Barney and Lane had scrambled into safety. Suddenly a cry of alarm rang out from below, and a responsive cry of horror came from the crowd of spectators on the shore. As the face of the rollway melted away and a view of the river was disclosed, Jim Lane and Barney O'Boyle were seen struggling in the water near the boom logs on the other side, while the avalanche from the rollway was rushing and heaving around them. Barney was evidently trying to help the stranger, who seemed hurt or exhausted. It looked as if in another moment or two both would surely be overwhelmed and crushed to death. The spectators on shore were paralyzed with horror—all but one.

A little woman with pale face and flying hair dashed from the crowd, and before any one could detain her, she was out on the writhing and rolling logs. She skipped from log to log like a fairy. Fear and love gave her wings. Reaching the edge of the rollway, which was rapidly melting away beneath her, she looked out upon the sea of logs, and for an instant her heart stood still. By a miracle she kept her feet that brief instant as she hesitated. What could she do? Could she do anything? A sense of her helplessness and of the almost certain death which now threatened her, as well as her lover, flashed through her mind, when, suddenly, a pair of strong arms seized her and bore her back toward the shore.

The schoolmaster, thrusting Robert Allen aside, had followed her with scarcely the loss of a second of time. He had not been quite so fleet of foot on the rolling logs; but he had been as heedless of danger, and her instant of hesitation had enabled him to catch her.

"Come back! You'll be killed! Don't you see Jim's gone to help Barney?" cried Waters, as he struggled back with the now almost helpless girl over the short but tortuous space between them and the shore.

A score of hands were outstretched to help. It seemed to Waters that he would never reach them. With incredible good fortune he had kept up thus far, springing from log to log as they vanished under his feet like a treadmill. Parson Allen had procured a rope and was just throwing it to him. What good would that do, he wondered, since both hands were busy holding Norine and maintaining his balance? The bank was almost reached—only a few feet farther. He pushed Norine before him. A cheer went up—too soon. His foot slipped, and in an instant he was lying prone on the logs and being carried down with the rolling mass. Norine fell at the same time, but near enough to the minister's outstretched hands to be dragged safely ashore.

Waters had fallen face downward across the logs in such a way that for a while his body remained at right angles to them and thus stayed on top of the rolling mass; but he was absolutely helpless.

At any instant his arms or legs were liable to be caught, and he would then be quickly dragged under and crushed. Suddenly the movement in the rollway became slower, and Waters struggled to regain his feet.

As he did so, a heavy log rolled upon one leg and pinned him down. Then the whole mass stopped as though unwilling to complete the tragedy it had begun.

The excitement caused by Norine's sudden dash and the schoolmaster's desperate plight had for the moment diverted attention from Barney and the stranger known as Jim Lane. Before help had reached them in the person of Jim Gyde, Barney had crawled out upon the boom logs and pulled Lane after him, with nothing worse than a ducking and a fright to show for his first experience with a rollway. Barney and Jim Gyde

16

quickly made their way to shore with the exhausted and crestfallen novice, only to find that a more serious disaster was threatening at that very instant.

"I'll have a word with you, Mr.—Lane, if ye plase, when we git through with this," said Barney, as he left the volunteer riverman and hurried toward the spot where Norine was the centre of an excited crowd.

"I'll be here," called Lane, following him, in spite of his wet clothes, to see what had happened.

Jim Gyde was there, already, striding up and down the bank like a madman. A fierce look of exultation blazed in his eyes when he caught sight of the schoolmaster half-way out from the shore and pinned down among the logs.

"He's a dead man the minute the logs start to roll again!" he cried. "Nothin' on earth can save him. What's the matter with them logs anyway? They're only half down. Why don't they roll?—why don't they roll?"

The bystanders stared at Jim in astonishment.

"Looks like ye're in a hurry for him to get killed, Bub," remarked old Doctor Landseer, whose son was with the drivers down the river.

"Sure, you're crazy, Jim!" exclaimed Barney. "We'll have him out o' that in two shakes of a stick. We kin go down there, the two of us, an' pull him out in no time."

"Shet up, you fool!" yelled Jim. "The minute you step on them logs down there, they'll roll again. Don't you see? They're jest hangin' now. What stopped 'em, anyhow? It can't be done. Nothin' can be done. Tech them logs, an' the schoolmaster an' us, too, will be rolled into jelly."

Jim swung his great arms in a frenzy of excitement,

and glared around at the crowd as if daring any one to contradict him.

"Bedad, I'm afraid ye're right; but we'll have a try at it, anyhow," declared Barney, as he examined the sloping bank of logs some hundred feet distant where Waters lay waiting for the help which he never doubted would come.

Ned Blakely, muddy, panting, dashed into the group.

"It's jammed! It's jammed!" he shouted. "Down by the bend—basswood-tree undermined by current— fell into river—caught the logs like fish in a net—river backin' up fast."

"Thet's what stopped the logs from rollin'," explained old Landseer, but nobody listened.

"The water's backin' up!" cried Jim again. "Soon 'twill lift these 'ere logs an' start 'em goin' again. The man that goes down there now is a——"

"Hero," spoke a quiet voice close behind Jim.

The young man whirled around, but no one acknowledged the interruption. Old Doctor Landseer, Jim Lane, in his wet clothes, and others were pressing upon him. Suddenly his eyes fell upon a little group which he had not noticed before. Norine was there, and Lettie Green, white and trembling—and there was another, whose face was turned first to him and then to the logs below the bank. An unspeakable agony and appeal was in those eyes; her hands were clasped, and she was leaning forward in breathless suspense for the issue of the dispute which seemed to her so strange at such a time. Jim staggered as from a blow. Hardly more than a moment had passed since he and Barney had come to the spot, yet it seemed as if a lifetime had rushed by. He shuddered as he glanced from Axcy to the schoolmaster. What was he doing?

Great God! Was he trying to murder the man who had given him the hand of a brother—who had been faithful to him even to the point of——?

"Here, Parson Allen! What are you doin' with that rope? I tell you it's impossible. Don't you see his foot's caught? What good is that? Git out o' the way, all of you! Give me that rope!"

Sweeping the crowd aside, and snatching the rope from the minister, who, regardless of Jim's wild talk, had been actively preparing to rescue Waters if he could, Jim sprang with his peavy down the bank and out upon the rollway. Before the spectators had time to realize what was taking place, he had fastened one end of the rope under the schoolmaster's arm and thrown the other end to the bank, where it was seized by the minister and Barney. Then with his peavy Jim sought to pry up the log which was pressing upon Waters. One end of it was under two other logs, and he could not budge it until they were removed. Without a moment's hesitation he drove his peavy into the green pine, and with a powerful twist sent one after another of the logs tumbling down toward the jam that now covered the river. Quickly he sprang to the great log which had caused the trouble, and, with a supreme output of strength, lifted it clear from its place, and Waters was instantly released. The next log above it slipped at once into the opening; another followed, then another, then more—scores—hundreds—the rollway was in motion again. Jim gazed at the form of the schoolmaster being drawn up out of harm's way. He ought to have watched his own footing. His eyes wandered to a group of faces on the bank—to one face. He ought to have been leaping nimbly from log to log.

The rollway could not go down very far now because of the jam. When it settled once more into its temporary quiet, Barney and others went out and picked up Jim Gyde's bruised and broken body and brought it tenderly to shore. Life was still in it—for a little while. The minister silently waved back the crowd that pressed around, while old Doctor Landseer made a hasty examination, shaking his head gravely as he did so. Jim turned his eyes wearily from one to another and then looked into Allen's face. The minister stooped closer, and listened.

"The schoolmaster," whispered Jim.

Waters, with his broken leg, was brought to Jim's side and placed in a reclining posture so that he could be as near as possible to the dying man. He grasped Jim's hand; their eyes met and looked into each other's soul. Waters could not speak for the choking in his throat. Jim's lips moved, and Waters bent nearer.

"You were true to me—in—everythin'?" asked Jim, painfully.

"Yes, Jim—in everything; but, oh, Jim! you've given——"

"It's all right, then," whispered Jim again; "an' she—" He stopped, and the gray began to creep into his face. "No, I won't say it," he added, presently. "You'll find out—Good-by."

"Good-by, Jim, you noble fellow—you hero—oh, it was too much, Jim!" said Waters, with a sob.

Jim smiled and turned from Waters to the minister. The latter motioned to Barney, and he helped the schoolmaster away, and spoke a quiet word to one and another of the crowd. In a moment Jim Gyde and the backwoods minister were left alone together. The young lumberman had found his "gold" at last. It was almost within his grasp, and it gleamed before his dimming eyes in the form of a crown.

Toward evening, after the jam had been loosened, and the remainder of the rollway broken, and the various gangs of drivers and rear-enders had the entire mass of logs under control, Barney returned to the village in search of Jim Lane. He found him in front of Pete's place explaining for the twentieth time to the gossips that came and went that he had retreated to the boom logs in the river, just as Barney had ordered him to do, but that the shock and upheaval caused by the downward rush of the second section of the rollway had thrown him off his feet, and that Barney, who had sprung at once to his rescue, had been pulled into the water in the effort to drag him up upon the boom logs.

"One moment, if ye plase, Mr.—Lane," said Barney, pushing his way into the group.

"Certainly; excuse me, gentlemen, I must speak with Mr. O'Boyle alone," and the man drew Barney away from the inquisitive idlers.

"Now, sir, Mr. Jim Lane, as ye call yerself, tell me what ye mane by follerin' me out onto the rollway," demanded Barney. "What divil's job were ye hatchin' up with Sam Hawkins the other night? What are ye doin' here with false whiskers? Begorra, who on airth *are* ye, anyhow?"

The stranger hesitated before answering, and eyed Barney contemplatively.

"Quite a batch of questions, and rather pointed; but I can't say that I blame you, considering all the circumstances. To begin with, I had reason to suspect, very good reason, as I thought, though it turned out to be based on a sad misunderstanding—that some one working near you had designs on your—well, we may say, life. I know now that the overtures made to him must have been as unsuccessful as similar ones made to me; but he was an utter stranger to me. I didn't know then that he was a hero."

"Jim Gyde! Ye mane to say—?" began Barney in great astonishment.

"Well, perhaps I didn't mean to say anything definite. We'll let that pass. It was rash for a 'tenderfoot' like me to venture on the rollway, I suppose. I yielded to an impulse, and for the moment I imagined —but we'll let that pass, too; likewise the 'job' you say I was hatching up with one Sam Hawkins. As to the—er—little additions to my hirsute adornment— well, that matter may as well join the others in retirement. My name—is Jim Lane. That is not true, but what's in a name? Perhaps this will do in place of one."

The queer stranger suddenly unbuttoned his shirt front, turned back one side, and revealed something fastened to it that caused Barney to stare in still greater astonishment. Quickly buttoning his shirt front again, the man continued:

"I'll ask you to say nothing to any one about that. I have, by the way, some news for you from Belfast, and if——"

"Belfast, did ye say?" interrupted Barney, excitedly. "Howly Saints! That same is where I came from, an' Miss Norine, too. An' ye have news from there, is it? Faith, I'm dyin' to hear it."

"Call in at Pete's place to-morrow evening about this time, and meanwhile remember that you don't know any more than any one else about Jim Lane."

Barney returned to the Hawkins farm with curiosity, wonder, and anxiety tugging at his heart. He could hardly wait until the time came to talk with the stranger at Pete's saloon. Early the following evening he repaired to the appointed place, only to find that "Jim Lane" had disappeared from Red-Keg, and no one knew where or when he had gone.

CHAPTER XVIII

LATE Wednesday afternoon, two days after the breaking of the rollway, a group of Red-Keggers was gathered in Jake Vogel's store talking over the funeral of Jim Gyde, which had been held that afternoon in Midland. Several of the party, including Jake himself, had just returned and stopped for a few minutes' gossip at the store before going home to supper.

"'Tain't many of us'll have two parsons to our fun'ral," remarked Ned Blakely, as he dusted off the top of a sugar barrel with his handkerchief so that he could sit down without soiling his best black suit.

"'Twant none too good fer Jim," said Vogel. "He deserved the big crowd, an' the two parsons, an' the wreaths, an' singin', an' all; though as ter the parsons, it couldn't a bin any ways else. Old Bill Gyde is one o' the pillers o' the church in Midland, an' o' course he had ter hev thet little Parson Hayward o' hisen. Our own Elder Allen went cause he's the only parson Jim ever had, an' you couldn't no more kep' him away than nothin'. They say he felt wuss over Jim than the old man did himself."

"Shouldn't wonder," declared Bob Landseer. "They wasn't much love lost 'tween Jim an' the old man. The boy was brung up on a stick till he got too big for it, an' the stick never had no taffy 'long with it. I hear thet Schoolmaster Waters is more cut up than anybody, though, an' fretted hisself near sick cause he couldn't git up an' go to the funeral."

"He has cause enough ter feel cut up," replied Blakely, "seein' es Jim got kilt savin' his life; but there's somebody else feels es bad es the schoolmaster, an' mebbe worse, ef what my Jenny tells me is true."

"Who's that?" asked several at once.

"Axcy Marthy," announced Blakely with significant emphasis, and the expression of one who has sprung a sensation.

"How's that? What's she got to do with it? They warn't engaged, war they?" asked the others, with satisfactory display of curiosity.

"No, they warn't; thet's jest it. She refused him, an' now she thinks he wasn't hisself on Monday on thet account, or he wouldn't a-gone down after savin' the schoolmaster. More'n that, they say she's sweet on Waters, an' thet Jim knew it when he went out on the rollway to pull him out o' the jaws o' death. Ef it's true, an' I don't doubt it fer a minute, Jim Gyde was a braver man than any of us knew."

"Amen! He certainly was," exclaimed Dan Underhill; "but I don't see the need of Axcy blamin' herself at all. It was all the fault of that pesky stranger, Lane, who had no business on the river. The whole thing started with him. What did he go out there for, anyhow, an' where in blazes is he now? He skipped out of town as suddenly as he skipped in."

"Ye might ask Barney about that," suggested Arch Fellows. "Him an' the stranger went off talkin' together by theirselves Monday evenin', ef I remember right."

"Barney don't know no more'n you or I do," declared Jake Vogel with some heat. "He yanked the stranger away to ask him jest the same questions you been askin' now. Lane put him off till the next day, an' then skipped. I saw Barney last night when he come down to see the fellow, an' Barney was disgusted clean through when he found out the chap had gone."

"Guess he had enough o' life in this region, after bein' near chawed up in the rollway," suggested Blakely.

"Likely he was afraid o' bein' locked up fer causin' the death o' Jim Gyde," said Landseer. "But he seemed ter take sech an interest in local happenings, he might o' took the chance an' stayed ter help put up Ros's new house. 'Twould only kept him here a week longer, an' a house-raisin' is es much fun es breakin' a rollway, an' less risk."

"Oh, let him go," exclaimed Vogel. "Ros will hev all the help he can take care of. Fer my part, I'm glad the close-mouthed stranger's gone. I jest see Barney, an' Farmer Hawkins, and Norine Maloney drive past on the way home from Jim's funeral. It's supper-time, an' I'm goin' in the house."

With this gentle hint, the company dispersed to continue their comments and speculations at their own tea-tables.

During the same afternoon a different discussion was taking place in Pete's saloon. Sam Hawkins and Billy Axford were in private consultation with Pete concerning the extra drain which had been made upon his supplies during the past week and the urgent need for replenishment. Pete was the only person outside of the Invincibles themselves who was kept informed of their business progress, and all other patrons of the "Mystic Brand" either procured their supply direct from him, or received from him the tip as to the right spot to find a cache in the woods. Even Pete was kept in ignorance of the location of the spring from which the

contraband liquid flowed, and he was quite content to
have it so.

While Pete and the two Invincibles were discussing
arrangements for filling his own barrel, and meeting
certain outside demands, Red Lampheer swaggered
noisily into the barroom and called for Pete. Ignoring
the presence of Sam and Billy, he made known the
fact that his crew up at Old Bloag's camp on the Tobacco was "stranded high an' dry," having exhausted
their own stuff and mopped up the last drop of the real
article in Sixteen; consequently he had been vociferously requested to "go down to Pete's an' bring up an
ocean or two ter set the gang afloat."

Pete winked at Sam and told Red that he could only
let him have a couple of demijohns at once, but that
in a day or two he would see that he got all he wanted.

"A couple of demijohns!" cried Lampheer, with a
volley of backwoods oaths. "D'ye think the boys
wan' ter make fools o' their mouths? They ain't 'nuff
in a couple o' demijohns ter give 'em all a smell. They'll
run me outer camp."

"Can't help it; stock's low," replied Pete, indiffer-
ently. "Might let ye hev three ef ye're in such a bad
way; but thet'll hev ter do ye till the day after termor-
rer. How are ye comin' on with ole man Bloag?"

"Nohow—may the devil roast him!" exclaimed
Lampheer. "The ole skinflint ain't ponyin' up a cent.
His logs is layin' on the skids an' in the woods, an' he
can't git 'em down the river this year, nohow; so he
says he'll keep the crew in camp an' not pay 'em a cent
till every log is barked to save 'em from the worms.
The boys ain't ready ter give in yet, an' the ole man's
logs can rot till they's skatin' in hell for all I care.
We'll see our money 'fore we bark a log."

"What ef he should cut off yer grub?" asked Pete.

"He's too smart fer thet. He knows we all 'd hev ter quit then fer sure, an' his logs wouldn't be wuth a cent. He couldn't git no other gang ter tech 'em ef he druv us away owin' our season's stakes. He reckons we'll come crawlin' to him in a few days axin' his pardin'; but he's missed his tally there. We're layin' ter wait till after the dance at Sixteen; then we'll tell the ole fool ef he don't pony up we'll skip an' leave his logs ter the worms, an' git the law onter him."

"What's the dance at Sixteen got to do with you all an' ole Bloag?" inquired Pete; and Sam began at the same time to show a lively interest in the conversation.

"What's it got ter do with us? Well, thet's a cool one! Don't ye reckon we lay out ter git an invite ter thet 'ere dance?" cried Lampheer, indignantly.

"Oh, like enough ye do," sneered Pete; "but I ain't heard any one say es how ole Bloag's gang o' shanty-men was wanted ter the dance."

Red Lampheer let out a yell of rage and a string of profanity as he demanded to know "why in hell he an' the boys warn't wanted."

"Mebbe thet's jest the place ye are wanted in; but I was talkin' of the dance. Ye know it's them as lives in these parts an' behaves themselves respectable who gits invites ter the dance. They'll be three or four boys ter every gal, anyhow, an' the ballroom ain't no place fer a big crowd. No offense, o' course," added Pete in a conciliatory tone. "I ain't never had an invite myself."

"Well, ye might es well tell the committee thet me an' the boys 'll git invites, or they'll be trouble," asserted Red, threateningly.

"Oh, come now, ye wouldn't push yer drive in where

ye're not wanted," urged Pete, more for the sake of argument than with a desire to preserve peace.

"Thet's what we'll do ef they try to give us a throw down," insisted Red; "so ef they want ter save trouble, let 'em send along the invites."

Sam had been listening with growing satisfaction. Things seemed to be shaping just as he would have them. Perhaps a word in season might help to bring matters to a head. He sauntered up to the bar and asked Lampheer to have one with him.

"You are dead right about the dance," he said, confidentially. "It would be an outrage not to send you invitations, don't you know. You see, the whole trouble is with the management. Barney O'Boyle is bossing the whole thing this year, and he has the swelled head. He thinks he's better than you and your men, and he is bound to keep you out. I heard him say that this dance is to be very select and exclusive, and that he wasn't going to allow any drunken shantymen near the place."

"Warn't goin' to allow any— Hell an' furies! We'll see about that. I never hed much ter do with Barney, but I thought he hed too much sense ter say a thing like that. We'll just about come down an' own thet dance, an' like's not we won't 'low any sech critters as Barney an' his crew in the place. You hear me!"

"It would be no more than right, I'm sure," declared Sam, hardly concealing his delight; "but you'll have to come prepared. Barney says that any drunken loafers who try to break in to the dance will have to fight him first."

"Fight him!" yelled Red Lampheer, beside himself with rage; "we'll fight him; we'll tear him into rags an' feed the crows. We'll teach him an' all like him to go easy with Red Lampheer an' his gang o' shanty-men. By——! You hear me!"

The irate shantyman tied his three demijohns on the back of his buckboard and drove off swearing vengeance and ruin for Barney and the rest of the Red-Keggers who should attempt to exclude the gang from the last dance and supper of the season, which was booked for a fortnight hence at the little village of Sixteen, some twelve miles up the river. Sam started soon after for home, congratulating himself on the chance which had thrown Red Lampheer in his way. As he passed the Maloney farm he saw Barney and Norine sitting together under the trees near the house. Just then Mrs. Maloney came to the door and called them to supper. Evidently Barney was there to spend the evening. The bitter hatred in his heart flamed up anew as he saw the happiness which he had been unable to interrupt and which interfered so provokingly with his own plans.

The Hawkins and Maloney homesteads were scarcely a mile apart as the crow flies, but a bend in the road added half a mile to the distance for those who did not care to tramp through the fields and a rough patch of woods. With Norine, Barney always took the longer route—alone, he used the short cut. Late that evening he was returning home across lots, whistling a gay tune, and utterly oblivious to everything but his own happy thoughts. The night was dark, but he knew his way, and went on unhesitatingly until he came to a narrow arm of the woods which followed a small stream across the Hawkins farm. Here the low ground on both sides of the stream was swampy and treacherous, being covered with fallen logs and pools of water. Special care was necessary in passing this spot, especially at night, and Barney began to pick his footholds more slowly. As he reached a large log which had been stretched across one of the pools for a path, he heard a rustling in the brush behind him. Thinking it might be a wildcat who had ventured down from the forest, he quickened his steps to reach the open. The next instant his foot tripped, and, unable to regain his balance, he fell heavily forward upon the log and rolled into the water. In a moment he righted himself and began to scramble back upon the log. Just as he threw one leg over it, another heavy log fell with crushing force, seemingly from the tree above him, and struck him down again into the swamp.

How long he remained there stunned he could not tell. When he regained consciousness, he found himself lying half buried in mud and water, his legs pinned down beneath the log that had fallen upon him. It seemed as if every bone in his body was broken as he struggled to throw off the weight across his legs. By slow, painful degrees, however, he succeeded in extricating himself and crawling up again upon the log which served as a foot-path. There he sat for several minutes to recover his wits and take an inventory of his bruises. Failing to find any serious injury, his spirits rose, and his anger, accordingly.

"What divil's work is this, begorra?" he muttered. "Sure, I heard some varmint rustlin' the bushes, or I'm a sinner."

He examined the log on which he sat, crawling along toward the further end. A tiny sapling was bent down across it and caught in the fork of a tree on the opposite side. Evidently it was this which had tripped him up.

"Some murdherin' spalpeen did that a' purpose!" exclaimed Barney, glaring around into the darkness. "Come out here, ye divil's whelp, an' let me see ye. I'll tache ye to set on a man in the dark!"

Not a sound came in response to his invitation, but he went on with increasing rage, "Begorra, ye're a cowardly hellyun, whoever ye are, an' I'll make it my business to find out. Ef thet log hed hit me square on the head, ye'd hev murder on yer soul this night, an' no mistake. Faith, the murder is there now for all ye know an' care."

As he vented his wrath against his unknown foe, Barney hurried as well as his sore joints would let him toward home. Suddenly he stopped short and clenched his fists. "By——!" he exclaimed through his teeth. "Ef it was you——!" No threat to suit his need came ready to his mind and he completed his limping walk to the Hawkins farm in silence, but the square jaw and clenched fists spoke a forcible language of their own.

"Lands alive, Barney! what's happened to you?" exclaimed Mother Hawkins, as he entered the sitting-room.

"Tripped on a log, an' fell into the swamp, Mother, darlint. Hit my head an' feel sore an' mad, but no bones broken. Sam home yet?"

"Yes, he came in a little while ago from his hunting trip—why?"

"Faith, I only axed. Good-night," and Barney hurried off to bed for fear the dear old lady might see the gleam of rage and suspicion that sprang into his eyes.

In the morning he was not much the worse for his mishap, save for a soreness and slight stiffness in his legs, and in the shoulder which received the principal force of the blow from the log. He waited around the house for an hour or two until Sam Hawkins came down to his breakfast. Then he walked into the room on some pretext, keeping his eye on Sam's face. He thought he saw him start and pale slightly, but otherwise pay no heed to his presence. Presently Barney went out without speaking. Since the previous evening he had weighed the matter carefully in his mind, and had come to the unwilling conclusion that it would not be wise to accuse Sam of an attempt on his life. In the first place, he had nothing himself but suspicion. He could not prove that he had been the victim of anything but a somewhat unusual accident. In the second place, Sam would undoubtedly deny with indignation that he had been anywhere near the place, or that he knew anything whatever concerning the affair. With so little to back up his accusation, his story would look too improbable, and Sam would be given the full benefit of the doubt. Clearly the only thing to do was to watch and wait.

CHAPTER XIX

Ros Whitmore had prospered during the two years since Farmer Hawkins had engaged him to clear the stumps from a section of his farm. He and his good wife Jule were hard workers and missed no opportunity to provide and save for their large and growing brood. The little cabin which they had erected out at The Corners, in the Sturgeon district, when they were among the first pioneers of the region, had long been too small. The time had come at last for building a house more suited to their needs and their position. The Whitmores were popular far and wide among young and old. It was a foregone conclusion that Ros's house-raising bee would eclipse anything of the kind seen in the township.

For weeks Ros had been selecting and bringing from the forest the best long, smooth pine-trees he could find whose diameter at the base was from a foot to fourteen or sixteen inches and tapered to eight or ten inches at a distance of twenty to twenty-four feet from the ground. As he intended to build a good "block" house, he flattened the logs with a broadax, cut them into proper lengths, and squared the ends to make them ready to be placed in their proper position in the house. For the less pretentious houses and for the lumber-shanties the ends of the logs only were squared, and on raising-day the logs were put up with the bark on. Thus they were rather uncouth in appearance, but answered the simple needs of the majority of small farmers. When properly chinked with clay or plaster, these log dwellings were warm and dry in winter, which was a great desideratum. Ros, however, was determined on a very different kind of house. He and his large family had lived long enough in the little rough log cabin of a pioneer. His new house would be one of the finest of its kind within twenty miles, almost as good as that of Farmer Hawkins. All the logs were nicely hewed and squared. The house was to be one and a half stories high, with real sawed rafters, shingles for the roof, siding for the gable ends, and all chinks filled with real lime plaster.

As soon as the logs were cut, trimmed, and ready to be put in place, Ros set a day for the raising, and every able-bodied man within reasonable distance was invited to be present and lend a helping hand. The Saturday following the breaking of the rollway had been selected as a convenient time for the many who had been engaged on the river and had not yet settled down to the regular spring work on their farms.

Raising-bees were always great occasions. The crowd never failed. Drawn by the certainty of a generous spread and plenty to drink, as well as by cordial neighborly feeling, and the unwritten law which governed such events, nearly all who could come did come. The jug was a potent factor. Custom had established it as an indispensable adjunct of every raising-bee, and many young farmers who would have been ashamed to be seen going into Pete's place, partook openly, and often too freely of his "Mystic Brand" at these gatherings, frequently taking their first lessons in dram-drinking. At the wind-up of a raising-bee the sober men were usually a small minority, and often serious accidents befell those whose nerves had been rendered

unsteady before the heavy work of the day was finished.
Ros was himself a temperate man, and did not approve
of the use of liquor, but at a time like this he felt compelled to yield to popular custom and demands. To
omit so important an item would be regarded as an un-
pardonable breach of hospitality, so he provided himself with several jugs of "Pete's best," which, as the
latter confidentially informed him, had been specially
procured the day before for this occasion. His wife,
also, made generous preparations for the great crowd
which was sure to be on hand. "Aunt Jule's" din-
ners were famous for their quality as well as for their
quantity, and there were many willing hands to help
her, because the women were glad of any excuse to be
present as participants in the activity.

Barney had recovered from his bruises sufficiently to
attend the raising. Indeed, his presence was regarded
as well nigh indispensable, because of his cool head,
his ready wit, and his universal popularity. Few, however, were prepared for the announcement made by
Sam Hawkins the day before the raising that he also
intended to go and help in the work, and that he would
do as much as anybody to help Ros Whitmore put up
his house.

"As to thet, we'll wait an' see," remarked Tom
Moore to Barney, and then he asked, "What idee hes
he got in his head, d'ye think? 'Tain't likely he's
grown fond o' work all on a sudden."

Barney's eyes flashed, and he clenched his fists, but
he merely replied, "Faith, ye'll have to ask me somethin' asier."

On Saturday morning Sam was astir fully two hours
earlier than his wont. Both his father and mother
marvelled at his unaccustomed activity, but were glad

to see it aroused in a good cause. Sam said very little to any one. He was ill-natured and nervous, and seemed to be enlisted in the day's undertaking not because he liked it, but in spite of his dislike of it. Yet no one had urged, or even invited him to attend the raising, taking for granted that it would be useless to do so.

Farmer Hawkins and Mother Hawkins, and Mr. and Mrs. Maloney rode over to Ros Whitmore's immediately after breakfast. Barney and Norine walked there together, while Sam went by himself, and arrived after all the others. Nearly two hundred men, women, and children had gathered on the clearing. Work was about to begin. Two layers of logs were already in place upon the foundation, and others were on the skids waiting to be moved up to form the third tier. The ever-present jug had taken its first round and was about to be placed in the cool shade of a hollow tree near by as Sam sauntered up.

"Seems I'm just in time," he remarked, taking in the situation at a glance. "Pass that jug this way before you set it down. It's good stuff. I can vouch for that, don't you know."

"How's that? What d'ye know about it, more'n anybody else?" asked Arch Fellows, who held the jug, eyeing Sam curiously.

"Oh, you know—that is, I heard Pete say he was going to fetch up from his cellar some of his best stock for this occasion," replied Sam, coloring with sudden embarrassment.

"Reckon ye got thet a leetle mixed, me boy," responded the other, handing Sam the jug "Pete told Ros Whitmore es how he'd jes' ordered this lot, special, from his agent for this raisin'. But it's good stuff, es you say, sure enough."

Sam took a deep draught of the liquor.

"Hurry up, Sam!" exclaimed Joe Reon in a half whisper at his side. "Here comes Barney. Ros hes appointed him his assistant superintendent for this job an' asked him to shet off the drinkin' until after the house is up—if he can."

Sam set the jug down with a fierce oath, and seemed on the point of defying Barney then and there, but just beyond Barney he saw the minister talking with Ros Whitmore, and he quickly edged away through the crowd.

"Pile in here, boys," called Barney, whipping off his own coat. "Begorra, this 'll be a foine big house, an' we must be after finishin' it before sundown."

Each man was given his place, and the work began in earnest. Five or six tiers were set and made fast without interruption. Then some one started the jug on its rounds again.

"Ye'd better lave the jug alone till the house is up," expostulated Barney; but it was of no use, for the fire had been kindled and the blaze must be kept up. Nobody was content to be left out after some had had their turn, so it was impossible to proceed with the work until all who wished had partaken a second time of Pete's "best."

While the lower tiers were being placed, the work was comparatively easy and safe. The skids rested at a gentle incline, one end on the ground and the other on the highest tier. The heavy logs were moved up this incline by the use of ropes pulled by those above, assisted by the strong arms of those below, who pushed as long as they could reach the rising log. As the walls grew higher and the incline of the skids correspondingly steeper, the work became more difficult, and the element of danger entered. Cool heads, strong arms and backs, and steady nerves were essential. Moreover, the quality of the work depended upon the carefulness used in setting the logs true and fastening the ends securely. Many a house and barn had suffered from neglect in these particulars, caused by too much attention to the jug.

Sam worked gingerly, and skipped from place to place with apparently no reason, never sticking to any one task more than a few minutes. He was gruff and irritable, and seemed to be dissatisfied with everything. Barney, on the other hand, worked with steady persistence, always at the hardest places, and ready to help wherever there seemed to be any danger of a log slipping. His hearty words of encouragement and exhortation, and his merry laugh and quick wit, inspired all with a greater willingness to work; but he could not persuade them to let the jug alone.

An old lady, a dear old soul, known by all as "Granny," lived in a shanty near by, and although more than eighty years of age, she was possessed of great vigor, and took as much interest in the house-raising as did Ros Whitmore himself. She watched the work from the laying of the first log, and as one by one the tiers went up, and time after time the "Mystic Brand" went around, she began to notice that the corners of the building were showing the effects of too much stimulation on the brain. The condition of "her boys," as she called all the men, worried her greatly, and finally she walked up to a group that had just gathered for another round of drinks and addressed them:

"Look here, boys, don't you think you ought to let me have thet jug for a while? Some of you will surely get hurted. Besides, don't you see what poor work you are doin' on Ros's house? Jes' let me keep it till after dinner, anyhow, and then if you *must* have it I'll give it to you agin."

"Hear what Granny says?" laughed Ned Blakely. "She wants you to give up the jug till arter dinner, an' I guess she's about right."

"I've got er holt o' this jug now, an' don't intend to let go yet," said Jake Vogel, good-humoredly. "But Granny's right, jest the same, an' she can hev it as soon as I get enough," and suiting the action to the word, he took a long "pull" of the stuff. "There," he remarked with a laugh, as he held the jug out to Granny, "I'll be good now. Ye got ter limber up a bit on these neighborly occasions, ye know. I've been ter lots of 'em, an' guess I know when it's time ter stop."

"Jake's a hog," said Tim Underwood, and reaching for the jug before Granny could get it, proceeded to demonstrate that he belonged to the same genus.

Barney and Ros were both getting out of patience, but the good-nature of the crew prevented any outbreak, and as they were all volunteers, extreme measures could not be taken. Even Parson Allen deemed it wise to refrain from remonstrance which would be listened to with perfect good-humor and respect, and then disregarded when his back was turned. Barney was constantly on the alert, and more than once he had sprung to the aid of some half-drunken workman just in time to save him from injury when he got into a dangerous position and had not wit enough to take care of himself. Finally Granny secured the jug, but by that time it was as empty as charity at a charity ball. By the time the noon hour arrived the house was about two-thirds up, and the work was beginning to go better, because one jug was empty and the other had been surreptitiously removed from its hiding-place and smuggled away.

The feast of the day was ready promptly at twelve o'clock, and the hungry men sat down to dinner at a long table made of boards and placed in the shade. White cloths covered the rough pine boards, and great heaps of substantial good things crowded each other from one end to the other. The women and girls bustled about to wait upon the workers, leaving their own repast until later.

Apparently all thought of the jug had been dropped, but as the men returned to the building, on their way a dozen or more of them ranged themselves along in front of Granny's place, and, to this good dame's utter disgust, demanded the article they sought. She argued with them for a while, but seeing argument useless, she finally produced it—empty. There were some who, forgetting that this was just its condition when surrendered to her, accused the dear old soul of dealing unfairly with them. However, Red-Keg being only a few miles distant, a courier was despatched with the jug with orders to lose no time in getting it refilled and back to the place.

The sun was well down in the west when the plates, or finishing logs, were to be put into their places to form the last tier upon which the roof was to rest. In order to raise these heavy logs, longer skids were employed, so that the incline should not be so steep. As before, two ropes were fastened at the top of the building, the lower ends were placed around the log at each end, and men were stationed at the top to pull on the ropes, while others remained below to assist in the lifting as far as they could reach. This dangerous work, which called for clear heads and steady nerves, was undertaken by men some of whom were scarcely able to stand erect upon the ground, so demoralizing had been the effect of the fresh supply of Pete's "Mystic Brand." Only those who had refrained from indulgence realized the gravity of the situation.

When the last log had been lifted and pulled to a point just above the heads of the men below, it was evident that the weight was too great for those above to master, but by a desperate effort they succeeded in pulling it up still farther.

"Boost 'er up, boys! I can't hold on ter this rope much longer!" bawled out Joe Reon at the top.

"Put the rope 'round yer waist," yelled Tim Underwood from below, laughing tipsily; "then ef the log comes down, you'll hev ter come with it. Haw, haw!"

The log dropped back a little till it was again within reach of those on the ground.

"Hurrah, boys, shove 'er up!" shouted Arch Fellows, giving it a boost, and away went that end of the log, while the other end, held above by Sam Hawkins, remained stationary.

This left the log in a most dangerous position, and cool heads were needed to avert a disaster, but the men became dazed, and the danger dawned upon their sodden minds too late.

"My God! boys, what are ye doin' down there?" yelled Joe Reon, who had actually tied the rope around his body as suggested, and was now struggling with all his nerveless strength to prevent the inevitable; "I'm fallin', an' the top log is comin' with me! Look out!"

Barney and Ros, seeing that some one was going to get hurt, both rushed toward the spot where the falling log must strike. Barney was there first, with quick brain and steady nerve taking in the situation at a glance. At the risk of his own life he pushed two men aside who would have been struck by the log in its descent, and then dodging under it, caught the man who was falling just in time to save him from striking his head on a sharp pine stump near by.

Sam, who held the rope at the other end of the log, braced his feet securely and held his end well in place, but just as the shout went up at the daring rescue Barney had made, Sam suddenly let his end go, which, released from duress, slid like lightning down the skid just as Barney was passing under it with Joe Reon still in his arms.

Every one supposed that the log was secure in Sam's hands, and no one had looked for it to fall. But Norine, who had been watching Barney's every movement, had come near to the scene unnoticed, and with quick eye she saw Sam let go of his rope, and almost before the log began to fall she screamed:

"Barney, quick, jump back!"

Without stopping to learn the reason, Barney obeyed his sweetheart's warning instantly, springing backward close to the wall just in time to avoid receiving the whole crushing weight of the log upon his head.

Ros Whitmore was not so fortunate. He had followed close behind Barney at the first sign of the danger. When Barney sprang back, Ros attempted to do the same, but he stumbled and fell to the ground. The heavy log came down upon his right leg and broke the bone below the knee.

Meanwhile, Sam stood above, watching the scene below, but forgot the slack of the rope, which he had gathered in as he had pulled up his end of the log, and which lay in loops and coils about his feet. As the log slid down the skids it jerked the rope with it, and the slack quickly becoming entangled around Sam's feet, pulled him unceremoniously from his position. No one was there to help him. Barney was still holding to Reon, whom he had the instant before caught in his fall. The rest were rushing to help Ros. Sam struggled for a brief moment to release himself from the ropes, and then, with a yell of rage and terror, came tumbling down. A large tub of mortar for filling the chinks between the logs had been started close to the wall just below Sam. The lime had just been slaked, and the sand was ready for mixing. Into this tub Sam fell headlong. The force of the fall was broken, but when Sam emerged from his lime bath he was a sight to behold. Sputtering, and spluttering, and howling, he rushed down to the brook near by and jumped in bodily, and began at once the task of cleaning the stuff out of his eyes and mouth.

A part of the crowd followed, forgetting even Ros's sad injury in this new diversion, and the more Sam raved and swore, the more the spectators laughed and jeered, for Sam was generally disliked by his neighbors, and they did not hesitate to blame him for his own plight. There was no excuse, they said, for his letting go of the rope, if he had had his wits about him, and that was the least that could be said. There were some who said nothing, but shook their heads gravely and turned away.

Barney had taken Joe Reon to Granny's cabin, where he had found the fellow to be more scared than hurt, and then he hastened to look after Ros, stopping on the way to see if Sam had been injured. When he saw the fun the rest were having at Sam's expense he withdrew to Whitmore's cabin, whither Ros had been carried. Already his brave and energetic wife had stripped the injured leg, and, with the help of Mother Hawkins and Parson Allen, was preparing splints and bandages. She knew just what to do, and wasted no time in useless lamentations or complaints.

"It is a very unfortunate interruption of Ros's home-building," said Allen to Barney, quietly; "but we may be thankful it is no worse. He will have the use of his leg again in time with the good care Jule will take of it. She is the best doctor he could have."

Barney said nothing in reply. He did not dare to trust himself, and the sight of little Tilly Whitmore standing by her father's bed and holding his hand tightly in hers while the big tears rolled quietly down her pale, agonized little face, was too much for him altogether. With a choking sensation in his throat, he hurriedly assured Ros that he would see to finishing the house, and that Ros needn't worry, and then broke away from the painful scene and went back to the work outside.

Sam and the rest of the men soon returned, all by this time being pretty well sobered up. Barney looked his enemy in the face as he passed him and saw the demon in the fellow's eyes, but said nothing. Sam was too badly bruised to resume work, and after a short rest started for home. The jug went around no more that day.

As Barney and Norine walked home together after the work was finished and the sumptuous supper eaten, they were unusually quiet. After walking almost half the distance, Norine, unable longer to keep her dreadful thought to herself, exclaimed:

"Oh, Barney! That's what he came for. He did it on purpose. I saw him——"

THE MORE SAM RAVED AND SWORE, THE MORE THE
SPECTATORS LAUGHED AND JEERED.

"Hush, darlint!" interrupted Barney, who had the same conviction. "Ye can't be sure. Let's not think of it. Let's talk about yer own swate self."

"And imagine," she continued, in only half obedience, "you thought I was going to the dance with him."

"Faith, I'm thinkin' thet was quare meself. But he'll not be there at all, niver fear, an' we kin have our fun better without him, eh, swateheart—thet is, ef we can have any fun at all when we'll be thinkin' of poor Ros lyin' home with a broken leg, an' his little mite of a girl cryin' her swate eyes out for him—all on account of thet—thet—*hellyun!*"

Having thus relieved a part of his pent-up rage through the safety valve of that one expressive word, Barney drew Norine closer to him, and spent the remainder of the time in trying to make her forget everything except himself and happiness.

CHAPTER XX

A DANCE and oyster supper at Sixteen was always an event which interested all the lads and lasses for miles around. To miss the last one of the season was a thing not to be thought of by any rational young person with nimble feet and a good digestion. The settlement which flourished under the name of "Sixteen," taken from the number of the township in which it was located, was about twelve miles from Red-Keg and nine miles from Farmer Hawkins's—a mere "stone's throw" for the active young lumbermen and farmers and their sweethearts. The festive occasion was always well attended, and fun and frolic were free and unrestrained. Barney O'Boyle was to be master of ceremonies, and he and Norine had been looking forward to the evening with more pleasant anticipation than ever before. It would be the first one for them to attend since the happy understanding between them. Barney had obtained Uncle Si's willing permission to take old Rock and the buckboard for the trip.

Norine came over early from the Maloney homestead "fixed up" for the occasion and looking very sweet in her holiday finery. Much of this finery was saved from last year and skilfully made over, but that was a woman's secret which others need not know.

Barney had carefully groomed Rock, dusted and polished up the buckboard, and arrayed himself in a new broadcloth suit, bought for the occasion, he said, but others thought it might have been purchased with an eye to a future use. Uncle Si was to bring the rig around from the barn when the young people were ready to start; but suddenly, while they were waiting, they heard his voice calling out in alarm:

"Barney, Barney, come here and help me with Rock. He's sick, an' I'm afraid he can't be taken out."

Hastening to the barn, he found that Rock was, indeed, a sick horse, and was now scarcely able to stand on his legs.

"Poor old boy, what's ailin' ye?" exclaimed Barney, as he stroked the horse's neck, which was covered with a cold sweat.

Rock turned his dim eyes upon Barney with a loving, piteous appeal for help, made an effort to lift his head and rally his strength, staggered a moment, and then fell upon the barn floor. Before anything could be done for him, he shivered once or twice, stretched out his limbs convulsively, and was dead.

"It's very strange. He was all right this afternoon," said the farmer, wiping away the suspicion of a tear, for good old Rock, so kind and gentle, had been the family horse ever since they came to the farm, and had become a great pet. They stood for some time looking down mournfully at the prostrate body, until Uncle Si asked dubiously:

"How will you go to the dance, now, Barney? It is a good nine miles, and the roads are bad out that way. You might walk, but Norine couldn't think of it. Poor child, she'll be so disappointed. It's too bad. Do you suppose you could get along with the oxen? Why not? They're a spry team, and would cover the ground almost as fast as Rock himself. The riding wouldn't be quite so easy, of course, but we don't seem to have

18

much choice now. You go and ask Norine while I hitch up. It's getting late."

Norine at first was scandalized when asked to go to a ball in an ox-cart with all her finery, but Barney finally persuaded her that it was the proper and only thing to do in such an emergency, and by the time Uncle Si came around with the big-eyed and gentle oxen, the couple had come to an agreement and were again awaiting him.

"You remind me of Priscilla and John Alden," laughed Mother Hawkins, coming to the door of the farmhouse to see the young couple safely off in their extemporized pleasure vehicle.

"Good-by, Auntie and Uncle. You're very good to help us out this way, though it seems queer to go to a dance in an ox-cart," said Norine, waving her handkerchief as they took their departure.

There was certainly something incongruous in the combination of broadcloth and ribbons with a rough ox-cart and heavy, slow-going oxen. Even Barney felt it as he urged his team into a livelier gait after leaving the farm.

"Git along there, Bill; gee, Bright, gee; can't ye hear? I'll be after givin' ye a taste o' this whip ef ye don't kape t' th' road better'n that. Begorra, did ye iver see so much trouble as I'm havin' with these oxen? Sure, they'll make me lose me timper, so they will," and Barney O'Boyle sidled closer to Norine, and encircling her waist with his arm, explained that he was afraid she would fall out of the wagon if he did not hold her in.

"Oh, you're a blarney," said Norine, coloring, but making no effort to unfold the brawny arm from around her.

Before long they were travelling over a very rough and winding road, one which had been used by lumbermen during the winter. While the ground was covered with snow this makeshift became a pretty fair highway for logging purposes, but when the snow and ice had melted, and the road-bed came to its normal condition, it could hardly lay claim to any particular merits for pleasure travel. While the right fore wheel of a vehicle might be on a protuberant root, the left one very likely would be down in a rut, throwing the conveyance somewhat out of equilibrium. In some places the right fore wheel of a wagon would be up, the left down, the right hind wheel down and the left up, all at the same time. In spite of it all, however, Barney and Norine were happy and in the best of spirits.

"Haw, Bright; haw, there; can't ye moind? Haw —" but before Barney could even disengage his arm from around his fair companion, to steady the awkward team, there was a crash and a spill—and Norine felt herself flying through the air as though shot from a catapult.

The wagon had struck one of the "bad spots," and the uncertainty of the road, together with Barney's excited vociferations, had frightened the oxen till they had "hawed" too much, and the "nigh" wagon-wheel had struck a root nearly opposite the one he was trying to avoid on the "off" side.

Norine landed a few feet away in a ditch of water, unharmed, much frightened, and very wet. Barney was likewise *hors du combat* on the other side of the road, while the ox-team took it into their heads to run, and run they did.

"Barney, come here, quick—come and help me," called Norine, bursting into tears, partly because she was frightened, and partly because her pretty clothes were ruined, and the prospects of a good time at the dance were rapidly fading away. In her present bedraggled condition she surely could not put in an appearance at the festivities.

"Where are ye, Norine; are ye hurt?" cried Barney, disengaging himself from a clump of briers into which he had fallen.

"I'm down here in the mud and water, up to my neck!" replied Norine through her tears; "and if you don't hurry I'll soon be drowned. It was bad luck for us to come out here in that old ox-cart."

Barney's clothes were torn and his hands and face badly lacerated by the brambles among which he had fallen, but he hastened to Norine and found her, not quite "up to her neck" in the water; but much the worse for her immersion in the shallow ditch, and too much frightened to help herself to dry ground. Barney quickly extricated her from the mire, and as he did so she exclaimed, half in earnest and half in play:

"You said you wanted to protect me from falling; and now see how you have done it. Just look at my clothes!"

"While ye're spakin' of clothes, look at mine!" said Barney, by way of apology.

Up to this time Norine had not noticed Barney's condition, but when she beheld him by the light of the full moon just rising, her own plight was for the moment forgotten and she was filled with alarm and sympathy for her companion. He was a fright! His new black coat was torn and muddy; he was minus his hat; his hair was tumbled, his face and hands bleeding, and a woebegone expression overspread his coun-

tenance, as he stood before Norine, and began to realize all that had come to them.

"What iver shall we do—" began Barney, and then
he suddenly awoke to the fact that his team was running away, and that he must stop it quickly, or a worse
accident might happen. Telling Norine to wait where
she was for a moment, and that he would be back immediately with the team and wagon to take her home
for dry clothes, he started up the road on a run after
the oxen.

By this time the team had a good start, and the usually gentle oxen were racing madly. The rumble of
the wagon could still be heard, with now and then a
crash as it met with some obstruction. The runaways
were nearing a strip of corduroy about half a mile in
length which had been laid across a treacherous swale.
Unless they stopped before reaching it there was
scarcely a hope that either the oxen or wagon could be
saved, as the "bridge" was narrow, and in their mad
rush they would surely go off into the mire and slime
of the lagoon, which meant certain death, because they
would quickly sink out of sight. Barney realized all
this as, with fear tugging at his heart, he bounded up
the road at his topmost speed.

"Whoa, Bright! whoa Bill! whoa!" rent the air as
he fairly flew over the uneven road. Strewn along the
way were evidences of the wreck the cattle were making of the wagon,—first the wagon-box, then one wheel,
then another, and it was soon apparent that all four
wheels had gone; but all the more desperately Barney
sped on, determined to capture the two oxen if possible, and whatever salvage remained of the cart.

He reasoned that the yoke and chain might still be
intact, even if the vehicle had been so rudely scattered.

He was nearing the runaways at every bound, but at the same time they were nearing the corduroy. An instant later he heard their hoofs and dangling chain clattering and clanking over the loose logs. He redoubled his efforts to reach them before it was too late. Arriving at the opening he saw his quarry only a little distance ahead, each ox making a crazy effort to crowd the other off the narrow bridge into the water. They were bellowing now with fright and fatigue, but kept on in their wild career. The middle of the bridge was reached, and Barney was almost upon them.

"Whoa, Bright, whoa! back, Bill, back! haw, Bright—" He was cut short. The hook of the chain had caught in one of the cross logs of the "bridge," and, before he knew what had happened, he was hurled headlong into the swale—chain, logs, cattle, and all in a frightful mix-up.

It so chanced that a loosened log landed near by, and as he gathered his few remaining senses he instinctively clutched at it, and before his feet became inextricably imbedded in the bog, he crawled upon its friendly side. He had been hurled head first, however, and was covered with mud and ooze from head to feet. His first thought was for his own safety, so he proceeded at once to secure it. Reaching the corduroy, he climbed up, and then looked around for his dumb charges. They had disappeared in the lagoon, and a few bubbles on the water alone indicated the spot where they went down.

Barney was at his wit's end to know what step to take next. In the excitement of the last few moments he had forgotten all about Norine, whom he had left standing in the road nearly a mile back.

He was nearly distracted with the course events had taken. The wagon had been smashed to smithereens, and the team of oxen were at the bottom of Sturgeon Slough. He was in a great dilemma. He could not think of going on to the dance, and he was ashamed to face Uncle Si. How could he explain such a dire calamity? How would Farmer Hawkins feel at losing his horse and his ox-team, both in the same evening?

Barney gazed wistfully at the murky water where the team had gone down. Mechanically he turned his footsteps toward the spot where he had left Norine so abruptly. As he passed one by one the pieces of wreckage strewn along the way he was filled with sorrow and dismay. He could scarcely realize the havoc wrought in so short a time. The wreck was complete.

Nearing the spot where he had left Norine standing he came suddenly to a realization that something else was wrong. She was nowhere to be seen, and repeated calls failed to get a response. He was nonplussed. Perhaps she had been injured by her fall, and had crawled away from the road and become unconscious. Again and again the woods resounded with his calls. He begged and implored her to answer if she were near, but not a sound broke the stillness of the night in response. He was some five miles from home and about four miles from the settlement of Sixteen. Help was nowhere at hand. The poor fellow was almost crazed by grief. He scoured the woods round about in a vain effort to find the lost girl. Once he thought he heard a faint call for help, but when he stopped to listen he could hear nothing, and was filled with apprehension.

While Barney was somewhat deficient in "school larnin'" he was a good deal of a philosopher. He saw that, direful as the incidents of the evening had been, the issue must be met, and the sooner Uncle Si and the rest became acquainted with the facts, the better it would be for all concerned. He therefore decided to return home with all haste, thinking, also, that he might find Norine there, or, perhaps, would overtake her on the way. Hoping against hope, he started on a run for the home of Farmer Hawkins, but saw nothing of Norine on the way, and his heart was sinking within him when he opened the door of the farmhouse. The peace and quiet that reigned within told him at once that Norine had not arrived there. Farmer Hawkins sat in his comfortable arm-chair, and Mother Hawkins was near by, busy with a basket of patchwork. Nero, the house-dog, was lazily stretched out on the floor at his master's feet, and Maltese Tabby was playing hide-and-seek with her brood of youngsters, assisted by a spool of thread which had dropped from her mistress's basket.

As the door burst open and Barney appeared, great consternation at once prevailed. The huge mastiff rose suddenly and made a rush for the supposed intruder. He was never friendly toward tramps, and his well-known antipathy kept the farm free from trespassers of that sort.

"Nero, lie down there! Aren't you ashamed of yourself acting so hastily," Uncle Si said, commandingly.

"Sakes alive, that's Barney! What on earth has happened to you? Where's Norine?" cried Mother Hawkins, dropping her patchwork over the floor as she hastened to meet Barney. She was trembling with excitement and alarm.

Breathlessly, Barney stammered out his woeful story. The farmer and his wife listened in amazement and sympathy, but when he came to the disappearance of Norine, Mother Hawkins could bear no more.

"Josiah, you go down to the village and rouse the

neighbors just as quick as you can. Maybe my poor little girl is dying out there in the woods. Don't lose a minute. Barney, get on some dry clothes and come with me," she said, almost hysterically.

"Now, Mother, you can't go out there in the night," protested Farmer Hawkins. "You haven't been feeling well for a month past. It would be too much for you. I'll get all the men I can. You stay here and wait for us."

"I can't stay here," exclaimed Mother Hawkins. "I must be doing something for the dear child. Perhaps I'll go down and keep her mother company. She'll be nearly crazy with anxiety."

"That's just the thing," agreed Josiah. "Hurry, Barney, we'll all go together and leave Mother at the Maloneys while we go on to rouse the neighbors. Has Sam been home to-night, Mother?"

"He came in about six o'clock and went to his room complaining of a headache and said he was going to bed and didn't want to be disturbed," replied Mother Hawkins.

Josiah hurried to Sam's room and quickly returned, saying that Sam was not there and his bed had not been touched.

"That's strange; I wonder where he can be," said his mother, half conscious of a vague disquiet in her heart.

"It's hard to say, but he'll turn up as usual when it pleases him," replied Josiah with a sigh; then, as Barney returned in his working clothes, and Mother Hawkins threw a thick shawl over her head and shoulders, he called to Nero, and they all started down the road toward Red-Keg.

Norine's mother was almost prostrated with grief and anxiety, and was bent upon starting out at once with the searchers, but cooler judgment prevailed and she was persuaded to remain with Mother Hawkins while the men searched for the lost girl.

In a marvellously short time Farmer Hawkins, John Maloney, and Barney, going in different directions, had gathered a party of twenty men, with half as many vehicles. The younger men were away at the dance; but Barney was overjoyed and not a little surprised to find Tom Moore at home, and ready to accompany him on the instant. Big Pete Murray, who would have been an invaluable addition to the party, had gone with his wife and his two daughters to the dance. Robert Allen had gone to Midland that morning to visit the schoolmaster, who was recovering from his injury in the rollway.

The moon was rising high in the heavens when the searching party, with lanterns and torches, arrived at the spot where the search was to begin. A signal was agreed upon to be used if any of the searchers were successful. Repeated shouts had failed to bring any response. Nero was alert. He ran around and around the spot where Norine was last seen, and then started off into the jungle, baying loudly as he went. He was evidently on the trail. On and on he went, further and further into the dense forest, till at last his baying was lost in the distance, even to those leading the party.

The brambles and briers were playing havoc with the clothing of the searchers. But that they were on the right trail there was no doubt, for here and there were found fragments of Norine's dress hanging to the briers which had torn them off as she went along. Tom Moore and Barney were in the lead, and when the baying of the mastiff ceased to reach their ears they hung to the trail just the same. The thought uppermost in

Barney's mind was that the girl had been bereft of her reason through fright and had fled through this terrible thicket not knowing whither. The woods were infested with wild animals and he dreaded lest she might have been torn to pieces.

After a half hour in the woods the moon was suddenly hidden by heavy clouds, and soon a drenching shower added to the discomforts and difficulties of the search, and to the fears for Norine. The route the mastiff had taken led deeper into the forest, away from habitations of any kind and into the dense woods where but few feet had ever trod; now across a tamarack swamp, now over ugly swales and watercourses filled to their brims by the spring rains and swollen by the present downpour.

The leaders at length reached a lagoon too deep to ford, a branch of the treacherous Sturgeon Slough. In the mud on its margin they discovered recent tracks— those of a woman and *a man*, or men. There appeared to be two. Intermingled with these were the footprints of a dog, which our searchers concluded were made by Nero. The latter were quite fresh, but the former had become nearly obliterated by the rain.

Tom Moore, who was an experienced trailer, was much encouraged by this find, but was considerably puzzled as to the identity of the companion or companions of Norine, and why she had companions. They were not made by the hobnailed boots of a lumberman. Who, then, did make them, and why had they come to this dismal and out-of-the-way place? Might it not be possible that the tracks were made at different times? No; for here, as Tom pointed out, after examining them closely by the light of the torches, were the men's tracks over the woman's, and a little farther on the

woman's tracks over the men's, showing clearly that
they must have been made by parties who were together.   No evidences of a struggle were apparent.

This muddy shore extended for some distance to the
left, and had been followed by the fugitives for its full
length.   It ended near a large, overhanging rock.
When this was reached the footprints were plainly
visible, as here they had been protected from the wash-
ing influence of the rain.

"Shoot me ef one of them boot-tracks warn't made
by Sam Hawkins!" ejaculated Tom, eyeing the ground
closely.   "Here's his mark plain es the nose on my
face—a star on the heel!   No one else es I know of
hes one like it.   Old John Harding, the shoemaker,
put it there only t'other day.   What on airth could ha'
brought him out here with that gal?   There's ben ugly
rumors about him an' thet gang o' his'n lately, an'
mebbe we're on their trail.   Ef thet's the case, Barney,
we must go back for reinforcements.   Them devils
may be up to suthin', an' we'd be no match fer 'em
alone.   Norine Maloney never kem out here of her
own free will and accord.   She's ben brought forcibly,
no doubt, afraid of her life.   By thunder! here's her
handkerchief, still wet with the poor gal's tears, thrown
down under this rock fer us ter find," went on big Tom,
excitedly.   "I tell ye she ain't fer away, nuther."

Barney was trembling like a leaf.   The thoughts
suggested by Tom, and the finding of Norine's handkerchief in this wild spot were almost too much for
his self-control.   He gasped a moment as if in mortal
pain.

"Give me that handkerchief, Tom," he said huskily,
and thrust the dainty bit of cambric into his bosom.
"Be the powers of hivin, Tom, let us kape on till we

find her. Begorra, it's me own doin's entirely as brought
her here, and we must find her or die in the attimpt!"

The two were now far in the lead. In fact, Tom
and Barney seemed to be the only ones who had kept
to the trail. The rest had wandered off in different
directions, scouring the woods around the spot where
Norine was last seen.

"Jest es ye say, Barney; but we're not very fer from
the dancers at Sixteen, an' we might run over there an'
git some help. These devils, whoever they be, are
desperit, else they wouldn't ha' sperited a gal off like
thet, let me tell ye; an' like es not her safety, her life
mebbe, depends on us meetin' 'em with a superior
force. I ain't ben runnin' 'round an' scourin' this neck
o' woods the last twenty years fer nuthin'; an' sure's
preachin' this is one o' them times when discretion'll
prove the better part of valor, an' don't you fergit it.
Still, Barney, old boy, ef ye say forrard, forrard's the
word, even though we meet Old Nick hisself," and
Tom looked inquiringly at his companion.

"Sure, Tom, ye're a better gin'ral then I am, so do
as ye think best; but fer the love of hivin, don't let us
make no mistakes," rejoined Barney, submissively;
then he added, "What on airth has become o' thet
dawg? He's gone entirely."

It was now nearly midnight. The rain had ceased
falling, and the men could make better progress. They
climbed upon the rock under which they had been
standing and soon reached a sand ridge which was quite
free from underbrush, and then made their way along
as rapidly as possible. Although this spot was fully
three miles back from any road, and no nearer to any
farmhouse or even lumber-camp, the two men were
surprised to see that there was a beaten path here,

which started from the edge of this lagoon, and extended back toward what were known as the burnt sand-hills. As soon as Tom made this discovery he told Barney to put out his light and move with great caution. The ridge they were traversing intersected another at the foot of the slough, and the latter could be followed up till it reached the settlement of Sixteen. At this intersection, the trail they had been following branched off toward the hills. The moon had now come out again in all its beauty and the night became as bright as day. They noted well the spot and then hastened in the direction of Sixteen. On the way they unexpectedly fell in with Jake Vogel and Dan Underhill, who also had become separated from the main party and had come around by a shorter route. Barney was for turning back at once, urging that four were enough; but Tom, whispering to him to say nothing of their suspicions, merely explained to the others that they were on the track of a party which might offer resistance and that as Sixteen was so near it would be wise to get assistance when they could. Jake and Dan approved of this plan, so they pushed on without further delay.

CHAPTER XXI

"LADIES give right hands across, don't get lost, be on time; the left hand back and don't be slack—balance four in a line," sang out the first violin, whose calling could be heard across the fields through an open window.

No sooner had that set been finished than a call for an "Old Mrs. Finnegan" quadrille was heard.

"Right ye are!" cried big Pete Murray, who was acting as floor manager until the arrival of Barney. "Form on for 'Old Mrs. Finnegan.'"

In a twinkling the floor was again filled and the music set agoing for this rollicking dance.

"Salute yer pardners. Left-hand around for Old Mrs. Finnegan. You've done it so well you may do it agin, agin! Forward all for Old Mrs. Finnegan. You've done it so well you may do it agin, agin! Balance all for Old Mrs. Finnegan. You've done it so well you may do it agin, agin! Allemand left for Old Mrs. Finnegan. You've done it so well you may do it agin, agin! Grand right-and-left for Old Mrs. Finnegan. You've done it so well you may do it agin, agin!"

Another set was ready and waiting to claim the floor the instant "Old Mrs. Finnegan" ended in a burst of laughter. The good-natured fiddlers swung into a new tune with scarcely a break.

"First lady lead up to the right; gent follow after. Balance all; swing 'em around," came in the regulation sing-song fashion from Dave Martin, who handled the bow on the first violin. "Allemand left; grand right-and-left. Swing on the corner," he bawled out in stentorian tones.

It was a jolly, rollicking crowd that had gathered at Sixteen in the only "ball-room" there. An extension of the tavern, used ordinarily as a dormitory for lumbermen, now cleared of the bunks and furnished with a row of benches placed around all sides of the room except on the end where the "fiddlers" were located —this was the ball-room.

The orchestra consisted of first and second violin and a bass viol. The veteran lumber-camp fiddler, Jose, fat and jolly, handled the second fiddle, and Arch Fellows the bass viol. Their repertoire included jigs, quicksteps, breakdowns, waltzes, schottisches, galops, etc., in great profusion. While in many respects the music was crude, it was remarkable how well some of those lumbermen could render the popular airs of the day merely by ear. Their remuneration depended upon the generosity of the dancers, who were expected to "chip in" when the hat was passed. A rough platform, consisting of loose boards placed upon several beer kegs, lifted the musicians above the crowd. They were further honored by being supplied with chairs— the only ones in the place.

On the present occasion, the dance was unusually well attended. The people came in all sorts of conveyances, from horseback to ox-carts. Some arrived on foot from distant points. There was no formality. The party was made up of all classes, from the shantyman who was "decent" to the boss lumberman and well-to-do farmer. Some came as far as twenty miles in order to take part in the hop which celebrated the wind-up of a prosperous logging season. Even some of the older people thought it not out of place to be on hand, and several gray-haired men and women were there to "trip the light fantastic toe." Ashbel Fair, "Babe" Strander, Rodney Bedell, and Bud Frazer had come seventeen miles from Midland and, with Grat Vogel, ruled the younger element. Pete Murray, with his wife Kate and his two buxom girls Katie and Sally, Bob Landseer and his wife Hetty, Ned Blakely and his wife Becky, Tim Underwood and Joe Reon were among the Red-Keggers present. Seward Rathaway had brought his cousin Lettie, who, in turn, had persuaded Axcy Marthy, with some difficulty, to go with them, insisting that the unhappy events at the rollway should not keep her from the dance, and that if she stayed away it would only make people talk.

Any of these events would be out of tune unless Barney O'Boyle had a hand in it. His presence often prevented mêlées which might have proved disastrous. His cool counsel and fearless ways gathered around him enough of the peaceable participants to resist the troublesome or boisterous ones. Whether the dance was held at Red-Keg, Sixteen, Beaverton, or any other place in the circuit, he was expected to be there. He seldom brought a companion, for he was too bashful to ask any of the girls, so this time, when it was known that Norine was to come with him, all his friends were on the *qui vive*.

The ball-room was barely large enough for two sets in a quadrille; even then it was difficult to keep to one's own set. The two sets would frequently get mixed in spite of all. This, however, merely gave zest to the occasion, and added to the general hilarity. The quadrille just finished had been one of the preliminary sets not on the regular order, put on to give the musi-

19

cians opportunity to "limber up" for the regular program which would begin upon the arrival of Barney. All knew that he had a long way to come, so they did not look for him very early; but as the minutes flew by until an hour had passed, and still no Barney, there was much "reckoning" as to what was delaying him. When nine o'clock came, Dave laid down his fiddle and, after a brief consultation with Pete Murray, announced that they would wait just half an hour longer for Barney; if he did not come by then the regular program would be taken up with Pete Murray as master of the evening. Thereupon the entire party was given up to a discussion of the failure of Barney and Norine to appear. The windows of the whole house were open, and eyes were at each looking down the only street in the direction from which the delinquents should arrive.

"Guess him an' Norine got sparkin' on the way an' fergot ter keep the old horse movin'," speculated Bob Landseer, as he turned away from the window. "I remember one night when me an' Hetty was goin' to church, our nag stopped, an' first we knew of it was when somebody comin' home from church hollered to us ter git outer the road. I says ter Het——"

The rest of his story was suppressed by the firm hand of Hetty herself clapped over his mouth, while a shout of laughter greeted the yarn and its interruption.

"Wal, I'll tell ye what I heard about a week ago, though I don't take no stock in it," said Ned Blakely. "It may not have anythin' ter do with Barney, an' I'd clean fergot it till jest now, but I did hear a rumor thet ole Bloag's gang o' shantymen, with Red Lampheer at their head, was talkin' about comin' down here to clean us out, 'cause they didn't git no invites. I haint heard nothin' more sence, an' I reckon they ain't nothin' in it, but then agin, mebbe they is."

Ned's statement made a decided sensation, and a dozen voices immediately demanded to know who was his informant.

"Es near es I can remember, 'twas Bob Simons, down at Pete's place," replied Ned. "He said Lampheer hed been there to git whiskey, an' raised ructions about the invites."

"Now ye spake of it, it strikes me I heard thet same thing," declared Pete Murray; "but let 'em try it on; bedad, they'll be more ructions raised than Red an' his hull drunken crew kin take care of in a week."

Although the belief was general that no such attack would be made, it was deemed wise to despatch a scout to reconnoitre. Steve Billings, the chore-boy at the tavern, was assigned to this task and promised suitable payment if he "kept his eyes peeled."

It was now half-past nine o'clock. Pete Murray announced that the dancing would be resumed without waiting any longer for Barney and Norine, so Dave Martin, Jose, and Arch Fellows vaulted to their places on the orchestra platform and reopened the ball with a varsouvienna.

"Dance a leetle, dance a leetle, and now you stop still; dance a leetle, dance a leetle, and now you stop still. Tra la, la, la, la! Tra la, la, la, la! Tra la, la, la, la! Tra la, la, la, la!" he sang out in unison with the music. A "Nelly Gray" schottische followed, and then a Virginia reel. In other parts of the house games were started,—spin the platter, blind man's buff, button, button, who want's to buy lead? The fun increased. All thought of interruption and disappointment was forgotten.

About half-past ten supper was announced, and a scramble ensued for seats, each man taking the lady nearest to him as the one he would escort to the table, in lieu of his regular partner. The supper was soon at its height, all hands discussing the bounteous repast with a relish born of good appetites. The dining-room rang with jest and laughter. Suddenly the door was flung open and Steve Billings rushed in panting for breath, his eyes bulging from their sockets.

"They're comin'!" he yelled, hardly able to get the words out, so great was his excitement.

"Who's comin'? Barney an' Norine?" demanded Pete Murray, imperatively, at the same time springing to his feet.

"The shantymen!" cried Steve. "They're 'bout half a mile up the road—more'n forty of 'em—drunker'n owls. They're stoppin' fer somethin'—I got near 'em by sneakin' through the woods the other side the road. They was fightin' an' yellin'—an' swearin' to tear the roof off the tavern—an' whale every son of a gun ter death what sassed 'em or tried ter stop 'em."

Steve panted out his sentences in short bits, trembling the while with fear, excitement, and a sense of his own importance at being the bearer of such sensational news. At once the room was in an uproar, all trying to speak at once to ask questions, give advice, threaten, joke, or sneer. Above the din, Pete Murray's voice was presently heard calling for silence.

"Boys!" he said in a quiet, commanding tone, "we mustn't be after losin' time in talk. We've got ter move lively an' git this shanty ready ter defend agin them barbarians. Listen ter me an' do as I tell ye, ivery mother's son of ye. Grat Vogel, you take Steve

an' go an' bolt and bar ivery door an' window in the
house, an' move somethin' agin 'em wherever ye can.
Rodney Bedell, Bud Frazer, Arch Fellows, Tim Underwood, Joe Reon, an' Seward Rathaway, grab holt of
anythin' ye can find for clubs, an' stand guard at the
windows here an' in the ball-room. Dave Martin, Bob
Landseer, Ned Blakely, Ashbel Fair an' "Babe" Strander will help me keep the door. The rest of ye stand
by ter help wheriver ye're naded. All the ladies will
stay right here in the dinin'-room, es fur away from the
pint of attack as ye can. Now," he added, as all hands
sprang to the places indicated, "let Red an' his little
s'prise party step up ter the office an' git their time;
we're ready ter pay."

A peri ιd of suspense followed. The men waited at
their posts, eager and alert, listening for the slightest
sound. The ladies, huddled over the remains of the
interrupted feast in the dining-room, exhibited remarkable coolness and courage. There was no weeping nor
wringing of hands, no outcries, nor insane supplica-
tions to be taken home, nor lamentations that they
had come. A belief in the impracticability of a hurried
or successful exodus at this juncture seemed to be
unanimous, and the righteousness of making as good a
defense as possible against the invading crew of semi-
barbarian and drunken ruffians seemed to be affirmed
by a general, if tacit, agreement.

Ten minutes passed without a sign of the enemy.
The strain of suspense was growing so severe that
nearly all were ready to welcome the attack simply to
be rid of the suspense. Presently Pete Murray exclaimed, impatiently:

"Sure, if the divils don't come on in one minute, I'll
go out there an' bring 'em, meself!"

The minute passed, and another, and still another. All was silent without.

"Come with me, Bob!" cried Pete at last; "we'll have a look to see what's kapin' thim. We can't wait much longer ter lick the smocks off 'em. If they won't come ter us, begorra, we'll go ter thim."

Pete opened the door and with Bob Landseer sallied forth in search of the marauders. About half a mile up the road they found them, as Steve had said, still engaged in a drunken quarrel. As the two skirmishers approached, they heard Red Lampheer asserting in a loud voice his right to continued dictatorship over the gang, as in camp, and insisting that he should have first choice for the "purtiest gal in the hull shanty" when they had vanquished the "mossbacks."

After satisfying himself as to the intentions of the gang and the cause of the delay, Pete advanced boldly into the road and called out tauntingly:

"Clear outer here, ye animals! What do ye mane, disturbin' dacent folks? We've been waitin' down yonder ter tache ye better manners. Come on, an' we'll show ye how ter dance in a way ye niver larned before." Then turning to Bob, he added: "That'll fetch the divils, ef they're comin' at all. We'll make tracks back ter the tavern an' be ready fer thim." Before the drunken shantymen realized what had happened, Pete and Bob were speeding down the road to Sixteen.

They were scarcely inside the tavern, however, before the raging, yelling mob came tearing after them. Ned Blakely, tall and lank, had charge of the door for the moment, while Pete recovered his wind from his run. Incautiously opening the door a crack to peep out, Ned suddenly found himself face to face with the ugly features of Red Lampheer, who at once tried to force an entrance.

"Git out of the way, ye scantling," he bawled contemptuously at Ned, "or I'll break ye in two."

Then Ned's stuff showed.

"I don't break easy," he retorted, as a long, slim arm, with a red, bony fist at the end thereof, shot out like a flash of chain lightning, the fist end taking effect full upon the flushed face of the burly intruder.

Red Lampheer, howling with pain and rage, fell backward into the arms of his companions. Ned, reinforced by as many of those inside as could crowd up, sought to take advantage of this temporary victory to close the door and bar it, but heavy-booted feet thrust in at the bottom, and brawny hands and fierce, brutal faces filling the space at the top made it impossible. The ruffians were only momentarily feazed by the overthrow of their leader. Red soon rallied, and with loud oaths started again to rush into the room. His followers came on *en masse*, and the fight raged hot about the entrance. First Pete Murray, then Ned Blakely, then Ashbel Fair and the other defenders sent the shantymen tumbling to the ground like weak children beneath the blows of their heavy fists; but as fast as one went down he was dragged or kicked away and another took his place. Suddenly a crash of glass announced an attack on one of the windows. It was followed quickly by the crash of a chair on the head which was thrust in through the broken sash. The situation was growing more perilous every moment. The women, with pale faces and dilated eyes, had shrunk close to the rear wall of the dining-room at the point farthest from the scrimmage. They made no outcry, but listened and watched with what interest in the result of the struggle may be imagined. Their defenders, with the single exception of Jose, the fat fiddler, who had mysteriously disappeared, and who, by the way, was found afterward asleep under a bed, were standing manfully up to the work in hand, determined to defend the citadel at any cost, although they could not tell how far the drunken fury of the shantymen would carry them. More than one regretted that they had not taken warning from the threat made by Red Lampheer and provided themselves with more effective means of defense. A single brace of revolvers would have proved more effectual than two score of fists. By a strange chance, there did not appear to be a single firearm in possession of either the defending or attacking party.

It appeared at length that a new scheme for forcing an entrance had been hit upon by the enemy. Three stalwart shantymen rushed in upon Pete at the same time and clinched with him, wrestling and tugging at the giant Irishman with all their might, and striving not so much to throw him to the floor as to shove him back from the entrance. In this they were completely successful, and the moment his place was vacant at the doorway three others rushed upon Ned and bore him struggling to the floor. Bob Landseer and Dave Martin in turn met a similar fate. Ashbel Fair was dragged outside. Before the remaining force within could rally to fill the breach thus formed, the horde of drunken, bruised, and yelling shantymen came pouring into the room, and the defenders were pushed back to the rear. Several brave fellows were already badly hurt, while a number of Lampheer's crew were still clinging to the arms, legs, necks, and hair of those who had been forced away from the door, rendering them helpless for the time. Ashbel Fair had come in again with the rush of

invaders and was now grappling with a wiry young
French-Canadian. "Babe" Strander was being pum-
melled about the head with huge fists by a burly logger
who knelt on his victim's body. Pete Murray was
down at last and giving four brutes all they could do to
hold him, but murderous fingers were clutching at his
throat. The outlook began to look dark; the enemy
outnumbered the defenders and fought with demoniacal
fury; the battle was almost lost—when unexpected
shouts were heard, and clear and distinct above the din
came the command:

"Loose your hold there, quick, or you die!"

Tom Moore stood inside the door with a cocked revolver pointed straight at the head of the ruffian who
was trying to strangle Pete Murray. Barney O'Boyle,
Jake Vogel, and Dan Underhill stood near him with
their revolvers levelled at Red Lampheer and his shantymen. Consternation seized the foe; they began to
fall away as if already they felt the cold lead in their
flesh. The hard-pressed defenders were electrified.
Pete sprang to his feet the moment the murderous
hands were removed, and pausing not an instant, as his
eye roved over the scene, cried out in a loud voice,
somewhat husky from the choking he had received:

"Now's the time, boys! Charge the divils!"

Immediately the swingle-like movement of his arms
recommenced. Shantymen began to fall around him
as decayed trees fall in the path of a cyclone. His
friends also were up and hewing away at the panic-
stricken foe. Barney, Tom, Jake, and Dan, putting up
their revolvers, joined with a relish in the feast of punishment, until the miserable wretches were cleared completely out of the tavern, and driven far down the road,
over the rude bridge spanning the creek, and on toward

the river, many of them begging for mercy, which none merited and which few obtained.

Not until the avengers had returned to the tavern to count the cost of the fight to their own side did any one think to ask Barney the meaning of his late arrival and of the absence of Norine. Even in the mind of the unhappy young Irishman himself the excitement and rush of battle had for the moment driven out all else. When, with the assistance of Tom Moore, he explained briefly the misfortune that had fallen, exclamations of astonishment and sympathy were heard on every side. It seemed as if that fated night had brought more than its share of evil, and some of the women whose nerves were already sorely tried began to sob hysterically. Seward Rathaway listened with fear, doubt, and indignation struggling in his face, but said nothing.

"We came here fer volunteers ter help run the rascals into their lair, ef they hev one, an' to find Norine an' take her home," explained Tom. "We don't know who the abductors are, though we hev suspicions. Hallo, there, Seward you here?" he exclaimed in surprise, catching sight of the young man for the first time. "You'll come with us, I spose; reckon you kin help as well as anybody." The significant tone in which he made the final suggestion was lost on all but Seward, who paled, and then flushed, as he replied:

"Certainly, I'd be glad to; but I must take my cousin and Axcy home; besides, I got a pretty hard knock on the head from one of those shantymen. I'm afraid I wouldn't be much good."

It was finally decided that the company should divide. All those who had suffered in the fight, or who were needed to see the ladies home, were to remain and take all the vehicles for that purpose, while those who were

"LOOSE YOUR HOLD THERE QUICK, OR YOU DIE!"

free from injury and obligation were to join in the
hunt for the lost girl if they were willing. Pete Murray, in spite of his rough handling, insisted upon joining
the searching party, and confided his wife and daughters to Bob and Hetty Landseer. Ned Blakely also
declared himself to be fit, and six others likewise, making a party of twelve, who declared they would thrash
every acre of woods until Norine was found. This arrangement settled upon, the party set forth, following
the ridge to where it intersected with the burnt hills.
Here Tom said that he and Barney would go forward
to reconnoitre while the others remained to follow when
the signal should be given. This signal was to be the
hooting of an owl, followed by a raccoon's cry. Tom,
from long years spent in the woods, was an adept at
imitating these sounds, making both so naturally as to
deceive even the owl or raccoon itself.

Barney and Tom moved stealthily along the ridge in
a southerly direction to the spot where the path had
been discovered. They followed this path till it merged
into the hill or ledge skirting the great swamp. There
all traces of it disappeared. They went cautiously from
side to side of the ridge, but not another sign of a track
could they find. The ground was all quite new to them.
They could be sure of their course only by observing
the stars. After traversing the ridge for a while they
concluded to return to their companions. It was useless to try to follow a trail on a rocky ledge at night.
Coming back to the rest of the party, they held a consultation as to the next step to be taken, and it was
unanimously agreed to wait for daylight before making
another attempt. The disappearance of Nero puzzled
them, and made the search more difficult.

At the first streak of light the whole party set out

again on the trail, thinking it wisdom to proceed then in a body. When they reached the ridge it was evident that the trail was lost there and could not be picked up again. They scoured the whole distance of three miles, spreading out from side to side of the ledge of rocks, scanning every foot of its surface in a vain attempt to pick up the lost trail. They peered into the swamp all along its margin for a possible opening, but none could be observed. It seemed evident that no foot could penetrate the swamp, which bordered the rocks on both sides, and no way of leaving the ridge could be found except the one by which they had come.

The sun had nearly reached the meridian before the tired and hungry searchers gave up hope of finding the lost girl. She could not have disappeared more completely if the earth had opened and swallowed her up. Utterly baffled, they turned their steps in the direction of the Hawkins farm to make their disheartening report and assist in any new plans that might be made to discover the secret which the forest and the swamp refused to disclose.

CHAPTER XXII

A PARTY of searchers, weary, crestfallen, muddy, and torn arrived at the farm of Mr. Hawkins on the afternoon following the interrupted dance and supper at Sixteen. The other searchers who had gone in different directions had returned several hours before. Mr. and Mrs. Maloney, Parson Allen and a score or more of neighbors were gathered there, anxiously awaiting the coming of the last party, and hoping against hope that they would bring Norine with them, or at least some tidings of her safety. Their story was heard with sorrow and alarm, which increased as the questions which came thick and fast failed to elicit any definite information or encouragement. The parents of Norine were distracted with grief and anxiety, all the more acute because Norine had never before been away from their protecting care for a single night.

Mother Hawkins was one of the most anxious inquirers for tidings of the lost girl. She seemed to be breaking down under a fear she could not repress. Learning that Barney and Tom had returned without any encouraging news, and that, indeed, their few discoveries pointed to foul play, the stricken woman unwilling to confide in human friends the inmost fears of her heart, raised her eyes to heaven and, while the tears rolled down her furrowed face, appealed to the unseen Father to spare her the added sorrows which she felt were near at hand.

Rumors, which could not be kept from Mother

Hawkins's ears, went from mouth to mouth that Sam
had not yet returned to his home since the night before, and that it was unfortunate he was not on hand
to help in the search and prevent suspicion from at-
taching to him. Some of the more reckless did not hesitate to venture the opinion that Sam Hawkins might
give the searching party certain valuable information.
These whispered remarks showed signs of developing
into threats, but as Tom and Barney said nothing to
substantiate the rumors, the majority gave the ugly
insinuations little credence. They stung his mother's
heart, however, like poisoned arrows. She had watched
all night, hoping that before morning Norine would be
safely returned. When Barney's home-coming blotted
out the last ray of hope she retired to the sitting-room
alone and gave herself up to sorrow and despair. The
minister followed, seeking to comfort her and keep
hope alive. She listened patiently for awhile, then
turning her weary, pain-filled eyes to his face, she said:

"You are very kind, Robert; you would save me
from the blow if you could; perhaps you believe all
will yet be well; God grant you may be right."

She rose tremblingly to her feet in the excess of her
emotion. The next moment the minister sprang forward to save her from falling, and placing her tenderly
in the big arm-chair, started to find Farmer Hawkins.

"Robert," she called faintly, as he was leaving the
room.

"Yes, Susan?" he asked, returning to her side.

"Do not let any of them know that I—that I believe——"

"I know, Susan; I will say nothing. Leave all in
God's hands, and trust in His mercy. He loves us all.
He saved even me, Susan," said Allen, gently.

Farmer Hawkins was greatly worried to find his wife failing so rapidly. He patted her face lovingly and urged her to keep up heart. "It's always the darkest before dawn," he said. Perhaps the sun would break through the clouds sooner than she thought. It was not time yet to lose hope. The cheery words cost the farmer an effort which well-nigh betrayed his own heavy heart to his wife. He found it hard to inspire her with a hope which he himself did not feel. Several recent happenings, of which his neighbors knew nothing, kept thrusting themselves into his memory, all pointing the same way. His tender pleadings with his wife were broken at last with a sob. He saw plainly that the strain of the past night and morning was proving too much for her feeble strength—that anxiety, sorrow, and shame were crushing her tender spirit. He looked appealingly to the minister; then by a common impulse they both knelt together near Mother Hawkins's chair and lifted up their burdened hearts to the throne of Him, who, having been "a man of sorrows, and acquainted with grief," is able also to bear *our* grief and carry *our* sorrows.

With the peace which seemed to be dawning in the loved face of his wife as they arose, Josiah saw something more which caused him sudden alarm. He hurried out to the veranda where several of his neighbors were still waiting, and exclaimed in a voice vibrating with anguish:

"I want somebody to go for the doctor, quick! Mother is ill; I'm afraid she's dying! Please hurry."

Every man sprang to get his horse, but Tom Moore, leaping into Vogel's buggy which stood waiting in the road, was off at a terrific pace before any of the others could get ready. In an incredibly short time Tom had found old Doctor Landseer, Bob's father, and brought him to the farm; then without a word of apology he turned the panting, lather-covered horse over to Jake Vogel to be sponged off and rubbed down.

Doctor Landseer came from the house half an hour later looking very grave. As the friends of Farmer Hawkins gathered round him with eager questions he raised his hand in warning.

"Sh! Silence—absolute silence!" he said. "It's very sad—very sad. The good woman is sufferin' from nervous shock an' strain. There was little I could do —very little. She may rally; then, again, she may not. Only her husband must go near her—an' her brother-in-law, the minister, of course. You better all go home. Noise or excitement of any kind might prove fatal. I regret to say it—it's very sad—but in her present condition even good news would be apt to have as serious effect as bad news."

The old doctor always self-important when speaking in his professional capacity, though unassuming enough at other times, was unusually set up at being called to visit so important a place as Farmer Hawkins's. He was genuinely sorry for the grief-stricken farmer, but his professional dignity asserted itself above all other feelings. He graciously condescended to ride back to Red-Keg with Vogel after his horse had rested, and promised to come out again with Bob in the morning.

There seemed to be little else that the neighbors could do for the time being in view of the probability, which amounted almost to a certainty, that Norine had not been lost, but had been forcibly taken away. It was decided, therefore, to leave the matter until the following day in the hands of Tom Moore and Barney to plan the next move.

Tom Moore, in his capacity as village constable, was ready and anxious to do anything that would throw more light upon the mystery. He did not care to accuse Sam until he had something more than a mere suspicion against him. Sam had a bad reputation, but there were many who, for his father's and mother's sake, if not for his own, would not believe him guilty of the dastardly outrage which had been laid at his door.

It was his unexplained disappearance, his well known antipathy to Barney, and his repeated advances to Norine, one of which had earned him a thrashing, that had caused him to be suspected of having a hand in the abduction of the girl. Big Tom and Barney had purposely refrained from mentioning the boot-tracks showing the star, and had also cautioned others to be very careful about spreading a report as to who was suspected; but the remarks concerning Sam were only partially repressed. Before Tom left for the village they had talked the matter over carefully and had laid plans for a campaign of search on their own lines, and determined to set about their work the next morning.

Doctor Landseer came early in the morning, and found Mother Hawkins very feeble and suffering great mental distress. He administered an opiate and cautioned Josiah again to keep from her everything of an exciting nature. Mrs. Maloney, her own heart torn with grief and anxiety, insisted upon relieving Josiah to enable him to get needed rest. With wonderful self-control she mastered her feelings, that she might soothe and comfort the sick woman with sympathy and tender ministrations.

Sam had not been seen since the night of Norine's disappearance. This fact counted against him strongly. On the other hand, the presence at the dance of Sew-

20

ard, by every one regarded as Sam's most intimate companion and confidant, together with his outspoken condemnation of whoever was responsible for the abduction, counted almost as strongly in Sam's favor. Those who had been most ready to point the finger of suspicion at Sam, were compelled to admit that he would hardly engage in so risky an undertaking without the knowledge or support of the other so-called Invincibles. When on the afternoon following the abduction Walt came up on the train from Midland, where he had been on a personal business errand, and also expressed unquestionable surprise and indignation on hearing of the affair, the case against Sam grew still weaker. Billy Axford and Sam himself remained to be heard from.

As soon as they could do so without attracting attention, Seward and Walt met in their room over Pete's saloon to discuss the matter in their own way. Their low, intense voices and angry gestures were strongly out of harmony with their professed ignorance of the whole affair.

A knock at the door interrupted their conference. Bob Simons stood there with a soiled letter in his hand.

Seward took it leisurely and then locked the door. He immediately tore the envelope open, read the note and handed it to Walt with an expressive "humph!"

"Come to the hunting lodge at once," the note said. There was no signature.

"Come on," exclaimed Seward. "The sooner we have this thing out the better."

By a circuitous route, with frequent halts, doublings, and constant watchfulness, the two young men made their way to the lodge in which they had entertained the detectives. Sam and Billy were waiting for them.

"What devil's work have you been up to now, Sam?" demanded Seward angrily the instant he opened the door. "I'm not going to beat about the bush, let me tell you; and what's more, if you have carried off Norine, I won't stand for it a minute; let that be understood."

"Just hold up there a minute, will you," replied Sam with provoking coolness. "Who said I carried off Norine? You are entirely too swift. Sit down here and we'll all talk it over together. Remember the motto of the Invincibles, ' no surrender.' How are you, Walt? Come sit down here, both of you."

Hour after hour passed. The four Invincibles continued in earnest consultation until late into the night. More than once the meeting threatened to break up in a row, but mutual interests, and more potent still, mutual safety held them strongly, and made a division the one thing to be avoided. Sam had told Billy sometime before that "if it comes to a pinch they must stand their share." Seward and Walt tried to dodge this share but saw no safe way to do so. When they parted in the morning, it was with a definite plan mapped out. Seward and Walt returned at once, by different routes, to Red-Keg. Sam and Billy were to follow later.

At Pete's saloon, on Monday afternoon, the second day after Norine's disappearance, the usual crowd of tavern gossips were gathered, discussing the mystery and waiting for any scrap of news that might find its way thither. The presence of Seward and Walt attracted some who were not accustomed to frequent the place, because it was hoped that they might throw some light upon the reason for Sam's continued absence. But they merely reiterated their belief that

Sam and Billy were on a hunting trip, and that they knew absolutely nothing about the abduction.

"Sam urged me to go with him out to the Big Salt on Saturday," said Seward, "but I refused because I wanted to go to the dance. I have every reason to suppose that he and Billy went, anyway, although I believe he wasn't feeling very well that afternoon."

"They must have gone," said Walt. "Billy told me they thought of it, and I suggested that they wait till Monday so we could all go together. I had to go to Midland, you know. He said he'd speak to Sam about it, and that's the last I—why, here they come now! By Jove! you see it is as we thought; they've just got in from their trip."

Sam and Billy came in attired in hunting garb, muddy and bedraggled, stood their guns noisily against the wall, and called on Pete to "set 'em up."

"Hallo, there, boys!" exclaimed Sam, addressing Walt and Seward. "You missed it by not coming with us. We had the best luck of the spring—two splendid big bucks. You must come out to the lodge as soon as you can and see them. Thunder! but I'm tired; Billy and I have been on the go from Saturday afternoon till last night, running those deer. Come up, and have something—what in blazes are you all staring about, anyhow?" he added, noting the significant looks bent upon him by the hangers-on.

"Hain't you two heard nothin' o' that lost girl?" asked Joe Reon, after an awkward pause.

"Lost girl!" exclaimed Sam with a great show of astonishment. "Who's lost?"

"Why, didn't ye know thet Norine Maloney hes disappeared es though the earth had swallered her up?" replied Joe.

"No indeed! How strange!" said Sam. "When was it, and how in the world did it happen?"

"No one seems ter know. She an' Barney started out ter the dance Saturday night in the ox-cart. They had an upset, an' while Barney was chasin' his team, Norine disappeared an' hain't been seen nor heard from sence."

The whole matter, so far as it was known, was then pretty thoroughly aired, Sam listening intently to every word.

"I say, Sam, come here a minute," whispered Arch Fellows to Sam, and jerked his head toward a corner of the barroom. "I don't mind tellin' ye thet your name is mixed up in this mess. Ef ye can clear yerself, now's the time to do it."

"Why, my friend, that's kind of you, don't you know, but you must be mistaken," replied Sam, flushing scarlet, and then paling.

"Unless you can show an allerby (I think thet's what they call it) there's trouble ahead fer ye. Don't let on as I've put ye on to this, but I want ye ter be on yer guard," and the two sauntered back to the bar and mingled with the rest.

"But I say that Sam Hawkins had nothing whatever to do with it!" Seward was just asserting. "He was off on the Big Salt hunting, as he says. I'll take my chances on that. What's the sense in calling a man a liar—and worse—when you have nothing to prove it. He is here, and can speak for himself. Oh, Sam, where are you? Here's a fellow who is trying to connect you with the disappearance of Norine. Come here and let us know what you have to say."

"Who says I know anything about this affair?" cried Sam, emboldened by Seward's companionship.

"If anything has happened to the girl ask Barney O'Boyle about it. He took her off Saturday night in an old ox-cart you say. The chances are that he quarrelled with her on the way—tried to force her to consent to his proposals, or something, and when she refused he made way with her; or else he lost her in the slough, and to save his own bacon he's trying to put suspicion on me. He's a——"

"Ye're a liar, and a coward! Ye wouldn't dare talk like thet ef Barney war here. I believe *you* know where Norine Maloney is if any one does," and Tom Moore at that instant stepped into the door, having been standing within hearing when Sam was making his dastardly charge against Barney.

This unexpected attack took everybody by surprise, and the crowd breathlessly awaited the outcome.

"Don't be too windy, there, Tom," exclaimed Seward, before Sam could reply for himself. "You know Sam is no knocker, and you take advantage of that fact. *You* just hold your peace, Sam, till I get through." Then turning again to Tom: "Whatever you may say don't change conditions at all. You've all heard where Sam was Saturday night and what he was doing. Here's Billy to prove it. I've known Sam for years; we've been intimate all that time. If he wants to make a fight of it, I'll join him, and meet any man or men who repeats the dirty lie again."

"Bully for you, Seward!" cried Axford. "That's the way to talk. I was with Sam Saturday night and I'm ready to plug the fellow that accuses me of having anything to do with the disappearance of the girl. Here's Walt, too. That makes four of us."

Walt said nothing, but he ranged himself beside the other three in tacit agreement.

A buzz of excitement went around, but no one had the temerity to accept the challenge thrown down.

Good-natured Tom Moore didn't want to fight. He merely wanted to save Barney from false accusations. He knew that Sam lied when he accused Barney. He could not prove anything further. In fact, the stand the boys had taken almost convinced him that Sam knew nothing of the matter.

"Gentlemen, I see you are all greatly excited over this affair, and if you will allow me my little say, I may throw a ray or two of light on this mystery."

One of the loungers, a tramp, who had been resting and dozing the greater part of the day at one of the small tables, pushed his way forward into the group.

"Saturday evening I walked all the way down from Sixteen, arriving here at about ten o'clock. On my way down the State road, when just this side of a long corduroy, crossing a deep lagoon, I heard an awful rumbling on ahead of me. I stopped to listen, and soon an ox-team came in sight running as though the very old Nick was after them. I stepped aside to let them pass, and soon I heard a man coming along, running at the top of his speed and yelling at the runaways. I was in a hurry and did not care to be delayed, so I again stepped to one side and the runner went by without noticing me. I had regained the road and walked scarcely a dozen rods when I saw a tall man step out from a clump of bushes. He started at a fast walk down the road, and I must confess I was a little startled to see him, and so remained behind in order to observe what was in the wind. A little farther down the road he came up to where a woman was standing. He approached her and held a conversation for a few moments, and then both of them started off into the forest to the west. From where I was standing (I didn't dare come too near) I could not tell whether she went willingly with the fellow or not. I could only see their outlines in the dark. I thought there was some mystery in it all, so I skipped out as fast as I could. I didn't want to be mixed up in anything like that."

The crowd listened and drank in every word. The Invincibles absorbed with avidity all that was said. After the stranger had cleared his throat he continued:

"I wouldn't have mentioned the matter only that I heard this young man here charged with having a hand in it, and this other gentleman swear that he was with him, and, that being true, he could not have had anything to do with the crime, as I saw only one man with the girl. I don't like to see a man charged with anything of which he is innocent," and the stranger looked longingly toward the bar.

"Stranger, you have relieved me of a great deal of embarrassment, don't you know," said Sam. "Of course time would have settled matters all right; but I might have been unpleasantly situated for a while, if it had not been for you and my friends here," and Sam grasped the hand of the shabby stranger. "Come up and have some of Pete's best. All of you have one on me." A rush was made toward the bar again, Tom only declining on the ground that he never indulged.

As the liquor disappeared down thirsty throats gossip was again let loose. The developments of the last few minutes had set all tongues to wagging.

"I want to know the name of my benefactor," said Sam to the stranger a little later.

"Oh, that don't matter much, my friend. I am nobody. I have been way up State for the winter and came down last week to Sixteen. Got on an awful jag there and saw snakes. Thought I saw a spider just now on your neck, and that reminds me," and the stranger gave an ominous shudder. " But this stuff of Pete's is a warmer, sure. Hadn't we better try another one?"

Again the treats went around at the expense of Sam.

"Speaking of my name, as I have said, that isn't much, but you are welcome to it such as it is. It's not long—simply Long, for short, or John Long, in full, and nearly always full, or willing to be. I expect to board a freight train down the line to-night, and I may never see you again, but I am so much obliged to you for your generosity. Say (*sotto voce*), you haven't a few pennies about you, have you? You know I may see those snakes again unless I am fortunate enough to be fortified against them," and Long looked furtively around as though he expected to see some just then.

"You see, my friend," his voice assuming a stage whisper again, " I am dead broke, or I wouldn't trouble a nice gentleman like yourself," and he cast an admiring look into Sam's face.

Sam reached into his pocket and gave the man a dollar bill.

"Kind friend, I will remember this, and some day I may be able to pay it back."

"Don't mention it. It's a mere trifle, don't you know, and you have already done me a great service," and Sam shook the outstretched hand of his garrulous friend.

Tom Moore had been watching the tramp closely for some minutes. When he was about to leave the place, Tom stepped up to him and brusquely said:

"Say, pard, don't take no offense; but I would like to ask ye a few questions. Ye say ye arrived here Saturday night about ten o'clock. Where'd ye sleep?"

Taken by surprise, the stranger began to stammer:

"You see, my friend—I—you—you know—or my friend here knows—that is—well—I was simply without a cent in the world, and a kindly barn out here on the outskirts of your hospitable village sheltered me from the inclemency of the weather while Jupiter Pluvius was drenching the land during the night."

"When did ye leave thet barn?" continued Tom, pointedly.

"Well, your honor—pardon me, sir; I thought for a moment that I was addressing a court—I left my temporary place of shelter this morning. Morpheus had taken such a powerful hold on me after I got nicely ensconced in the depths of that sweet hay, and, having empty pockets, I let him hang on as long as he would," and the tramp looked pleadingly at his interrogator.

"Hev ye any objections to lettin' me see the bottom o' yer boot?" again asked Tom.

"Not the slightest," and the tramp raised his foot from the floor. All eyes were now turned toward this couple.

"Jest as I thought! Do ye see thet, boys?" and Tom pointed to the heel.

There in plain sight was a star!

"Thet's enough," resumed Tom, "ye may put down yer foot; but I want ye to come with me," and the big fellow had a pair of handcuffs snapped upon the tramp before he could even utter a word of protest.

"What does this mean?" yelled the crowd, as Tom and his prisoner started for the door.

"It means that I have arrested this man for abductin' or otherwise disposin' of Norine Maloney," said Tom, with decision, as he marched his prisoner over to the lockup near by, the crowd following, hooting and yelling, and with cries of

"Hang him!"

"String him up!"

"Give 'im to us! We'll fix 'im!"

"Hold on. We must have no blood on our hands," exclaimed Seward to the crowd, and the Invincibles quickly surrounded Tom and his prisoner. "Justice will be done, and we'll see it through to the end. We will have no mob violence. This man's punishment will come soon enough when he is proven guilty."

The crowd, numbering by this time a hundred people, fell back to let the law take its course, and Constable Tom soon had the unfortunate wanderer securely under lock and key in an old log shanty which was used as a jail when occasion required.

CHAPTER XXIII

Tom Moore hastened to find Barney to boast of his capture. There seemed no doubt that he had the right man. As his belief in the tramp's guilt grew stronger, the defense offered by Sam assumed proportionately greater value. Hadn't he proved an alibi? Were not the hunting boots he wore free from the telltale star, while the tramp's boots had them? Was not Sam's story of how his time had been employed since Saturday night much more credible than that told by the tramp? All these points Tom laid before Barney, but the latter seemed unconvinced.

"What did the tramp say for himself?" he asked.

"Oh, of course he denied the hull thing, an' stuck to it," replied Tom; "but I reckon Jedge Frost will git it outer him at the hearin'."

The young Irishman shook his head gloomily. He could see no light on the dark mystery. The uncertainty regarding the whereabouts and fate of Norine was preying upon his mind. He could see the girl standing in the road where he had left her; her appealing voice still smote upon his ears, and he could not be comforted. He fully realized the sorrow his misfortune had entailed upon others, and also the loss of property by his beloved employer, who bore the blow uncomplainingly. He could see the suffering of dear Mother Hawkins, who had been indeed a mother to him. He could see also the heart-sorrow of the parents

of his betrothed. His bride-to-be had disappeared—
was perhaps dead—and there was lost property to make
good. In the last two days he had become melancholy,
almost morose, and took little interest in anything except how to find Norine.

Tom and Barney, who stood talking out near the
road, were so absorbed that they did not hear a light
footstep behind them. It was evening, and darkness
had already fallen.

"Mr. Moore, excuse me for interrupting, but have
you had any news from Norine? I saw you passing
our place, and thought you would be here and might
have more information by this time, so I came up to
see. We are so much worried about her." Lettie
Green had approached the two men, and now looked inquiringly at the burly constable. She did not look at
Barney. Her heart was too full of sorrow at the loss
of her friend; moreover, there were other thoughts in
her mind which she hardly dared to consider, even in
secret.

"We hev no perticular news of her, but we are sartin
thet we hev her abductor safely behind the bars, Miss
Green," answered Tom, politely.

"What! Sam Hawkins—in jail!" and she grasped
the gate to keep herself from falling. "What will
become of his poor old mother?" and Lettie burst into
tears.

"Be calm, Miss; *he* isn't the guilty one. What made
ye think he was?" and Tom looked at her in amazement.

"Why, Mr. Moore—I—I—really—somebody said
that it was Sam," and her face crimsoned deeply, while
she gave a sigh of relief.

"No, no, Miss Green; we hev found a tramp who

we think hes abducted or possibly murdered the poor gal. We will know more about it tomorrer."

"Oh, I hope she isn't—I hope she's safe," exclaimed Lettie; then thanking Tom, she went to the house to inquire after Mother Hawkins. Receiving an assurance that she was quietly resting, the young woman started down the road toward her home.

She seemed to be walking in a haze. She was oblivious to all things around her. A great tumult was going on between heart and brain. She was sure that Sam Hawkins was the culprit, even though some one else had been arrested on suspicion. Should she tell what she knew of Sam's eagerness to prevent Norine from going to the dance with Barney, or should she shield Sam and let an innocent man suffer? Although at her last meeting with Sam he had grossly insulted her, she had forgiven him in spite of herself. Why was it that she still held to the love that had well-nigh wrecked her life? Why was it that the hate which, at the moment of his insults and taunts seemed springing up in her heart, died away so quickly? Surely he did not mean half of what he had said then in anger. If only she could see him alone again, her tenderness and forgiveness would win him back. Perhaps, after all, he was innocent of the dreadful thing that had been done. Why should she suspect him, if others did not? He needed a loyal friend now in the time of his trouble. Might she not find comfort and joy herself in standing as his champion? Ah, let him try her and see.

Thus musing, she was walking slowly homeward. The road led through a dark patch of wood before reaching her home, and as she neared this spot she suddenly came to a standstill. She dreaded to go through. It was dark, and the woods seemed unusually gloomy.

Thoughts of Norine filled her with apprehension. She stood at the outskirts of the wood, hesitating. She could hear her heart thump at every pulsation. A terrible dread crept over her, and she was about to turn and fly back to the home of Norine, when she heard some one coming through the glen. She was now helpless from fright. She essayed to move or cry out, but stood like a statue. Soon the outlines of a man could be seen coming toward her, and a moment later, to her great relief, she saw that it was Sam. With a cry of joy she rushed to him, her fear having departed with his advent.

"Oh, Sam, I never was so glad in my life. I was so frightened at this lonely spot just now, and you came just in time to save me from losing my self-possession. Why, Sam, what's the matter? Are you not glad to see me?" and Lettie drew back a step as Sam impatiently motioned her aside.

"Don't know why I should be," he said gruffly. "I suppose you've been up to Norine's or to our place to blab what you know. Have you?" his voice was thick, and even in the darkness Lettie discovered that he was the worse for liquor, and was in an ugly mood.

"Sam, please don't talk that way to me. I have done nothing to deserve it. I have not breathed one word against you, nor told anything I know. As soon as I heard of the trouble, and found your name being drawn into it, I prayed that you might be able to clear yourself."

"I would rather have you use your wits and help me, and do less praying," sneered Sam. "I'm not out of this scrape yet, even though they have got a tramp in jail. I need friends still, and if you're as smart as you're supposed to be, you'll think of some way to help

me. That tramp says he came down here Saturday
night, and on the way saw a man come out of the woods
and meet Norine and then go back with her. He says
he went past this way about ten o'clock. If his story
holds water, he'll get off and they'll have to find the
other man. Can't you find somebody, your Aunt Lydia,
or somebody else, who will swear they saw the tramp,
short, dark suit, slouch hat, pass here *this morning*, or
last evening? That'll bear out Tom Moore's idea and
upset the tramp's yarn. He's no account anyhow, and
a spell of boarding at the State's expense will do him
good, don't you know, m' dear."

Sam's tone was growing confidential and coaxing as
he thought his plea would succeed. It was too dark
for him to see the look of horror which had come into
Lettie's face as she listened.

"Sam!" she gasped, "would you have me ask some
one to swear to a lie? Oh, you don't mean that!
What if the poor man is really innocent? Why are
you so anxious to convict him? Is there no other way
for you to shield yourself? Does it mean that you—
oh, Sam! did you——?"

"That's enough!" interrupted Sam gruffly. "I
didn't ask you to preach. Of course I've got to shield
myself the best way I can. I thought I could count
on you to help me, as you pretended to care for me.
S'posing I did do it, isn't that all the more reason for
needing help? Are you going to do as I ask or
not?"

"You know, Sam, I want to help you; but don't ask
me to commit another crime to cover up one already
committed. Oh, Sam, is it too late for you to set right
whatever you have done, and restore Norine to her
parents, and to—to—Barney? What do *you* want of her,

Sam, when she has no love for you? Tell me where she is. Let me go to her, and my word for it, Sam, I will have her return and clear both you and the poor tramp. Besides, no one need ever know that she was really abducted. Let me manage it, Sam. Return her through me to Barney. By so doing you may save your dear mother's life. Do you know she now lies at the point of death, brought there by the thought that her only son has been guilty of some unnamable crime?"

"Mother sick, did you say, and on my account?" said Sam uneasily. "I don't see why she should worry about me. I know enough to take care of myself without being tied to her apron-strings."

"That may all be very true, Sam," the girl continued, "but you have caused her great suffering, and the doctor says she may die at any moment."

"Hang it all! She seems to think I'm a baby yet," and his lips curled in annoyance at the thought.

"But, Sam," and Lettie placed her hand tenderly upon his shoulder, "don't you love your mother? When she is gone, Sam—when she is gone—it will be too late to show her the tenderness that she hungers for now. She yearns for you, and the agony of the thought that you have done such a dastardly——"

"Don't be too ready with your adjectives, please; something unpleasant about them, don't you know," broke in Sam, sneeringly.

"I beg your pardon, Sam; I do sincerely. My only thought was to save you from further trouble and your mother needless suffering. Sam, I would do anything in honor for you, because—Sam—because—" and she twined her arms about the neck of the one who was still her idol—"because I—I—love you——"

"Don't be a fool, Lettie! I've got other things to

21

think of now," and he roughly disengaged himself from her embrace.

Lettie drew back quickly, her face scarlet. For a moment she was speechless. Then tears of pain and mortification sprang into her eyes. Controlling herself at last, she said:

"Mr. Hawkins, forgive me. I did not mean to force myself on you. Perhaps my zeal for your well-being has made me forgetful of my own dignity. You knew long ago that what I said was true, and you must remember what *you* said; but I will never repeat it, or give you any further uneasiness on that score. I can not leave you now until you promise me not to injure Norine. Will you take me to her and let me save you from further disgrace?"

"No! You may as well say no more about that," answered Sam, angrily.

"But," she persisted, "will you tell me where Norine is? Is she safe and well? And—will no harm come to her?"

"That is none of your business. You do as I tell you and don't interfere further," answered Sam, petulantly.

Lettie's patience was sorely tried. With some show of returning spirit, she asked: "What if I should refuse to do as you say, but should tell all I know about this affair? If I am asked in court, shall I not have to tell the truth? If I thought that you had wronged or injured Norine, I could never rest till the wrong was righted—even though——"

"It took me to prison? I know what you were going to say," and, rushing forward in a sudden spasm of rage, Sam seized the girl by the throat and bore her to the ground.

"Tell on me—will you? Tell on me?" he hissed through his clenched teeth. "What if I should choke the last breath from your lying throat?" and his brutal nails sank deeper and deeper into the delicate, quivering flesh. "Will you do as I want you to, or will you tell on me, you false hussy?"

Only a choking gurgle came from the distorted mouth. Suddenly Sam released his hold and peered into the face of his victim. It was purple; the tongue protruded, the bulging, unseeing eyes stared at him in the growing darkness. He sprang to his feet and looked hastily around.

"My God! I've gone too far!" he muttered, shaking like a leaf. He stooped and gazed searchingly at the prostrate figure.

"Lettie! Lettie!" he whispered hoarsely, shaking her in a vain effort to bring some response; then in a sudden panic of fear he sprang to his feet and hurried away from the spot.

Lydia Green glanced at the clock and remarked a little nervously that it was time for Lettie to be back at home. Seward Rathaway was there, waiting for her also.

"She ought not to have started out so late to go alone up to Hawkins's," he said. "It is a good two miles up there and the road is dark and lonesome enough for men, to say nothing of a girl."

"I know it," admitted her aunt, "but the poor girl is so upset about Norine; and after she heard that Sam was suspected of having a hand in the abduction she wished to go. I urged her for a while to keep away, as they had trouble enough of their own. But when she saw Tom Moore go by, she was sure he had some news, and then she *must* go, so at last I gave in. I am getting to be a little worried about her now, though."

"Well, Auntie, I'll take a stroll up the road to see if I can meet her. Hope *she* hasn't been abducted," and with a forced smile he sauntered away.

When he reached the glen, Seward thought he heard angry voices; listening more intently he became sure of this, and hastened to investigate. As he drew near the spot whence came the sounds of altercation, he discovered that his cousin and Sam Hawkins were wrangling about something. He could not catch what was said and hesitated to interrupt a private conversation. At that moment the voices ceased, and after pausing a few moments to hear whether there would be a renewal of the dispute, he went forward in time to see Sam start off up the road alone. Lettie was not to be seen. Puzzled at this, he quickened his pace, and was about to call to Sam when he stumbled over a prostrate form in the road.

It took but an instant to discover that this was his cousin, whom he was seeking.

"That arch fiend has been doing some more of his hellish work! Lettie, Lettie, are you hurt?" and, stooping to raise her, he uttered a cry of horror.

Hastily raising the limp form to a sitting posture, he chafed her temples and her hands and sought as best he could to restore life to the apparently lifeless body. Soon he felt a quiver; then she began to gasp and moan.

"Thank God, she lives!" he exclaimed. "Heavens! what a narrow escape."

Without an instant's delay he lifted his cousin in his arms and hastened back to his aunt's home. Not a moment must be lost. When he reached the house, Aunt Lydia was outside, waiting for him.

"Here, Auntie, get some hot water bandages at once and put them around Lettie's neck. Not a moment for questions! I'll tell you all about it later!" Lydia Green was a methodical woman, and although greatly unnerved at the sight of poor Lettie's condition, she saw the necessity of prompt action. In a few moments the compresses were ready.

"Keep these up, Auntie, till I return. I must go for the doctor," and away Seward sped toward the village. When he returned post-haste with old Doctor Landseer, Lettie was just regaining consciousness. As she opened her eyes and saw that she was in her own home, she smiled in recognition of Seward, who was bending over her; then she closed her eyes once more.

"She has been strangled, Doctor—" Lettie's eyes opened again and looked so pleadingly into the eyes of Seward that he quickly understood their eloquent entreaty.

"As I was saying, Doctor, she was strangled and left for dead on the road." Again an agonizing look of appeal arrested Seward's words. He returned the gaze, and smiling tenderly at his cousin, who in her extremity desired still to protect the man who had so nearly killed her, nodded his head knowingly.

"The poor girl is dazed at the experience she has gone through," said the doctor.

"Yes. I saw two men—" those eyes were now again looking him full in the face—"they were, I think, attempting to abduct her when they heard me coming, and fled up the road. I shouldn't wonder if they belonged to some gang, and are the same ones who kidnapped Norine Maloney Saturday night." Seward again glanced at the upturned eyes, and saw there a look of gratitude.

His first impulse was to denounce Sam and have him brought to justice; but he could not ignore the plainly expressed wishes of his cousin, and so refrained from carrying out his intention, which he admitted to himself, on second thought, might result disastrously for more than Sam.

This unhappy youth, meanwhile, had hastened away from the girl whom he supposed was dead. His first impulse was to flee and escape all his troubles at once; but a moment's consideration convinced him that this would be the most dangerous course he could pursue. It would amount to a confession of guilt, and the chances of capture were too great. Better face it out, throwing suspicion elsewhere if possible.

"I had to do it in self-defense," he told himself. "She would have blabbed on me. Well, now she can't —that's one comfort. After all, it's better as it is—for another reason—if only I can keep them from suspecting me—bah! I'm trembling. This will never do. Can't afford to be chicken-hearted. There's no time to lose if I'm going to start things going my way."

Thus musing he approached his father's farm. Some one was just coming down the road. Sam braced himself with an effort. In a moment he recognized Tom Moore and called out to him in as off-hand a manner as he could command:

"By Jove! Tom, deuced glad to see you, don't you know. I thought for a while to-day, though, that you had it up your sleeve for me, and was believing the vile rumors set afloat by busybodies—by my enemies, don't you know. But I forgive you freely, Tom, for you had a duty to perform, and did it nobly. How fortunate that you were there to unmask the villainy of that tramp just as he was going to slip out of your fingers. Quite a clever catch. Really good in the fellow, though, to run such a risk for a stranger; eh, Tom?"

"Yas, it wus good in 'im, I 'low," said Tom, extending his hand to Sam, "an' o' course he must hev justice done 'im, fer all he's nothin' but a sneakin' tramp. How I come ter get onter him was the stars on his heels. You know you hed some put on your'n an' thet's how I come to suspect ye. I saw them marks 'way out at the foot of Sturgeon Slough, in the mud, an' when thet stranger begun ter talk I begun ter look at foot-gear. I looked at your'n an' saw ye hed on yer huntin' boots. I concluded to onct thet they were not your tracks. But when I saw his'n my eyes bulged out like saucers, fer I knew I had 'im jest es plain es though I hed already seen the telltale stars. When I saw 'em, *then* I was sure enough of my man to put on the bracelets. My! but the feller must be a cool one. He ast ter hev a jug o' Pete's best laid in with 'im fer the night, an' ter accommerdate 'im I gave 'im one. But say, Sam, forgive me fer whut I did, won't ye? I'll acknowledge my mistake afore the hull Kag, ef ye say so," and Tom gave a twist to Sam's hand.

"That is all right, Tom. I harbor no ill-will. Mistakes will be made, don't you know, and honest ones, too. By the way, better keep your eye out for a couple of suspicious fellows down below. When passing by the Wilford road I saw two men who looked as though they wanted to avoid me. After I had passed they went on down the road, and you may overtake them. There seems to be a gang of strange men in the neighborhood just now. When do you have a hearing for your prisoner?"

"To-morrer, I think; an' be on han', will ye—you an' the rest o' the boys? The people are hard set agin 'im down 't the Kag. You fellers did nobly to stan' by in thet storm o' this afternoon, an' we may need ye agin," said Tom, as he started down the road.

"Yes, we will be there. We want the poor devil to be humanely treated, even though he is guilty. We may be able to touch his heart, so he will tell us what has become of his victim. Poor girl, I can't rest, wondering where she is. Well, good-night, Tom; we'll be on hand bright and early," and the two men parted.

"Deuced good luck that I met him," muttered Sam, nervously. "Now if he stumbles over that fool down there in the road he'll connect the find with those suspicious persons that I didn't see. That was a clever thought. I hope the chump will believe it."

While the conscienceless wretch was congratulating himself on his astuteness, he was treading, unknown to himself, on the crust of a slumbering volcano.

CHAPTER XXIV

"Now to keep up the bluff," thought Sam as he continued his way toward his home after parting with Tom Moore. "It would be a good stroke just now to mollify that confounded Irishman. He's hatching up trouble, I'll be bound. Wonder if I can get around him. Perhaps I might try on a pious dodge for a few days till this thing blows over. 'Twould please the old lady and shut Barney's mouth. If I can only keep out of the way of Allen, it may work."

Sam found himself getting into deep water. The thought of coming into close contact with the minister frightened him almost as much as the possibility of discovery. His parents, the neighbors, and even Barney might believe him if he should profess a change of heart, but could he look into those deep, honest eyes of the minister and make him believe such hypocrisy? Of course, if he could manage to avoid him—. There was not time now to plan a definite course; here he was at the gate, and Barney was standing there alone, disconsolate, and absorbed in his unhappy thoughts. Sam hesitated a moment, then accosted him with a bold display of cordiality.

"Hallo, Barney. What are you doing out here in the dark? Come into the house, man, and cheer up. Brooding won't help matters."

Barney moved away from the gate without replying, but the other refused to be repulsed. He extended his hand and exclaimed:

"Come, Barney, why can't we be friends? We have had our outs long enough, and I want to tell you of my sorrow at your misfortunes. Cheer up, for I feel sure that before long Norine will be safely restored to us. When the screws have been tightened upon that hobo down there in jail, he will weaken and tell us where she is."

The young Irishman hesitated. His heart was bursting with grief and self-blame. He had been standing alone in the darkness ever since Tom had left him, brooding over the unhappy event of Saturday night, and racking his brain for some plan by which he might find Norine and restore her to her stricken parents. He had hardly heard Sam's first greeting, and when he did at last grasp the meaning of the words he was puzzled and embarrassed rather than pleased. The enmity between him and Sam was one which could hardly be brushed aside in a moment, especially when Norine, whom Sam had so recently threatened, was mysteriously missing. Moreover, suspicion had fastened itself in Barney's mind so firmly, that even Tom's report concerning the tramp had hardly removed it. Still Sam's words seemed fair enough, and Barney was not at that moment sufficiently attentive to discern the false ring to them.

"You an' me ain't got much ter shake han's on, I'm thinkin'," said Barney, slowly. "They tell me a tramp's after bein' jugged fer doin' thet cowardly work night 'fore last. Tellin' ye the truth, I 'spected some one else. I don't want ter do ye any injustice, an' I hope ye had nothin' ter do with the matter, but ef ye did— I'd brek ivery bone in yer body!"

"Of course, Barney," replied Sam, ignoring Barney's lack of cordiality, "matters *did* look dark for me, don't you know, especially after that little difference of ours. I can't blame you for your suspicions. But thanks to the acuteness of Tom Moore I have been cleared even from suspicion. Shall you attend the hearing to-morrow?"

"I intind to be there," replied Barney, shortly.

"Here comes father," said Sam, looking up. "Well, father, how are you to-night, and how is mother?" he continued, as his father approached.

Farmer Hawkins was taken by surprise and did not answer at once. He peered at his son, trying to make out his face in the darkness. Sam's tone and manner were so unusual that he was at a loss to account for them. When he replied, his words came slowly, with a deep sadness and solemnity which struck a chill to his son's heart.

"I'm afraid your mother is dying of a broken heart, Sam."

All of Sam's easy manner and forced carelessness of tone seemed to slip away from him in a moment. A sinking sensation almost like faintness possessed him and made it hard to speak, but he managed to falter, hardly knowing what he said:

"I'm sorry, father—I suppose I have been a little wild—but I never meant any real harm. I—I hope you—or mother don't believe I had anything to do with —the disappearance of Norine. I—really didn't. Tom has just been telling Barney that he has captured a tramp and can prove he is the guilty one. It was hard for me to be suspected, but I suppose it was my own fault—and I've made up my mind to—to—well, you know, to turn over a new leaf, and try to—to—oh, be better, you know."

It seemed impossible to get his sentences out, as he

began to realize, with a sickening disgust, how thoroughly he despised himself. When his father put his arm tenderly around his shoulder and exclaimed in a voice choking with joy, "God help you, my son!" the shame and desire to escape were almost too much for him; but his father drew him on to the house. In the sitting-room they paused.

"Wait here a minute, my boy; I want to see Mother."

In the sick-room he stood looking down on the closed eyes of his wife for a moment or two. Presently she looked up into his face wistfully.

"Mother, dear," he said, "are you feeling strong enough this evening to talk a little?"

"Yes, Josiah; have you any news from Norine—or —or Sam?" A heartful of longing spoke in her feeble voice.

Josiah drew his chair close by the bedside, while Mrs. Maloney went to the window to look out into the night. He reached over and took his wife's hand in his and gently stroked it. He wanted to speak, but at each attempt a great lump came into his throat, and he could not utter a word. Finally, raising the feverish hand to his lips, he kissed it again and again, and then broke down completely, the tears welling from his eyes and falling upon the hand he held.

"What are you crying for, Josiah; any bad news?" and she placed her disengaged hand softly upon his head.

"No, Susan, no bad news; but I was wondering if you could bear to hear some *good* news?" and he gazed tenderly at the sharer of his joys and sorrows.

"What is it, Josiah? Tell me," and the eyes brightened.

"Our Sam has returned, and he hadn't anything to

do with taking Norine away. Besides, Susan," and he clasped her hand tighter, "he says he is sorry for being so wild, and is going to try to be a good son to us in our old age."

A heavenly light shone in the eyes of the sick woman, but no other emotion was perceptible.

"Where is he, Josiah?"

"In the sitting-room; shall I let him come in here?"

"Yes; let him come to me—my boy!"

As they entered the sick-room the aged mother looked longingly at them and beckoned them nearer. Sam hung his head, unable to meet that pure gaze. He moved nearer the bed, but did not offer to speak. As he beheld the change which had come over his mother's features since he last saw them, only two days before, his heart began to throb, and he reached out and took her by the hand.

"What is it, mother?" His voice was choking.

"Sam, darling, kneel down by the bedside as you used to do when a child. There, that is right. Take my hands in yours, my boy; hold them tight. I feel that I can not be with you long. Sam, is it true that you are converted and are going to live an upright, useful life?" The mother gazed longingly at her wayward son.

"Repent, repent!" came the voice of conscience, grown suddenly bold. But the sight of a struggling girl pleading for life, and another face, distorted in agony, rose before his mind, and he would not listen to the "still, small voice." Yet he stammered almost inaudibly:

"I'll try, mother," and bowed his head lower.

"Josiah, turn up the light! It is dark, and I want to see you and our boy kneeling together."

Josiah, doing as he was bidden, came to the bedside and there knelt in silence.

Mrs. Maloney, a few minutes later, came softly over to where they knelt, and, touching the elder man on the shoulder, bade him rise. As he rose, the hand which had been placed on his head fell listlessly on the bed. Mrs. Maloney then touched Sam, also. All was solemn and quiet. With bowed heads the two stood for an instant. Hearing sobs behind them, they raised their heads and turned to learn the cause. Mrs. Maloney stood there, her face suffused in tears. She pointed mutely toward the bed. A beautiful smile played over the features of wife, mother, and friend.

"Great God! is mother dead?" and the wicked and hardened son fell prone upon the bed, tears coming thick and fast as he gave way to an agony of remorse. Then a horrible thought came rushing into his heart. Over and over he repeated to himself with a terrible conviction, "Now she'll know! she'll know!" All his crimes would be revealed to her. She would know that he had knelt by her dying bed with a lie upon his lips. He scarcely realized the infinitely more dreadful fact that an angry God saw him and knew him through and through. It seemed more real, more shameful, that the mother who had just placed her hand on his head in blessing, who had smiled with a holy joy in the belief of his innocence and conversion, could now see him in all his black-hearted hypocrisy. An awful fear that he was lost beyond hope, shut out forever from the heaven to which his mother had just gone, overwhelmed him. Even the timid voice of conscience was still. He trembled, fearing to rise and face his father. For a long time he remained, hiding his face in the bedclothes. At length he lifted his head furtively and found the room was almost dark. Mrs. Maloney had turned the wick of the lamp low and left the room. Farmer Hawkins was still kneeling by the head of the bed absorbed in his great sorrow. Sam rose softly and tiptoed to the door. Without a sound he turned the latch and passed out of the room. Then, grasping his hat from the little table in the hall, he fled from the house like an evil spirit.

For more than an hour he wandered restlessly about the farm in the darkness. He dreaded to sleep in the house where every object, every sound, every shadow would remind him of the mother lying there still and cold. He feared that her spirit might come to his bedside and charge him with his horrible sins and his hypocritical lies. More than once he was on the point of yielding to an impulse to go to the village and spend the night in Pete's place, lulled by strong drink; but the sight of an agonized face, with protruding tongue and bulging eyeballs, confronted him. No, he could not pass that spot on the road by night, even to escape from his present plight. Finally he crept into the barn and lay down in the hay until daylight came. As the first rays of light penetrated the little square gable-window he left the barn, taking care not to be seen, and hastened by a circuitous route to Red-Keg. He roused Pete and made him give him a breakfast. The troublesome thoughts that had haunted him the night before had slipped away with the darkness. What a fool he had been, he told himself, to give in to such mawkish sentimentality. It was a desperate game he had to play, and it required all his nerve and self-possession. Much remained yet to be done. It was necessary to brace up and be ready to meet all questions and repel all attacks.

Before the morning was far advanced he learned that

Lettie had been found and was on the road to recovery. The news at first brought him relief and fear. At least he was not a murderer; but had she told, or would she tell, who had made the attack upon her? When, however, he heard that it was Seward who found her, and that they had given out a statement involving two unknown strangers, he smiled grimly, and congratulated himself on the fortunate coincidence that their fiction agreed precisely with the one which he, on the spur of the moment, had given to Tom Moore. He was at a loss to know whether or not Seward suspected him. Never mind; he would find out soon enough.

The attack on Lettie, coming so soon after the abduction of Norine, created not only an unparalleled sensation, but a feeling of alarm on behalf of the other young women of the neighborhood. The Red-Keggers and others for miles around were wrought up to such a high pitch of excitement that an informal meeting was called before noon at Jake Vogel's store to form a vigilance committee for protection and for hunting the scoundrels down. Seward Rathaway was present, and at his own request was placed on the committee.

Before the meeting adjourned, Barney arrived from the Hawkins farm with the sad news of Mother Hawkins's death. He had heard, also, of the attack on Lettie, and was filled with new dread lest Norine had suffered in like manner. Although he and Tom Moore had bent every effort and taxed their ingenuity to the utmost, they had been unable thus far to get any trace of the missing girl. John Maloney, with several of his neighbors, had continued to scour the woods, but with no better result. The only immediate hope of learning anything seemed to lie in the possibility of getting the tramp to tell something more than he had done; but

Norine's father and Tom Moore had cross-questioned him in vain.

The death of Mother Hawkins and the attack on Lettie Green led to a postponement of the hearing before Justice Frost until Thursday morning. The whole village turned out to honor her memory. Robert Allen had been with the bereaved husband from the very first, and had comforted him by sharing his grief and pointing him steadily to the source of all comfort. Josiah had often asked for his son, but Sam avoided him now as carefully as he avoided the minister. He would have stayed away from the funeral if he had dared; but he feared to attract notice and suspicion, so at the last moment, when the opportunity for conversation was at an end, he came to the large room in the ell of the house where the ceremony was to be held, and took a place in the doorway. Even Joseph Waters, the schoolmaster, whose leg was only partially recovered, managed to come in a buggy with the help of crutches, and the more indispensable help of Axcy Marthy. It was evident to all that they understood each other perfectly, for they made no secret of their love. Ros Whitmore was unable to come. The broken bone was not yet firmly enough knit together to allow moving. He sent his wife Jule in his place. Lettie Green was there, her throat still bandaged. Sam did not see her when he entered. Indeed, it had not occurred to him that she might be present. At one end of the long room was the coffin surrounded with spring flowers. Near it, with bowed head, already in the winter of life, sat Josiah, in the presence of a host of his friends—yet so lonely.

Robert Allen stood up silently before them all for a moment or two, seeking to control his own feelings.

22

He asked some one to start the hymn, and Dan Under-hill, in a rich baritone, began, rather huskily at first, but gaining in volume and melody as he proceeded:

> " Asleep in Jesus! blessed sleep,
>   From which none ever wakes to weep;
>   A calm and undisturb'd repose,
>   Unbroken by the last of foes.

> " Asleep in Jesus! peaceful rest,
>   Whose waking is supremely blest;
>   No fear, no woe, shall dim that hour
>   That manifests the Saviour's power."

Several verses of the hymn were sung. As the last words died away, the minister began to read quietly from the fourteenth chapter of John's Gospel. In a few simple words he brought the promise in the eight-eenth verse home to the sorrowing hearts before him. "I will not leave you comfortless." The love of friend for friend, of parent for child, of husband for wife, was a precious thing, and the breaking of such ties was for the moment grievous; but the love of Christ, the per-sonal companionship with Him, was far more precious, and nothing could separate us from the love of Christ. When the companionship of the dearest on earth was taken away, the personal presence of Christ would more than compensate. "I will not leave you comfort-less: I will come to you." What heart could be lonely with such a tender, loving companion, walking with us when we walk, sitting with us in the stillness of our chamber, helping us with our burdens? "In my Fa-ther's house are many mansions . . . I go to prepare a place for you." What better preparation of a heav-enly mansion could there be than the placing in it of the heart's loved one to welcome home him who should come after? "Let not your heart be troubled, neither let it be afraid." The minister's voice thrilled with meaning as he repeated the verse.

"There are things which trouble us and make us afraid at times," he said, "—things far out of the common little affairs of life. Such things have happened among us during the past few days. We have seen two of our number—tenderly nurtured lambs of the flock—cruelly seized upon,—one of them torn from her home and taken away to what fate we know not; another barely saved from death inflicted by brutal hands. Our hearts are troubled and afraid. We know not what to do. We have searched and have not found. What shall we do?"

The minister's voice suddenly rose to a cry full of solemn prophecy, which rang through the room and pierced the inmost hearts of all who heard it.

"Listen to the Psalmist!" he cried: "' Shall not God search this out? for He knoweth the secrets of the heart.'"

A moment of awe-filled silence followed. All eyes were riveted on the minister; thus none of his hearers noticed a pallid, cringing, trembling figure slip away from a seat near the door, and disappear.

"' Let not your heart be troubled, neither let it be afraid . . . I will not leave you comfortless: I will come to you,'" continued the minister, with another sudden change to tenderness. "We need Christ's presence and His comfort at just such times as this, if ever at all. If we will accept it, He will be as good as His word and give us the help and comfort we need. He is ready to employ His power where our weakness has failed; to apply the balm of His love where our hearts are bruised and sore. Let us sink our sadness and fear in the fathomless ocean of His love."

After a more personal tribute to the beloved wife whose body lay peacefully in the casket, but whose spirit had gone to one of the many mansions in the Father's house, the minister closed the service with a tender, heartfelt prayer for a fulfilment of the promise which had been brought to sorrowing hearts in that hour

In the long line of mourners who passed before the casket for a last look at the face they had all loved so well, the only son, for whom the mother's heart had yearned and broken, was not present. If any noticed his absence, they held their peace. Robert Allen, too, held his peace, but something he had seen within the past hour had brought him more sorrow than the death and translation of his friend and sister Susan Hawkins.

CHAPTER XXV

"In the case of the People of this Commonwealth against John Long, is the defendant present?" called out Judge Frost, glaring over the crowd in his primitive little court-room, the next afternoon.

"He is, your honor," replied Tom Moore.

"Bring him to the bar. Is this the prisoner?" and the judge looked over his goggles at the man before him.

"I'm the man, your honor, and I've been waiting the pleasure of this court for three days," said the prisoner, glibly.

"Never mind that, sir; you are charged with a most heinous crime, a most abominable offense against the peace and dignity of a great State. What have you to say to the charge, guilty or not guilty?"

"If it please your honor, would you kindly inform me what this dreadful charge might be?" inquired the prisoner, in a tone of friendly curiosity.

"The charge—the charge—" sputtered the judge, whose temper was becoming ruffled, "why, that you did with malice intent deprive one Norine Maloney of her liberty—and that you are now detaining her against her will——"

"Where, your honor? In the lockup, where I have been staying for the past several days? Oh, no, not for Joseph! Not that I know of," and he smiled triumphantly at the judge.

"That feller's a reg'lar Tartar, he is," some one in the crowded court-room was heard to remark.

"Silence in the court!" thundered the judge, and the stillness that followed was oppressive.

Then after readjusting his spectacles, which had barely escaped a fall on the floor during the excitement, the judge glanced again at the paper which he had in his hand, held it out at arm's length in order to read it, and then looking over the rims of his glasses directly at the prisoner, who was the calmest one in the whole room, he continued:

"As I was saying, you are charged with a diabolical crime whose foulness smells to heaven. Constable," turning his gaze from the prisoner to Tom Moore, "where are your witnesses?"

"I hain't got many witnesses, jedge; but this feller's got stars in his heels, an' me 'n Barney seed tracks out on the Sturgeon Slough as jest fitted 'em, an' I 'low 's he's the chap as made 'em—right there 'long side o' Norine's dainty little footprints. Here's Barney as 'll tell ye the same thing."

"Come to the stand," said the judge, looking toward Barney. "Now, you have heard what our court officer has said—what have you got to offer against this man?"

"Sure, Tom's told the truth, jedge. We saw those star heels out there in the mud," said Barney, hesitatingly, for he was not ready yet to be too severe on the tramp, in the absence of more conclusive proof.

"Now, sir, what have you to say for yourself?" and the searching steel-blue eyes of Judge Frost again peered at Long, seeking to pierce the prisoner's mask of effrontery.

"Judge—your honor—you seem to have the upper hand of me at present. In other words, the weight of evidence looks to be against me so far. I came as a stranger into your community, and have no witnesses to speak up in my behalf. I do not hanker to be made a celebrity, and if I had gone along about my business instead of interfering in other people's affairs from the kindest of motives, I wouldn't be in this scrape. Judge, I swear that I had nothing whatever to do with the disappearance of this young lady, and haven't any idea where she is now. I wish I did, your honor. If you will permit me, I——"

"I'll permit you to keep silent," interrupted the judge. "The evidence says you're guilty. I don't know whether you are or not, though I have my opinion. I'll bind you over to the Circuit Court in October to find out."

"Thank you, your honor; does that mean that I am still detaining the young lady against her will, and am I to keep possession of her till October?" timidly put in the prisoner.

"I'll fine you for contempt of court," shouted the judge, "if I hear another word out of your head!"

"Your honor, will ye fix a bond for this prisoner?" asked Tom Moore.

"Yes. Five hundred dollars!" and the judge looked defiantly around the room, not dreaming that the bond would be forthcoming.

"Please make out your bond and release the prisoner in my custody," spoke up Walt Haywood from the back of the room, to the great surprise of judge and spectators.

The bond was filled out, and, in lieu of real estate, a cash deposit to the amount of the bond was accepted. In a few moments the prisoner walked out of court a free man.

"My friend, whom have I to thank for this great kindness?" said Long, addressing the constable.

"He's one o' yer friends. Ef it hadn't a' been fer him an' his pals ye'd been strung up the day I put the bracelets on ye," rather testily responded Tom, for he was apparently displeased that the prisoner should be released on bail at all under the circumstances, as there had been no further developments in the case, and it might yet prove to be something worse than a mere abduction.

Approaching Walt, the released prisoner was very profuse in his thanks for the disinterested kindness that had been shown him.

"I assure you, my friend, upon the honor of a gentleman, that I appreciate your kindness, and shall bear you in mind when I get possession of my baronial estates in old England. For the present, however, let us adjourn court to Pete's. That's something tangible, at least. (*Sotto voce.*) I came pretty near seeing 'em again last night—sh—" and with a wild look around as though he expected to "see 'em" again, he grabbed the arm of Walt for protection.

Walt good-naturedly assured the fellow that he was all right, and, as suggested, an adjournment was taken to "Pete's place." All the boys were present, and as further demonstrations were about to be made which boded ill for the tramp, the whole party proposed to give him safe conduct to the saloon at least, and thither many of the crowd followed. By the time all hands had taken several "nips" around, his trampship began to get loquacious.

"Gentlemen," he said, "I am a stranger here in a strange land. I came among you peaceably enough, but through some unfortunate incidents or circumstances I have been the subject of suspicion and arrest. Gentlemen of the jury—I mean gentlemen of Red-Keg

—I have been released on bail, and now whither shall I
go? I have no money and I have no work. I assure
you, gentlemen (although you would never suspect it),
that I would work if I could get work to do. I have
worked in all sorts of places, from a sawmill to a watch-
factory, and if there is any gentleman here who dares
offer me work I'll stay with him till court sits in October, be this same person a parson, or a bunco-steerer,
or a representative of any of the several grades between
these two stations."

Here, again, he cast wistful glances toward the bar,
but, no one offering to treat, he again directed his remarks to his benefactor, and asked his advice as to what
it was best to do.

"If I should leave town," he argued, "I might never
return again, and in that case——"

"I would be just that much out," laughed Walt.

"Exactly, exactly. Now, sir, I am accepting my liberty in good faith. I have nothing to fear from a trial,
and if the people here would care to have me incarcer-
ated till this court sits, why, gentlemen, I will return
to my late dungeon and there remain for the law to take
its course," and, in a spirit of submission to the powers
that be, Long held his hands in front of him as though
expecting to have the manacles replaced.

"Very well, then, no one seems to wish my return;
so, unless labor of some kind is offered to me, I must
take up the thread of my interrupted journey and proceed to-night *via* some hospitable way-train, securing
a reserved seat upon the trucks of a freight-car. To
guard against thirst, gentlemen, I always carry a
convenient flask with me. It is now empty (and so
am I), and who speaks first for the privilege of filling it?"

Several responded, and a broad smile came over the face of the man.

"Thank you. I don't want to slight any one. I keep these for just such emergencies," and a laugh went round as he produced three other flasks of similar shape and size, and those who were a short time before eager to lynch the fellow, now vied with each other in rewarding him for his ready wit.

When the bottles were all filled and returned to his capacious pockets, he cast more longing looks toward the bar.

"What, haven't you enough yet? We'll get the hose and attach one end to your mouth and the other end to a barrel. How would that suit you?"

"Just the ticket, boss; just the ticket," and the man's eyes bulged with delight.

"Well, come and have one with me," said Billy.

The tramp obeyed with alacrity, and, resuming the place he had first occupied near an open window at the end of the bar, he set his glass in front of him and gazed at it affectionately.

"You see, sir, I have an awful—awful thirst on me," he said, "and I didn't care to tap those bottles while the fountain flowed so freely near by. I'll keep them till I am out on the desert, so to speak, and there is no other reservoir in sight. Again I thank you all, gentlemen, for your most magnanimous consideration of my frailties. And to this especially kind friend, to whom I owe my liberty, I am more than grateful," and he grasped the hand of Walt, who stood near him.

"That's all right," responded Walt; "but why not give us your pedigree, and tell us where you came from and where you are going—that is, if you are cruel enough to skip your bail?"

"Certainly, with pleasure; you are entitled to it, my dear sir; but first, if you don't mind—you know talking is dry work—and——"

"What! you don't mean to say your glass is empty again!" exclaimed Walt, regarding the tramp in surprise. "You have a thirst, surely. Well, Pete, fill him up again, and give him enough to last this time."

Pete laughed, and filled the tramp's glass to the top with "Mystic Brand." The man seized it with an unsteady hand.

"Thank you, my good and generous fellow!" he exclaimed, thickly; then letting his gaze wander over the crowded barroom, he cried out, banteringly, pointing toward the door:

"Oh, I say! there's the honest, but unfortunate man who t-testified against me in the court. Now, my frien', I don't bear any ill-will. Come an' join me in some of this excellen' beverage. I trus' one of these very gen'rous gen'lemen will stan' treat on my 'count."

All hands turned and saw Barney sitting at a table near the door. He made no move or reply except to shake his head to signify his refusal of the invitation. The tramp pressed his invitation.

"Don't hang back m' man! A drink of this," and he flourished his glass, "will help you t' forget all your sorrows. They say I am de-de-tainin' your sweetheart. It's a lie—I mean a sad mistake. Come here an' sh-shake han's, an' les be frien's."

Barney rose angrily to his feet as though to leave the saloon. The crowd watching him thought there might be a quarrel, and one or two stepped toward him to interfere. Suddenly, however, Barney sat down again, looking more surprised than angry.

"Ah! but tha's good for what ails me!" exclaimed

the tramp, as, attention being again directed to him, he set down his empty glass and smacked his lips with great gusto, while Walt and the others stared at him in amazement.

"You wan' know m' pedigree, an' where I came from," he continued. "Well, mos' es'mable frien' an' ben'factor, all I know is I came hither from thither, an' thence I shall go forth from hence by the firs' frien'ly fras' feight—I mean the frirs' fenly fash freight—or something like that. M' name, you have; m' res'dence —wherever th' night closes 'pon me; my oc'pation— had so many, don' know which the lash one was; m' people—they don' know me 'cause m' close ain't good 'nough; but le' me tell you m' frien's—these patched trousers cover an hones' (hic) heart. Wha' you laughin' at, mister? It's a fac', I 'sure you. I don' look han'some, but I'd rather (hic) be a good mushroom, growin' on a dung-heap than a bad egg in a good shell. Some day I'll compel m' fam'ly to reco'nize my rights an' return me t' the rish b'ronial eshtates in m' mother coun'ry—merry ol' Englan'. Then m' frien'," growing confidential, "I wan' you t' come over there an' be m' honor' guesh. It will (hic) give me the greatesh pleasure to welcome you."

"But what about your other friends here? Would not all the Invincibles be welcome?" asked Walt.

"Mosh assuredly, m' frien'—mosh assur—(hic)—ly. Guesh that lash imbiba—(hic)—tion wash too much for me," replied the fellow thickly, and he began to reel heavily.

The Invincibles consulted among themselves hastily and decided to get rid of the fellow as quickly as possible, so, taking him by both arms, they escorted him out of the saloon. Barney, who had remained at the table near the door watching the proceedings but saying nothing, started up as though to speak when the tramp and his escorts passed, but quickly changing his mind, he sank back in his seat and waited until they had all gone out. Then he arose, left the saloon, and strode rapidly away, his face flushed with suppressed excitement.

When the Invincibles and their protégé reached the road, the tramp turned to Walt and insisted upon shaking hands with him again.

"How 'm I to repay you, mos' noble frien' f' thish— (hic)—kin'ness?" he sputtered.

"That's easy enough," replied Walt. "We will see you safely to the railroad station, and when your train of palace cars comes along you may take your choice of bumpers or trucks."

By the time the station was reached, however, the tramp was in such a helpless condition that after a conference among the Invincibles, it was decided to remove him to their private room, over Pete's place, and back they dragged him to this hostelry.

"It would be suicidal for him to attempt to board a train in this condition," said Seward, "and murder for us to allow it. We'll take him upstairs, where he can sleep it off undisturbed. At the same time," he whispered to Walt, "we have a little business to transact while we're all together."

After considerable tugging and boosting the tramp was smuggled into Pete's place by a back entrance to escape the eyes of the remaining loungers, and was stowed away on the cot heretofore used more than once by Sam for a similar purpose.

"He's good for all night," remarked Walt, as stertorous snores came from the couch. "Light up, Billy;

it's getting dark. Don't go, Sam; we've got some fig-
uring to do, and need your help. We'll have Pete send
up some grub."

Bob Simons was called and given instructions. Soon
the four Invincibles were seated at their light repast,
the door was locked, and Sam waited for the storm
which he knew was about to break upon his head.
Walt was the first to speak.

"We've got to look things squarely in the face and
decide on some way to get out of the snarl we're in,"
he began. "The sooner we do it the better. If we
could have stuck to our profitable business without
being hampered with side issues and private affairs we
should have been all right. Those spies of Uncle Sam
gave us a clean bill of health. It isn't likely we would
have been bothered on that line again in a hurry. But
the president of our company allows himself to get off
the track on other business. I call this plagued love
affair business because I don't think he's the man to go
to such extremes for a simple sentiment. There must
be something more in it. I wouldn't care for that, if he
had been content to work his scheme, whatever it was,
on the outside; but in spite of our refusal to have anything to do with it, he goes ahead and springs it on us
behind our backs. Before we know it, we are mixed
up in the matter, and have to stand for it or throw up
the whole concern at the risk of making him blab.
Now there's the devil to pay with all this excitement
over Norine. If we don't look out, the chickens will
begin coming home to roost. I don't call it a square
deal. Our business is at a standstill. We don't dare
to go out to the island for more stuff while the woods
are full of searchers. Yet the only thing to do, so far
as I can see, is to return the girl at once, provided it

can be done safely, and she will promise not to blab. What do you say?"

Sam had been drumming on the table in an effort to appear unconcerned while Walt was speaking. He now surprised the others by sitting erect in his chair and looking around defiantly at his companions as he replied:

"This practically places me on trial, I suppose. All right, go ahead, fret, accuse, curse; but remember, we are all in the same boat, and if you think it's going to sink, and have any plans for getting out, present them. If not, better hold your tongues. There's nothing to be gained by pot calling kettle black, don't you know. Funny what a spasm of virtue has taken hold of you because you think *I* have made a mistake. Maybe I have; anyhow I'm sorry it had to turn out this way. I don't like the excitement any more than you do; but we're in for it, and may as well make the best of a bad job."

"Talking of excitement," said Seward, slowly, "that damnable attack on my cousin Lettie was about as bad as anything could be, and doesn't make it any easier for us to get out of our fix, even though I did manage to get myself put on the vigilance committee. If they can find the wretch who did the thing, he will probably swing from a good stout limb in short order."

"The poor girl had a narrow escape. Have you any idea who were the perpetrators?" asked Walt.

"I know—the perpetrator," said Seward, looking Sam full in the face. "Is it necessary to mention any name? We ought to have no secrets from each other, but so far as the public is concerned, I left the matter with Lettie. It was through her love, poor girl, that you were spared, Sam. Now I warn you to get out of this Norine affair as quickly as you can."

The discussion continued hour after hour, mingled with bitter accusations and recriminations. Billy at first took up Sam's defense, but after a while he found it more to his interests to keep silent.

Sam fought his battle alone with less and less assurance until he was driven to yield every point.

"I am for giving Sam just one chance to redeem himself," said Seward. "If he will set his wits to work to restore the girl, without exposing the rendezvous, or revealing our connection with the matter, I, for one, will vote to overlook the past. Then we can decide whether he shall resume his position as leader, from which I now consider him as deposed."

"Well put," agreed Walt. "What do you say to that proposition, Billy?"

"Agreed," he answered.

"Very well, then, Sam. Can you return the girl safely—*safely, mind you*—to her parents, and have no one the wiser as to where she has been?" asked Seward.

"That's a hard nut to crack, don't you know," replied Sam meekly, "but I'll try. After all, I suppose she will be glad enough to get away without peaching on us."

"Don't wager too much on that, Sam. If she can be induced to keep still, it certainly will not be out of regard for you. It will be to save your poor old father," answered Walt.

"One thing is certain," said Seward, "you must return Norine, and that at once, or within a reasonable length of time. By another week, say a week from to-night, we must make the attempt. We will all go out to the south shore—" He suddenly hesitated, looked hard at the sleeper on the couch, who was snoring like a porker, and then, satisfied that the tramp was oblivious to all the world, proceeded: "Sam, you stay around the Keg—I am managing this campaign now— Billy and Walt shall go up to the hunting-lodge, and I'll stay around home. By the time the week is up all will have quieted down and we can safely make the trip. Be there at daylight, and at sunrise we can fire the salute. Pomp will hear it, and will soon be with us. We can then complete details as the emergencies require. What do you think of the plan?"

There was nothing better to offer, so Seward's plan was adopted, subject to change if circumstances should require.

They had remained talking all night, and it was not until near morning that their protégé showed signs of returning consciousness. With the first symptom of this return they directed their attention to him and ceased their palaver.

"Had a good sleep, have you, pard?" said Walt, who first observed his awakening.

"Yesh, but *awful—awful* thirsty. Where's Pete?" and with groggy eyes he looked around the apartment.

"Pete's to bed, but if you want an eye-opener, there are your bottles yet. Better take a little bracer, and get on the train due here at four o'clock. Pretty early, but we'll go with you," said Walt.

Without further ado, the program was carried out.

Ere long the tramp was bundled onto the train, and the Invincibles breathed more freely.

23

CHAPTER XXVI

THE people of Red-Keg and all the surrounding region were thrown into a state of renewed excitement by the arrival, on the morning following the tramp's hearing, of another stranger, and the posting, a few hours later, of a notice on Vogel's store and other places offering five thousand dollars reward, and no questions asked, for the safe return of Norine Maloney. The news flew in all directions that Orrin Maloney, brother of John Maloney, and son of a wealthy manufacturer who had just died in Belfast, Ireland, leaving the bulk of his vast property to his two sons, had come in search of his brother, arriving just in time to help in a still more thorough and aggressive hunt for the lost girl. The offer of a reward and a description of Norine were sent far and wide. New parties were organized. The woods were beaten for miles around, until it seemed as though even a rabbit could not escape. Sturgeon Slough was dragged, and out-of-the-way places were searched. The activity and hopefulness of the big-hearted Irishman—Sir Orrin, as the Red-Keggers dubbed him — seemed boundless. Every one caught the contagion, and worked with a fresh determination, which lasted for fully three days. Orrin was indignant that the tramp had not been held. He offered another reward for his apprehension and return to the custody of the court.

The Invincibles were in a constant state of alarm

lest some of the searchers should stumble upon their
secret rendezvous, or lest the tramp should turn up and
clear himself, or lest suspicion should again fall upon
them. The day was approaching which they had agreed
upon for making the attempt to get Norine off their
hands. They did their best to foster the spirit of dis-
couragement with further searching in the woods, hoping to clear their own way. Indeed, the searching parties soon came to the conviction that they had done all
that was possible in this direction, and before the week
was up, nearly all had abandoned that line of search.
Walt and Seward insisted that Sam stick to his agreement.

"If we could only manage it some way by which we
could get hold of that reward at the same time, it
would compensate in part for the loss of the girl,"
urged Sam, thinking regretfully of the stake for which
he had risked so much, and which was about to slip
from his grasp.

"I have no taste for any further complications," de-
murred Seward. "The one thing I am anxious for is
to get Norine safely off our hands, and we do not know
yet whether we can even do that. If we get out of
this scrape with a whole skin, that will be reward
enough. You can't expect anything more."

"I have been thinking we might tell Norine that we
would return her to her parents on condition that she
would pledge herself on her honor to tell nothing, and
then we might arrange with one or two of our middle-
men up in the Big Salt—for instance, Pierre Badeau, to
meet us at the usual place and take this new product
of our island to the market, get the reward, retain a
share for his trouble, and turn the remainder over to
us for our trouble. He could spin a yarn about being

the go-betweens for two professional kidnappers up in the next township, and the chances are the story would go down. You know the notice says no questions asked."

" I don't know but that might be feasible," said Walt, doubtfully. "I don't hanker for any more complications, either, but the money would come in very handy just now, after paying out that five hundred dollars to let Mr. Tramp escape, and they say Orrin Maloney has barrels of it. I'll agree to it if Seward will."

But Seward refused, positively.

While the Invincibles were worrying and planning, and the friends of Norine were making conspicuous efforts to discover some clew to her, and the vigilance committee was exerting itself to catch the miscreants and protect the neighborhood from further acts of violence, Barney O'Boyle held himself aloof as much as he could from his neighbors, and avoided the questions and commiserations that came from all sides whenever he went abroad. Usually cool, collected, and undisturbed, he was now completely overcome with grief. The illness and then the death of Mother Hawkins, together with the uncomplaining sorrow of Uncle Si, cut him to the heart; the hopeless grief of Norine's parents smote him like a barbed arrow. Yet, neither they nor Orrin Maloney had a word of blame for the manly fellow. They knew that all this sorrow and trouble had been brought about through no fault of his. He had expected nothing less than a mild censure, to say the least, but when all concerned had shown such magnanimity toward him, and confidence in his honor, his grief was all the more poignant, and he recorded a vow with himself that come what would he would never rest till

the lost girl was restored to her family, or the mystery
of her taking off unravelled

It was a busy time on the farm, and the spring work
must be done. Without consulting Farmer Hawkins,
he purchased from his own savings a new yoke of oxen,
and worked incessantly during the hours of daylight.
He scarcely touched his food, and when evening came
he attended to his usual chores; then taking a lantern,
he went out alone to search the woods for a trace of
his lost sweetheart. The failure of searching parties
did not convince nor deter him. All night long he
tramped up and down through forest and swamp; following the original trail back and forth, and then
branching out in every direction; peering under bushes
and brambles and dragging ponds and lagoons, sick at
heart, but determined to keep on. For more than a
week he had been out every night, sometimes with
others, more often alone, going each time in a different
direction, farther and farther, and with less and less
hope of success, yet without a thought of abandoning
his search. He had not said a word to any one, until
Uncle Si, noting with alarm his haggard looks each
morning, insisted on his taking more rest. Then Barney poured out his pent-up feelings and told of his night
searches. Uncle Si expostulated with him.

"You ought not to do that, Barney. You can't
stand it. Suppose you should get off in the wilderness
alone somewhere and give out. It is unlikely Norine
is in the woods now. Whoever took her away has got
her in safe-keeping—that is—if she is still alive.
Orrin's reward will bring her to us if anything will.
You must take care of yourself, or you won't be fit to
meet her when she does come."

Barney thanked his kind employer and friend, but

he would not be dissuaded from continuing his search. He could not bear to think that perhaps his darling was lying out there, cold and wet and dead, and no loving hands to place her in her last resting-place. So again he started out on his weary tramp. He always carried his revolver with him, for he knew the woods were full of prowling animals. He also had his hunting-knife, and he knew no fear as he hastened along to the point whence he was to begin the night search.

"Oh, Norine, darlint," he cried aloud, "will these eyes iver see ye agin? Shall I iver spake into yer livin' ears the sorrow an' love of me heart? Sure, it's no fault of yours that ye're not this minute safe under yer mother's roof. There's some dark diviltry here, an' begorra, if I could lay these two hands on the cowardly varmint as sperited ye away—" his eyes gleamed fiercely, his breath came in short gasps, his hands clinched till the nails nearly cut through the flesh of his horny hand—"I'd niver rest till he was strung up by the neck an' left fer the crows to pick his worthless bones." The words came from between his clenched teeth, and the utterance of his rage in the darkness and the wilderness, like the safety-valve of an engine, relieved the pressure within.

For some time he strode on in silence, and then burst out again:

"Sam Hawkins, I hate yer infernal looks. I—I—. They all say ye didn't do it, an' ye pretind to be turnin' over a new leaf, but I feel in me heart that ye *did* do it, an' that ye know where the darlint is now. Ye must be a sneakin' hypercrit, an' the divil's own, besides. Why was ye so anxious to git rid o' thet tramp? Ye knew he was innercent, an' if he stayed here, they'd be after provin' it. Ye wanted them ter kape on thinkin' he done it, an' so ye helped him to skip, you an' yer friends."

He had reached the spot where he was to take up the search for the night, and was just stepping from the road, when there came wafted to his ear the maudlin tones of a drunken man singing "The Falling of the Pine," one of the popular lumber-camp airs. He had no desire for such a companion at this time, so he made haste to get out of the way before he should be seen, and into the woods he went on his melancholy quest. Not a spot within reach of the rays of his lantern, or lighted by the moon, which had helped so greatly during the past few nights, now escaped his attention.

As he hunted, his thoughts ever returned to Norine, and the last moments he had spent with her on that memorable night. She had fallen into the water, and was cold and wet. How long could she survive the cruel exposure, even if nothing worse had happened to her? But perhaps Uncle Si was right, and she was being taken care of, and would be returned in order that her abductors might secure the reward. Then his thoughts flew to the scene in the saloon after the hearing of the tramp in court.

"Begorra, there was somethin' strange about thet tramp. The crowd thought he was drunker'n a owl, but I'm thinkin' *he didn't drink a blessed drop*. What did he dump the stuff outer the winder fer, when he thought nobody was lookin'? Maybe the boys thought he was drunk, maybe not. He's sure enough up to some game, good or bad."

An hour passed, and Barney was still hunting. Another hour found him thrusting, poking, tramping. His long partial fasting, and the ceaseless toil and worry were beginning to tell upon his strength. He felt a weakness unknown to him, the strong, robust young Hercules, the envy of every youth in the township.

"H—o—o, h—o—o, hoo—hoo!" came to his listening ears as he was retracing his steps toward an overhanging rock which he had passed some time before. He was now intent on looking around that place again and still more thoroughly. He reached it and made a detour to the south among the tanglewood. He had not proceeded far when the doleful and ominous hoot of the same owl again arrested his attention.

"H—o—o, h—o—o, hoo—hoo!" came the mournful dirge, and for the first time in his life the notes struck a chord in Barney's breast which caused him to shake with apprehension. He was not frightened, but under the tense condition of nervous strain under which he was bearing up, the sound thrilled him through and through, and he took the hooting as a portent of coming disaster.

As the notes died away he thought he heard a crackling in the underbrush just a little way ahead of him, and stopped to listen. With unreasoning hope springing in his breast he rushed forward toward the spot whence came the sound, calling the name of Norine at every bound. A moment's thought would have told him that Norine could not possibly be wandering at night in the forest alive after more than a week had passed.

As he neared the spot he again stopped to listen, and this time he distinctly heard the "ughf, ughf" of a bear, which came from the clump of bushes not fifty feet ahead of him.

What if this beast had overtaken Norine and torn

her in pieces, was the first thought that entered his
mind, and, with a cry of desperation, thinking nothing
of the possible outcome, he rushed with maddened fury
in the direction of the beast. It was a large fellow of
the black variety, and ordinarily would have run away,
but Barney's onslaught was so fierce and determined
that the animal had no alternative but to turn and defend himself against the charge of his mad antagonist.
Rising to his haunches he met the onslaught with a
swingle-like motion of his ponderous paw. Barney, his
blood up, had not moved with his usual caution. He
had unsheathed his knife and made his rush, hoping to
catch bruin at a disadvantage. But the bear was too
quick. His paw struck Barney's knife-hand a terrible
blow, knocking the knife away and rendering that hand
practically useless. Too late our hero had measured
the strength of his foe, and the bear, now himself enraged to the fighting-point, made another pass at Barney, who fortunately dodged just in time to escape its
full force upon his head, which no doubt would have
concluded the conflict then and there in favor of bruin.

Barney had dropped his lantern some distance back,
and the oil, running out and igniting, presented a weird
spectacle of the surrounding wood, but at the same
time distracted for an instant the attention of the bear
and gave Barney a chance to draw his revolver and
again force the fight with his huge antagonist. The
bear's last blow had deprived Barney of his hat, but
had not hurt him, and while the bear had his attention
drawn to the blazing oil, the desperate man took aim
at the heart of the beast and pulled the trigger.

With a yell of rage the monster was again upright,
with froth-flecked mouth and gleaming eyes. He
aimed another blow, which failed, and then the two

met in a hand-to-hand and desperate struggle for the mastery—a powerful brute pitted against a human antagonist, both goaded to desperation.

Barney grappled with the fellow, and the two rolled to the ground, the former on top. His pistol had dropped from his hand, and there in the dead of night, the light having burned out by this time, leaving the combatants to trust to the moon, the two fought and struggled for supremacy. With a power born of love and a determination to live to avenge the wrongs of his loved one, the brave man knew no fear, and with a mighty power for an instant beyond even his ordinary strength, he grasped the throat of the beast with his uninjured hand and the other he wound around a sapling near by.

His grip upon the throat tightened. The animal writhed and twisted in his agony. But just as Barney felt that the victory was his, he relaxed his hold, as the terrible strain was more than he could stand. The bear, who had almost ceased to struggle, now made a last ferocious effort, in a twinkling breaking the hold upon his throat, and with a terrible growl fastened his jaws upon Barney's arm. Fortunately for Barney he had on his leather hunting-coat, or the arm would have been torn in pieces. Bruin, now evidently aware of his ascendency, paused a moment to contemplate his prostrate foe, or to get breath, the while holding the arm like a vise, and growling ominously.

Barney, weak and trembling from lack of food and rest, was for the first time unnerved. He felt that having no weapon within reach, the fight was greatly in favor of the bear. The pain caused by the sharp teeth on his arm and the almost paralyzed condition of his other hand from the first blow of the bear was excruciating, and a groan of agony escaped his lips. Further than that he remained silent, while the big beast, seemingly satisfied with the advantage he had gained, did not crowd the fight. Barney realized this, and with pain shooting through every nerve he heroically held his peace and did not move a muscle. How long he remained in that position he did not know, but soon he realized that a lethargy was creeping over his already benumbed senses, and he was yielding to over-wrought nature.

Suddenly, without warning, he felt the bear release his hold, and at the same instant a stream of something hot and foaming struck him full in the face. He was aroused at once from his lethargy, and sat upright. The bear had rolled over on his side, while the hot blood still flowed from a knife wound in his throat. Standing over them Barney observed the dim outlines of a man, holding a murderous-looking knife which was dripping with the life-blood of the quivering beast at his feet.

"Seems to me you have had a pretty narrow escape, eh? Let me help you to your feet now you are free from the embraces of that fellow," and Jim Lane, the man whom Barney and Jim Gyde had saved from death in the rollway two weeks previous, rolled the carcass away from Barney and reached out to help him up.

For a moment Barney was too much dazed to speak. But as he gazed at the dead bear, and then at his rescuer, his thoughts returned. Peering into the face before him, he recognized Mr. Lane, and reaching for his hand he squeezed it as heartily as his remaining strength would permit.

"Misther Lane, ye're an angel o' mercy. Ye dropped down from hivin just in time to save my life. Do ye remember the young lady ye saw with me down at the rollway? Well, that same girl is lost in these woods an' I'm looking for her, in the course of which I came across this varmint, an' but for your help, I'd been a goner, sure."

"That's all right, Mr. O'Boyle. I have only, in a small way, been repaying a debt of gratitude which I have owed you ever since the day of the rollway, so please only consider this a partial payment on account —nothing more. I happened to be out in these woods on private business, and getting lost, I thought it wisest to just stop where night overtook me and trust to daylight to get out of the tangle. I had climbed up among the branches of a big hemlock, cut a few boughs, made a bed, and was about dropping off in slumber when the report of a pistol aroused me. I jumped up, saw a large blaze over in this direction, and heard you and the bear struggling, but before I could reach you the blaze went out, and but for the labored breathing and growling of the bear I would never have found you. The fellow was too intent on finishing you at his leisure to notice me, so when I was near enough to see just the situation of affairs, I made a lunge forward with my knife and luckily reached a vital spot without touching you."

"Mr. Lane, I — why, I believe I am going to — to——"

In a moment the strong man dropped in a heap at the feet of his rescuer.

From a pool of water near by Lane fetched his hat full and bathed Barney's face. Then from his pocket he took a flask and was about to place it to the lips of the prostrate man when he opened his eyes and sat up.

"Faith, it's nothin' at all, only a little dizzy. The beast did give me quite a squeeze, an' I've been on the go the last few nights, an' not much appetite to eat. Guess I ain't meself."

A few moments' rest and a draught of cold water restored the young man somewhat. He looked closely at his companion, whose face was now clearly revealed in the moonlight.

"Why did ye quit the Keg the day of the rollway without kapin' yer appointment with me?" he asked abruptly.

"Well, I did leave without much notice, I confess, but you know men in my particular line of business," and he tapped the left side of his coat significantly, "are liable to receive sudden calls. I found it necessary to catch a train before the time of our appointment."

"Ye said ye had news fer me from Belfast, ef ye'll remember. Would ye mind tellin' it now? A friend o' mine hes come from there since I saw ye, but I hain't heard him mention yer name."

Lane sat silent for several minutes as though debating with himself, then he said impressively:

"Barney O'Boyle, I have learned many things the past few weeks, and some of them concern you very closely. It is a little premature to disclose them just now, but very soon you shall know all. In the mean time I wish you to discontinue this search for Miss Norine, and leave the matter in my hands. If I had known you were coming out here at night I should have told you to give it up before now. You can accomplish nothing."

"Fer the love of hivin, man! What do ye mane? Is she dead?" Barney sprang to his feet, and grasping Lane by both shoulders, gazed into his face with terror-stricken eyes.

"Your sweetheart is alive and safe," replied Lane.

"Alive! Safe! Say that again! Oh, blissed Saints! Say it again!" and then he proceeded to make any repetition impossible by clasping his long arms around Lane, and, with a new-born strength, nearly crushing the breath out of his body.

"Let me go! Great Cæsar! Let me go!" gasped Lane, struggling out of Barney's frantic embrace. "It is true; Norine is alive and——"

"Take me to her this blissed minute, man! What are we loafin' here for? Alive! Safe! Come, we'll have her home before mornin'. Which way——"

"Not so fast, my friend. I only know that she is safe. I do not know yet exactly where she is. I am close on the track, however, and shall find her before the week is out. Meanwhile you must get some rest and be ready to help me when the time comes. Be assured I shall call on you to be present at the finish. Until then you must appear to know nothing at all. Even the joy you can not help feeling at the knowledge of the dear girl's safety must not show itself at home nor in the village. It might arouse suspicion that would spoil our plans."

"Ye mane——"

"Never mind what I mean. It is most important that you do as I tell you. The suspense will be over soon and the guilty ones brought to justice."

"The guilty *ones?* Then the tramp——"

For answer, Lane put his hand to his face, and turned his back to Barney. In a moment he confronted him again.

"You!" cried Barney, astonished.

"Yes, your honor," laughed the newly made tramp. "I skipped my bail, but I shall be on hand before the October term."

"Faith, I spotted ye in Pete's gin-mill the other day, when ye were fakin' the boys, but I couldn't make out yer game, an' I hed no idea 'twas Jim Lane. Ah, but ye're a cute one. What brought ye out here?"

"You shall have the whole story in a few days. Now I want you to share the comfortable bed I have made in the hemlock branches yonder. There is room for two, and you are too much used up to walk back home to-night.

In a few moments the two men were comfortably ensconced in their rustic retreat, and Barney was soon dreaming the sweetest dreams for many a night.

CHAPTER XXVII

NORINE woke from a heavy sleep of utter exhaustion and rose with a start to a sitting posture. What had happened? or had she been dreaming? A vague sense of trouble or sudden accident oppressed her. She would go to her mother at once and let her laugh away the feeling. Then her eyes began to take in strange surroundings. Rocky walls and ceiling; a bright cloth hanging in front of an opening and flapping idly in the draft; soft skins of various animals scattered over the rough floor; a low couch piled with cushions upon which she had been lying; the subdued light coming from some unseen source—all these things mystified her, and filled her with alarm. Where was she? How did she get here? What was she to do? A little cry broke from her lips involuntarily. At the sound Nero sprang up from a rug upon which he had been keeping watch, stretched himself, and uttered a welcoming bark. The presence of Nero in such a place puzzled her, but also reassured her. Surely wherever he was with her she must be safe.

Suddenly a recollection of a terrible night rushed over her; bumping over a rough road in an old ox-cart; a crash, followed by a fall into mud and water; an apparition of Barney standing before her, torn and muddy, and then flying down the road like a mad man; a man springing unexpectedly from the darkness and dragging her into the forest where another man met them and urged her on; a cry for help, and a cruel bandage over her mouth; a long, hurried tramp through brambles which tore her clothes and scratched her hands, through rain, and mud, and swamp; the sudden appearance of Nero; a strange boat ride through tall rushes; a big negro woman who hugged her; and then—oblivion.

She shuddered as she looked again around the strange room, which she now saw was a cave. She dreaded to see Sam Hawkins confront her. But no, she was alone with Nero. The great dog came up, and, placing his head in her lap, looked with his soulful eyes up into hers. He wagged his tail with delight, and seemed to be telling her that he would protect her with his life.

Rising to her feet, Norine essayed to walk, but her sore and weary limbs refused their offices for an instant. This movement revealed to her the effect of the hardships which she had passed through during the night. She looked at her clothing. Her pretty dress was torn and covered with mud. She noticed, likewise, that her hands were badly scratched, and every joint of her body was stiff with pain. She sank back upon the couch too much frightened even to cry.

Presently the sound of voices reached her, and bending her head to a listening attitude, she caught notes of music coming from a distance, but still distinct and sweet. It was an old negro melody, and was being sung by two voices:

> " You ask what makes dis darky weep,
>   Why he like oders am not gay—
> What makes de tears roll down his cheek
>   From early morn till close ob day?
> My story, darkies, you shall hear,
>   For in my mem'ry fresh it dwells ;
> 'Twill cause you all to drop a tear
>   O'er de grave ob my sweet Kittie Wells."

24

Norine listened, bewildered. She had often heard that old melody, but never so tenderly sung as now. The sweet voice of the soprano reassured her, as it told her that one of her own sex was near, even though the color of her skin was not the same as her own. The bass voice was powerful and melodious. After a brief interval, the song went on:

> "When de birds were singin' in de mornin',
>   And de myrtle an' de ivy were in bloom,
> De sun on de hill tops was a dawnin'
>   It was den we laid her in de tomb."

The pathos that came with those tones told the lonely girl as plainly as words could do that she had nothing to fear, at least from those tender hearts near her, and she began to hope that after all she would soon be free.

After a while she made another attempt to move, determined to explore her surroundings at any cost. Nero stayed at her side as she painfully walked about in her rocky prison. Then she lifted the bright cloth and made her way out through the opening into a larger room. The profusion of animal rugs here startled her again, but, observing an exit through which the sun was shining, she hastened to it to get once more into open air, away from those enchanted caves.

As she stepped outside she drew a long sigh of relief, and inhaled a deep breath of the spring air. A scene of beauty lay before her. The budding trees lent their fragrance to the air, and birds and squirrels enlivened the scene with their songs and chatter. The sloping sward looked green and lovely. It was perfect, as only Nature could make it. The magnificent trees which dotted it here and there were beautiful to look upon, and supplied an ideal setting to the scene. The rippling, gushing waterfall was a delight to eye and ear, and Norine gazed upon all that was thus unfolded to her senses with mingled wonder and admiration.

Suddenly Nero looked up, and in an instant was bounding down the winding path which led to a little copse or thicket, upon reaching which he gave vent to a series of short sharp barks. A moment later the owner of a dark visage, bedecked with a large bandanna, came sauntering along the path singing snatches of plantation melodies. Nero had evidently bestowed his friendship without delay or reserve upon this new acquaintance, who had given him such a generous repast the night before, for he was now very demonstrative in his expressions of pleasure.

"Whar yo' missus, Nero? Hab you done run away f'om—? Wy, bress my stahs, here she be," and old Sue brushed out her apron and gave a tightening twist to the bandanna. "Is yuh done waked up, honey? It's pas' noontime. Ise so glad to see yo' pretty eyes," and she made a courtesy to the young lady who had been thrust upon her motherly care.

Norine sprang toward the kindly negress and grasping both of her big brown hands gazed eagerly into her face.

"Oh, tell me what all this means," she begged. "I am sure you must be kind and good or Nero wouldn't like you so. Tell me why I am here and how I can get home. My mother, and—and folks will be so frightened."

"Bress yo' haht, honey. Didn't Mars Sam done tell yuh dat yo' be queen yere?" answered Sue, her eyes opening wide in surprise because of the apparent ignorance of her charge.

"No, indeed, he didn't, and I didn't come here willingly. He brought me by force, he and his friend Mr. Axford. He is a very wicked man. I must go home at once. Tell me how I can get away—oh, do! do!" she exclaimed with renewed terror, as the black woman began shaking her head and turned as if to leave her.

"I don't know 'bout dat, honey," she said, kindly. "Can't talk dat-a way. Come wid me an' I'll get yuh yo' dinnah. Den yo'll feel better."

"I don't want to eat here," cried Norine in anguish. "I must find my way through the forest to my mother. Where is the man who was with you last night? Can't he help me?"

The negress put her arm gently but firmly around the trembling girl and patted her pretty, rumpled hair.

"We'll talk 'bout yo' mammy while yo' eatin' yuh dinner, honey. Yo' shuah mus' eat, or yo' kaint walk a step f'om here. Yo' needn't be a'feared. Ole Pomp an' Sue'll take good cayah yuh."

Unable to resist the gentle, coaxing voice and the strong arm of the negress, Norine submitted to being led back into the grotto. There Sue set before her a dainty meal, comforting her all the while with cooing words and caressing touches. The poor girl's confidence was soon won. It seemed unlikely that the good-hearted woman would refuse any help that lay in her power. Norine determined to find out all she could about the strange place to which she had been brought.

"Where are we, Sue?" she asked. "It seems so different from everywhere else. Are we far from Red-Keg?"

"Ah mus' confesticate, honey, as ah doan know. Yuh see, honey, me an' mah ole man come yere f'om

away off, an' w'en we come, den Mars Sam an' de rest
ob de boys done an' fotched us yere in de night wen it
wus dahk as Egypt, an' ah doan know how to get out.
Mah ole man be blin' foh shuah, an' o' cose he doan
know nuther. Ah doan keer, missus, as long as de
boys are so kin' to us."

"And are the boys kind to you?"

"Yas, missus, dey be berry kin' to us. Only we be
prisoners, shuah!"

"Who are these boys, Sue; the only ones I have
seen are Sam Hawkins and Billy Axford. Are there
more of them, and who are they?"

"Dar am Mars Sam, Mars Seward, Mars Billy, an'
Mars Walt."

"What! do you mean Seward Rathaway and Walter
Hayward?"

"Yas, honey, dat's dere names."

"Lettie's cousin!" exclaimed Norine. "Can he have
had anything to do with this?"

"Don' know who Lettie is," replied the woman.

"No, I suppose not. What do the boys do here?"
asked Norine.

"You is gettin' exquisitive, honey, an' if ah should
tell you—mah head would shuah fall inter de ribber!"
said Sue with a frightened look in her calm eyes.

"Well, what do they intend to do with me?" insisted
Norine, making another tack in her conversation, not
wishing that such a calamity should fall upon Sue on
her account.

"Wy, you's to be queen, honey; to rule ober us," replied Sue, brightening again.

Under other circumstances Norine would have
laughed merrily at such a grotesque idea; but now even
the sight of a tattered and soiled gown on the figure of

an acknowledged queen did not bring a smile to her face.

"Where is your husband, Sue?" she asked. On being told that he was down at the boat-landing, Norine insisted upon being taken to him at once. Sue reluctantly obeyed, and in a few moments they found Pomp lolling on the greensward near the water. Hearing their footsteps, he arose and turned his face toward the newcomers, waiting for their approach.

"Hey, Pomp, dis am de Missus as hab come down to see yuh," broke in Sue.

"Hit am a great honah to receib yuh, Missus; an' Pomp hol's hisself yo mos' humble subjec'," replied this worthy, bowing low.

"If you are my subject, then," exclaimed Norine, "I command you to take me away from here or tell me how I can get home. I must go to-day. If I should stay here another night, it would kill my poor mother."

"Ah's awful sorry, Missus; but ah dassent tell yuh nuffin. Yo' see ah hab no recumlection in dese cases. Ah—yo'—doan yuh see, honey—Pomp lose his head in de ribber ef ah tell yuh too much! 'Sides I don' know where we is mahself, an' ah couldn't fin' mah way out'n heyuh ef ah tried."

Repeated entreaties and tears failed to accomplish anything. Old Pomp and Sue showed every evidence of sympathy for the unhappy girl, and were untiring in their efforts to make her comfortable, but either they could not or feared to assist her to leave the island. In response to inquiry she learned that her captors did not expect to return for a week or more for fear of being followed. She hoped some of her friends would find her before then. Her parents and Barney, she knew,

would be frantic with grief and anxiety over her disappearance, not knowing whether she was dead or alive,
and she longed to send some message of comfort to
them. No way for doing so presented itself, and not
a particle of information as to her whereabouts could
she get from the two colored people, who really seemed
to be as much in ignorance as she. Each morning she
told herself that surely some one would come for her
before night; but each evening despair settled down
more heavily upon her and she sobbed herself to sleep
among the cushions of her couch. Barney she knew
was hunting for her night and day. She felt it. Her
father and the neighbors, too, would leave nothing undone to find her; but she wondered and grew discouraged as day followed day with no sign of a rescue party.
Perhaps they were near at hand. If only she could
make some signal that they would see or hear. She
hunted through the grotto, but could find no fire-arms.
Every day she wandered about the island seeking for
some point of escape, but the swamp surrounded it on
all sides. She spent hours on the top of the hill in the
middle of the island, straining her eyes in every direction over the swamp and forest, but could see nothing
which indicated a relief party, because she could see
only the tops of the trees and the tall waving swamp-
grass.

Norine soon learned that there was a fine garden on
the island, and Sue occupied much of her time caring
for this. Pomp had done the spading for it, and Sue
did the planting and then nurtured the young plants as
they came forth.

While wandering one day further than usual she discovered the secret of the island. For a while she was
nonplussed at her find, but it was not long before she

divined its meaning. That portion of the island was rocky like the part in which the grotto was located, but its abrupt side came down to the edge of the swamp, leaving only a narrow way in front of it. Norine at first hesitated about venturing upon this narrow path, but finally she yielded to curiosity and the hope of escape, and went. She found that an excavation had been made into the face of the cliff, and therein were queer looking receptacles, vats, coils, and retorts, which were new to her. But the smell of spirits convinced her that she had discovered a distillery. The fires were out, and all was silent. It was evident to her mind that it was at least temporarily abandoned, because the boys were away. Directly in front of the still was a dock and on this were stored casks and bottles and boxes. A branch of the canal ended at this place. At the end of the dock was a boat somewhat larger than a canoe, which was no doubt used for transporting the product of the distillery. It was held with chains, and these in turn were locked securely; so Norine saw no escape from that source.

One bright afternoon, as she was taking her accustomed walk around the island, Norine again wandered down toward the still. She mounted the dock, and then stepping down into the boat, sat there a while listening to the song-birds and the chatter of some blue-jays hovering near. She was thinking of Barney, and wondering if she would ever see him and her mother and home again, when in her sadness there came to her the words of a favorite refrain, and involuntarily she began to sing in a sweet voice the song which had stirred the hearts of thousands—"Dreaming of home, dear old home; dreaming of home and mother." As she finished the first verse, her voice broke in a sob, and bowing her head on her hands, she gave way to a flood of tears.

Hearing a splash in the water beside her, she raised her eyes and was about to utter a scream, as she beheld in the water before her a man, immersed nearly up to his shoulders. A warning look in his eyes, as he placed one hand on his lips to command silence, restrained her; but she stood up and looked more closely at the intruder, at the same time making ready to flee if necessary. A moment's inspection, however, revealed to her astonished gaze the man whose life Barney had saved at the rollway some weeks before—Jim Lane, of Belfast.

"Are you alone?" were the first words he uttered, and these almost in a whisper.

She felt like shouting out in joy at the sight of a rescuer, as she at once believed him to be, for she saw in his face the honest candor of a man she could trust. But discretion controlled her, and she answered in a low tone, her eyes brightening through her tears, that others were not far distant.

Then in a few words she explained her position, and in the mean time her visitor clambered out of the chilly water and stood upon the boat in the warmth of the bright sunshine.

"How did you get here?" Norine asked, full of eagerness and curiosity.

"I have swum and waded I don't know how far. Many a time I was almost ready to turn back, for I could see no evidences of life on either hand, and I didn't know what I was getting into. Finally I came to a fork in the stream, and here I was nonplussed. I was chilled and almost exhausted, and at the same time discouraged, for I thought I must be on the wrong track. Even the banks of the stream showed no touch of a human hand or foot, and I was about to retrace my way when I heard some one singing. I followed the sound and here I found you. I am so thankful. You were brought here by Sam Hawkins and his pals, were you not?"

"Yes; but how did you know it? Are they discovered?"

"No one knows of it as yet but myself. Never mind how I found out. I did not know exactly where you were hidden, and I wished to find you before those young scoundrels returned. I have been hunting through the swamp and forest of this region for nearly a week. What a wonderful hiding place this is to be sure."

"Tell me about my dear parents—and Barney. Are they very much worried?" pleaded the girl.

"The blow has been almost too much for them, but they are still doing everything conceivable to get news of you. Your Uncle Orrin from Belfast has come and is with them, helping and comforting surprisingly. As for Barney, the poor boy is crushed with grief. He has been hunting far and wide through the wilderness every night, and going without food, until he was nearly dead with sorrow and exhaustion. Last night I found him in the forest in the embrace of a great black bear, and I finished the beast just in time to prevent him from doing the same for Barney. I sent the boy home this morning to get well, telling him that you were safe, and that he must leave me to find you."

The tears rolled down Norine's face as she listened to the recital of the sorrow of her loved ones, and she murmured, "Poor dear mama and papa," and then to herself, "Poor dear Barney."

"Well, my friend, I am warm and must now start away, because I don't want your guardians to discover me. Remain here and be patient till you hear from me again, and do not give any hint of my visit. The old darkies are kind, you say, so you will be all right."

"Oh, they are so kind to me. Don't let any harm come to them!"

Lane promised that he would endeavor to protect the colored couple, and then shaking hands with Norine, he turned to let himself down into the water. Before doing so he glanced for the first time at the cliff, and then with a sudden sniff at the air, he almost shouted, so intense was his excitement.

"Ah! What is that?" he exclaimed in a suppressed voice, as he pointed to the cave.

"That? Why, I just discovered it myself for the first time the other day. I think it must be a distillery," and as she spoke Lane bounded past her, and in a twinkling was inside the cavern.

"Just what I have been looking for for the past year, and here I have stumbled upon it by accident," and he looked eagerly around at his find, noting the piled sacks of corn and the great still.

To delay there any longer might endanger complete success, and so bidding Norine good-by until he should see her again under more favorable circumstances, he clambered off from the dock into the canal.

"Keep a lookout for Pomp," warned Norine. "He is on the river most of the time. He is totally blind and can't see you, but his hearing is very acute. Be very careful."

It was well that the advice was given, for otherwise Lane, no doubt, would have returned with more haste than prudence, and thus would have been heard by the ever alert negro. Just as he came in sight of the forks of the canal, he saw the old boatman paddling along toward him, his boat keeping as unerringly in the middle of the stream as though he could see.

Lane stopped, crept up close to the bank, and allowed the old darky to pass. When he was out of hearing the tedious journey was resumed, and before sundown the detective had reached the landing; tired, cold, and hungry, but more than satisfied with his day's work.

CHAPTER XXVIII

THE day after the surreptitious visit of Jim Lane, Norine was walking with Sue just after sunrise toward the top of the hill which was near the centre of the island. Hope had been planted by Lane's visit and had grown over night into vigorous life. The beautiful morning cheered her. All nature seemed to smile its glad greeting to the glimmering sunlight that shone in brightness around, and she responded with a cheerful face and lighter heart.

While they stood gazing around the horizon to the southward, Norine espied three puffs of smoke, as from a gun, and then two more in rapid succession. Scarcely had the eye beheld, when the ear took up the following report.

"One, two, three; one, two," she said, as she took note of the strange occurrence. "Do you know what that means, Sue? Is it a signal?"

"It am de boys, it am de boys!" fairly yelled Sue, and without a word further she rushed down to the landing where Pomp was just pushing off his boat. Norine followed more slowly, with fear springing anew in her heart. Could it be that Mr. Lane had failed? What did it all mean?

It was, in fact, the Invincibles returning to the island. According to the agreement made at their conference in the club-room over Pete's saloon a week previously, they were all at the place of meeting on time. Each had arrived at the landing by a circuitous route, and just as Norine and Sue reached the top of the hill, Seward raised his big Colt's revolver and fired five shots. This was the cause of the commotion on the island.

Pomp made haste, and in due time, though it seemed an age to the nervous boys, the canoe came near, and then, to make sure, Pomp gave the raccoon signal while yet under cover. It was answered promptly, and the canoe and Pomp came into sight. The boys sprang in hurriedly.

"Shove off!" commanded Seward.

"Hands up!" came as a thunderbolt from a clear sky. "The first man who moves is a dead un."

Without delay the Invincibles, including Pomp, raised their hands high in air.

"Bring that boat of yours to shore and disembark, please, and be quick about it."

For the first time all eyes were turned toward the speaker. About a hundred feet away, with muskets levelled at the culprits, stood five resolute men, and at their head was John Lawrence, otherwise known as "John Long," the clever detective, who as a tramp had gone to sleep in the den of the Invincibles but a week before, and as "Jim Lane" had met with an accident in the rollway.

"The game's up, boys," said Walt, with resignation. "Might as well surrender." Then, turning toward their captors, he coolly asked: "What is it you want, and under what charge are we held?"

"Up with your hands, there, you black nigger!" spoke up a gruff voice as Pomp had unconsciously lowered his hands for a minute.

"Yas, Mars, I is hab 'em up," and the poor darky trembled with fear pitiful to behold, for he expected a bullet through him at any moment.

"We have warrants for the arrest, dead or alive, of Walter Haywood, William Axford, Seward Rathaway, and Samuel Hawkins, issued out of the United States District Court, upon the charge of operating an illicit still and disposing of the products thereof contrary to the statutes of the United States," announced Lawrence.

"We have also a warrant for Samuel Hawkins for the crime of abducting, with malice *prepense*, one Norine Maloney.

"Also, another warrant for the said Hawkins, charging him with a felonious assault upon the person of one Lettie Green, with intent to commit the crime of homicide.

"We have other warrants, but I guess you've heard enough to convince you that you will have to come with us. You will please step forward as your names are separately called," and he then proceeded to call the roll. One by one they came forward to receive the bracelets, the rifles still levelled at their breasts.

A look of stoicism crept into the faces of the first three, and they made no attempt at resistance or protest; but Sam's face was the picture of despair. He was trembling violently, and as his name was called, he suddenly jerked down his hand, drew his revolver, and pointed it at his head. As his finger pressed the trigger his arm was thrown upward by a quick blow of a rifle in the hands of Tom Moore, who had been watching Sam closely and sprang forward just in time. The bullet flew harmlessly over his head, and his hands were soon fast in the handcuffs.

"Come up here, you imp of darkness—come up here!" and the owner of the gruff voice stepped toward the darky, who was trembling from head to foot, his teeth chattering, and his knees fairly shaking together.

"Doan yuh see, Mars, ah am blin'?" and poor Pomp
rolled his eyes and moved his head from side to side in
abject terror.

"We have no charge against that helpless old man!"
said Lawrence, sternly. "Let him go back to his
home. Mr. O'Boyle, if you will come with me, we will
take this boat here with our colored friend, and he will
guide us to the retreat where we shall find the young
lady you seek." Then turning to Tom Moore, he added: "Constable, under no circumstances allow these
men to escape. Keep them well guarded till we return,
which will be in a very short time." Then he laugh-
ingly drew from his pockets four familiar-looking flasks
and exhibited them to the prisoners. A faint smile appeared on the faces of Walt and Billy as they recognized the flasks, which were still full.

"I never indulge, boys, though sometimes, in the
line of business, I have to go through the motions."

So saying, he tossed the flasks into the swamp; then
stepping into the boat with Barney and the negro, he
pushed off toward Mystic Isle.

As soon as Pomp had left them, Norine and Sue returned to the top of the hill. The negress gave the
girl a pair of field-glasses and pointed in the direction
of the landing.

"I'm sure, Sue, that there are more than four men
down there," she exclaimed at last. "I can even see
the shimmer of the sun as though along gun-barrels.
There must be trouble. Yes, there are nearly a dozen
men, but I can not recognize any of them."

Suddenly a single pistol shot was heard. Then all
was quiet.

As she waited, the minutes seemed like hours to
her, but at last she heard the voice of old Pomp calling

in great excitement: "Missy Norine, come down yere, quick," and, losing no time, she was soon at the landing.

There was the boat; there was Pomp swinging his arms wildly and shouting to Sue; there was her friend Mr. Lane—there was Barney!

In an instant she found her "home" in his strong embrace.

In front of Pete's place a small group of idlers sat smoking, chewing, and gossipping. Old "Leatherback," a tanned and wrinkled lumberman, whose nickname suited him to a dot, was complaining because Pete had just refused him a third glass of whiskey on the plea that his stock was unusually low.

"Hain't got in a supply for some time, ye know. My agent hes been unable ter 'tend ter bus'ness fer nigh on two weeks. Last I heard, he was countin' on startin' up agin this week. Reckon we'll be able ter stock up soon now," explained Pete.

Old Leatherback squinted at Pete out of the corner of his eye, and remarked:

"Thet 'ere 'agent' o' your'n is a mighty fly critter; I've heerd ye talk about 'im a good deal, but I never sot eyes on 'im yet. Where's he keep hisself?"

"Like enough thet's his business," said Pete, shortly. His love for imparting information seemed suddenly to have deserted him.

"Hear anythin' 'bout thet Maloney gal all this rumpus is about?" asked Old Leatherback, after a pause, looking around at the loungers.

"No, ain't heerd nothin'," answered Jack Mann. "Why, are ye figgerin' on winnin' thet five thousan'?" he queried with a sneer.

25

Leatherback rolled a monster quid out of his mouth, deposited it on the bench, gazed at it a moment, and finally picked it up and tossed it into the road. Then he spread his legs apart, placed his elbows on his knees, poked his head forward, and squinted into the faces of the two men before him. Presently he said, sententiously:

"Five thousand's five thousand."

After a silence of some minutes, Pete ventured a remark.

"Jes' so," said he.

Another pause. Jack Mann fidgeted a bit but said nothing. Pete waited. Leatherback pulled out his square of tobacco, cut off a fresh hunk, and stuffed it away in his cheek.

"I been thinkin'," he began slowly; "I been thinkin'—thunder!"

Leatherback's intended revelation of his thoughts was interrupted by the sudden exclamation because he caught sight of a horseman dashing down the road at breakneck speed.

"Well, in the name of all darnation, Joe, what's up?" asked Leatherback, as Joe drew rein before the Keg and sprang from his horse.

"Up? Everythin's up. Norine's found, the Invincibles hev all been taken prisoners, an' Tom Moore an' his posse hes' 'em, an' is bringin' the hull kit of 'em in, —an' they've got the bracelets on—Sam Hawkins, an' all the rest."

As Joe Reon shouted out his exciting news, neither he, nor the loungers at the Keg, noticed a trim little figure just passing or the other side of the road. She stopped an instant to listen to Joe, trembled a little, and then hurried on, and was quickly out of sight.

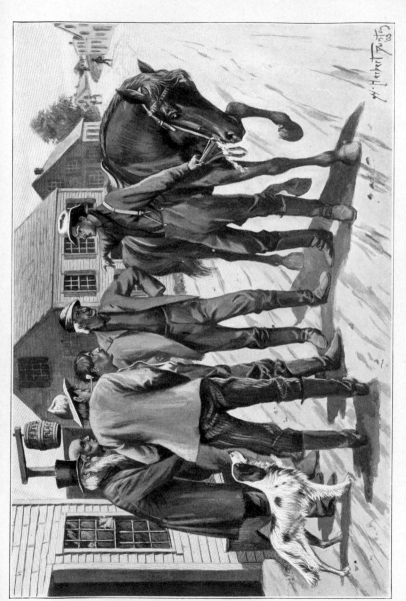

"WELL, IN THE NAME OF ALL DARNATION, JOE, WHAT'S UP?"

Norine and Barney had reached home by way of the crossroad from Wilford, and thus had avoided the village and the curious eyes of the gossips. The joy of home-coming would be marred by a crowd of intruders if they were seen. The Hawkins farm lay between them and Norine's home, and Uncle Si would be the first one to know of the return. Fearing that the sudden excitement might be too much for the old man, Norine waited in the orchard while Barney went in to find Uncle Si and break the news. He dreaded to tell him that his only son was indeed the guilty man, but he hoped to soften the blow, as any one else might not do. He found Farmer Hawkins in the barn and greeted him with a cheery "Good-mornin'," although it was well toward noon.

"Good-morning, Barney; where have you been? You must have started out long before sun up. I didn't hear you."

"Yes, Uncle Si. It was airly business I was after attindin' to. Ye didn't see Sam last night or this mornin', did ye?"

"No," replied Mr. Hawkins, with a sigh. "He spent the night with Seward, I suppose. You haven't heard anything unpleasant about him, I hope?" he added anxiously.

"Faith, I've been so taken up lookin' for Norine, I don't consarn meself much about Sam, unless followin' him would lead me to her," replied Barney, evasively.

"Do you really think he did it, Barney?" The old man's voice trembled. This was the first time the subject had been spoken of so plainly between them.

"Sometimes I hevn't thought so, an' sometimes, begorra, I hev," admitted Barney, and then he continued: "That tramp yarn don't seem to hold water, an' there

ain't any one else as I know of, who was set on havin'
Norine agin her wishes, or who hed a grudge agin
me."

Farmer Hawkins groaned at this plain statement of
his own fears, and said: "That's so, Barney. I've
thought of it again and again, but Sam has been quiet
and sober lately, and has been at home most of the
time. I had begun to hope that he was really innocent,
as he claims. It would be dreadful, Barney, if he——"

"There, Uncle Si, don't be after feelin' so bad.
Sure, ye done your duty by the lad. Ef it should turn
out that no harm hes come to Norine, an' that she
comes back safe home, it wouldn't be so bad."

"God grant it!" exclaimed Uncle Si.

"Ef ye could only see the darlint this blessed minute,
sure she'd make up for the sorrows the boy hes brought
ye by his doin's."

"She is a sweet girl, Barney, and it would be a great
comfort to me to see her again safe an' sound. I love
her almost as a daughter. But it has been so long now
since she was lost, I'm beginning to lose hope."

"Faith, ye must niver do that. Look at me. She
is the light of me eyes, an' I'm sure this very minute
they shall feast themselves on her swate face agin.
Begorra, we hevn't looked for her enough. We've
been lookin' away off in the woods an' the swamp.
More like she's nearer home. Hev ye looked in the
attic, Uncle Si, an' in the barn, an' in the garden, an'
in the orchard? Hev ye——?"

Uncle Si stared at Barney in amazement, and the
suspicion began to grow that his mind had given way
under the strain, but Barney seized him by the arm and
continued:

"Come, this blessed minute, Uncle Si. We must

make up for lost time. Sure, she must be *somewhere*, and, by hivin, we'll find her in a jiffy!"

Dragging the astonished farmer once around the barn, he poked hurriedly into the hay-loft, into the corn-barrel, into the oat-bin; then out across the barn-yard into the garden, dodging under syringa bushes, and lilacs, and through the grape arbor, continually repeating, "She must be *somewhere*, and I know we can find her in a jiffy, you and I!" Soon they reached the fence separating the garden from the orchard. Pulling Uncle Si through the little gate, Barney hurried him on. The old man was now certain that Barney had gone crazy, but the latter kept insisting, "Sure, she must be somewhere, an' you an' I will find her." They dodged among the trees, Barney now and then telling Uncle Si to look up into the branches to see if he could see Norine. At last they came to the corner of the orchard where Barney had built a little secluded rustic seat for himself and Norine that same spring. With a last cheery assurance that Norine "must be somewhere, an' most likely *here*," Barney suddenly brought his friend and employer to the rustic seat, and Norine sprang from it and threw her arms about Uncle Si's neck with a glad cry of greeting.

The old man looked from one to the other of the young people with tears in his eyes, but Barney grinned and remarked boastingly, "I told ye she would be likely near by, an' that we would find her in a jiffy ef Uncle Si took a hand in the sarch; but we mustn't stop here. Sure Norine is wanted at home to bring joy to the eyes an' hearts of her own parents an' Uncle Orrin. Come along, Uncle Si, an' we'll tell ye the hull story on the way."

"I thought you were crazy, lad—but, thank God!

you wasn't," said Uncle Si, as he prepared to accompany the young people to the Maloney homestead.

The first to arrive at the home of Norine to congratulate her upon her rescue was her friend Lettie Green, who had overheard Joe Reon as he told the news to the loungers at Red-Keg. She kissed Norine affectionately; but there were tears in her eyes, and she hid her face for a moment on her friend's shoulder. Norine stroked her hair and hugged her close, but said nothing, feeling that it was hardly the right moment for confidential words on a subject so painful as that which she knew brought those tears to Lettie's eyes.

While the family group discussed the affair and plied Norine with questions, Lettie sat silent a little apart, busy with her own thoughts. The crimson came and went in her cheeks, and she seemed restive and uncomfortable, but she made no move to depart until Barney, who had remained for some time after Uncle Si had returned to his farm, excused himself, regretfully, saying that he must get to his work, and would come again in the evening. As he arose to go, Lettie excused herself also, and asked if she might walk up the road with him part of the way.

"Sure, Miss Lettie, I'll be plased ter have yer company," said Barney, cordially; but as they walked along together, neither seemed very much to enjoy the other's company. Lettie, particularly, was embarrassed, and found it more difficult than she expected to speak of the things in her heart.

"Barney," she began after a long silence, "you are glad to get Norine back again, aren't you?"

"Indade, Miss Lettie, I am, an' no mistake. Sure, we're all mighty glad, I'm thinkin'."

"Then you can afford to be generous and forgiving, can't you, Barney?" pleaded Lettie. "I'm afraid— Sam—will need all the mercy and forgiveness we can give him, poor boy."

"Ye may well say that, Miss Lettie, but it's mighty little mercy he's showed to others, an' it's mighty little he nade ask for here. The sooner he's put where he belongs, the better it will be for all consarned."

"But, Barney, you know we are told to forgive our enemies and do good to them that despitefully use us."

"I don't know so much about that, an' I can't say es I ever heard that sayin' quoted by any except them es wanted to save themselves from somethin' they desarved to get; but, sure, there'd be plenty to do good to Sam ef all he'd despitefully used should follow that rule. He broke his poor old mother's heart. She's gone. But there's others. He tried three times to kill me. He stole Norine away, an' dragged her through the forest an' swamp, an' kep' her away all this time from her home. He tried to kill yer own swate self, an' came near to doin' it. He hes——"

"Barney! How did you know *that?*" exclaimed Lettie, with a sudden alarm ringing in her voice.

"Sure, everybody knows it—or soon will. That was one o' the charges for his arrist. It strikes me, Miss Lettie, you hev es little cause es any to be asy with the rapscallion. He's bad clane through, an' ain't worth your trouble."

"Oh, Barney, have pity, if not for his sake, at least for the sake of his poor old father. I'm afraid this blow will kill him, if he is not comforted. He has been a kind friend to you. Now in his time of need, you can repay his kindness on his son."

"Faith, Miss Lettie, you're right about dear old

Uncle Si, but what can I do? Sam hes got himself into the clutches o' the law for a list o' crimes es long es my arm. It's no grudge o' mine thet'll be holdin' him. He'll likely get his desarts for all I can do to help or prevint. Sure, nobody knows it better than his father, God help him!"

"At least you can refuse to press any charge against him yourself, and you can persuade Norine to do the same—please, Barney."

"An' goodness knows there'll be no nade for me to priss charges, or for Norine to priss thim for thet matter. He was caught rid-handed, ye might say, an' ef that ain't enough, he was heard to tell the Invincibles all about his own doin's, not forgettin' the attack on yerself."

"Who heard him?"

"The tramp, no less. He was a sure enough detective in disguise."

"Then I must find him, too," said Lettie with a little groan of despair. "But you will do as I ask, Barney?"

"I'll have to tell the truth when they ax me. But I'll not be too hard on the varmint (beggin' yer pardon) for your sake an' Uncle Si's."

"Thank you, Barney; and you will speak to Norine about it, too?"

"Faith, you better spake to her yerself, with yer persuadin' ways. It would be hard for me to put much feelin' in the job, I'm thinkin'."

And speak to Norine she did. No sooner had Barney left her to enter the Hawkins home than Lettie hastened back to the Maloney farm. The two girls went off by themselves and talked the matter all over, and Norine was soon persuaded to refrain as far as she might be allowed to do from pressing her complaint against Sam. She was moved by her friend's distress and forgot for the moment her own and Barney's wrongs. So these two loving and forgiving girls planned how they might help the wretch who had so ruthlessly injured them both. Lettie, in her innocence, believed it would be enough to win over those who had suffered most at Sam's hands, and those who were immediately instrumental in his arrest, to secure his release. After Norine's assurances her heart felt somewhat lighter, but she determined to see Tom Moore and Mr. Lawrence before any legal steps could be taken, so she made all haste to the village of Red-Keg, arriving there early in the evening. She was almost exhausted, having walked to and fro many miles during that sad day. To each of the men she poured out her heart without reserve and pleaded for mercy for the man whom, though so unworthy, she still loved. Tom, big-hearted, honest, and susceptible to the pleading of the unfortunate, especially when in the person of a beautiful girl, listened with a show of sympathy, which was really nothing but pity, and then said that he had a painful duty before him, that he would be held strictly responsible for the performance of it, but that, while he could not escape it, he would do no more than the law required, and that without malice or desire for vengeance.

The generous and sympathetic form of Tom Moore's assurances made up to some extent for their lack of satisfying substance, but prepared Lettie for still further lack of real success with Mr. Lawrence. He explained to her, as kindly as he could, the necessary attitude of the representatives of the law toward one who had committed so many serious crimes against the community. He showed her that it was a matter which was not limited to the persons immediately concerned, but that the county, state, and nation shared in the injury inflicted upon the individuals. He pointed out the enormity of the offenses, and showed her that to let them go unpunished would be to commit another still worse crime against the community. Poor Lettie was in despair.

"Mr. Lawrence, what you say is all very true—too true. He is branded with a series of terrible crimes, but I know that he is not all bad—that if he is given another chance he will see the error of his ways and be a better man hereafter. Oh, Mr. Lawrence, have mercy," and she clasped his hands in hers, and with eyes suffused in tears begged for leniency to the man who but a few short days ago had ruthlessly strangled her and left her for dead upon the roadside.

Mr. Lawrence had great things at stake. He had prided himself on this job, and hoped to gain official recognition, but the pleadings of this fair young girl unnerved him, and bidding her go home and rest, he promised to do all he could compatible with public safety and his professional honor. He did not think it necessary to pain her further by pointing out how little that "all" would necessarily be.

With a "God bless you!" she left him, feeling that he would prove a friend in the hour of great trouble, and who would at least see that justice should be ered with mercy instead of a desire for vengeance. At last, weary and footsore, she returned to her own home. Robert Allen was waiting for her. He had heard of her efforts in Sam's behalf, and with his own heart full of yearning for the unhappy youth, he had hastened to give the brave girl such sympathy and help as lay within his power. When he left her, late in the evening, both were comforted by a mutual understanding, and hopeful that the plans which they had settled upon might lighten the hand of justice on the man they both loved.

CHAPTER XXIX

Justice Frost had never been called upon to hear so important a case, and his little court-room was entirely inadequate for the crowd which gathered the next morning at the hearing of the Invincibles. The whole neighborhood was in a fever of excitement and curiosity, and the big constable, Tom Moore, found some difficulty in getting his prisoners through the throngs which surrounded and filled the court-room. Sam held his head high with a defiant air, yet so thinly veiled was this expression that all knew it was assumed. Seward, Walt, and Billy appeared more resigned. They were not so heavily burdened with guilt as was their fallen leader, and they were indeed glad that the suspense was over and that Norine had been restored. Uncle Si sat there bowed with grief and shame. He seemed to feel in all its intensity the disgrace which had fallen upon his son. Barney and Norine showed plainly that they did not share the relish for the affair which so large a majority of the spectators enjoyed, and that they would rather be anywhere else than there. Poor Lettie Green was nervous and haggard, having passed a sleepless night after the wearisome day which had preceded it. The minister sat close by her side and spoke to her frequently in a low tone.

Promptly at ten o'clock Judge Frost took his seat, wiped his spectacles, placed them with deliberate care upon his nose, and without uttering a word gazed over the rims at the four prisoners, collectively and individually, for some moments.

Judge Frost had been chosen by his neighbors in that farming and lumber region to be justice of the peace, but legal practises were little known and less observed. There was no practising attorney in the village, and Judge Frost, who had been proven to be an honest and merciful man, and a lover of justice, administered cases which came within his jurisdiction with an unrestricted hand and in his own way. Usually when an evil-doer trespassed State laws, however, Judge Frost simply examined the accused and their accusers, and if the evidence was sufficient he held the prisoners for trial in the Circuit Court, which convened at Midland, the county seat. This was the procedure which he intended to follow in the present case. After his scrutiny of the four young men, he said slowly and solemnly:

"Prisoners at the bar, stand up!"

They all arose and listened to the reading of the charges, and each in turn, to the surprise of many of their neighbors, pleaded "not guilty."

It was generally believed by those who knew how clear was the case against them that they would plead guilty and throw themselves upon the mercy of the court.

"Bedad, they're as guilty as the divil!" exclaimed a voice in the back of the room.

"Constable, take that man out!" thundered the judge, glaring in the direction of the offender.

"Who was it, yer honor?" asked Tom, though he thought he recognized Pete Murray's voice.

"Find out!" exclaimed the judge, turning again to the prisoners. As the disturber did not declare himself, and as Tom Moore could scarcely move through the densely packed crowd, he took the liberty of disregarding the judge's commands.

"Prisoners, be seated. We will now consider the evidence upon which you are being held for the several counts against you, beginning with the case of Sam Hawkins, who is charged with illicit distilling, abduction, and attempted murder. What we want to know about now is this abduction. Barney O'Boyle, take the stand."

Barney elbowed his way to the witness stand through a crowd, all of whom were his friends, and many a pat on the back, or hearty word, was given him on the way.

"Barney O'Boyle, what can you tell us in this case of the People of this State against this prisoner charged with the abduction of Norine Maloney?"

"Sure, yer honor, I was goin' to—I mean, he—that is, I— Begorra! I can't tell a blissed thing."

"What! Can't tell anything about the abduction of your sweetheart—I mean of Miss Maloney!" exclaimed the judge in astonishment.

"Well, ye see, yer honor, there's poor old Uncle Si, the best friend I hev in the world, sittin' there, lookin' so old an' heart-broken; an' there's Miss Lettie gazin' at me with them big eyes o' hern all red with cryin'— sure I can't say a word agin that varmint, knowin' that 'twould be like stabbin' the hearts o' them two."

"But we must have the truth. Justice demands it. Come, speak out and tell what happened as you know it," insisted the judge.

Barney was embarrassed and uncomfortable in the extreme. He shifted from one foot to the other, gazed at the ceiling, and back to the faces before him. Suddenly his face cleared and he turned to the judge.

"Ye want me to tell ye all I saw, yer honor?"

"Yes, tell the truth and nothing but the truth, no matter whom it hurts."

"Well, yer honor, I saw Norine with me that night, an' then I saw she warn't with me. I swear I didn't see Sam carry her off, an' I didn't see him with her when I found her agin."

An audible grin rippled over the court-room, but Barney's face was as serious as an owl's. The judge looked at him sharply, and said:

"Don't trifle with the court, sir."

"No, yer honor," said Barney.

"Is that all you can say?"

"Yes, yer honor; I'm losin' me mimory."

"Stand down, sir."

"Sure, thet's what I'm doin' now, yer honor, only it's up I'm standin'."

"Take your seat, sir!" roared the judge.

"Yes, yer honor."

Barney had managed to keep his eyes away from Sam during his testimony, and had not noticed the surprise, shame, and relief which swept over his face when the man he had wronged declined to accuse him. These fleeting emotions quickly lost themselves in the sullenness in which he had taken refuge since entering the court-room. But Barney did not fail to see the tears of gratitude which filled the eyes of Lettie and old Uncle Si, and he felt rewarded.

Tom Moore being next called to the stand said he could tell nothing except as to the capture of the prisoners and the finding of Norine. He could not swear from his own knowledge that Sam Hawkins had done the deed imputed to him.

"Who is there to accuse this young man? If you're

all going to flunk when you come to swear I may as well let the prisoners go at once. But perhaps Miss Maloney will come to the stand and enlighten the court a little," and his piercing eyes sought this young lady.

She came slowly forward, amid the most breathless silence. Sam had forgotten his defiance, and was aroused out of his sullenness. He trembled before the girl who a short time ago had been in his power.

"Miss Norine," said Judge Frost, kindly, "please tell the court from the beginning all that happened to you Saturday night, May 6th."

Norine was surprised at such a comprehensive command, when she was expecting only a simple question, and she hesitated. Then, seeing Lettie's eyes fixed appealingly upon her, she said:

"Must I tell it, judge? Please, I'd rather not."

"You certainly must," said the judge. "We have got to get at the bottom of this affair some way, and you can tell more than any one else. We cannot excuse you."

Seeing that there was no escape Norine narrated the events briefly but truthfully. Not a sound but her voice was heard in the court-room. Sam sat through the recital like a statue of stone. Norine mentioned no names, until, at the end of her story, the judge insisted that she name the persons who had carried her off.

"One was Billy Axford—and the other—was Sam Hawkins," she answered so low that only those very near her could hear the names.

"Very well, that will do."

John Lawrence was called to the stand, and as he took his place many recognized him for the first time as the tramp who had been arrested for the abduction of Norine and released on bail furnished by the Invincibles. The significance of that "generous" act at once became apparent.

"What have you to offer as a reason for holding this man over to the Circuit Court besides what has been said?" asked the judge.

"Your honor, it is not my desire to persecute this young man, and it pains me deeply to bring more sorrow to those who have already suffered so much through him, but I am a representative of the government, and have sworn to serve it faithfully, and it is my duty to charge Sam Hawkins with robbery of the United States mails."

The witness was interrupted with a buzz of astonishment which swept over the crowd at this unexpected announcement. Judge Frost pounded on his desk and called for instant silence. Mr. Lawrence continued rapidly:

"I have in my possession evidence that through this robbing of the mails he discovered that a legacy was coming to Miss Maloney. He hoped to marry her and thus get possession of her fortune. Failing to secure her hand in a legitimate way he sought to obtain it by force, and hence the abduction."

If a bomb had burst in the court-room those present could hardly have been more astonished, and no heed was paid to the calls of the judge for silence. To add to the excitement, Lettie Green, who had been listening with white, drawn face and staring eyes to the testimony, suddenly uttered a moan and fell fainting to the floor. All was at once confusion, some crying one thing and some another. Even the judge forgot for a moment his dignity and sprang to his feet, ordering the crowd to make way so that Lettie could be taken out

26

into the air. But it was impossible to force a passage through the press of spectators within and those who were pushing from without, eager to hear something of the proceedings. A glass of water stood on the judge's desk, and Barney seized it and passed it to Norine, who bathed the poor girl's face until she regained consciousness. Then Lettie refused to listen to any suggestion of retiring from the room. She would be all right soon, and must stay, at any cost.

Sam, meanwhile, was shrinking in his seat, pale and trembling, his face twitching nervously. This new charge was unexpected by him, also. When order was restored Judge Frost commanded Lawrence to continue.

"There is a man in the room who will corroborate me, I think. But before he is called I wish to depose further that not only Sam Hawkins, but Seward Rathaway, Walter Haywood, and William Axford are charged with operating an illicit distillery in this county on what they have styled 'Mystic Isle.' I ask your honor to hold them for the United States District Court on that charge. Now, if your honor please, we will listen to Orrin Maloney."

The judge immediately summoned Orrin to the witness stand. He identified a letter as having been written by himself to Barney O'Boyle, and which Lawrence then testified that he had seen Sam drop in the woods. The four prisoners here, as with one accord, sought the face of Lawrence, and at once recognized their former guest, whom they supposed had been disposed of by their cunning ruse.

There being no other witnesses, the judge asked if any one had anything to urge why the prisoners should not be held for trial. There was an oppressive silence for a moment, then Lettie, gathering strength by a sudden effort, rose tremblingly to her feet, and faced the judge. Even then she was unable to speak at once, and turned an appealing look upon the minister, who, without a word, arose and stood by her side.

"May it please your honor," she began in a low tone, which gradually grew stronger as she continued, "I stand before this court knowing only too well how—how—dreadful are the—the crimes charged against the —Mr. Hawkins. One of those—charges is for something in which I was the only sufferer. The charge is made on hearsay only. For myself, I do not join in this charge. What he did, I provoked him to while he was not himself, and I was to blame. The others— Norine and Barney—do not press any charge. The prisoner's dear old father is here to join with me in a plea for mercy. Sam is all that is left to him now. Do not break poor old Uncle Si's heart. Oh, judge, be merciful! be merciful!"

"Amen!" said Allen, earnestly.

The tears were streaming down her face as Lettie sank into her seat. There was breathless silence now in the court. Even the stern judge was driven to conceal his emotion by blowing his nose vigorously. Sam opened his mouth as though to speak, but no word passed his lips. A deathly pallor overspread his face, and he seemed about to fall. Every one waited with tense feelings for the judge's reply. He spoke very kindly but firmly as he said:

"My dear young lady, I feel the deepest sympathy with you and good Farmer Hawkins, although there is nothing I can see in the behavior of this prisoner which would call for clemency, or entitle him to such forbearance as you and these others whom he has wronged are disposed to show him, but whatever I might be willing to do for your sake, and for the sake of my friend the prisoner's father, I don't see how I can interfere in this case. The prisoners have all pleaded not guilty, and the law says they must be tried. The evidence is too strong for me to dismiss it. If they had pleaded guilty and thrown themselves upon the mercy of this court, there's no telling what I might have done, except in the matters which concern the United States mails and the internal revenue. Even there, a recommendation of mercy from this court on account of the prisoners' youth and the fact of this being their first offense might accomplish something; but they have pleaded not guilty to all the charges, and I am afraid I can do nothing, in view of the evidence, but hold them for trial."

"Your honor, may I speak with the prisoner—Mr. Hawkins, I mean?" asked Lettie.

"Yes, for a moment."

Lettie made her way to the bench where Sam was sitting and began to whisper earnestly in his ear, heedless of the many curious eyes which watched her. Sam listened with a dogged air at first, but in a little time his spirit seemed to melt within him. His lips moved and an indistinct sound came forth; then raising his fettered hands to his head, he broke down completely and sobbed like a child. Lettie waited. Presently she placed a soft little hand on his arm. He started, and suddenly sprang to his feet, exclaiming excitedly:

"I am guilty, judge, guilty! Oh, yes, far more guilty than you think—than any one thinks—even this noble little girl here, who knows I am vile enough. Everything charged against me is true. A good deal more might be charged if some persons cared to speak

"I AM GUILTY, JUDGE, GUILTY!"

—Barney O'Boyle there, for instance. It's all true. I am a scoundrel, a coward, almost a— Oh, I can't say it. This angel here says you would show me mercy if you could. I don't see how you can, I don't see how Barney could, or Norine Maloney, most of all how this girl here at my side could. But if you can, judge, in spite of all my wickedness, be merciful—if you can, because of my full confession, coming so late, save me from a part of the punishment I deserve, I beg you to do so, not for my sake—I am not worth a single kind thought—but for the sake of my poor old father, whose heart I have almost broken, as I broke my saintly mother's—for his sake, and for the sake of this angelic, long-suffering, and forgiving girl—*my wife!*"

He stopped for want of breath and stood trembling, his eyes fixed on the judge, seeing nothing else. The spectators, the witnesses, the other prisoners, the judge himself, were dumb, paralyzed, with amazement. Only Lettie seemed to grasp the situation.

"Your wife!" she cried. "I thought——"

"Oh, yes! I told you I was guilty even more than you could think," Sam said to her; then turning again to the judge, he went on: "Nearly three years ago, when I came home from college, I met Lettie, and we loved each other—at least I thought so at the time. I took her to a minister and we were married secretly. I made her swear solemnly not to reveal the secret under any circumstances until I should give permission. In a short time I regretted what I had done, and to free myself, I told her that it was only a joke—that it was no minister at all who had married us, but that some day we would be married in earnest. I held her to her oath of secrecy, however, and she has been true to it ever since, although I have given her more provocation than most women would ever endure. I lied to her. The marriage was a genuine one, and if I ever get free from the penalties of my crimes I shall spend my life in an effort to make up to her all that she has suffered on my account, for I love her now if I never did before. I am in your hands, judge, to do with as you see fit."

Sam sat down beside Lettie, who was weeping hysterically.

Judge Frost was rubbing his eye-glasses as vigorously as Lady Macbeth ever rubbed her guilt-stained hand. The scene in the court-room was indescribable. Meanwhile, Seward, Walt, and Billy whispered together, and then stood up.

"Your honor," said Seward, "we beg to withdraw our plea of 'not guilty' and substitute a plea of 'guilty'!"

"That is my wish," said Walt.

"And mine," said Billy.

The three boys sat down.

At last the "damned spot" in the eye-glasses seemed to be "out," for Judge Frost adjusted them again to his nose and rapped loudly on his desk.

"Silence in the court!"

The silence was instantaneous and oppressive.

"The charge against Sam Hawkins for assault, with intent to kill, upon his wife, otherwise known as Lettie Green, is dismissed.

"The charge against Sam Hawkins, which charge should extend, but does not, to William Axford, for the abduction of one Norine Maloney, is dismissed.

"The charge against Sam Hawkins for robbing the United States mail, and the charge against the four prisoners for operating an illicit distillery shall be tried in the United States District Court. I reserve the right to send with the papers such communications of my own as I may see fit.

"For the time until that court meets, the prisoners are released without bail, in the custody of Thomas Moore, who shall be responsible for their appearance when the court convenes.

"This court is now adjourned."

CHAPTER XXX

Two men walked slowly along a narrow logging road which wound here and there through the forest. The younger of the two saw only the wreck of all things present, with nothing but humiliation, disgrace, and ruin as his lot. The other man, looking beyond the unsightly path of the whirlwind, saw the star of hope shining brightly, and caught the glimmer of a happier day about to dawn for the young man at his side. He was speaking quietly.

"After all, notwithstanding the distress we all felt, there was a great deal of joy in the occasion. It may look dark to you now; but the day will come, I believe, when you will mark the 18th of May, 1871, as one of the happiest days in your life."

The elder man paused; but no reply, no contradiction, no question came from his companion. Presently he continued:

"It was joyful for several reasons. You have been frightfully handicapped for a long time. I know very well that more than once you have really wished to escape from the path you were treading. Secret things held you back. Enterprises to which you felt yourself hopelessly committed could not be given up. You were not strong enough. While immunity lasted it was so much easier to increase your burden than to lessen it. I tell you, my boy, sin is the worst handicap any man can have. It is like the mythical 'old man of the sea.' The time comes when the burdened one cries out in terror and despair, 'O wretched man that I am! who shall deliver me from the body of this death?' Well, now, don't you see how the very completeness of the exposure has cleared the way for your escape? The secret enterprises being ruined can have no further hold on you. It isn't necessary to plan, or worry any longer over them, nor to commit new sins in order that old ones may remain hidden and prosper. So far as they are concerned, you are free to start anew. Aren't you glad to be rid of them?

"More than that, you confessed, publicly—made a clean breast of it—to those you had injured, and righted a great wrong to your angelic little wife. That was cause for joy, surely. It put you right in line for forgiveness, and I don't know of anybody but will forgive you, or has forgiven you. The best of it all is that this confession to men will make it easier for you to take the next and more important step—confession to God. That will bring you not only forgiveness, but a thorough cleansing away of the stain sin has made upon your soul. The promise is that 'if we confess our sins, He is faithful and just to forgive us our sins and to cleanse us from all unrighteousness.' More than that, He will obliterate the sin altogether from His memory; for He has declared 'I will forgive their iniquity, and I will remember their sin no more.' There is the greatest of all joys for you, my dear boy. Come, won't you join with me right here and ask for it?"

The young man's temples throbbed; his throat was parched and aching; he longed to feel the relief and joy the minister had spoken of with such quiet confidence, but it seemed beyond his reach. The simple power to yield had not come to him. For a few moments he moved nervously. Then he realized that the minister was waiting for him to answer. His painful embarrassment increased. At last, in an agony of spirit, he cried out:

"I can't—I can't! It's too much; I'm an outcast; I am ashamed!"

"Nothing is too much for Him, Sam," answered the minister, putting his arm about the young man's shoulders in affectionate entreaty. "If your earthly friends know how to forgive, shall not your Heavenly Father, who loves you far better than they do, forgive you even more gladly? It is the outcast whom He calls first and receives most lovingly. It is the coming to Him of such a one which causes 'joy in the presence of the angels of God.' We must all be ashamed when we look at ourselves, but He bids us look at Him, and tells us 'though your sins be as scarlet they shall be as white as snow; though they be red like crimson they shall be as wool.' Oh, Sam, He loves you so! He knows that you've fallen, and hurt yourself so badly that you need help. His hand has been stretched out to you for some time through the hands of friends here who love you. Just take hold and you will be lifted up. Others have been as deep in the abyss as you. The Saviour's love reaches to the uttermost. Just try it and see."

A dry sob was the only reply Allen received as he paused a moment. A gentle urging of his arm, however, found no yielding yet. From one anxious heart an eager appeal ascended that moment to the throne of power.

"Listen, Sam, I want to tell you the story of one young man who lived some years ago in a city in this State. I know all the details from personal knowledge and from friends of the young man. I will call him simply B. for the present. His father sent him to college and gave him every comfort. He studied law part of the time, but gave more of his time to pleasure and dissipation with careless fellows. After he graduated he started in business, with his father's help. Then he won and married a beautiful girl, one of the tenderest and most faithful ever given by God to any man. He loved her, but he loved himself more. Fondness for indulgence and bad companions caused him to neglect his chosen profession. The neglect brought speedy failure. A chance came to him to go into the hotel business. Again his father helped him with money, though disapproving the enterprise. B. saw that more money could be made from a bar than from the legitimate end of the business, and by degrees the bar became the chief feature of the hotel. Then B. decided not to bother with any hotel, but to run a saloon openly. He had been sinking rapidly in the social and moral scale. His own dissipations increased. He was cruel to his gentle wife. His father's gray hairs went down in sorrow to the grave, whither the delicate mother had preceded him. B. went from bad to worse, but his faithful wife stuck to him, ever trying tenderly to lead him away from his evil life. Her own heart was breaking with shame and disappointment, but she never reproached him. One night, as he reeled into the room, drunk and ugly, he found her weeping, and struck her a cowardly blow in the face. She turned her sad eyes full upon him with a look that made him grow weak and sick. He felt as if he had smitten an angel. Without a word she set his supper before him and retired to her bed. He fell into a drunken sleep in his chair and stayed there until morning. Only once, through the fumes of liquor, there came to his stupid brain the sound of his wife's voice calling his name with an agony of appeal. He growled and went to sleep again. When daylight and appetite roused him, he went, with an ugly word on his lips, to waken his wife and complain because his breakfast was not ready. He found a babe and its mother, both lying dead."

The minister's voice had grown strange and husky. He turned a pale face, and eyes glowing with a fierce light, upon Sam, and seized the young man's arm.

"Sam, have you ever done anything as wicked, as loathsome, as that?" he cried. "Could the great God who is angry with the sinner every day ever forgive so foul and cruel a crime? Was it for such an outcast that God allowed His only Son, His dearly beloved Son, to die in agony on the cross? Ah, Sam, it was for just such a vile outcast as that; and He stretched down His ever loving, tender, bleeding hands to lift up that outcast from the deep pit into which he had fallen; and then, just as at other times, He used the hands of one of His servants on earth to do His work.

B. was then keeper of a low saloon of the most infamous character. After his wife's death, he had moved into a hovel, and lived in loneliness and filth. One night in winter he was staggering blindly along in the middle of the street through the snow and sleet, ready to end his wretched life in the gutter if he should chance to fall and lie unnoticed until morning. A man saw him and, taking pity on his miserable condition, helped him home, built a fire in the cheerless hovel, made hot coffee and forced him to drink it, and stayed with him until he was sober. Then he spoke words of cheer and encouragement to the outcast, urged him to reform and be a man, and offered to be his friend, not only in secret, but openly, before the world which despised him.

"B. was astonished, almost overcome, by such kindness. His better nature was touched; but he cried out despairingly: 'It's too late! I am an outcast! What is the use, now?'

"'It's not too late,' replied his friend. 'While you live, you are not an outcast from God's mercy. You are a child of the King. You have an immortal soul, and it's worth saving.'

"B. began to cry like a baby. Then he almost drove the good man away, declaring that he could not reform; his only means of livelihood was tied up in his saloon; that was all his property; he was committed to it, and must stick to it till the end.

"But God's hand of mercy was still reaching down for the outcast. The good Samaritan would not desert him. Again and again he saw B. and urged him with inspired persuasiveness to turn his steps into the upward path of manliness and honor. The temptation came to B. to sell his saloon, and follow after his friend; but he could not make himself believe that he would find much satisfaction in a new life haunted by the knowledge that he had freed himself from the 'body of this death' only by fastening it upon some other wretched man. If it meant damnation for him, would it not mean the same for another, and could he buy salvation with the price of his neighbor's soul?

"One night the sleeping town was roused by wild cries in the street.

"'Fire! Fire! Fire!'

"The alarm-bell in the church steeple rang out. Crowds of hurriedly dressed people thronged to the fire. A block of old wooden buildings was burning fiercely, and before anything could be done to arrest the flames the entire block was doomed. B.'s saloon was in the fated row, directly in the path of the conflagration. The red tongues of fire came nearer and nearer, eagerly devouring the dry timber.

"'Where's B.? Let's save his liquors!' cried voices in the crowd. 'Here, boys, lend a hand, and we'll yank some of them kegs of old rye out in the street before they're all burned up!'

"Half a dozen men sprang to the door of B.'s saloon, broke it in, and in a few moments several kegs of liquors of various kinds were on the street, while ready hands were about to tap them for the benefit of the crowd.

"Just then a cry of furious rage sounded above the roar of the flames and the babel of the crowd. The next moment B. stood in the midst of his kegs and barrels, swinging an axe above his head.

"'I want every one here to understand that this is *my* property, and I'll brain the first man who dares to touch it!' he cried, and there was a flash of determination in his eyes which awed the crowd and made them hurry to stand back. They thought the threatened loss of his saloon had bereft him of reason, and that he was about to wreak his insane wrath on the spectators. None were prepared for what he did do. Raising his axe aloft, he brought it down with all his strength again and again upon the kegs and barrels, destroying them utterly and letting their contents flow out into the mud and snow of the street. When this task was finished he looked around at the raging fire, gazed a moment at his saloon, now enveloped in flame, then fell upon his knees in the street, and poured out his heart in thanksgiving to God for having done for him by fire what he could not do for himself—remove the obstacle which had hindered him from starting in the right way.

"Through all the hard struggle which followed, B.'s God-sent friend stood by him, lifting him up, holding him up, encouraging him by word and by deed. Not a single reproach for the past came from his lips. Always it was hope and purpose for the future. Yet he and the one dearest to him had suffered from B.'s wicked life."

The minister paused, so much overcome by his own recital that for the moment he did not notice how it had affected his companion.

"Sam," he said at length, "you know some of the persons in the little story I have just told you. The angel wife who died with her babe in the night was your dear mother's sister Ruth. The good Samaritan, who in Christ's name lifted up the wretched outcast, was your own father. The unhappy drunkard, whom God in His great mercy saved from such a depth of sin, is now a redeemed man, and is here to-day pleading with his younger brother to come to the same loving Saviour."

Sam stared at the minister in amazement and unbelief.

"What! was it you?" he whispered.

"Yes, Sam, I travelled the path you have been pursuing, and now the way of escape by which I came out of darkness into the light is open to you. Will you come?"

The minister's arm again tightened lovingly with a persuasive pressure. This time it met no resistance; and two souls found a bethel in the midst of the pine-forest.

CHAPTER XXXI

PEACE again brooded over village, farm, and forest. The excitement which had disturbed the Red-Keggers during the spring subsided. Farm activity engaged everybody's attention. The four Invincibles no longer occupied a prominent place in the public mind. Tom Moore, acting upon the minister's suggestion, had taken their paroles, only requiring that each man should report once a day to him, or other appointed deputies, in order that he might keep posted as to their whereabouts. Sam and Seward found work to do at their homes. Walt and Billy hung about the village, or helped in such affairs as interested them.

Sam only of the four seemed greatly affected by his position. He went quietly about the farm, working industriously, but seldom speaking to any one, and keeping to himself as much as possible. He seemed crushed and ashamed. His father's kindness touched but did not cheer him. Tender, faithful Lettie did her best to bring him brightness and hope. Farmer Hawkins even suggested that she come to the farm at once and make her home in the place that would be hers when he should pass away; but Sam would not consent to any arrangement of the kind until after his trial. He could not bear the thought of establishing a home circle to be broken by a sentence to a term in prison. Measures had been set on foot by the minister and others to secure a pardon for the young men. If these should succeed—but the chance was not great enough to justify anticipating such an outcome. Lettie was compelled to bide her time and hope for the best.

Early in June two quiet weddings supplied pleasant gossip for several days. At Hal Marthy's farm Axcy and Joseph Waters joined hands before Parson Allen and in the presence of a chosen few of their friends, and then began life together in the modest home which the schoolmaster had provided. A few days later, in the home of John Maloney, a tall, wiry young Irishman, beaming with pride and joy, claimed his blushing bride. After the ceremony he fairly hugged the stalwart minister for speaking those "blissed words" which gave him the right to say "my wife" to the happy little woman at his side.

The skies smiled with unclouded face upon happy and sad alike. As June advanced, men looked more and more anxiously for a cloud to break that unchanging smile. A breath as from a furnace swept over the land. Rain came not upon just or unjust. Before July was half over the oldest inhabitants declared it was the hottest and dryest summer ever known in that section. Crops withered and died under the blighting fierceness of the sun. Domestic animals suffered from lack of water. The wells on farms and in the villages dried up. Creeks and rivulets, usually well filled until August, became empty channels. Even the pretentious Tittabawassee and its largest tributaries shrank within their banks to narrow, muddy, sluggish streams. One could walk for miles upon the Sturgeon's clay and gravel bed without wetting the soles of his feet.

At Red-Keg and Midland the cry for water was universal. The scarcity amounted to a famine. Wells heretofore had been not much more than superficial affairs, usually from six to ten feet deep, but supplying

27

abundance of water for all purposes. These were now dry as powder-houses. It became necessary to strike deeper, and well-diggers were in great demand. So few were available, and their charges became so high, that many farmers undertook to dig new wells for themselves. More often than not they had their trouble for nothing.

Farmer Hawkins was more fortunate than most of his neighbors in that his well was deeper, and the supply lasted, with careful economy, through the summer. Several times it seemed on the point of failing, but slowly filled again, over night. Barney O'Boyle sank a well on John Maloney's farm near one which had run dry. He dug down through hard-pan about twenty feet until he came to a flat rock of limestone. No apparatus being available for drilling through the rock, poor Barney was well-nigh discouraged at the prospect. The rock covered the whole bottom of the well and was as dry as dust. In desperation, he called for a crowbar and began sounding the stone. It gave back a hollow sound. A few vigorous blows with the crowbar soon convinced him that he could work his way through the apparently thin layer of rock. He struck still more rapidly, throwing his whole strength into the blows. Suddenly the crowbar slipped from his hands and disappeared through a hole in the rock. Then a column of pure, cold water spouted up, drenching Barney to the skin and nearly drowning him before he could get to the top of the well. The crowbar was never found, but John Maloney was blessed with an ever-flowing well of water, which, springing up in the midst of a parched and burning land, was a veritable godsend to his less fortunate neighbors, who sought in vain to find the meanderings of his subterranean stream.

The great huckleberry marshes out in the Sturgeon district became so dry that, where the previous year hundreds of bushels of the luscious berries had been picked by men, women, and children, who earned a good income thereby, this summer only a few of the bushes, in the wettest spots, got beyond the flowering stage. Likewise the raspberries and blackberries were blighted by the drouth, and the sand-ridges upon which they throve luxuriously in a moist season became little more than desert wastes.

In the forests the pitch oozed from the barks of green trees, filling the heated air with a fragrant aroma. The beds of pine-needles and mosses which had lain for years, retaining moisture for the use of the trees, became like tinder-boxes. As a result the earth around the tree-roots grew dry and powdery.

August passed in panting, shimmering heat. September brought a few half-hearted showers which tended only to aggravate conditions, until the people were almost ready to give up hope. By the first of October a general feeling of depression had settled upon the entire section. On every hand praying people besought God for relief, but still no rain came, and day by day the drouth strengthened its deadly grip.

Then alarm suddenly took a new turn. The atmosphere grew hazy and smoke-laden. Disquieting reports began to come from different quarters that the forests were on fire, and that the fires were spreading with great rapidity. Preparations were made to flee, or to fight for homes and lives. All through the section which included Red-Keg large quantities of timber had been cut down during the previous winter, and the dried, pitch-filled limbs and needles which littered the ground would burn like oil. Only those homes which stood in the midst of wide clearings could be regarded as comparatively safe. Even then it was necessary to burn away with great care acres of dried grass and grain which might offer means of communication for the onrushing conflagration. Houses and barns closely surrounded by the forest were in imminent danger. As the fires drew nearer many a farmer and lumber-owner made haste to cut down and drag away valuable trees in the hope of saving their homes.

Farmer Hawkins surveyed his grounds with anxious face. He noted the direction of the wind, and the increasing smoke in the sky. His buildings were all far enough away from the limits of the forest for safety, but he hated to sacrifice the beautiful and stately trees in which he took so much delight. Early one morning he shook his head gravely and said to the minister:

"My old pets have got to go, Robert. Let's have it over with at once."

Before noon not a single tree was standing within a thousand feet of the house.

John Maloney had a more difficult task. His clearing was not yet so broad. If it were not for the fact that the last winter's cut of timber had been taken from the acres nearest his farm, for the purpose of cultivation, his case would have been almost hopeless. He and Barney, with such help as they could get, worked desperately night and day to drive the edge of the forest back beyond the danger line. Ros Whitmore, strong and courageous again, helped Maloney, or Farmer Hawkins, or any others who needed help, with as much energy as though his own home were concerned.

"'Twould be a waste o' time an' strength to do anythin' out to Th' Corners," he said. "We're shet in on three sides by pine-woods, an' nothin' short o' twenty men could make a clearin' there big enough ter keep the fire off ef it hed a mine'ter come. Men are scarce now, an' they's too many places where they hev a better chance. Mebbe the fire'll skip us by. Ef it don't, we'll hev ter skip ourselves an' let the shanty go."

His friends knew very well that he would not talk with such seeming indifference of his fine new home if he had not canvassed the situation thoroughly and found it absolutely hopeless. Finding no help for it, he bravely concealed his own sorrow and helped those who had some chance of saving their property. Andrew Green was in similar hopeless case, and realizing it at the very beginning, moved his family and goods to Midland. Many others did the same.

By the end of the first week in October a lurid glow was seen at night in the north and west. The heat and smoke became almost unbearable. Bandages were kept over the eyes and mouth. Refugees came from all directions, hurrying toward Midland. The conflagration swept on apace, sometimes in wide swath, sometimes in long, narrow arms which wormed their way onward, leaving irregular paths of destruction behind. Communities joined together for a common onslaught upon the devouring flames. Bands of men hurried from place to place to beat down the fire wherever it specially threatened. The lack of water greatly hampered the work and caused fearful suffering, but the sturdy farmers and woodsmen fought on bravely, desperately, unceasingly, to save their homes and their loved ones.

The former Invincibles earned a new title to the name by their unyielding, untiring efforts in the common cause. By tacit agreement they banded themselves together for the fearful work, and in the most dangerous places displayed a reckless valor which earned the admiration as well as the gratitude of those who a few months before had welcomed their downfall.

The very air seemed filled with fire. From tree-top to tree-top great balls of flame would pass, often jumping over an open space of several hundred feet to a pitch-laden tree, which in a twinkling would burst into a seething column of fire from root to topmost branch. Here again the swirling flames would gather themselves into huge balls to be tossed about by the wind and dropped wherever a waiting tree or building offered food for the ravenous element.

> " From fiery night to morning,
> From flaming dawn to night,
> Rolled the resistless tide of fire
> In roaring waves of light."

Red-Keg and Midland were both threatened with destruction, although both were providentially spared. At the latter place the citizens turned out in relief brigades to plough out around the town and in every possible way seek to prevent the flames from getting a hold upon the frame dwellings which composed the town. Church bells were kept ringing and whistles blowing to guide people thither who had been driven from their homes. Landmarks were burned away and there was no visible means by which refugees could tell whether they were going north or south.

The tide of fire was sweeping over toward the State road from the Big Salt district. Already the woods a few miles above the Hawkins farm to the north and out toward Wilford were blazing. The bands of fire fighters were retreating before the awful foe. Pete

Murray, Tom Moore, Barney O'Boyle, Ned Blakely, Dan Underhill, John Maloney, Ros Whitmore, the Invincibles, and a hundred more were contesting every rod of ground wherever a chance of rescue or home-saving presented itself. Several farmhouses had been saved by heroic efforts. Many others were lying in blackened ruins. The men were nearly exhausted; their eyes were red and swollen, their throats parched, and their hands frightfully burned and blistered; but there was no thought of surrender.

Monday afternoon, October 9th, a company of Red-Keggers, almost ready to drop with weariness, and the pain of their burns, was resting for an hour or so at the Hawkins farm to gather a little fresh strength for the further efforts which they could not avoid. News had just come from the telegraph office at the railroad depot that the whole of Michigan was on fire; then the same was said of Wisconsin; then that Chicago was burning, after which dreadful news, all communication with the outside world was cut off.

"Must be the end o' the world's comin'," said Ned Blakely in awe-struck tones.

No one scoffed. The thing seemed frightfully real, and the same belief had forced itself into many minds.

"Our times are in His hands," said Allen with quiet but solemn voice. "When He comes, may He find each of us ready, doing his duty to the last, courageous and true. Let us commend ourselves to Him, and ask for strength for the work which lies immediately before us."

In a few earnest words the minister lifted the brave but fear-laden hearts of that little band to the throne of Him who said to the tempest, "Peace, be still," and who gives peace to meet the direst human need.

Seward Rathaway, who had been to the village and returned with the latest news, had reported also that the fire was working round to the Sturgeon district and might hem them in if they were not careful.

Ros Whitmore had spoken several times during the day of returning to his home to take his family out of harm's way. Now he announced his intention of going out to The Corners at once.

"Not thet they's any immediate danger. I told Jule ter git the kids an' the things in the cart an' go down ter the Keg ef the fire seemed ter be comin' thet way. Jule's set on takin' keer o' the house ter the last; but she won't run no resk, I reckon, with the kids. I'll run out an' see thet they're all right. Ef the fire's got 'round to the Sturgeon, it's time they made tracks out o' there."

"You may need help; I'll go with you," said Allen, "and perhaps Sam may like to go;" but Sam could not be found. No one remembered seeing him since dinner.

"Never mind, ye may be sure he's needed wherever he is," said Ros, as they started off in a buckboard.

Driving down past Maloney's farm to a point just above Andrew Green's deserted house, they turned into the narrow winding road which led some five miles out to the Sandytown settlement. Ros Whitmore's place was about half a mile nearer the State road, and near the intersection of the Sandytown and Wilford roads. It was thus referred to as The Corners.

Ros and the minister pushed on with all possible speed, alarmed at the smoke which seemed to grow thicker as they advanced. When scarcely a mile from the State road they met Jule with the children and a wagon-load of household goods coming rapidly toward them. The good woman was pale and weeping, and the smaller children huddled to her with frightened faces.

"The road's cut off, Ros!" cried his wife. "The fire ran around us before we knew it. We'd never got out alive but for Sam Hawkins, who rushed in jest after dinner an' hustled us all into the wagon. Then he came part way to see that we got through. But the woods on both sides of the road jest below The Corners is all afire, an' he had to lead the horses through by the bridle." Ros had been looking hastily over the little group while listening to his wife's excited narrative. Suddenly he shouted, a quick note of anxiety in his voice:

"Where's Tilly?"

Jule began to cry hysterically again and wring her hands.

"We had to hurry so!" she wailed. "We all thought she was in the wagon. She wasn't in the house when we left. We were sure she was in the wagon. We were all so excited, and had to start all in a minute. Sam went back to find her—he swore an oath he'd find her an' bring her to me this very afternoon—he went back—through the fire."

Ros groaned in an agony of fear. Here were his "ninety-and-nine," saved almost by a miracle; but his father's heart yearned for the one wee lamb that was missing. Bidding Jule drive on at once to the village, Ros and the minister lashed their horse forward in the hope that they might pass the burning barrier across the road and reach the threatened road. Before they had gone two miles farther, however, they were stopped by a fiery wall, advancing toward them, which made progress in that direction utterly impossible. Ros looked at the minister in mute and hopeless anguish. Without a moment's hesitation, Allen sprang out of the buckboard and bade Ros do the same. Then he turned the horse around, fastened the reins to the seat, and with a slap and a quick word sent the animal galloping back down the road.

"This arm of the fire is coming around from the east," he said. "It may not have reached the Wilford road. You know the logging path through to there. We may get around to The Corners that way. I doubt if the fire has got to your place yet."

While he spoke, the two men were hurrying to a little path which led from the road zigzag through the forest. Apparently a temporary shift of the wind had driven a narrow tongue of fire out from the main conflagration in a westerly direction. This puff of wind had now died out, and the fire was probably working south again rather than continuing to the west. It was upon this theory, at least, that Allen based his calculations. There was no time for weighing chances. He had seized the first that suggested itself. Through the forest, already stifling with smoke and heat, they plunged. Before they had gone a furlong the place at which they had entered was in flames. In half an hour they reached the Wilford road and hastened on. As they neared The Corners, the smoke became more dense, and showers of sparks fell around them. The father's heart sank in his breast. The minister was troubled with another fear, also.

"Look!" cried Ros, pointing through the woods to a red glare which grew nearer and brighter each moment.

"Look!" cried the minister, pointing to a terrible figure which came staggering down the road holding something in its arms.

"I DES LOVE HIM, I DO!"

Ros looked; then with a glad cry he sprang forward. "Tilly! my baby! my darlin'!" he shouted.

Without a word the terrible, staggering figure laid the child unhurt in her father's arms. Then he reeled as if about to fall.

"Sam! my hero!" cried the minister, supporting the burned and exhausted man. "You must not give out now. We need you. Come, Ros, hurry! We'll cut through at the first opening to the Hawkins farm. There's no place any safer than that."

"Let me run, papa, I'm all right," begged little Tilly. "I went to find my kitty an' when I comed back, mama an' ev'ybody was gone. I was des goin' to cry when my teacher's Mister Hawkins comed an' said he'd take me to mama. Oh, my! but he was aw-ful burned an' sore, an' I wanted to get him some water, an' some o' mama's mutton tallow an' cream, but he wouldn't wait for the leastest thing, but des grabbed me up an' run. An' we had to go fru a dre'ful fire. I was afraid, but he said he couldn't help it, an' it was the on'y way to get to mama. He took off his coat an' wrapped it all roun' me, even my head, so's I couldn't hardly breave, till we got fru the fire; but his hair an' eyes an' han's got more burned—poor man! He must be awful good. I des love him, I do—most as much as I do my teacher."

The little girl wriggled herself out of her father's restraining arms, and running to Sam caught one of his hands in hers and kissed it tenderly. Then she gazed at it a moment in silent pity, and the tears ran down her cheeks.

"Oh, it's so sore!" she said. "I must wrap it up des like my mama does in soft rags with plenty of mutton tallow and cream."

"'Inasmuch as ye have done it unto one of the least of these, ye have done it unto Me,'" said Allen, close to Sam's ear. "Those words of the Saviour are spoken to you, Sam."

The little party hurried along with as much speed as the suffering man could maintain, and soon came to another path which took them through the woods to the Hawkins farm. There Sam's burns were dressed and he was put to bed, while others fought the fire-fiend for two days longer, until the pitying heavens poured down the blessed rain and stopped the carnival of destruction.

Several days passed, and the telegraph lines were restored. Among the first to use them in the little Red-Keg railroad office was Robert Allen. Ros Whitmore, Tom Moore, Justice Frost, Pete Murray, and several other men were with him. Their business required an unusual amount of ticking on the little instrument. Then Robert Allen suddenly disappeared without telling Sam or Farmer Hawkins where he was going. He might be gone a week, perhaps longer, he said; but he hoped to be back in time to help Sam through his ordeal at the United States District Court.

The date fixed for the sitting came all too soon. Even the great fire caused no postponement. Parson Allen had not returned, and Sam, who was barely able to go to Midland, both hands still swathed in bandages, nerved himself to take the punishment he had earned. Every influence possible was exerted in behalf of him and his companions, and their services to the community during the fire were urged as an offset to their offenses; but the clemency of the court could not grant more than a lightening of the sentence. After that had been pronounced, Sam was given an hour to be alone with his father and Lettie; then he must go away. The minister came just in time to join the sorrowful little group. He appeared to notice nothing amiss and advanced with a pleasant greeting.

"How are the burns, Sam? Healing nicely?"

"Better, thank you," replied Sam, adding sadly: "You came too late for the trial. I suppose you know the result."

"Yes, I know; but perhaps I am not too late. You still have a few minutes left to read this," and he placed a long envelope in the bandaged hand.

Sam looked at it helplessly a moment, and his hand trembled. He held the envelope toward his father, who removed the paper, opened it, and tried to read, but his eyes were dimmed with tears. Lettie could not wait. She leaned over Farmer Hawkins's shoulder and took one long look. Then she snatched the paper excitedly.

"A pardon!" she cried. "Look, Sam, it's a pardon! Oh, it's all over, Sam, it's a pardon!" and she fell on her knees and spread the paper on Sam's lap.

The young man gazed at the paper a moment, then at the happy, excited face of his wife, and into the quiet, strong, tender face of the minister. At last his eyes rested again upon the paper in his lap.

"Pardoned!" he whispered. After a pause, he added, softly, "by God and man!"

"Yes, Sam," said Robert Allen, "and may the Lord bless thee and keep thee; the Lord make His face to shine upon thee and be gracious to thee; the Lord lift up His countenance upon thee and give thee peace."

And the deep bright glow in the young man's eyes as he lifted them once more to those of the minister—his friend—his brother—testified eloquently that the prayer for blessing was already answered.